Cybil Raven: Miracle at St. Rita

Volume 2

Cybil Raven Chronicles

Tony Timbol and Crystal Craven

To Jennifer,
thanks for
being a great
customer,
enjoy the read.
Tony

St. Johns, FL 32259
www.verilogos.com

Printed in the United States of America

First Printing October 2011, Second Printing March 2012

ISBN: 978-0-9831333-1-5 (eBook)
ISBN: 978-0-9831333-3-9 (Paperback)
LCCN: 2011927033 (eBook)
LCCN: 2011934654 (Paperback)

Tony Timbol and Crystal Craven

www.tonytimbol.com

https://www.facebook.com/TonyTimbolAuthor

Cybil Raven Chronicles:

Cybil Raven Beginnings, Volume 1

Cybil Raven: Miracle at St. Rita, Volume 2

http://www.facebook.com/CybilRavenChronicles

www.cybilraven.com

Prologue

From the huge oak tree the large blackbird quietly surveyed the garden. Its tree perch stood at the wood's edge next to St. Rita, Savannah's orphanage for girls that would soon close. Long shadows cooled the building and clouds further dimmed the light. The bird looked left, past the dock which gave access to the channel flowing into the Atlantic. Storm clouds on the horizon approached, driven by strong winds from the east. Every few seconds, from within the cloud's shape-shifting billows, flashes of light burst forth giving form to the blackness. Minutes passed and then the glossy bird lifted its head to attention, flapped its wings once and flew straight up into the sky, leaving its favorite sitting place, the crook where the single massive, moss-draped limb joined the trunk. The limb, too thick even for a tall man to wrap his arms around, hung heavy over the old brick well beneath it. Seconds later, out of the gray-black sky a brilliant lightning discharge struck the exact spot where the bird had sat, scorching the surface. Yet no thunder reverberated. The bird stopped in mid-flight, turned and looked back briefly before it continued its ascent.

這種籽的宇宙倍到自己,把它必須死團圓,它可以活,要改變,成為它的意思。

—Adamic Scrolls, First Verse, Seventh Scroll

In the side of a steep granite mountain in the surrounding terrain of Umbria, Italy, about 70 miles from Rome, a monastery barely made its presence known. Its facade measured three stories tall and in the center, near the ground, heavy wooden doors were circled by a stone arch. In the stone, intricate carvings of trees, birds, animals and men intertwined, weaving a story. Above the arch was a curious four foot by eight foot rectangular opening. Every few minutes one or more species of birds left and entered through the opening. The rest of the monastery was buried in the mountainside, as if the granite had swallowed it up except for the facade.

The monastery, originally part of the St. Augustine Order, was occupied by an unknown group of unusual monks that included men and women. The building overlooked a valley where the city of Cascia was founded and where St. Rita, the Saint of Impossible Causes, was born.

A long stone path, winding and less than two feet across, led up from the valley floor, ending at the monastery doors. A man, slim and fit and dressed for hiking, climbed the path carefully since it was still slick and wet from the summer morning dew. He encountered no meadows, trees or bushes, only dirt, boulders and sharp-edged rocks. Stopping to rest for the third time, he was halfway there. He adjusted the fit of the heavy backpack, tightening its hold. His red-and-black right-hand wrist tattoo glistened from sweat. He continued upward.

An hour later the hiker knocked on the imposing monastery door. A small, red blinking light to the side caught his eye. Recessed inside a hole in the stone arch, a tiny video camera stared at him.

Fallujah, Iraq

2003

Cybil Raven's deep-blue eyes scanned the pitch-dark horizon through the Blackhawk helicopter's open side door. A few dots of lights spotted the edge of the sky. Flying at this low altitude and looking down, she could discern rusty oil barrels containing small fires, their light revealing grungy alleys strewn with trash, tires and broken-down cars. Small groups of Iraqi men gathered around the impromptu flames. Looking at her wristwatch she read the time: 0230 hours. The chopper, part of an air convoy, streaked through the dark: destination, the northwestern edge of the Sunni Triangle. The wind, tunneling by loudly, and the rhythmic beating of the blades cutting the night sky shook everything, even the back of her seat. Some of the wind currents swept into the transport's interior, flapping the loose edges of her desert camouflage uniform. The shifting and moving helicopter banked and turned with practiced ease; in a combat zone you never flew a straight line. This strong, almost violent, motion jostled riders. Strands of dark-chestnut hair had fallen out of her ballistic helmet, blocking her vision. Frowning, her eyes flashed lighter for a second before she grabbed her helmet with one hand, lifted it and pushed her hair back underneath with the other. *Almost there.*

The corporal took a deep breath to awaken her senses. The 0100 briefing at base had taken longer than usual. The mission was crucial. The Snake's mobile IED factory had proved slippery; several prior missions had failed to find anything but sand, bad-smelling camels and closed-mouthed Sunnis. Cybil looked around the cabin again at Charlie, Sam, Curtis and the captain. They sat at the bulkhead behind the pilots, all her brothers from the 82nd Airborne Division. Curtis was new, a replacement for Danny, who didn't return from the last mission. Cybil thought, *Let's all get back.* The captain caught her glance and nodded.

The captain had hand-picked Cybil for the day's mission. Her intelligence and insight made her invaluable as a communications specialist. He wanted a thinker to evaluate the voice traffic, to listen to what was going on—not a message robot merely relaying what was being said. She was the best, her intuition sharp. Unfortunately, that had made his clumsy advances obvious. When she, the only female in the company, had been assigned to his unit, he thought her an overachieving little girl, lost, hiding in the Army, a California beauty pageant winner trying to prove herself more than a pretty piece of ass. She'd proved him wrong. He smiled at her and raised his right hand to his brow in a small salute.

Cybil nodded back and couldn't suppress a half-smile. He was tough and demanding on the job, yet the captain played fair. He gave her opportunities to excel while never making it easy. She liked the captain, who was tall, well-built and single. But romance on the battlefield could be complicated; lust among a band of brothers and sisters knots things up. And the person in her mind more than anyone was not her captain. Cybil took a breath in and closed her eyes. *Why was Holden gone, especially after Dubai? Dubai.*

Cybil's hands moved to her knees. She started rubbing the outside of her thighs, instinctively doing a quick pre-combat check. Left hip pocket: compass. Left cargo pocket: flask from the captain. Right hip pocket: memo pad with half-chewed pencil. Right cargo pocket: the photo. She stretched her hand out and let her fingers strum the top of her sheathed calf knife, military issue, just below the knee. She pulled up her hand to feel the photo, her fingers closing in on its edges … taken in Dubai during last month's leave when they ….

The chopper's interior red light began flashing, signaling their imminent landing. Seated next to the flashing light, the captain beamed a blood-red face.

Within minutes the chopper and the rest of the convoy landed behind protective dunes bracketing a dried-out riverbed.

"Smells like the rest of the damn desert. Sandy, acrid and dry," she commented as she unloaded camp gear with the rest of her team. The other choppers, spread across the desert, were doing the same.

Within an hour the camp was set up and the team assembled, ready to leave. This spot sat close to a village of friendlies, according to recon. But the mission had to be completed by dawn; eager for U.S. dollars, the locals would be up with the hot sun, trying to sell their goods to rich American soldiers.

Cybil had lined up everyone's communications gear by rank, the captain's at the end of the table, everyone else's in line behind his. She had checked each unit carefully, each passing her test. Each soldier picked up his unit without confusion; they knew Cybil's categorizing methods. After assembly they streamed into the moonless desert from the camp, night vision goggles on. They were only a few miles from the objective.

Inside the tent, Cybil started her work: relaying instructions, clarifications and commands. She watched the mission clock. Timing was crucial; the strike was set for 30 minutes before sunrise, on the dark side of dawn. On cue, her heart began racing as the team started their approach to the target, voice traffic slowing. Sitting there staring at the console, headset on, microphone inches from her mouth, her brother's voices fading in the air, she started sweating. She mopped her brow with her forearm sleeve. Down her front and back, the sweat formed into drops which trailed down and joined others as if on a march. The sweat overpowered the last molecules of her deodorant and she wrinkled her nose at the result. She glanced up to see streaks of light coming through the command tent's faded, yellowing window flap as the sun breached the horizon. The 82nd Airborne's boot should be on the Snake's head right about … now.

*

"Boots on the ground is the only way to win a war!" Cybil had heard this often during Army basic training. And her brothers' boots had stomped on the head of the Snake.

Walking up to the captain's tent, she nodded to the armed guards on each side of the entrance.

Stepping through, Cybil said, "He's a little scrawny for a master bomb maker, isn't he? And it stinks in here. That ain't you, Captain, is it?"

She smiled at her commander and then looked over at the Snake, hands zip-tied behind him, sitting quietly in a folding chair with his head down. He slowly raised his head and looked at her, unsmiling. His dark face brooded, narrow and triangular. Cold eyes over a pointed nose peered at her. A trimmed beard set him apart; most locals kept scraggly facial hair. He blinked once, lowered his head and closed his eyes.

She had come to deliver written orders from FORSCOM about the Snake. Special black, unmarked helicopters would soon pick up what the team had obtained.

"Yeah, turns out Mr. Al-Mahdi's days of causing a ruckus are over," the captain said, looking over the orders and signing a confirmation receipt.

Al-Mahdi squirmed, his chair moving a few inches as his sandals scratched at the fabric under his feet.

The captain smiled at Cybil. "On the way out, tell the guards to send in that kid with figs and cheeses, I'm hungry. They can get some coffee and bring me back a cup. I'll keep an eye on this ass-hat," he said.

She returned a thin smile, turned on her boot heels and walked out of the tent. The guards soon followed her, eager for a break. Twenty yards away they turned right, toward the mess tent. She kept walking.

"Shit! I forget the message from the colonel," Cybil said aloud. The division commander had sent the captain an "attaboy" along with an invitation to dinner. He wanted Cybil to verbally deliver it.

She turned around and started back in the direction of the captain's tent. Getting closer, she saw a small Arab teen step out; he looked left, then right and took off running over the dune behind the tent.

"What the fuck!" Cybil ran to the tent while shouting for help. Other soldiers walking nearby stopped, looked over at the running female and took to a sprint, converging on the tent. Cybil closed to within ten feet when Al-Mahdi appeared at the tent door, holding in his left hand a large knife red with blood. He looked straight at her and smiled. Cybil's eyes widened and she accelerated towards him. He raised his left arm to strike, but Cybil was too quick. She barreled into him head first, the top of her helmet sinking into his stomach before he could bring the knife down. They tumbled together into the tent. She rolled to her right and sprang to her feet. Her knuckles were white as they gripped the now drawn calf knife in her right hand. But there was no need.

Al-Mahdi lay still on the ground. A deep gash across his chin, under his lower lip, was bleeding. He had come to rest right next to the tent's main pole. He moaned. The guards returned and ran into the tent. One went directly to handcuff Al-Mahdi, kicking away the large knife lying near the Snake's hand.

The other guard went over to the captain, who was face down on the tent floor. The guard knelt next to him and gently rolled him over. The guard's head dropped for a second. He then looked up at Cybil and shook his head. The captain was dead, his neck sliced open, face covered in blood. Cybil drew in a quick breath, almost a gasp. *Control*, she told herself. Cybil looked at her commander and friend and didn't say a word. Going over to his cot, she grabbed a blanket and placed it over his body.

"You will all pay, you dogs!" Al-Mahdi spat out.

The guard had made him stand up.

"You think this will stop me?" he said. "Allah is on my side. Your God is nothing. It is only the beginning."

Allah, God, Jesus, yeah, right. Cybil approached him, her eyes drilling into his. The other guard had moved over to Al-Mahdi and held him tight. The sound of helicopters grew by the second, the tent walls quivering as the wind from the flying transports filled the camp.

"Beginning? Your time here ends now," she said, her eyes flashing bright. Raising her right hand she slapped Al-Mahdi hard across the face.

Al-Mahdi's head was turned by the force of the blow. He slowly turned back to face Cybil. Fresh blood oozed from his gash. He looked back into her eyes and blinked, unsure. Then his face turned darker and he grimaced. "American bitch, how dare you strike me! This I will not forget, ever!"

"Take him out of here," Cybil said to the guards.

The guards grabbed Al-Mahdi and shoved him out the tent entrance, to the waiting helicopters and escorted him through the swirling sand. Her fellow soldiers poured into the tent to secure the area for the investigation. She walked past them.

Corp. Cybil Raven stood outside her captain's tent and watched the choppers take Al-Mahdi into the air. The rotating blades drew dust and sand that circled up, then down around the choppers, forming a halo. The light from the risen sun scattered through the chaotic particles. She stood there for some time watching the helicopters rise and speed away, becoming smaller and smaller and smaller. *No time for tears*. She couldn't wait to get back to base, to take a hot shower, reread Holden's letter and wash off this day.

Savannah, Georgia

Present Day

1

Despite weeks of planning, the early morning photo shoot at Forsyth Park in Savannah, Georgia, started late. The lighting equipment had not been set up as scheduled. The makeup girl called in sick and Jimmy Gordon's new digital SLR burned out two memory cards. Furthermore, the night before, pranksters had poured soap into the large centerpiece fountain, their shoot location. Park workers had begun to neutralize the foaming mixture with special additives, but bubbles still formed and lifted into the air from the splash pool's surface. A small cloud of different-sized bubbles rose and drifted in the light morning breeze over to the woman in the wedding dress.

Cybil Raven stood watching one large bubble drift over to her. It neared her face. As it approached she smiled, blew at it, stopping its flight midair. It shimmered in the morning light. Through it she saw a magnified snapshot of the dense woods of the park, dark colors mixing with the soft-yellow morning light. Rainbow colors traced the edge of the suspended traveler. She raised her hand and with her index finger poked the bubble; it exploded, disappearing into the wind along with her "Gotcha!"

Cybil stood opposite the fountain, on its west side, near a weathered wooden bench. She wished to sit but couldn't. The wedding gown she wore, a form-fitting pearl white Vera Wang, a rental for the shoot, restrained her. So she stood quietly, firm and strong, at rest, as she had done so often at Ft. Bragg and in Iraq. Her hands folded lightly together below her midsection. Two strands of white pearls lay in a double curve at the base of her neck. The strapless, form-fitting silk bodice of the gown wrapped itself around her torso, outlining her small pear-shaped breasts.

She leaned slightly forward and, lifting her chin, took a deep breath through her nose. The scent of hyacinth in its morning bloom brought a smile. Her early morning runs in Savannah had become pleasing scented tours until the morning traffic belched odious gases. She glanced down at her backpack on the bench. Inside it were her purse and iPhone. Her chest rose and fell as she sighed and looked over at Jimmy, her photographer.

Jimmy, on the other side of the fountain, had his cell phone jammed to his ear while moving his free hand in frantic motions. His slim build leaned forward like a slash as he paced quickly, head down toward Sasha, his assistant, about 30 feet away. She was kneeling, adjusting the lighting stand anchors to the just-arrived equipment. As he talked into the phone his hands whirled about, almost striking Judy in the face as he walked by her. Cybil's friend, artist and part-time shoot coordinator leaned back to avoid the potential slap. Turning her head to look at Cybil, she shrugged her shoulders and lifted her fully tattooed arm to wave.

Cybil returned Judy's wave and then brushed away a few tiny bubbles. Her smile faded as she shifted her feet, cocked her hip and folded her arms in front of her. The gown was a two-part dress with bodice floating over a lace-over silk skirt that followed her slim athletic build. A fly buzzed her face and she swatted at it before lightly touching the delicate white lace headpiece to adjust it.

Two thin veils streamed from the headpiece to her mid-back. She shifted her weight again and her eyes scanned the park. Her face presented a balanced oval. Perfectly centered, her nose descended to just above delicate lips colored in red for today's shoot. Her sapphire-blue eyes, observant to the surroundings, shimmered with raw intelligence.

Looking down at her open bag on the bench, she wanted to reach for her iPhone to check messages. William had been an ass when they had talked last, jealous about the wrap party photos from her last shoot. *He should have called already.* Across the fountain and down the boulevard, a couple of Park Service cops providing security stared at her, mouths slightly open. Glancing in that direction Cybil smiled and chuckled before scanning the park again.

She looked over at Jimmy, Judy and Sasha and watched him bounce back and forth between them, his hand waving widely as he talked on the phone. He glanced over at Cybil and gave her a "We'll get started soon" wave and added a few head nods. She waved back.

Cybil viewed the morning sky. It was pale blue but starting to deepen, much like the desert mornings in Fallujah. She frowned. Holden would jog with her early, to start the day together. Cybil shook her head.

The air had the slight chill of early spring. She took a deep cleansing breath, as yoga had taught her, to center herself. Her eyes settled on the top of Forsyth Fountain, to the classical Greek figure of a woman in military stance holding some sort of rod or flag. Cybil cocked her head slightly. *Good to see you again, lady.*

The figure seemed to be protecting the fountain, maybe the square, maybe the city. The wind picked up and she could smell the bougainvillea and magnolias from around the nearby Confederate Memorial. The wind brushed her forehead and she felt it touch her lips. Her veil rose up slightly and then rested on her shoulders and back. The hair on Cybil's neck rose as if a chill had passed over her, but this wind was warm and a little moist. A small dark shadow passed over the statue, moving from the feet toward its head; maybe from some large bird, she thought. She blinked, her eyes scanning the landscape. She felt a need to be ready. *Nothing here, nothing coming, just us,* she thought while fighting the feeling.

Looking up at the lady, she took in the woman's flowing robe which hung tightly around her body and appeared to cover her breasts. But Cybil noticed the nipples were prominent, disproportionally so. *Horny Michelangelo*, she thought, and Cybil's half-smile turned into a little laugh.

"Let me check my tweets," she said out loud and reached for her iPhone inside her bag.

It had settled deep, near the bottom and under her wallet, change of clothes, prescription pain meds, flip-flops and iPad. Pushing aside what she didn't want, she felt around for the rubber edges of the iPhone's protective sleeve till she found it.

She touched the screen, fingers sliding where they had to, making sure her automated tweet engine would post her scheduled messages and music selections throughout the day. During busy weeks like this she programmed five to 10 tweets to run per day. When not too busy, she posted personally. With a large following eager for Cybil Raven Tweets, Facebook posts and music recommendations, she didn't want to disappoint.

Scrolling through, she saw the day's first two messages had tweeted, plus her Song of the Morning, which would also stream to Facebook.

@forsyth fountain for wedding dress shoot, cool this morning...

@early am light is great!

Ladies (Put a Ring on it) by Beyoncé

Typing in an impromptu manual tweet, she sent it into the stream: Lighting late ☹

Cybil also checked if William had texted. "Yes!" she said, spotting several texts in a row from William Gaston, her latest and most serious boyfriend. Head down, she proceeded to read:

Cybil, meant to text before
still dealing w mom's money men in NY
big mess with will issues
miss u back nxt wk

Cybil's shoulders slumped. *No apology for the argument.* She started to sit down but stopped halfway. Her head dropped further and she started chewing on her lip. She tossed the phone into her bag. Crossing her arms she leaned to one side, resting on her left leg, hip tilted. Holding herself, her right hand touched her left bicep. Her fingers strummed her tattoo, hidden under heavy makeup, above the elbow. She pursed her lips and puffed out a short breath while looking into her bag. *Cigarette. No*.

"My dear, frowns like that will simply add wrinkles as you get older," a familiar voice said to her. She looked up.

"John! How are you?" Cybil said to a plump man holding a leash that was connected to a little dachshund. "And you brought Lyle."

"He got tired of the park next to the house, so I brought him here for variety," John Block said. "My, that is a gorgeous dress. Can you keep it after the shoot?"

"Not this time," Cybil said.

John, a few inches taller than Cybil, and heavyset, leaned to one side and then another, taking in the whole view. He looked up at her and said, "Pity, I would have loved to borrow it and surprise Derrin when he came home. Would need to let it out quite a bit, though. Maybe that would be a big enough hint."

John laughed, as did Cybil. Smiling at her first friend in Savannah, she recalled when they had met. His architecture firm commissioned a multimedia ad campaign to build their brand outside of Savannah. Atlanta was where the auditions were held. Cybil almost didn't get the job but his vote broke the tie among the partners. At the wrap party after the filming, huddled in a corner with martinis, they talked for hours. Mostly about love for fashion and food and wine, but when they talked about family they connected and found much in common. John's younger sister had died from childhood leukemia, the same type Cybil had survived. Later when Cybil visited Savannah and John, he took to her like an older brother showing her the city and introducing her to his business network, which included William. When she moved to Savannah, John helped her get settled.

Lyle pulled at his leash, straightening it taut as he sniffed around bushes next to the bench. John, dressed in a plaid three-piece suit, lifted his confederate blue-gray fedora and wiped a sweating brow with his forearm.

"Walking this larger park always makes me perspire. I prefer the smaller one next to the house. I'll let you get back to work. Lyle probably needs to take care of business," John said. "Plus, we wouldn't want any yellow stains on the dress—would ruin the look." John walked past Cybil, following Lyle.

She reached out and squeezed his shoulder as he passed. "We need to get together soon, okay?" she said, smiling.

Dragged by Lyle a few feet farther, John glanced over his shoulder. "You bet, my dear, soon! Kiss, kiss!" He puckered his lips a couple of times.

Watching her friend continue down the park boulevard, she shifted to her right side. Her face felt warm and she could feel sweat starting to form on her brow. *Check makeup*. She bent down to reach into her bag and fumbled around for her case, when she heard a loud slapping sound. Straightening up, she looked in its direction in time to see a small woman falling to the ground. A large man stood over her, shaking his fist.

Cybil hiked up her skirt, kicked off her heels and ran toward the couple in double-time.

2

"What will happen to us?" Sofi said.

She looked up at Sister Anne and Sister George in front of her. Sister Anne looked back at Sofi, smiled and knelt on one knee in front of her.

"And how's Robby this morning?" Sister Anne asked, touching the stuffed rabbit in the little girl's arms.

Sofi, wearing the same clothes as the day before, a flower-print tank over her ever-present jeans, held one-eared Robby tight against her. Cotton spilled out from the poorly stitched hole where the ear once was. Her friend Cecilia, twice her size, stood next to her. The big girl's scarred left hand rested on Sofi's shoulder. Cecilia rocked back and forth, her mouth slack open. She tapped her leg in no particular rhythm with her palm. Thump. Thump … thump, thump … thump. Two roller suitcases, one small, one large, sat next to the girls.

"Cecilia's worried, so she packed for us," Sofi said, sighing.

Sofi's chin dropped to her chest. Her lower lip covered her upper one as if to comfort it. Squeezing the tattered Robby harder, a small puff of cotton blew out. Sister Anne watched it float down, as did Sofi. It landed on the floor between them, on the worn seal of St. Rita's Children's Home, open since 1875 to house Savannah's orphan girls.

"Why is Cecilia worried?" Sister Anne said, standing up and looking at the last special needs child at St. Rita.

"Oh, we talked about going to Florida to be with her sister," Sofi said.

"Why? You and Cecilia live here," Sister Anne said, clenching her teeth. Cecilia's older sister had been dead for years.

"But we can't stay here," Sofi said. "I heard voices saying the children had to be …." Her eyes looked up and to the right, searching.

"To be what, Sofi?" Sister Anne said.

"I think renvated. Yes … renvated!" Sofi said, smiling and stamping her foot on the hardwood floor. Her footfall echoed in the lobby.

"Could it be, relocated?" Sister Anne said, lifting her eyebrows.

Sofi and Cecilia liked to play hide-and-seek in the large lobby and in the hallway next to the kitchen and near Father Michael's office. Sister Anne supposed that Sofi had overhead loose talk.

"Maybe?" The little girl looked to the side, her smile fading.

"Sometimes grown-up talk can be confusing," Sister Anne said, nodding her head.

Sister Anne forced a smile and then knelt again to the child's level, looking into her eyes. She placed both hands on Sofi's shoulders, which felt bony and thin. Cecilia started to rock faster, moving her feet back and forth. Sofi glanced over her shoulder toward her friend and then back to the nun.

"Sofi, you know God will take care of you and Cecilia, you can trust him," Sister Anne said.

Sofi, unsmiling, looked straight at her and said, "Cecilia needs to go pee."

Sister Anne pursed her lips and looked up to see Sister George, leaning on her cane, standing behind Cecilia and Sofi. The older nun had come downstairs with Sister Anne to find out about the early morning voices in the lobby.

Sister George patted Cecilia on the back and said, “I’ll take you to the restroom now.”

Sister George took Cecilia’s hand. Her cane tapped every other step as they both went toward the hall restroom.

“Let’s sit over here,” Sister Anne said, pointing to the lobby bench near the tall, wooden, front double doors.

The large, square lobby reflected pre-Civil War design of southern plantation houses. Several tall stained-glass windows lined the walls. Morning light streamed through them, painting a bright row of colored squares across the wood floor. The plantation house had been donated to the diocese after the Civil War.

Sister Anne picked up Sofi and placed her gently on the bench before sitting next to her. Sofi scooted forward and sat on the edge, her short legs dangling. She swung them back and forth. With the movement, the little girl’s thin, wheat-colored hair, hanging past her shoulders, swayed. It had not seen a comb that morning.

“You must not worry, Sofi, God will take care of you. He never leaves you,” Sister Anne said.

Sofi’s head moved side to side as she looked down at her swinging legs. The dress hem below her knees rode up above them every time she swung her legs.

“But people leave, my mommy did. You won’t leave me, will you?” she said.

Sister Anne shifted forward. Her hands had been folded neatly in her lap. They reached for the bench beneath her for balance, fingers gripping tight. Her head dropped and she closed her eyes as she leaned. The bench creaked under the shifting weight.

She took a breath and looked up, across the lobby, her eyes sad. The floors had just been polished, the old wood smell mixing with the lemon-scented wax. It tingled her nose and she exhaled to clear it. Her sight settled on the centerpiece stained-glass window, the one installed there by the Sisters of Mercy after they moved into the donated home, and land, that eventually became St. Rita. The large multicolored window depicted clouds, the sun, rays of light and a huge white dove diving down from Heaven. The morning light had shifted. The dove had darkened to a dull gray.

Sister Anne swallowed, coughed. *I'm not the one to ask about leaving.*

Sofi turned to face Sister Anne, her eyebrows rising. Sister Anne gave a small smile. Sofi stared at her, saying nothing and looked down. Her legs had stopped swinging.

"I guess God is tired of taking care of us," Sofi said.

Sister Anne's shoulders slumped. "I'm not sure about that, but one thing is sure. …"

Sofi looked up. Sister Anne lifted her shoulders and put one arm around Sofi, squeezing her tight.

"We'll have a nice breakfast and leave tomorrow alone," Sister Anne said, smiling.

"Can we eat pancakes and bacon even though it's Tuesday?" Sofi said.

"Of course," Sister Anne said.

Sister George and Cecilia came back to the lobby. Fiddling with her dress, Cecilia trailed Sister George. Sofi jumped off the bench, her shoes tapping her steps as she ran toward them. Sister Anne got up and followed.

Smiling, Sofi ran up to Cecilia and said, "Sister Anne said we're going to have pancakes and bacon this morning—let's go!"

Cecilia grunted her approval. "Ess, ess, ancakes!"

Sofi grabbed Cecilia's hand and turned toward the dining room. She looked back at Sister Anne, who was smiling, and Sister George next to her.

Sister George stared straight ahead. "Pancakes and bacon on Tuesday, Sister Anne?"

"I don't care about the expense," Sister Anne replied, her voice rising. "I don't understand the trustees' report on the finances. It doesn't make sense.

"What do you mean?" Sister George said.

Sister Anne flung her hands over her head and said, "Things changed so fast. It certainly wasn't because of what we spend on these kids. When I came here I was told this work needed organization, not money."

Since she had been in the order close to seven years, Sister Anne's relative youth and military background had brought her to certain assignments. With fine red hair cut short, framing delicate Irish features, she seemed fragile, unassuming, a pushover. Yet things got done despite stressful circumstances, with few if any complaints from co-workers. Sister Anne was assigned to St. Rita, to help Father Michael improve and expand. The last thing she'd expected was to be involved with closing down a much-needed home for orphan girls.

Sister George nodded. "Okay, let's feed them well this morning. They've been up early and must be hungry."

They followed Sofi and Cecilia to the kitchen, passing by the stained-glass window. Drifting morning clouds had blunted the rising sun's intensity. The wind picked up, a rustling sound filled the hall, and the windows creaked under the changing air pressure. Sister Anne felt a light touch on her neck, as if the breeze had come inside. She glanced toward the window again; she swore the dove turned black for a second.

3

Stavos Gruner sat with his legs crossed, leaning back. With one arm resting along the back of the lone red velvet couch in Saya's Bottle Service Only lounge, he looked at ease. This particular grotto was reserved for him on Thursday nights, his favorite evening. He disdained the crowds on Fridays and Saturdays, of SCAD (Savannah College of Art and Design) college kids and overdressed, late-30 cougars in heat prowling for young men. Seated next to him with one hand on his thigh, a tall, skinny blonde who looked European or Slavic leaned forward to fetch Gruner's drink. Her large breasts nearly spilled out of a red cocktail dress a size too small.

He took the tumbler from her and drained the anise-flavored ouzo, on ice, allowing it to flow over his tongue. It was his third of the night. As she leaned back her hand slipped between his legs and she brushed him gently before sliding her hand back atop his leg. Smiling, he held the glass to his mouth and his tongue darted through it looking for the last ice cube, nearly melted. Finding it, he sucked it into his mouth, crushing it and swallowing the remains.

Next to the table, at military rest, stood Kurt, Gruner's perimeter bodyguard, ex-West German military police. He looked well-dressed except for the tight fit. Kurt tried in vain to hide a muscular upper body under off-the-rack jackets. He needed a custom fitting. Kurt adjusted his jacket, and the strap of a black leather gun holster peeked out. It melted into the black silk shirt he wore, as intended. He frowned as he looked across the dance floor, toward the entrance and the single staircase, the only exit to West Broughton Street. He squeezed his arms inward so he could feel the presence of his Heckler and Koch HK45 Compact. He didn't like that Saya had but one entry, one exit; it complicated his job of always making sure Stavos had an escape route. Kurt's father, ex-Stasi, East German Secret Police, told him bedtime stories about the escape routes from East to West he found and closed, often with people trapped in them. Stavos listened to Kurt's concerns but said not to worry, that if they needed an escape route at Saya, they'd make one, with Kurt in the lead.

"STAV! STAVOS!" A voice boomed. Its owner had just made his way through the sparse dance floor at the Saya Lounge. Asian themed with various-sized Buddhas watching from the walls, Saya drew an eclectic mix from all the cliques within Savannah. Blaring through the wall speakers the thudding music filled the room. Tonight's DJ hand-picked heavy bass-loaded tunes remixed from Lady Gaga.

The man's words registered but his bear-like open arms spoke louder to Stavos, who looked up and smiled broadly recognizing Vasily.

Next to Gruner sat his personal bodyguard, Markos. Dressed in a dark suit, white shirt and no tie, he looked relaxed in the dimly lit lounge. Stavos always had the overhead light turned off in his grotto. Seeing Vasily approach, Markos, wide as he was tall, stood up and put himself in front of Stavos. The bodyguard quick stepped in front of the approaching Vasily, which made him stop outside the grotto entrance curtains. He stood under one of the bright hanging pearl-stranded lights.

Vasily smiled and raised his arms parallel to his shoulders. Markos, now close to him, moved his large hands, patting him down. He moved fast and touched lightly, having done this many times. Markos turned back to look at Gruner and nodded his head.

Stavos looked up at his old friend, now a deal broker. Vasily's blonde hair and square head shone under the light. Mangled ears on each side looked like crushed flowers. Stavos and Vasily had met in the ring as Army boxers, as part of the goodwill exchange between Russia and Greece. They became friends, despite fierce fights in the ring, because of a common interest in selling contraband. Vasily stood erect, still looking fit. He stared at the blonde on the couch but without lust.

Stavos looked over at his arm candy for the night and tilted his head to usher her away. She looked from the new arrival to Stavos, grimaced and got up quickly.

"I'll go to the ladies room now!" she said with a sniffle, wiping her nose.

"Good idea. Here." Stavos grabbed her small hand, which was swallowed by his two large ones, nails manicured. Hidden from view, he placed a small plastic bag with white powder in her palm.

She smiled and leaned down to whisper in his ear. Her heavily applied J'Adore perfume reached his nose. "You are such a great guy!"

Stavos took a deep breath, tasting her scent. "I know," he said.

She moved in closer, her warm breath landing on his cheek. "Don't get all tired tonight talking business. I've got a friend we can hook up with later. She's interested."

She licked his ear, twirling her tongue around his lobe. Stavos grinned and nodded his head. She moved away, stepping past the small table in front of the couch. On the dance floor she passed through a group of dancers now hopping to a quicker beat.

Markos moved to the couch and sat at the end. Vasily seated himself close to Gruner but turned his head to follow the arm candy's swinging and shapely rear end. The clinging thin red satin showed no panty lines as she walked away.

"For a Greek bastard, you do good with the bitches. Tits on a stick, I remember that's how you like them," Vasily said as he watched her disappear down the long hallway to the restrooms.

"Vasily, tell me, what do you call a beautiful girl in Russia?" Stavos asked, waiting a second.

Vasily turned toward Stavos and he shrugged. "What?"

"A tourist," Stavos said and started laughing. Vasily joined him, letting out a low rumbling, coughing laugh.

"Yes, yes, and all my girls are tourists visiting Russia," Vasily said, joking about his "trade."

Stavos motioned to the assigned barmaid, his hand bidding her over. The owner made sure one worker focused all evening on Stavos's reserved lounge. Quickly, a $30-bottle of Armadale vodka appeared along with another bottle of ouzo. The owner kept a case of the Greek imported liquor on hand exclusively for Gruner.

Vasily poured the ouzo into Stavos's empty tumbler. The aniseed, licorice and mint scent tinged by wintergreen and fennel floated upward. Vasily sniffed at it.

"Don't know why you like this candy drink," Vasily said.

Stavos poured the expensive vodka into Vasily's glass.

Vasily picked up his glass, Stavos his, and toasted to his friend's health in Russian: "Твоё здоровье!" Each drained their drink and set their glass on the table.

"It's good to see you, Vasily. What can I do for you?" Stavos said.

Normally he calls, rarely visits, almost never at night, Stavos thought, staring at him with narrowing eyes.

Vasily's face grew serious. "I have a new partner needing shipping, usual cargo, schedule most important, no delays. Interested?"

Stavos leaned back and smiled. "Yes, more business for both of us. Usual finder's fee for you?"

"I was not sure I was going to recommend you after the last shipment," Vasily said with a calm voice. He picked up his glass and twirled the liquid around.

Stavos's eyebrows pinched downward, his smile disappeared. He bent forward. In the darkened grotto, his face came into a beam of light from the next booth. "What do you mean?" he said.

"One lost shipment in a year I can understand, risk of the business, but two in six months," Vasily said, shaking his head side to side.

That son of a bitch Roger! The missed drops, Stavos thought. Stavos blinked a few times and rubbed his chin.

Despite being in his mid-fifties, Stavos maintained a full head of dyed black hair, professionally styled and slicked back, which gave him a sleek look. Short, neat sideburns faded into light-gray stubble over a strong chin. His black eyebrows drew your notice to dark stabbing eyes.

"Vasily … Vasily …." Stavos let the name linger like he was talking to family. He placed his hand on his guest's shoulder, close to the neck, squeezing gently. "I am so sorry for that, but it did not cost you a thing. I made good on my guarantee, as usual," Stavos said.

"The money, I could not care about," Vasily said. "The shipment was a test from this partner and now I am not sure I can bring him back. He was willing to pay triple the normal shipping charges."

Stavos paused. Roger's face now filled his mind. Stavos tightened his lips and ground his teeth. That marina rat had cost him. His mind focused on the lost profits.

Through a thin smile Stavos said, "Tell your customer the next shipment is free—goodwill. If it's to his liking, then he can pay two, not three times."

He knew the three times offer was a lie. Vasily always tried to up his take.

Vasily said nothing. His head turned right and left, scanning the Saya Lounge dance floor. The music had moved to a heavy rap beat and dancers moved frantically to the rhythm.

On the street above, a few walkers strolling by heard the loud music and looked through the open entrance to a stairwell leading downward. A small sign, hard to see, hung on the brick façade. Saya had been constructed below a historic building on West Broughton Street. You took steps to a basement lounge well decorated with teak and rosewood. The white pillars lining the dance floor supported the low wood ceiling. Across the ceiling, strategically placed hanging pearl-stranded lights supplied minimal illumination. People liked the dark.

"Okay, I will tell him. Maybe I can get him back," Vasily said. "I will let you know soon."

Stavos's guest stood up, brought his right hand to his temple and saluted goodbye. Turning on his heels, Vasily walked across the dance floor, dodging couples and free-styling singles before going up the steps.

Stavos had remained seated and barely moved through Vasily's departure. Eyes staring straight into the crowd, Stavos was not looking at anyone or anything in particular. He lifted his right hand and ran it over his hair, which didn't need adjusting.

Kurt moved closer, anticipating some instruction; he had learned to read Stavos's moods. Markos leaned forward, moving his large rear end to the couch's edge, his thick legs planted like trunks.

The arm candy returned and proceeded to sit next to Stavos. He looked up at her with unblinking, cold eyes. She knew better, nodded and puckered her lips to air-kiss him from a distance, mouthing the word "Later." She turned and found an empty seat at the bar next a good-looking couple. Stavos kept a casual eye on her and the couple, his mind on Roger. Shots appeared before them, on the bar, and they drank and looked engaged in conversation. After a few minutes, the arm candy's hand found a place on the woman's back while they were talking. Her thumb moved up and down, caressing the woman's bare back. The women smiled at each other. Soon the three got up and left together.

Stavos grinned and turned his face toward Kurt.

"Kurt?" Stavos said.

"Yes."

"Tell me again your thoughts on Roger."

Kurt shook his head. "I know he's been with you a long time, before me. But he's sloppy, imprecise in his execution. Even with simple plans I give him. It's gotten worse lately."

Stavos put his hands on his knees. His chest heaved as he took a long breath. "I want to talk to Roger tomorrow," he said.

"I'll get the boat ready in the morning then," Kurt said.

Stavos nodded and then turned to Markos. "Get Roger to join us in the morning, leave now. We'll meet you at the boat."

He raised his arm again toward the attendant, pointing to the table needing to be bused. Markos stood up, looked over at Kurt and down at Stavos. He smiled. He stepped away and moved deliberately through the dancing crowd, who instinctively moved out of his way. As he reached the steps leading out of Saya, he looked back to the grotto but couldn't see inside it. He turned and walked up into the Savannah night.

4

A man sat on a bench near the fountain, watching Cybil run toward the couple. Dressed in hiking shorts and a blue long-sleeved soccer jersey, he lifted his hand to adjust mirrored aviator sunglasses. Behind the mirrors his eyes followed her from left to right. Her reflection traveled ghostlike from one lens to the other.

Moves very well, even so dressed. He closed his eyes for a second and took a deep, slow, calming breath. He stifled his impulse to move. *I am here to observe and report, I cannot interfere*, he told himself again as he had many times since arriving in Savannah. He'd said it this morning during prayers, back at the sparsely furnished rented apartment. With a shawl over his head and on his calloused knees, he connected to the transcendent and pondered this confusing assignment, so far away from Cascia in Umbria, Italy, and his brothers and sisters in the Order.

A couple walked by, looking at a map of the park while talking. The man looked at the woman and pointed at the central fountain, which sprayed water and mist in all directions. Next he pointed to the Civil War Confederate Memorial, past the park's amphitheatre, along the main boulevard.

The man on the bench thought, *Tourists with an interest in history. What you should be worried about is the future.*

As if they had heard his warning, they glanced over at him. His arms were spread-eagled across the bench's back. He looked relaxed. His right sleeve had ridden up, revealing a sliver of an intricate black-and-red wrist tattoo, which caught the couple's attention. He noticed their eyebrows rise in interest and calmly brought his arms down, resting one in his lap and the other on the backpack lying next to him.

She is quick, a few seconds more. His gaze followed Cybil, waiting for her to reach the couple, a tall, fit man in a business suit shaking his fist over a shorter woman on her knees, sobbing. As he focused on the model in the wedding dress, he smiled, not noticing the dark shadow that had traveled on the sidewalk by his feet.

Overhead in a bright sky, the sun reached higher than the morning clouds. A large blackbird flew above the fountain toward the forest. It reached the trees, darting and dodging expertly between thick limbs and thin branches. It found a perfect spot high within one of the many large oak trees common to Forsyth Park. The bird had a perfect view of the man on the park bench and beyond him, Cybil Raven.

5

Four Months Earlier

The new cell phone vibrated on the kitchen table where he always sat for breakfast. Vasily saw "UNKNOWN" on the display but knew it could only be "him," since he had given him the phone and only he ever called on it. Picking it up, the "import specialist" pressed Answer.

"Yes," he said, and then took a full bite of scrambled eggs. Vasily's face screwed up. *Too much salt.*

"This is Mr. Kasen," said the now familiar voice with an English tinge.

"Yes. Yes, how can I help you," Vasily said, gulping the eggs.

Holding the phone to his ear, his other hand grabbed a half-full vodka bottle sitting on the table. He emptied it into a torn-open half-gallon orange juice carton. Lifting the carton, his hand made small circles, swirling the mixture and splashing the contents. A couple of drops escaped from the container and plopped next to his plate.

"I'm not sure if you are a consumer of news but if you have read the papers the last few days, the story of the warehouse raid affects our arrangement," he said.

Vasily's eyebrows rose and he looked across his apartment, to the coffee table in front of the couch. On it, scattered newspaper sections lay covering the laminated wood table. *Warehouse?*

"Yes, Yes. I read about it," Vasily said, lying.

He got up, took a big gulp from the carton, the bitter taste telling him the juice should have been thrown out. Walking over to the coffee table, he sat down on the couch and rustled through the papers trying to find the story.

One section from two days ago lay underneath the table. Above the fold, a photo showed the bashed-in side of a warehouse, curling twisted sheet metal, shattered overhead windows, and shards dangling that were barely connected. The headline over the picture read: "Authorities raid suspected smuggling operation: three suspects dead."

The article described a raid on Warehouse 50, located at the Port Newark Container Terminal, less than 13 miles from Ground Zero. A joint task force of FBI, Port Authority Police and Homeland Security had secured the warehouse after an armed confrontation with three suspects believed to be local organized crime. The three dead suspects perished under sniper fire when they shot at the authorities after the assault vehicle breached the warehouse walls.

Vasily gave up on his search and said, "Please continue, Mr. Kasen."

"I may need to rely on your services farther south. Do you think your friend can handle my volume and timing?" Mr. Kasen said.

"Sure, sure, he can!" *Bigger cut for me.*

"I am unconvinced. My contacts tell me he has a small operation and my work is extremely important to me. I cannot tolerate failure," Mr. Kasen said, his voice slowing.

Vasily started to sweat. Even though alone, he looked right, then left. His mind reached for anything so as not to lose this premium paying customer. *What did Stavos say last time we drank—got drunk? Lying, they can tell. Shades of personal truth, they can believe. Yes!*

"Mr. Kasen, my friend expanded his operations over the last year. He and I worked together in the Mediterranean helping others with their import needs. His father was a fisherman who taught him all about the sea. His boats are the fastest and best equipped, very low profile. He is now the southern operator most discriminating shippers go to. I give my personal assurance he will succeed for you … and your cause," Vasily said, adding the last part on a guess.

Silence for 15 seconds. Vasily's heart beat faster … 30 seconds. Vasily looked at the phone. It was still connected.

Mr. Kasen's voice started steady and even. "Very well, I must insist on a test. … It must succeed before I will commit to this friend of yours."

"Wonderful!" Vasily said louder than he wanted to. He grimaced, shaking his head.

"I will contact you in a week with the details of the first test. Goodbye," Mr. Kasen said before disconnecting.

Vasily leaned back on the couch and puffed out a few breaths.

Leaning forward, he fished his personal cell phone from his bathrobe and punched Stavos's speed dial number.

The phone rang once, twice. Vasily reran the words in his head: *I will test first. Damn, Stavos's boat missed the other client's drop last month.*

Stavos's smile came through with his loud voice: "What do you want, you Russian dog!"

6

Cybil reached the sobbing woman sprawled on the ground. The large man who had slapped her had moved a few feet away and glared at the woman, his arms folded calmly across his jacket. He turned toward the woods, looking away, and didn't notice Cybil's arrival. She released her grip on the white skirt and it straightened out.

Cybil bent over the woman, who was now sitting up with her face in her hands. Tears dripped between her fingers onto her grass-stained dress slacks. Cybil put her left hand on the woman's shoulder and gave a light squeeze.

"Are you all right?" Cybil said in a low voice.

The woman nodded meekly.

Cybil glanced at the boyfriend or husband staring into space. Her eyes narrowed, her breath slowed. She could feel her right hand tighten into a ball.

Turning back to the woman, Cybil said, "Only little boys with little minds strike a woman, let alone anyone else."

The woman looked up at Cybil for a few seconds. Her face grew sad.

"Is this the first time?" Cybil said.

"No, it's not," the woman said in a low voice.

Cybil guessed she must be in her 40s. She had a slight build and was nicely dressed for office work. Volunteering at the Crisis Center had taught Cybil that domestic abuse lives in all classes of society and before victims can think about change, they need to get away to be safe.

Helping her up, Cybil brushed off the grass that had been sticking to the woman's blouse and slacks. Cybil smiled at the woman and held her shoulders with both hands. The woman wiped the remaining moisture from her eyes. Cybil turned and waved at the two public service cops, one heavyset, one thin. They had drifted about 100 yards down the boulevard and were looking at the Confederate War Memorial, thus they missed witnessing the violence. After her wave, they walked toward her. Jimmy, Judy and Sasha stood by the bench near Cybil's bag and were looking around. Jimmy turned and saw Cybil. He gathered Judy and Sasha and started toward her.

From behind Cybil came a man's voice: "What the hell are you doing?"

The woman looked over Cybil's shoulder and her eyes widened. Cybil turned to see him approaching. At about six feet, he stood half a foot taller than her. The woman, shorter than Cybil, started to speak.

Cybil said, "Let me talk to him."

Stepping forward in front of the woman, Cybil said, "Sir, it might be best if you and your companion had some time and space apart to calm down."

"What fucking business is that of yours? And what's with the wedding dress?"

Cybil took a deep breath. With a half-smile, she appealed again. "Sir, no need to be rude. I will help her get home and you can catch up with her at a later time."

When the man drew closer a mix of his body odor and a whiff of gin reached her nose. She opened her mouth to breathe, avoiding the smell. Cybil forced a thin, polite smile, turned her back to him and faced the woman. He snorted several times and his breathing quickened.

"Is there someplace you can stay, sort things out?" Cybil said, hopeful for a smart reply.

"My sister's place," she said.

Cybil smiled. She looked to the public service cops who were some 50 yards away and moving toward them in no hurry. She and the woman started walking to meet the approaching policemen.

"Debra, don't you walk away from me!" the man shouted.

Cybil, walking alongside the woman, shook her head and whispered, "Ignore him."

Cybil heard a quick shuffle of feet against the rough concrete. She felt a sweaty hand on her left shoulder, closing a strong grip. She stopped.

Jimmy, Judy and Sasha had closed the gap no more than 20 yards away. They froze in their tracks.

"Uh-oh, not good. Big mistake," Judy said.

Sasha looked at Judy and laughed. Jimmy sighed and his arms dropped to his side.

"See that smile?" Sasha said, pointing out Cybil's face beaming a mischievous grin.

"Yep, here it comes," Judy said, her voice rising as she observed her friend.

Cybil's left arm shot straight into the air. The man looked up for a second, long enough for her heel to stamp hard on his left instep, directly below the ankle.

"Aaaahhhhh!" the man brayed.

He reflexively bent over, easing his grip. Cybil's left arm cartwheeled back in a long arc, forcing the man's arm under hers. Her other hand grabbed his wrist, bending it unnaturally into a practiced aikido hold. Both his knees struck the ground with a thud. The model in the wedding dress continued the move, her wrist hold tightening. The swoosh of her silk skirt was barely noticeable as she slid to his side, bending him low enough to place her bare foot at his shoulder. Stretching his arm straight and bending his wrist to the point of breaking, she pushed her foot farther in. Flexing her toes she noticed her red toenail polish and smiled, thinking, *I could pop his shoulder out, that would calm him down.*

The small woman standing by had a smile on her face and a quizzical look as if she had never seen her man in such a position.

"Are you going to behave? Or will I have to press assault charges after you get out of the hospital with a dislocated shoulder and broken wrist?" Cybil said, her voice betraying her enjoyment.

"Okay, okay. Debra, I'm sorry, I'll catch up with you later," he said.

Cybil pulled his arm a little more and the man grimaced.

"Yes, ma'am, yes, I mean it. I'll make no more trouble," he said.

Cybil released the hold and jumped back at the ready. The public service cops, Jimmy, Judy and Sasha arrived at the scene.

The man got up and looked at the group. He gingerly moved his shoulder and held it with his other hand. He looked at Cybil with a confused look, shaking his head. He frowned, nodded to Debra and limped away toward Park Avenue.

"Is everyone all right here?" the heavy cop said.

"Glad we were able to get here in time," the thin one added.

Cybil glanced at their direction, one eyebrow rising.

"If you could see that Debra, here, gets to her car, it will help," Cybil said.

"We sure will, miss." Both cops smiled at Cybil but didn't move.

Cybil lifted her hands, shooing the cops away like children. They followed Debra, who was walking toward Gaston Street.

Smiling at the shoot team, Cybil said, "Let's get back to work, shall we?"

7

Driving over the last bridge before the mainland, the van reached the apex, bringing the outline of Savannah's downtown in full view. Sister Anne thought she saw the top of St. John the Baptist Cathedral. After pushing all the buttons on the vehicle door handle, she lowered the windows. Fresh air rushed in to sweep away the river's rotten-egg smell that had crept in. In the morning, gases from decaying algae on Savannah's waterways filled passing cars making the trek from beach to downtown. Feeling the wind rush around the interior, she took a breath. The sulfur smell had dissipated.

The van sped downhill and moved onto the tree-lined Victory Drive, or 80, as the locals called it. Reaching Abercorn Street she turned right, toward Calhoun Square and just past it, Lafayette Square, picturesque urban parks well maintained by the city. Lafayette sat next to St. John the Baptist Cathedral, her destination. She had an appointment with the bishop to talk about St. Rita's closing.

She parked behind the Hamilton Turner Inn, a three-story bed-and-breakfast next to Lafayette. The inn's exterior, even from the back, looked well maintained. Smooth white alabaster walls were bordered on the corners by off-set gray bricks. Walking up Macon Street she reached the corner and turned left toward the inn. Arriving early she had time to see Tim and Georgia, the innkeepers, the family that had adopted Emma from St. Rita.

The inn's French Provincial architecture looked new despite ancient details. Walking by the black wrought-iron fencing, she moved up the stairs to the porch. Three layers of recessed arches framed the door, focusing attention deep into the lobby where, behind the main desk, Tim and Georgia greeted their guests. Longtime owners, they worked hard for the repeat business the centrally located B&B brought in year after year.

When they had adopted several years ago Sister Anne handled the matter and found herself also "adopted" into the family. As she entered the empty lobby, she walked toward the front desk. Savannah's tourist season had not yet started and the place lacked the usual noisy voices, suntan lotion smells and crying babies.

"Sister Anne!" Tim yelled from behind the counter. His smile spread across his plump face.

Sister Anne exhaled as Tim's bearlike embrace squeezed her against his chest. His fresh white shirt had a clean smell, as if just washed at the inn laundry. Tim, over six foot and a half, stood a foot taller than his friend. He stepped to the side and gave her a strong shoulder squeeze while looking down at her.

"Georgia's out shopping. Can you stay for lunch? She'll be right back," Tim said.

"I'd love to, but I have an appointment with Bishop Cantwell," Sister Anne said. "I parked behind, is that all right?"

Tim released his hold and stepped back. He raised his hand, stroking his chin. His smile faded and his eyes lost some light as he said, "It's about St. Rita, huh?"

"Yes."

"Do you think the bishop can do anything?" Tim said.

"I don't know. Father Michael and Reverend Scott don't know I'm here, but they will soon," Sister Anne said.

"Father Michael and Reverend Scott," Tim said their names in a low voice, shaking his head.

He moved his hand from his chin and patted his chest a few times. He opened his mouth to say something but stopped, pursing his lips. Sister Anne looked at Tim, waiting.

"Never mind. When you come into town again, let Georgia and me know ahead of time and we can make plans. We can tell you how well Emma is doing," Tim said.

"Okay, I will," Sister Anne said.

She strode out the lobby doors and stepped down the steep stairs, picking her way carefully. Her flats clicked against Lafayette's brick pavers as she made her way across stopping at the fountain in the middle of the Square.

The water smelled fresh, aired by the fountain's labor. Glancing over her right shoulder toward the cathedral, she sighed and looked down at her dress. Opting not to wear a habit today, she had picked a dress that could have used ironing. She smoothed a few wrinkles. Not liking how it lay, she smoothed it again then a third time. Looking to see if anyone was around, she reached underneath her blouse to adjust her right bra strap which had fallen off the shoulder. Small-chested, she often wondered why she even bothered. Still trim from her days in the Army, she kept in shape by running. Sister Anne's demeanor didn't shout "nun." She looked like a pretty young woman with fine red hair who dressed modestly for the times.

Water cascaded over the fountain's three tiers and splashed into the basin, a circular pool approximately 30 feet across. The falling water created ripples, moving out and coming back crossing each other, creating unpredictable patterns. Sister Anne gazed across the basin and around, back to the water in front of her. Dried leaves floated on the surface, bobbing with the ever-present ripples; scattered coins shimmered at the bottom. She bent down and reached a few inches into the water to touch one. The water was cold and the coins deeper than at first look. *I'll get wet*. The ripples she caused pushed the leaves away, floating, drifting.

Money's out of reach. She turned and walked toward the cathedral.

*

Forty-five minutes later, the appointment with the bishop over, Sister Anne returned to the nearby square's fountain. Seated on the circular pool's brick wall, she looked back at the cathedral. Two tall spires reached up into Heaven, one on each side of the main structure. Small crosses were atop every converging point. The restoration in 2000 had helped it stay pretty, if only on the outside.

Sister Anne folded her hands in her lap and threw her shoulders back, straightening her spine. She pulled her flat, firm stomach in. Her chin moved up and her eyes looked straight ahead but at nothing in particular. Her feet were together, heels touching. *Why am I sitting at attention?* Images of drills and lectures at Ft. Bragg flashed through her mind.

*

At one particular class on Unit Cohesion she remembered not paying attention when the instructor went over the material that Anne felt was obvious. Seated next to a row of windows, she looked through the glass to the practice fields and also saw her reflection. Her face appeared to her, floating. Her jade-green eyes peered at her narrow, oval face. *Like your typical Irish lass, pixie nose and all,* she thought.

*

The leaves of a large oak tree swayed back and forth and the sound of their struggle against one another brought her back. The strong breeze pushed through the treetops. Old leaves fell, no longer needed, a few landing in front of her feet. She could smell the water behind her. The gentle cascading sounds didn't soothe her, though. She let her shoulders drop, her feet shifting wider for balance.

Reaching into her satchel past personal items (including her ever-present mints) she pulled out a new composition book. She had made a few fresh scribbles and notes on a page from her meeting. She ripped that page out and crumpled it. She dropped it on the brick wall but then a puff of wind pushed the wad to the ground, next to the leaves. She left it there.

The breeze picked up again, rustling through the trees. Sister Anne felt the wind on her cheeks and smelled the aroma of vegetation and soil traveling in the air. On a blank page, she started to write her prayer to God. At the convent, she learned that writing out prayers slowed the mind and "gives your soul space to breathe before your thoughts ascend …" Sister Marjorie, her favorite instructor, had said.

"Our Father, who art in Heaven," she wrote, and then stopped. Sister Anne bowed her head, closed her eyes and took a deep breath. Opening her eyes and gripping her pen, she wrote more discourse than prayer: "I cannot understand why this is happening—greater purpose? Shutting down St. Rita?"

Sister Anne looked up, her eyes searching for words. She looked down to keep writing. "Everything has a reason—cheap slogans of faith! Those who conclude as such are like cheating schoolboys who copy the answer out of a book without working out the sum for themselves."

Gripping the pen harder, she pressed down, almost breaking through the paper.

"I hated it when the Army field chaplains told this over and over during hospital visits. Telling young soldiers trying to figure out how to go on without their legs—everything has a reason—COP-OUT!"

She glanced at her satchel and noticed the Hello Kitty decal Sofi had stuck on the flap. She smiled and kept writing.

"Sofi, Cecilia and the other children have a place with me and the Sisters. The foster system is so unpredictable. I am sure a good family will come and take Sofi into their arms BUT NOT IF SHE'S NOT THERE! The bishop, Father Michael and Reverend Scott have done nothing but tell us we have to go. I wish they would go to ..."

Sister Anne stopped writing. She grimaced. *I can't wish them harm.* She resumed her writing.

"I left all that I loved for you. It was my choice. Wasn't that enough? What about them. They have no choice. What will happen to Sofi? Cecilia so depends on her. If they are split up, she will not do well. They are like sisters."

Stopping, Sister Anne looked up from her notebook. Tears formed and a few dropped onto the pages. She put her pen to paper again.

"Are you crying, God? Do you even feel anything?" Sister Anne wrote quickly, her pen breaking through the paper. She stopped and took a breath. *I'm sorry.*

She continued writing: "God, please act, show me about love, show Sofi you are not tired of us. A check for a million dollars in the mail today—would be a good start."

Sister Anne smiled and wrote: "Dear Lord, you know everything and run the universe, but a little attention to us down here!"

Like all husbands I wonder if he ever really hears me. She looked at her watch and closed her book.

Sister Anne stood up, slid the book into the satchel and slung it over her shoulder. Through the treetops the bright sun cast light cutting into the heavy shade. She took a step but stopped short. A small dark shadow appeared at her feet and moved fast toward the large tree she had passed earlier. The shadow climbed the trunk and rested on a thick limb where it met its maker, a large blackbird.

Interesting. She walked back toward her car, her route taking her by the strange bird. As she went past she felt a need to look at it. It didn't move except for its head, which followed her direction. The sound of her flats echoed, surprising her. A few more steps and Anne stopped again.

Her heart was beating faster. Her breath grew shallower. Turned fully around, she looked directly at the blackbird. It flapped its wings once and then flew straight up, making its way around the tree limbs between it and Heaven. It made no sound as it flew. *Strange.* Anne's eyes followed it up through the treetops and finally across the sun. Her eyes squinted as she raised her hand to shield her face from the bright rays.

Pausing, she told herself in a low voice, "No, no, it can't be. That part of my life is gone, so how does that help me now?" Anne looked down and around the square, unfocused, blinking.

A couple walking their dog turned to stare at her for a second and then continued following their pet.

Sister Anne stood still. Exhaling, she looked across the square, through the trees, to the brightly lit cathedral. She crossed her arms and held herself close as if a cold chill passed. With her left arm folded over her right, her left hand rubbed just above her elbow.

She spoke again, her voice trailing off. "She won't see me or want to hear from me, let alone help. Cybil hates me!"

8

The warm wind on Stavos's face felt familiar, reminding him of the stiff trade winds off the coast of Greece. His father had taught him to sail on their small skiff. Now he sat in his custom-made fishing chair at the bow of his 50-foot cruiser. At 11 years old he could navigate the local waters and find prime fishing locations. His father taught him many good things on their trips—reading the sea, fishing wisdom and gutting fish quickly—but most outings ended badly.

When the beer ran out the arguing began. One fight ended with Stavos flipping over the side into the water after a punch in the face when the boy complained about his father's drinking. The boy learned what he needed that day.

Gruner's yacht, its name, *μοίρα*, written in blood-red Greek lettering, knifed through the Savannah River channel powered by twin 400 HP inboard engines, top of class. Today the Atlantic, their destination, appeared calm. A passing commercial fishing boat sent a small wake toward them but it had no effect on the large advancing boat. The sun had no company in the cloudless sky. Stavos rose from his chair. He stepped to the front bow rail. The wind picked up as the ship increased its speed beyond the outer markers. Gruner's jet-black hair, thick with gel, stayed unaffected by the breeze. He passed his hand over, smoothing nothing amiss. Large, muscular hands powered by thick, wide forearms gripped the railing. He leaned forward. Years of dock work in Greece had chiseled a lean, powerful upper body with a tapered lean waist. His handsome tanned face and well-dressed habits, at every occasion turned heads, male and female.

He thought of that silly ship movie a few years ago, the one Michelle liked. "I may not be King of the World, but Savannah is mine. Soon the whole South," he said to the wind.

He took a deep breath and he gripped the rail tighter.

Gruner turned around and sat on the rail, looking back toward the wheelhouse where Kurt steered. His blonde, thinning military buzz cut over a square head made him look like your typical cop. Except for the twisted nose. Too many fights, more with his fellow cops than suspects, littered his work record. The last fight, over a fellow MP's wayward wife, left the jealous husband in a coma and ended Kurt's law enforcement career.

"Kurt, are we going to be on time?" Gruner said. His deep-black eyes peered at his employee but then he smiled.

Kurt, who kept the Stavos crime business machinery on schedule, preferred printed sea maps and rarely used the GPS. The last time he did, he had programmed the wrong digits for latitude and they got lost for a few hours.

The ex-MP shook his head and frowned. "Not my fault, but it will not happen again. You have a memory like a woman, Stavos."

Stavos clapped his hands and laughed. Markos laughed also. At the back of the boat with a beer in hand, Markos looked imposing, even sitting down. When he stood, his thick arms seemed less to hang than perch off his shoulders. He looked like a walking block of marble whenever he moved.

"Yeah Kurt, we need to be on schedule, like Roger does!" Markos's chest heaved as his laugh grew louder.

He lifted his beer bottle, drinking the remaining bitter contents. He tilted his large head, completely bald, to the left, toward their passenger. Just then the ship raised up a few feet in the water due to a swell. It lifted the boat before it splashed down. Water sprayed onto the stern, much of it landing at Roger's bound feet.

Sitting next to Markos, Roger sat with hands and feet tied with plastic zip ties. The ridged vinyl had cut into his skin. Dried blood had coagulated under his right eyebrow in a clump. His right eye was swollen shut. On the left side of his face, blood slowly dripped from a deep cut at the corner of his mouth, which was starting to heal. He kept licking his lips every few seconds, tasting salt air mixed with his fresh blood. The cut spanned from the corner of his mouth to the middle of his cheek. It looked like a knife had been dragged through it.

"Can I have something to drink?" Roger said. "Please."

Bending over an open cooler at his feet, Markos tossed his empty in. It clinked against the other empties. Reaching in, he brought up another beer for himself. He shook it and opened it in Roger's face. The jet rush of cold ale sprayed into his eyes and burned them. Roger pecked in the air to drink what he could before it spilled onto the white vinyl deck.

"Kurt, about how much longer before we get to Cutter's Point?" Stavos asked.

"About another hour," Kurt said.

"Okay, I'm going to close my eyes for a few minutes," Stavos said.

The warm sun, the sea, just like back in Thrace, Stavos thought for a moment. He leaned back in the fishing chair, at ease. He drifted off thinking of home, the food, Mother. His peace, as usual, was interrupted by his father's big, rough-hewn hands hitting him.

9

After the late starting photo shoot, Cybil raced home, not wanting to miss meeting Sebastian and June at the bus stop. At breakfast she had promised to walk them home, a rare occurrence given her schedule. She grinned, recalling how the photo shoot went from a disaster to success despite the interruption. Driving faster than she should on Gaston to catch I-16, *Promises are to be kept,* she thought.

Slowing her breathing, she replayed the incident at the park. The 30-minute drive to her home in Southbridge, Savannah's semiprivate golf community, gave her time to reflect. As she passed through the Whitaker intersection she looked right, down the road. It was too far to see the Aikido Savannah Dojo on Broughton Street. *Was too slow engaging the wrist grapple and lock. Got to schedule a workout with Sensei Dan. A pro would have blocked it and knocked me on my ass,* she thought.

The statue at the fountain at Forsyth Park remained on her mind. Cybil could almost feel the wind on her lips and the chill she'd felt when the shadow crossed over it. Goose bumps again appeared on Cybil's arms. She checked the sky. *Nothing here, nothing coming.* She glanced at her iPhone resting in its cradle. *Must not text while driving. But I can still read.* She pulled it out to check while her eyes darted down and back up to the windshield. Cybil navigated through heavy traffic, her reflexes sharp, her blue BMW responsive as she weaved through traffic and passed slow cars clogging both lanes.

Passing by a large car moving slowly, she saw an old man at the wheel. Cybil looked into the rearview mirror and stared with irritation at new wrinkles around her eyes, this year's edition. Genetics, nutrition and controlled partying had kept obvious aging at bay, but at 31 she was pushing her luck. Most models had an expiration date of 29, an unwritten rule at agencies.

Looking down to her iPhone, she punched her steering wheel Bluetooth button since it was quiet enough; the BMW's top was up.

"Call Sensei Dan," she said.

The auto dialer kicked in right away, reaching out to his private cell number. The phone rang twice. Cybil looked at the dashboard clock and hoped she wasn't bothering him. Dan, a devout Muslim convert from Vietnam, kept to a disciplined schedule, only booking sessions between his five daily prayers.

The phone clicked on. "Hello, Cybil," Dan said.

"Did I interrupt anything?"

"Not at all, just gearing up for another session. I have a class with eight- to twelve-year-olds. Sebastian could be a great student. He has your moves. He's fast for Pop Warner football," Dan said.

"Still thinking about it. Can you fit me in for a session? Need to brush-up."

"Sure, I have an open slot Friday afternoon, will that work?"

"Can't check my calendar while driving but I'll text back."

"Works for me," Sensei Dan said.

"Bye now," Cybil said, punching the hang-up icon on her steering wheel.

She glanced down again at her phone's call history and noticed a missed call from a familiar number. She pressed Call Back.

"Hello, Covered Dish Kitchen Goods. May I help you?"

"May I speak with Miss SE, please. I want to schedule a Covered Dish Party," Cybil said.

After a pause, then a few clicks, Cybil's iPhone flashed twice. A small icon in the Japanese language appeared on her display. "I'll transfer you now."

A raspy woman's voice came on the line: "That was quick."

"Hello to you too, by the way. Have you learned to boil water while running this new business?" Cybil said, smiling.

"Funny girl, you know I hate cooking. I thought the contractors would find the humor in the unit's call screening. Wait till next month. You'll be calling into an adult novelty store. You can then order properly sized companionship," Sonja said.

Cybil laughed, “So, what’s up?”

“Since this is now a secure line, I may have an assignment for you,” Sonja said.

Cybil’s heart jumped. Her recent cyber security work had been boring. Simple network analysis of suspect financial transactions. The U.S. District Attorney had given her a lame assignment chasing down forensics on mortgage and finance companies with maybe a link to money laundering. She had found nothing solid and had to tell him it was a dead end. It was interesting because the name of an attorney she knew, Blitz Thompson, came up a couple of times. But it evolved to nothing substantial.

“Remember the work you did for the A27 Jump Jet Contract? It is similar but with a Department of Homeland Security twist,” Sonja said.

Cybil paused. *A27 Jump Jet.* “Okay, I get it, good, look forward to it. I’ll send you a prelim plan on my first read. I’m good to go,” Cybil said, exhaling. She shook her head.

“A full briefing download is ready,” Sonja said. “I’m texting you the access codes now. Memorize them, they self-delete as usual. Say hi to the kids for me. They’ll be home soon.” She hung up.

Sonja’s remarks reminded Cybil of how close private contractors are watched. It unsettled her, but that’s the price to pay.

Cybil held the phone until the text came in and she easily memorized the 13-digit access code, courtesy of unit memory training. A rest stop sign whizzed by. She bit her lip and looked over to her purse and thought about a cigarette. Feeling warmer she punched the fan setting to high. Her chest filled with a slow breath.

Her mind began touching on memories around the A27 Jump Jet Contract investigation. Her heart beat faster. Shifting position she moved her lean legs nervously. Licking her lips she could feel the dryness and a taste … vanilla? A warm feeling turned into an ache a few inches below her stomach, making her uncomfortable. She accelerated unintentionally and then upon noticing, slowed the car. Her time with the 82nd Airborne Division was made with that project. That was when she met Holden.

A call came in, the speaker rang. She pressed Answer, glancing at UNKNOWN on the dashboard display.

A tractor trailer started passing her car, the wind and noise building as the large tires rolled over Georgia asphalt.

"Cybil Raven," she said loudly.

"Hello Cybil, it's Anne," the voice said softly. The outside noise overwhelmed her voice.

"Who, Jan? Could you please speak up, it's noisy, " Cybil said, not recognizing the caller.

Sister Anne spoke louder: "It's Joy Anne Holden, Cybil. It's very nice to hear your voice again."

Cybil now heard clearly and said nothing. Immediately she slowed and caught the approaching off-ramp to the rest stop. Following the road to the parking lot she quickly parked the car, screeching the tires as she mashed the brakes hard. A couple feeding two small children at a picnic table a few feet away turned their heads to see the sound's source.

The caller continued. "Has it been so long that you don't remember my voice?" Sister Anne said.

"I hear you. What do you want?" Cybil said. Her voice was cool as she leaned back and took the call she had promised herself she never would take.

10

The clanking anchor chains threading down to the water woke the napping Stavos. His head snapped up to attention. He took a quick deep breath and blinked his eyes at the horizon. Darkness began spreading up from the edge of the sky; the sun had just set. He licked salty lips. His throat was dry. The rattling stopped when the anchor hit bottom, holding the *μοίρα* (*Destiny*) at Cutter's Point.

About 15 miles offshore, this spot had become Stavos's favorite fishing zone where he caught marlin, 'cuda and dolphin almost every time. Plenty of sharks, too, roamed these waters. Here he also conducted "other" business.

Soon enough, Kurt, on orders, chummed the waters, tossing in chunks of bloody fish tails and heads. Stavos walked over to the large deep bucket and grabbed one of the two gaffs latched to the side of the wheelhouse. Poking into the bucket, he hooked a large piece and lifted it slowly. He pointed the gaff and looked down its length over to Roger, before flicking the whole thing into the water.

"Roger …" Stavos said as he slowly approached *Destiny*'s passenger near the stern of the boat. He motioned to Markos, "Stand him up."

Markos pulled him up, jerking him quickly to his feet.

"Stavos, you know I'm your best runner," Roger said.

"Roger." Stavos stopped in front of him, within the personal space most people find uncomfortable.

Roger recoiled at the smell of vermouth and gin on Stavos's breath.

"Do you not remember our last …." Stavos paused and looked up, his brow creased. Then his face relaxed and he smiled. "Conversation. I thought you left persuaded."

Roger grimaced at the memory of Stavos, Markos and Kurt "talking" to him about last month's missed pickup. It took him a week to recover. He still insisted it was not his fault.

"Stavos, the damn shore cops were all over the boat next to mine taking down that jackass wife beater," Roger explained. "He had to pick that night to get drunk and knock three teeth out of his wife's mouth. I couldn't load the diving gear at midnight in plain sight of them. Who goes out diving at midnight?"

"Are you complaining about circumstances?" Stavos said. "They are irrelevant to your performance."

"It cost ME a lot of money. Disrupted my schedule. Schedule is very important. It is what makes my services special to my customers. They like my delivery guarantees," he said.

Losing the smile, he reached out slowly with his right hand and gently patted Roger's arm below the shoulder a few times. Staring into his employee's face, Stavos narrowed his eyes.

"Vasily is an old friend and he's very well connected. He tells many about our reliability and speed, you know, like Fed Ex. When it absolutely has to get there, Stavos will get it there for you. You missed Vasily's pickup. Like the one before," he said.

"God, please don't do this," Roger said, shifting his feet. His sandals slipped on the deck, wet from spilled beer and the occasional wave splashed on board. His mouth dry, he coughed. So much sweat was pouring down his back that his soaked red-and-blue patterned Hawaiian shirt couldn't hold any more moisture. He fell backward into Markos.

Markos leaned in and whispered something into Roger's ear. Roger began shaking. Then the large bald enforcer pushed him forward.

Stavos's eyes grew large, his shoulders pinched up and he raised his right arm high. He slapped Roger across the face with the back of his hand. The force of the slap tore away the crust above the eyebrow and blood gushed again, some of it into Roger's eyes, making him blink.

"Never, never tell me what to do and don't ever talk to me about no damn God. Look around, do you see him?" Stavos smiled and looked over at Markos.

Markos laughed and glanced at Kurt, who stood at the boat's steering wheel, keeping a lookout. Stavos glared at Roger.

Roger's trimmed gray streaked dark beard contrasted with his dyed blonde ponytail. Plenty of sun, sailing and surfing had wrinkled a previously young, slender face. The acrid smell of pot, mixed with sweat, wafted from his shirt. Roger turned his face away from his boss.

Stavos felt his chest and throat tighten and his head twitched to the right almost reflexively. He couldn't remember specific beatings from his father; they blurred together, except the last one when he sunk his knife into the bastard. He'd had enough of the beatings that came with talk of God's purposes and threats. Bullshit then and bullshit now. Stavos laughed and was joined by Markos.

"Let's finish our business together," Stavos said.

Staring into Roger's brown eyes, his employer turned his head slowly side to side. Stavos's lower lip protruded and his face looked lost in thought as he scanned his hired hand's face. Roger's eyes opened wider in expectation. He knelt in front of Roger, on one knee, as if tying his shoe. Roger looked down and saw Stavos was wearing boat loafers. Roger blinked a couple times to clear his vision of the blood. Stavos seemed to adjust his pant leg and stood up. He took a couple of steps back. His right hand was hanging loosely, his left hand brushed his hair back.

"You cost me a lot of time and money. After tonight's business I'll need some remuneration for my troubles," he said, looking past Roger's shoulder. "Markos, what did you tell me about his little girl, the one who dances with Kurt at the club."

"Boss, that little peach is young and juicy, what Vasily looks for. With just a little fuzz." Markos chuckled, a big smile on his face. "She will fetch a great price and will be blowing oil-rich rag heads for years."

"You leave her the fuck alone!" Roger screamed. "I swear to God I'll kill you, you fucking animal!" Roger lunged toward Stavos.

Markos had tied a thick, bright-yellow tow rope several times around Roger's chest and waist and held on to it. Roger's thin 150-pound frame jerked to a stop, useless against his captor's bulk and strength. A few more feet of rope threaded down to the deck from Roger's waist. They had been expertly knotted to four 50-pound kettle bells, the exercise kind with a loop handle. They looked like grotesquely large fish line weights.

Stavos stepped forward and pressed his body close to Roger's. He felt the sweat-soaked shirt through his own. His left hand grabbed Roger's ponytail, pulling down hard. Roger's head snapped upward. Breathing fast into the sky he noticed the thick Milky Way cutting across the sky, the stars seemed to move away from him. He began to shake even more.

"There is no God on this boat but me," Stavos said as the knife in his right hand plunged slowly past skin and muscle to Roger's liver.

Roger grunted, trying to speak, but the pain stomped on his words. He struggled, to no effect. Markos had moved up and his huge hands easily held Roger still. Stavos always took his time, making sure to enjoy every second.

The pain grew as the knife worked its way in. Roger's grunts confirmed the effectiveness of a liver stab, a preferred military close-quarter attack technique. The trauma so severe that victims can barely let out a sound, it's taught as an excellent method to quietly penetrate a guarded compound's perimeter. Stavos learned enough before washing out of the Greek army.

The blade stopped when the hilt reached the stomach wall. It lingered, as Stavos made sure to move the steel back and forth as if carefully carving his initials into Roger's vital organ. All the while he looked into Roger's eyes. The right side of the crime boss's mouth lifted into a crooked smile. He pulled the knife out at the same pace. When he had extracted it, Markos released his grip and the profusely bleeding man dropped to his knees, gasping for air, bent over, coughing.

All Roger could think about was Jenny. What he had done? He remembered visiting one of Vasily's spas in Macon, or was it Atlanta? His mind was unclear. His taste ran toward older women, Russian. He had declined the young Czech girls. Eager to please, they were too much like his teenage daughter. He remembered that Vasily had Middle East operations. In his daze, he thought he saw Markos and Kurt breaking into her room, knocking over precious fragile possessions, the kind 16-year-olds love. He saw a boot landing on the floor, crushing her favorite stuffed animal. He felt woozy, drained. He stared at Stavos's left knee, the pants water-stained.

"Kurt, throw me a towel," Stavos said.

Kurt, still looking at the horizon, bent down and picked up a small towel. The moon had risen, the light bright enough to read a newspaper. The moonlight shone on the white towel as it flew at Stavos. He snapped it up in midair. Stavos used it to slowly wipe the knife blade clean. He sopped wetness from his dark silk shirt and, bending over, patted his pant leg at the knee. He folded the towel and dropped it to the deck, over spilled blood. Kneeling on it, he lowered himself to talk to the bent-over Roger. Stavos returned his knife to its ankle sheath.

"It will be over soon. The cool water will refresh you," Stavos said, smiling.

He placed his left hand on Roger's shoulder and gave him a paternal squeeze.

Stavos stood up and walked to the wheelhouse to confer with Kurt about that night's drop and pick-up. Lifting the ship-to-shore phone next to the wheel Stavos dialed. He wanted Vasily to understand there would be no more problems with shipping performance, he could pass that on to whomever.

Looking to the stern of the boat, Stavos raised his hand and pointed the thumb to the water. Markos nodded. With little effort, Markos lifted Roger and heaved him overboard. The resulting splash licked the side of the *Destiny*. Roger floated, treading water, but with bound hands and feet, struggled. Markos, with a little exertion, picked up the tied together kettle bells and tossed them into the water. They raced to the bottom, dragging Roger underwater as his scream trail of bubbles disappeared into the dark depths.

After a few minutes, a handful of bubbles broke the surface. One large bubble remained drifting, the image of the moonlit *Destiny* floating on its convex surface. The ship's engines rumbled as it moved away. The reverberations traveling over the surface toward the eyeless observer burst it, returning it to the sea.

11

Sister Anne stared at the stained-glass dove flying down from Heaven as she waited in the St. Rita lobby. She knew the board meeting would start at 2:00 pm. Her eyes moved left, off the dove and onto the dusty grandfather clock ticking down to the appointed time, its hands at five till two. *Almost time.*

Just 30 minutes ago while standing at the upstairs hall window and wiping the dusty glass, her gaze had followed Father Michael, who walked down the porch steps and into his car to leave for the meeting. She thought, *Can't do a thing*, as she finished her chore and headed downstairs. Still bothered by her earlier difficult phone call with Cybil, she walked into the quiet lobby thinking it would bring her peace. It had not.

*

"The St. Rita Children's Home board meeting will come to order," Father Michael said as the clock in the conference room at the Oglethorpe Club reached 2:00 p.m. He picked up a small black wood gavel and banged the table three times. Each rap echoed harder than the previous one, the increasing sound sharp and insistent.

The priest in charge of St. Rita sat at the head of the table, the chair's usual position during these meetings. A three-ring binder sat in front of him, its spine labeled ST. RITA BOARD BUSINESS. Next to it sat a spiral-bound leather planner open to today's date. The Rev. Randolph Scott had taken a seat at his right hand. The white-haired Father Michael, ex-football player from Notre Dame and Jesuit graduate, glanced over to the group standing together beneath the large portrait of General Oglethorpe. Fred Drayton, Sally McIntosh and Mrs. Montgomery formed a small circle talking to each other in hushed tones before the gavel stopped them. They looked back at Father Michael and Reverend Scott, who were talking to each other. Father Michael kept talking to his old friend Scott but kept his new board members in his peripheral vision.

In the left-hand corner of the room the recent additions to the board, Andrew Cramer and Michelle Duval, stood looking relaxed. Both had been selected by the chair last year, to replace Mrs. Gaston and Mr. Bryan who had passed away unexpectedly. Andrew and Michelle moved toward the conference table and took their seats at the other end. Directly opposite Father Michael, Michelle looked at him with a small smile. His eyes glinted pleasure.

The board members, under the portrait, moved to take their seats. Mrs. Montgomery, in a flower-print dress, sat next to Fred. Her plump face turned toward him. Her wide-rimmed, silk-flowered straw hat tipped forward, almost falling off. She tipped it back with a fleshy hand.

Fred looked at her for a moment and then turned to the chair, "Father Michael, I'd like to be recognized."

"The chair recognizes Fred Drayton, Drayton Foundation," Father Michael said, his voice formal, eyes business-like. Dark, trimmed eyebrows underneath a full head of white hair, combed straight back, contrasted sharply. The priest looked down to the binder and made a note for the minutes.

Fred said, "I—no, we three—find it deplorable that the financial management of this longstanding institution has led to today's proceedings."

He sat back and crossed his legs. Noticing some loose grass on his pants cuff, he brushed it off. His golfing shoes from the morning round at Henderson Golf Club were still on. He saw the group looking at them. He changed position and brought both feet under the table, and leaned his tall frame forward, his hands landing on the table with fingers spread wide. His head turned toward Father Michael.

"Do you not agree, Father Michael?" Fred said narrowing his focus on the man's white collar.

Father Michael stared back, his tapered jaw visibly clenched. Broad-shouldered with a slender waist, the priest kept in shape. He leaned forward quickly but then took his time to sit back.

Mrs. Montgomery and Sally both nodded in agreement to Fred's statement.

Sally McIntosh, blonde and petite, in a navy-blue business suit with white pinstripes, added, "This is just a tragedy."

"Before we take up the tabled motion to close St. Rita, I'd like to introduce a motion to open an independent investigation," Fred said. He looked over to Reverend Scott.

"Fred," Reverend Scott said, "Father Michael and I have already given you the independent audit report from Hanson Smith & Co., done last quarter."

Scott turned toward Father Michael. “Father Michael, what date was that report provided to the board members?”

Father Michael opened his planner and leafed through several pages. “November 14, last year,” he said.

“Thank you, Father Michael. The report shows nothing out of order except for the decimation of our endowment over the last two years. Many, many charities, Jewish and Christian, invested heavily in Bernie Madoff's funds and lost out. Then the recession hit. Many of our generous families simply could not keep up their commitments,” Reverend Scott said, looking down the table.

Mrs. Montgomery’s eyes turned down. Sally’s head bobbed up. Her blue eyes, peeking out from well-cut blonde bangs, scanned left to Fred and then right to Reverend Scott. Sally, a Savannah attorney, specialized in adoptions and provided pro bono legal counsel to St. Rita.

Sally raised her hand and said, “Reverend Scott, it’s not only that, but St. Rita has not changed with the times. There are many families seeking to adopt children but St. Rita’s refuses to consider some of them. If it did, additional support could come in from other communities in Savannah,” she said.

“I will not call them families,” Father Michael said, his voice full of displeasure. “The Church will not condone placing young children in immoral situations, to be used as sexual devices.”

“Oh my God, Father Michael,” Sally said, raising her voice. “You can’t possibly believe that. Alternative families care for and love children like traditional families.” She looked at Reverend Scott.

Reverend Scott sighed and put his elbows on the table. “Sally, placing children with nontraditional families works for some state agencies. Regardless of the merits, that policy would never clear our diocese leaders in Atlanta. Plus, it has little to do with why we have to close.”

“Make your motion or withdraw it, we really need to move on,” Father Michael said.

In a clear voice, Fred stated, “I move to open an investigation, using an outside of Savannah firm, to determine why St. Rita is in this position and if there are any alternatives to closing.”

“Is there a second?” Father Michael said.

“Second,” Sally said without delay.

“Is there further discussion of the motion on the table?” Father Michael said.

“I’d like to know what Andrew and Michelle think,” Sally said.

She stared at them, seated together as they had always done since they joined the board.

Michelle scooted forward, almost slipping off the leather chair, her tight skinny jeans sliding her to the edge. Catching the table with her hands, she chuckled. When she pushed herself back up, her full breasts, under a tight-fitting silk T-shirt with a deep V neck, moved enough to wag the visible tail of the snow leopard tattoo running across her cleavage.

“I trust in what Father Michael and Reverend Scott think is best,” she said.

“Same here,” Andrew said.

Light complexioned, with sandy-brown hair atop a wide forehead, Andrew grinned while looking at Michelle. He then glanced at Sally. With plaid shirt tucked into jeans and a denim vest, he looked more at place in a fraternity house than in a boardroom.

Sally rolled her eyes and looked at Fred and then Mrs. Montgomery, who was frowning.

"All those in favor of the motion, please raise your hand," Father Michael said.

Sally raised her hand first. Fred followed and then Mrs. Montgomery. Sally glanced at Reverend Scott, who looked down at his hands, folded on the table. He made no move. Andrew and Michelle leaned back.

"The count is three for the motion. All those opposed to the motion, please raise your hand," Father Michael said.

Andrew, Michelle and Father Michael each raised their hand in unison. The room grew silent as everyone stared at Reverend Scott.

"Randolph?" Father Michael asked, with a puzzled look.

He and Jamison Randolph Scott had been friends for a long time. Reverend Scott looked over at Father Michael and then stared down into the highly polished boardroom table. He could see his face, which looked tired and old. He slowly raised his hand, as if it weighed more than it did.

"The motion is defeated, four to three," Father Michael said.

"We will now take up the tabled motion from the last meeting to close St. Rita Orphanage and relocate the remaining residents to other facilities," Father Michael said, his voice calm.

Sally's chin dropped to her chest and she slumped in her chair, sighing out loud. Fred shook his head side to side, lips pressed together. Mrs. Montgomery's hand patted her face and muttered "Oh my, oh my."

Andrew and Michelle exchanged small smiles. Father Michael continued the proceedings until he gaveled the meeting closed with one loud smack to the table.

*

At that moment in the St. Rita lobby, the grandfather clock struck 15 times at 3:00 p.m.. No one was there to hear it.

12

While resting her chin in her left hand, Cybil picked at the blackened snapper on her plate. Earlier the steam coming off the fish had smelled pungent, nutty and sweet from the paprika and chili powder. Now the barely eaten cold fish, chewed corn cob and untouched salad sat waiting for her. She pushed the plate away. Seated in a window booth at Tubby's Tank House in Thunderbolt, she glanced out looking for her.

Was hungry. Cybil took out her iPhone and scrolled down her tweet stream. Five new followers plus several posts from friends trailed one from her agency that promoted her recently filmed commercial, now past post-production.

CybilRaven: I just became the mayor of Tubbys on @foursquare!

AnonTattoo: New artist added, see her work at http://anonymoustattoo.com

PremierModels: Sandals Resorts national commercial starts next week; see Cybil strutting on the beach now at their website. http://www.sandals.com

She paused and then touched her display to bring up Pandora and post a new music selection to Facebook. Scrolling through her lists, she found what she wanted and typed in her post.

CybilRaven: Pumped Up Kicks by Foster the People

Closing twitter, she reread Anne's text sent after their phone call: Thanks for agreeing to meet, see u Fri 6:30 @ Tubbys

The clock on her phone read 6:10 p.m., 1810 hours.

"Not hungry today, honey?" the server said as she walked up to the table.

Cybil, a regular at Tubby's, looked up at Phyllis, the owner's daughter.

"That's a pretty black dress. Silk, right?" Phyllis said.

"Thanks, and no, not really. It's Egyptian cotton specially treated to look like silk," Cybil said.

"Oh well, here's your check, dear. Take your time," she said, placing the ticket near the iced tea glass.

Cybil looked at the bill. *Time. I thought we had time.*

Her eyebrows scrunched, her breathing got quicker. She reached down and rubbed her thigh where she used to keep the photo, in her uniform's right cargo pocket. The fabric under her hand felt cool. Her lips pinched together. Standing up, she snapped the ticket off the table, walked to the cashier and paid the bill. She turned around and quickly walked out the door, right into Anne.

"Hi!" Sister Anne said, smiling.

Cybil's eyebrows rose. A few inches taller than Anne, Cybil looked down into her eyes. *Still jade green.*

"Hello, Anne. It's been a long time," Cybil said, unsmiling.

Cybil stretched taller, tensing up. She saw Anne had dressed casually in a light green blouse tucked neatly into form-fitting chinos. She had stayed trim. On her feet, dark, low-heeled pumps. Her reddish hair styled short, with bangs, looked different from her Airborne days. A large silver cross hung on a pewter chain resting between her breasts.

"Yes, it has. But like I said on the phone, I hope we can set aside what happened. Something's not right. I'm worried about Sofi, Cecilia and the rest of the children. I hope you can help," Sister Anne said.

"You threw a lot at me over the phone. Not sure why you called. I almost cancelled," Cybil said, lying about not wanting to come.

A couple walked up to them from the parking lot, wanting to enter Tubby's. Anne and Cybil blocked the front door.

"You're early," Cybil said.

"I didn't want to be late," Anne said, her eyebrows rising.

Cybil motioned with her right hand for both of them to walk down River Street. She had suggested meeting at Tubby's near the museum, a favorite of her kids and a short walk from the restaurant. Anne knew the area as well. She had taken some of St. Rita's children to the museum on field trips. The Mermaid and Dolphin Museum had been in Thunderbolt for some time before they built the marina next door. They turned and walked side by side. A minute of silence passed before Cybil had to speak.

"Early was hard for you at Airborne," Cybil said, looking down.

Sister Anne looked at her and smiled. "Yeah, I had a little problem with time, but you cured me of that with the morning ice ritual. Remember how pissed I got."

Cybil returned her gaze. "It took a week," she said. "Then one morning I showed up and you were all dressed, ready for PT. Handed you the glass of ice water. You held it for a few seconds and grinned. I could have sworn you were going to throw it in my face."

"I thought about it," Anne said, chuckling.

Cybil smiled back. She had met Anne at Airborne school; the only other female in the company. Impressive for someone not coming through ROTC. She had opted for the Army, disappointing her family in Boston who couldn't understand her turning down a track scholarship. Still, she wasn't as fast as Cybil.

"But I'd have run you down and when I caught you," Cybil said, softening her voice.

"Yeah, and kicked my ass and then made me work the compass on push-ups. You did outrank me then," Sister Anne said.

They had reached the museum, a small one-story building, mostly windows set in red-brick walls. A silver tiled slanted roof shone in the setting sun. Neatly trimmed hedges reached to the windowsills. A large wooden carved sign, colorfully etched with a blonde mermaid with hair flowing, swimming happily with a dolphin, stood on posts in the front yard.

"Oh, it's closed. We're late. I forgot the times," Sister Anne said, looking at the empty parking lot. She glanced at the sign: OPEN 9–5 MON.–THURS., 9–3 FRIDAY.

Cybil started to laugh but stopped before Anne could see her.

Looking across the road, Cybil could see the river running by Thunderbolt. This was a small river community, one of many around Savannah connected to the Atlantic by winding waterways and tributaries. These alternate routes gave boaters, fishermen and anyone else access to the Atlantic. Savannah's water routes snaked their way around secluded islands, hidden inlets and smelly marshes; they interlaced through the seaside city. This particular waterway ended near Sister Island before it spilled into the ocean.

"There's a sitting area with tables and a bench. Over there, next to the chainlink fence, and the river," Cybil said.

She looked at Anne, who was peering in a window. Anne turned and made a small skip before settling into a quick walk toward Cybil.

Cybil's eyes grew wide with remembrance. She had learned to like that small movement during that month at Ft. Bragg. At first she couldn't stand this wispy redhead who kept falling behind. Cybil excelled in PT, class and field work, way beyond many of the "boys," but Anne's difficulties reflected on Cybil since they were the only "girls" there. When Anne strained her thigh muscle and needed rehab, Cybil felt compelled, though reluctant, to help her "sister" recover and improve. Anne resented the help but accepted it. Yet during that week in rehab Cybil and Anne became friends, not merely fellow soldiers.

As they reached the tables, Sister Anne said, "This is nice," then took a seat on a weathered gray wooden bench.

The bench and two marble tables rested on a concrete pad surrounded by tended landscape. This quiet picnic spot stayed cool in the waning of the day due to passing ocean breezes working upriver. Cybil stood next to Anne as the wind fluttered her black dress, pushing it tight against her body.

"You look good," Anne said.

Cybil ignored the compliment and sat down next to her. She looked through the chainlink fence, out over the water. Relaxing she smiled enjoying the breeze. The river flowed left to right, no boat traffic now. Muted sounds of banging and metal repair work, deep in the nearby marina hangars, traveled to their spot.

"The marina next door does a lot of work on expensive yachts," Cybil said, turning her head to look at Anne.

Anne turned to respond but didn't. Cybil's blue eyes caught the lowering sun, grew brighter, and Anne's breath held for a second as she recalled the first time she really noticed them, during rehab at Ft. Bragg.

*

"I want to stop. It's hurting." Anne had been pedaling hard and her legs were starting to throb.

Sweat dripped from her forehead, pinging the exercise bike's dashboard. It read: 20 minutes. *She's pushing me too hard.*

"Oh, please! Don't be such a candy-ass," Cybil said. "Ten more minutes spinning. Work through the pain and you'll accomplish something rather than quitting, as usual."

Her face full of hurt, Anne stopped pedaling immediately and looked up at Cybil. They had gotten to know each other, eating together after rehab, getting drinks off base. She had opened up to Cybil about her parents, their expectations, her attempts at finding something to do with her life. Cybil listened actively, asking questions, offering opinions but careful not to judge. This began to draw Anne in.

She learned soon Cybil had a weakness for cranberry vodkas. More than a few times Anne had to help her back to the barracks to tuck her in. When she didn't drink too much, Cybil talked freely about her ambitions, career goals, less than ideal upbringing and douche-bag men that couldn't compete with her and only wanted one thing. Anne began to understand her.

Anne's look at the mention of quitting surprised Cybil. Soon her fierce blue eyes softened, shimmered and apologized. In a way Anne had never seen. It was right there that Joy Anne Holden started to battle her feelings for the dark-haired corporal.

*

Coming back to Thunderbolt, Anne said, "I've never been on a yacht before, have you?"

"Yes I have, several times. Yachts make great backgrounds for photo shoots. And rich guys like to impress you on dates by inviting you for a sail," Cybil said smiling.

A 40-foot white, streamlined cruiser came around the bend, cutting through the center of the river. They watched it pass. A couple of guys in the back sat while a large man steered at the helm. The name came into view, written in a foreign language.

"Like that one," Cybil said, pointing. "I wonder what her name is."

"The language looks Russian but I don't know it. Greek is the only language I've studied," Sister Anne said. "To become a nun means learning how God speaks to us in many different ways and tongues."

God. Cybil stood up and glanced back at Anne for a second. Then she walked a few feet to the chainlink fence and reached for it. Both hands landed on the mesh, her fingers interlacing through the open steel, squeezing down hard. Her head dropped.

"What's wrong?" Sister Anne asked.

Cybil stayed quiet for a long minute as she gripped the fence.

She let go, turned around and faced Anne. She walked back to the bench and stood tall in front of her, almost at attention. Anne remained seated, looking up, and folded trembling hands in her lap.

"I can't believe you just call me, after all this time, to ask for help. You left. I never saw it coming. A shitty nothing note under my bunk pillow," Cybil said, her voice rising. "I read that fucking note a hundred times and it said the same thing every time I read it, nothing."

"But Cybil—" Anne said.

"Don't interrupt! Let me finish!"

Cybil looked at Anne directly. "You don't leave your battle buddy behind. We went through a lot at school and then in Iraq. Then Dubai. Preparing for that last mission made me realize I wanted future with you. But then you leave."

Cybil's voice trailed off. *Hold on*. She looked away, folding her arms. Turning toward the marina, Anne was to her right.

"Then on the phone, a few details about your life after you left. Talks with Chaplain O'Reilly you never told me about. Doubts you never shared. Going back home. Finding God, becoming a nun. A NUN!" Cybil said.

Anne was quiet, thinking that Cybil needed to vent.

"Worst of all, Annnnneeee," Cybil said, turning back toward her with a flushed face, "you're here in Savannah for over a year working at St. Rita, find me on the Web and don't contact me at ALL. What kind of person does that?" Cybil stared with lit blue eyes.

Anne looked down at her hands, which were shaking. She blinked a few times, her lips pressed together. She took a short breath. *Father*.

"Cybil, ummm, uuuhhh," Anne said.

A few tears collected under her eyes. She rubbed them away with her fingers.

Anne looked straight up into Cybil's face. "I'm, I'm sorry. I guess I … I'm only thinking about it now."

"St. Rita is closing and you don't know why. Your neat little God-ordered life is ending here in Savannah. Then you come to me for help because you think something's wrong. If your God is soooo BIIIGGG, sooooo in charge, then why is this happening to little Anne?" Cybil said, her voice harsh.

"I believe I was directed to contact you," Anne said, holding her emotions in check. *Can't take much more.*

"Really? You'll need to tell me how because I really don't give a damn right now. You can get 'direction' to use me, as if I could or would help, but for over a year you were not 'directed' to talk to me!"

"This was a bad idea. You're not going to hear me out," Anne said, standing up, her knees weak, face warm.

"That's right, leave. Like before. Don't stand up and face reality, go back to your holy crutch," Cybil said.

Anne and Cybil faced each other in silence. Anne's eyes steeled at that last comment. She wanted to yell back but wouldn't. She frowned, turned and walked back to her car.

Cybil stood there, hands at her side, looking at Anne walking back up River Street at a quick pace. She folded her arms and leaned to one side, breathing heavily. Her jaw clenched, teeth grinding. Then Anne walked out of view. After standing in the same pose for five minutes, Cybil turned and slumped onto the bench, cradling her face with her hands. Her heart raced. Her face was dry; no tears fell, the heat of rage evaporating any betraying wetness.

God, thanks a lot, you SOB.

13

The Middle East, three years earlier

"The trigger mechanism is key to the success of the device," Al-Rashid said.

His right hand rose to the old dusty chalkboard where he had drawn his simple schematic. He held his open hand there, the scarred palm connected to four fingers and a stump of a thumb. Crooking his index finger he knuckle-hit the slate, the sound sharp and loud. A small puff flew off the diagram and floated into the ceiling.

Al-Rashid smiled, seeing all eyes turn to the diagram. This assembled group of 15 trainees had come from all over the region, expenses paid by his Iranian mentors. All sat on the floor, on top of their prayer rugs, in two rows. All but a few wore the traditional thobe, the long white cotton garment for Muslim men. The two that caught his attention wore jeans and white shirts, Western clothing.

The large room at the madrasah held plenty of space for prayers. The white alabaster walls looked freshly painted. Trimming the room near the ceiling, arch cutouts in alternate blue-and-white block patterns let cool air flow in, warm air rise up and out. A large open rectangular space, acting as a window, interrupted the line of cutouts; it faced the city, allowing a visible skyline for the students to see.

"Teacher?" Jamil said, raising his hand high.

"Yes," Al-Rashid said as he stepped toward the group.

"How is this particular method an improvement over recent modifications?" Jamil said.

The rest of the room stirred. A single fan blew warm air from the corner near the front of the class. Dust hung in the air, scattering light coming in from the cutouts. Several students shifted their sitting positions scuffling along the floor. Other students looked at each other, nodding. Safir and Abdul, both in jeans in the front row, sketched on their notepads while talking with each other.

"Good question," Al-Rashid said.

He stroked his trimmed beard with his left hand. His white kufi, or prayer cap, fit snug on his head. Tilting his head downward, Al-Rashid seemed to hover over his tall thin body. His dark triangular face looked up.

"This version provides for three paths of detonation. Think of it as a three-headed snake that can strike from anywhere. The first trigger is an encrypted radio frequency that cannot be jammed. It is on frequencies the West thinks we do not know about. It has a range of 200 yards. Once the access key code is entered, false signal detonation is a thing of the past."

He rubbed his hands together, caressing the remainder of his thumb.

Across the room, heads bobbed up and down. Smiles broke out on many faces. Safir and Abdul continued their private discussion, pointing to each other's notepads on their laps.

"The second head of the snake," Al-Rashid said, smiling as he spoke, "is the mercury motion sensor. If the radio trigger fails to detonate in the timed cycle, for whatever reason, the motion sensor is activated. It is very sensitive. For precaution, there is a 180-second delay from activation to detonation to allow you to shake or push the device and leave the area. The digital countdown clock then starts working downward. Once triggered, there is no stopping."

The room buzz grew louder as the students digested the additional information. Safir raised his hand.

"Yes, Safir?" Al-Rashid said.

"Teacher, the wiring from the motion switch is exposed and easily cut. Does that not weaken this head?" Safir said.

"Very observant," Al-Rashid said.

Abdul nudged his friend, and both looked forward with thin smiles.

"Yes, it does, but the wiring is connected to the third head of the snake, just for this purpose," Al-Rashid said.

"Why?" a voice from the back of the room said.

"Let us imagine the Americans or Europeans or Saudi dogs have reached the device and have cut the wires. If for some reason they have jammed the frequencies and the motion sensor wires are cut, everyone will think the danger is passed," Al-Rashid said.

Abdul spoke up, putting words in the teacher's mouth. "The countdown clock appears to stop. That is on the surface, but it resets to 3 minutes waiting for a GPS shift."

Safir looked over to his friend, a single eyebrow raised.

"Yes," Al-Rashid said, "your understanding of the bypass is correct. Once cut, the passive GPS sensor activates. The Americans especially will want to move the device to one of their facilities for study. They will put it into one of their vehicles, likely a large van or truck full of fuel."

Al-Rashid smiled, walking back to the chalkboard. Despite the heat, he wore a dark overcoat that flowed behind him as he moved. Long, sharp collar points pushed outside the lapels.

At the board he pointed to a circuit path connecting to the GPS sensor circuit.

"Again, if the radio trigger fails or the motion sensor wires are cut, it activates the other head of the snake." Al-Rashid paused. "At the same time."

"Allah Akbar! Allah Akbar! Allah Akbar!" broke across the room as fists rose. The air was hot with sweat, pungent from the excitement. A beam of light, from the window above the cutouts, had spread across the room, cutting its way above the learners. One after another they pumped their arms in repetitive celebration, each thrust illuminated by the sunshine.

After a minute the room calmed down and Al-Rashid continued.

"After they think they have disarmed the device, as is their pattern, they will relax, cordon off the area, bring in their forensic experts, and lots of other people. Crowds will likely form to watch, but be kept at a distance, about 100 yards usually. They will remove the batteries, assuming the power source is gone, and they will miss of course the disguised batteries still connected," Al-Rashid said.

Abdul spoke, interrupting again. "And as the device is transported, passing through the watching crowds, and has moved 100 yards, it detonates, a custom-made car bomb."

"Yes!" Al-Rashid smiled. "The last head of the snake will strike in complete surprise."

The chants praising Allah began again and moved through the room. Safir and Abdul got up and approached Al-Rashid at the front of the class.

Safir spoke first. "The Hadeaa plan will succeed. The devices will work beyond expectation. This plan is blessed by Allah with intelligence and detail."

"We wish to learn and be part of this glory," Abdul said, nodding vigorously.

Al-Rashid motioned for them to step aside so he could talk to the class. His bony hands with long fingers, nails well trimmed, touched each other tent-like in front of him as he addressed the room.

"We will now stop for prayers and then you may leave," he said, looking up through the window facing the city.

Visible through the opening, the city's prayer tower, topped with a small golden minaret dome, stood tall and observant. The sky shone clear blue, cloudless. Typical city noises—the din of car horns, street talk and children playing—drifted into the classroom. The wail of the tower horn signaling prayers echoed across the city, deep in Yemen, on the Arabian Sea.

Turning to the two young men, Al-Rashid said, "Come back this evening."

14

Cybil's sky-blue BMW sped down Victory Drive away from her meeting with Anne. Several cars leaned on their horns, blaring at her, as she aggressively cut through traffic. Speeding between lights, Cybil hit every red one along the way. After the sixth screeching stop, she banged the steering wheel with her fists and screamed several expletives. The muffled sounds, through rolled-up windows, traveled to a minivan in the next lane.

A soccer mom with a pack of kids gave her a weak smile and then waved before accelerating at the next green light. A loud honk from a pickup truck behind Cybil drove her foot against the gas pedal as she glared in the rearview mirror. Her hands tightened their grip on the Italian leather steering wheel cover, a gift from William.

Finally pulling into her driveway she punched the garage door remote Open button. The car slowed until the lime-green tennis ball hanging from the ceiling touched the windshield, keeping the front bumper precisely 18" from the back wall, as she had measured. Slowly, her head fell onto the steering wheel. *Why now?*

Getting out, she slammed the door and stood there. Looking around the neat garage with closets, filled toy bins, hung bicycles and sports gear organized by height, she felt little comfort in the controlled look.

"Humph," she snorted, and took a quick breath. The plastic smell from the third refinish of the bright, oil-resistant epoxy floor, done last month, still lingered. By the door into the house, the "outside" refrigerator kicked into cycle, the low rumble of its motor felt through the soles of her feet. She opened the door and reached into the fridge and grabbed a chilled bottle of white wine and stepped into the house.

Carol, her neighbor, watched the kids when needed. Walking next door to pick them up, Cybil kept the small talk brief. Soon all three were back home and into the nightly ritual of snack, bath, bed and a story. Except for Sebastian, who opted out of story time; too tired, he said. He did tell his mother about his new comic book drawings advancing his story of the boy astronaut. He asked if Tom, Cybil's retired NASA engineer friend, would visit again and tell him more about space. Cybil said she'd check the next day. Sebastian smiled and told her how much he missed her, and a huge hug and kiss from her followed. He laid his head down on a personalized pillowcase embroidered with stars, moons and galaxies, and yawned. She stayed a few minutes, watching him fall asleep before going to June's room. Cybil sighed as she dropped onto June's bed to read her a story.

June, dressed in her pink-and-white cotton pajama set with the short sleeves, had tucked herself in and waited. Her usual glass of water, which she got for herself, sat on the nightstand along with a neat pile of tissues. Next to it, her Dragon Ball Z Kai trading cards stacked high. Looking at the cards, Cybil recalled giving up trying to keep her from watching the violent cartoons, but Carol's older boys next door treated June like a little sister when her kids stayed over. June watched when the boys watched. She started following the martial arts combat story line, which she enjoyed. *I would probably like it too,* Cybil thought.

"Are you okay, Mommy?" June asked.

She doesn't miss a thing, Cybil thought.

"Yes, Mommy's just a little tired. It was a long day. What story would you like to hear tonight?"

Cybil looked at the small cubby within the nightstand where June's books were kept. Disney character stories, Dora the Explorer, American Girl and a few oddballs from Grandma. No books from Grandpa, who had remarried and never showed any interest.

"Make one up," June said, smiling. "Like the one Mr. Tom did for Sebastian."

"Honey, I really can't tonight. I had a hard day, lots of grown-up talk about work and stuff. How about a Dora story?"

She reached for one of the well-worn volumes.

"Can I make up a story?" June asked.

Yes, but quickly. "Sure, let's hear it," Cybil said, and reaching her finger out, touched June's little button nose with a playful tap.

The little girl shook her head, beaming, her short blonde hair rustling around her narrow face. "OOOKKKAY. … Mommy went to work today. She got all dressed up. Pretty Mommy and the picture man danced in the fountain and all got wet. He dropped the camera and was sad," June said.

"That's so good, sweetie. You have an imagination," Cybil said, rubbing her daughter's bare arm.

"The picture man went away sad but Mommy stayed. Mommy's friend came back from far away to help Mommy look for the picture man's camera," June said.

Cybil blinked a couple times and looked at her daughter.

"Mommy and her friend dove under the fountain, swam and swam, like a dolphin and a mermaid, but the sharks came and almost ate them!" June said.

"Dolphin and mermaid?" Cybil said as she stopped rubbing her daughter's arm.

"Yes, but Mommy rammed the sharks and saved her friend. The end!"

Immediately June reached out both arms, stretching them toward her mother. Cybil bent down, letting the little girl's arms wrap around her neck, and then kissed her on the cheek. She sat up after laying her daughter down. June turned on her side and smiling, stared at her trading cards. Shaking her head about the story, Cybil looked at her daughter.

Soon June's breathing got slower and deeper and her eyes closed. Her mother rose slowly not to disturb her and left the door slightly open. Both kids preferred the hall light to nightlights. It helped them find her room on nights they couldn't sleep, when the nightmares about the big tree in the garden occurred.

Cybil walked into her master bedroom and went straight to her large walk-in closet. She took off her black heels and looked for their appointed space. A three-tier shoe rack organizer housed all of the model's many shoes. Fashion modeling required proper footwear and time management. With her shoes placed neatly into rows by season, style and color, she could quickly get to the pair to best match her outfit. *Ah, there they go.*

After undressing and a long hot shower, she put on her silk bathrobe and finished her nightly face cream routine before going downstairs. In the kitchen, she poured her favorite Sauvignon blanc into a long-stemmed wine glass, took a sip and brought it with her to the family room. Placing it on the end table she plopped herself down at the end of her couch.

"Damn it! Ouch," Cybil said, pulling a plastic football from under her butt. She threw it across the room. It landed near the wall, underneath the wall-mounted LCD TV.

She reached over to the end table for her iPod and earphones and selected a quick playlist: some Nora Jones, Dispatch, and several Jack Johnson tunes.

She plugged in the ear buds and turned the volume up. Cybil's head began moving slowly and smoothly back and forth. She stopped long enough to pick up her glass and take a long sip. *Yes.*

As the wine took the day's edge off, she thought about William and their last argument. She replayed Anne's phone call, their meeting and how she yelled at her. *Should leave it like that ... can't.*

Looking across the room to the large lithograph of her Savannah *Skirt!* magazine cover next to the TV, she smiled, then frowned. William had been at that shoot at Hilton Head and stayed over for the night. The great sex was a short memory, as they fought all morning. He had to leave for his damn sailing tour. He could have said something the night before. She started breathing harder, her eyes narrowing, complexion flushing. Reaching into her bathrobe pocket her hands found the loose Percocet tablets. She drained her glass, washing down two tablets.

Damn, where's the phone ... oh, car. She dragged herself off the couch. On the way to the garage she put down her empty glass on the kitchen counter. She began to twist and shimmy to the music all the way to the BMW. At the car, she opened the door several times as if dancing with it. After getting the phone out of her bag and putting it into her other bathrobe pocket, she stutter-stepped back into the kitchen, but tripped on the doorstep. Agile despite being tipsy, she caught herself on the counter with both hands on the edge as in a push-up pose, the bottle of Blanc in front of her. *Oops. Ha, ha!*

She filled the glass again and made her way back to the couch, dance-stepping all the way, mixing tango and salsa moves. Checking the couch for any more toys, she carefully lowered herself, glass in hand, back in the same spot. *Not fair.*

Her smile gone, she pulled out her iPhone. She went to her pictures folder, organized into 20 subfolders, each clearly titled by subject except for one marked DELETE SOMETIME. She tapped it once.

Browsing over the photos of the weekend in Dubai, Cybil's eyelids started feeling heavy. She sighed several times. Slumping down and stretching out her legs, her head rested on the couch's back. She brought the screen close. Over and over she looked at the 30-odd photos, stopping at the one taken at Sultan's Bistro at Dubai beach: both of them were seated at a table littered with coffee cups and half-eaten pastries.

In the photo, they had pushed up their sleeves and curled their arms in a bodybuilder biceps pose, fists clenched, Cybil's left elbow touching Anne's right elbow, both arms forming a V. Above each elbow, a brand-new tattoo commemorated the weekend.

Identical, the new ink art shone on both arms. The design had twin dolphins swimming next to each other, both riding the waves represented by three blue lines. The dolphins were not quite side by side; you could say one was chasing the other. Anne and Cybil, both smiling, looked at each other with their eyes locked.

Cybil's eyes slowly closed as she drifted off into her haze. *Why now?*

15

"Damn her!" the priest said, slamming his fist on the dresser. His reflection in the tall attached mirror wobbled and Father Michael stared at himself until his image settled. On the dresser top he noticed the mess his strike had made, scattering the last few lines of coke he had brought that night.

Scraping them together to save what he could, he looked over his shoulder to the bed. *Good, she's still sleeping*. The clock on the nightstand next to her head read 11:30. As usual he had arrived at eight o'clock. Shaping two lines from the remains, he snorted one. His head snapped back as eyes grew wide. The room expanded and his image in the mirror flexed larger. *She shouldn't have talked to the bishop*.

Walking backward from the dresser, he watched himself. His naked chest over a thin waist matched by muscular arms showed an upper body lacking typical middle-age spread; he admired the leftovers of earlier athleticism. Sitting gently on the bed, he put his hands on his knees and closed his eyes trying to imagine Sister Anne without her clothes on. *The bitch*.

The bishop's phone call, before dinner, took forever as he got chewed out for not managing expectations. He could handle the bishop but he did not want an outside, independent investigation he couldn't control. *That must not happen*.

The half-naked priest looked up from the edge of the bed and saw his sitting reflection. He drew a breath through his nose; his nostrils flared, the insides raw again. Waking, Michelle sat up and the sheet dropped from her breasts. She moved over to hug Father Michael from behind, looking over his left shoulder into the mirror, her face next to his, smiling. Her left arm moved around to his front, gripping his left pectoral. She traced her finger along a thin, ragged scar that went from his left nipple to below his collarbone.

"This is what Stavos did?" she asked, her voice tender.

Father Michael's face went pale for a few seconds before his color came back. "Yes."

Michelle held him tighter. She moved her head over to his right shoulder and looking into the mirror, peered into his eyes. Her short black hair with blonde streaks, styled into an upsweeping brush cut, matched the pierced Goth look underlined by the small silver ball loop eyebrow piercing. She held his gaze for a second, smiled and lifted herself onto her knees. Her hands, on either side of his neck, began massaging him. Her full breasts cradled the back of his head; her nipples, both pierced with silver loops, stood erect. The tail of the now fully visible snow leopard tattoo started near her cleavage. The creature's twisting body and legs embraced her right breast as his massive mouth, teeth and jaws devoured her shoulder. The priest grinned at her in the mirror.

She pulled herself tighter against him, leaning her head downward and whispering, "Did I do good at the board meeting?"

"You did very well. Andrew also. We got want we wanted," Father Michael said.

"Cool!" Michelle smiled, bouncing on her knees, flexing the bed. She slowly massaged his temples, pressing closer. He could feel her flat, tight stomach against his back, her bellybutton piercing ragged and sharp. He reached behind to grab her leg below the knee, rubbing gently. Her skin was so soft and warm.

"One more time? I think I have a few minutes left in me," Father Michael said with a wide, wicked smile in the mirror. *Viagra's a blessing.*

Michelle kept massaging his neck while moving her body slowly against his back.

"I'd love to, baby, but Stavos told me yesterday he wanted to see you tonight. He wants to meet us at St. Rita at two. I'm supposed to drive."

She felt him tense up. Father Michael shook his head.

"Baby, relax. Stavos promised us a trip after all this business. Bermuda, remember. No one will know what you do plus the beaches are top optional," Michelle said, with a wink.

Father Michael smiled and exhaled a deep breath.

Fifteen minutes later Michelle left her second-story midtown apartment first. She got her car, parked several streets over, and drove it to the front entrance. Father Michael, watching from the window, timed his arrival and jumped into her car. After turning down a few streets, they reached I-80 and headed for St. Rita on Wylly Island. Father Michael looked straight ahead, the night's pleasures fading while thinking, *What does he want now?*

On the island's main road, they drove until reaching the turnoff to St. Rita. Clicking the lights off, she turned down the driveway. Small knee-high solar lights formed a chain of dim illumination leading to the main building. She guided the car carefully down the winding road to St. Rita.

About 100 yards from the front porch Father Michael said, "Stop here, we'll walk."

Darkness dominated the windows of the main orphanage building and both wings. A single flashlight beckoned to them from grounds beside the left wing, near the chapel. When the pair approached the signal light, Stavos, Kurt and Markos appeared.

They stood under a small lit bulb hanging over the door of a large metal shed. A rake leaned against the side wall where large garden hoses hung on several hooks.

"Father Michael, thank you for joining us," Stavos said. He nodded to Michelle.

Stepping closer to the group, in a low voice Father Michael blurted out, "What are we doing here! We are closing next week, why the rush, couldn't you wait?" He looked from Markos to Stavos.

Markos shook his head.

"No," Stavos said, "I couldn't. I wanted to see the dock personally. Father, you know better my impatience."

Stavos, standing in front of Father Michael, leaned over and with a finger touched the priest's collarbone.

Father Michael lurched back. Stavos smiled, turned and walked toward the dock, which was farther down the garden path and past the well.

"I'll stay here in case anyone comes out, so I can explain," Father Michael said, huffing.

Markos, Kurt and Michelle joined Stavos. They passed the area near the old well. The brick-lined well, with a bucket and overhead pulley, had no purpose; city water supplied St. Rita now. It was located next to a large prominent oak tree.

Markos looked up into the branches, took a few more paces, then looked again. He picked up his pace and closed ranks, moving closer to Kurt. Stavos saw this, as did Michelle.

Michelle leaned over to Stavos. “Is he okay?”

“He will be. He’s very superstitious. Hates blackbirds, thinks they are bad omens. His mother’s poor choice of bedtime tales. He was probably looking for them. In prison he killed a fellow inmate who tried to spook him about it. The idiot pretended to be a fortune teller predicting a blackbird’s visit. Markos broke the man’s neck in seconds,” Stavos said.

They passed by the well, barely visible from the illumination coming from the shed. Michelle glanced at it.

Stopping, she said, “Keep going, I’ll catch up.”

She ran over to it and looked down, smiling. Her head turned left and right at the ground until her eyes found a dead branch. She picked it up and tossed it into the well. Leaning over it, she turned her ear to listen. Several seconds passed and she nodded her head. She jogged down the path to rejoin the group.

“What the hell was that about?” Kurt said.

“I love wells. Had a deep dry one near my house growing up. This one’s still wet at the bottom. Love to hear things hit after a drop, like frogs and wounded birds that can’t fly. Damn sheriff boarded mine up after a stupid kid fell in. Ruined my fun,” she said.

As the group melted away into the dark, Father Michael began pacing and sweating. The heavy dew of the night clung on everything, plant and animal. He could feel moisture forming around his neck and trailing down his chest. The scar, like a tiny dam, held the wetness for a second before it spilled over, draining down. His stomach gurgled; he had not eaten since before going to see Michelle. He reached up and rubbed his scar through his clerical shirt and remembered.

*

Markos pinned Father Michael's arms behind his back and squeezed again, forcing the priest's head down. He was breathing hard. Kurt's last blow to his stomach had doubled him over. The priest's head rose to look at Kurt who then stepped aside. Behind him Stavos was kneeling, seeming to tie his shoes. He then stood up and approached. The group filled Michelle's small apartment. Stavos had sent her away for an hour.

"Father Michael. A priest does not make that much money. So please tell me again why you are able to be so nice to my Michelle, plying her with gifts and coke for so long?" Stavos asked.

"My parents left me a trust fund." The priest swallowed a few times trying to find some saliva.

"Father, you know lying is a sin. My Andrew, so good with computers and pharmaceuticals, tells me otherwise. You are a son of the working-class Irish, a pipefitter family. Sons like that rarely inherit anything more than wrenches and tool belts." Raising his voice, Stavos leaned in close. "Now don't lie to me again about the St. Rita accounts."

Father Michael smelled alcohol and cologne coming from his tormentor.

Stavos reached out to the priest's shirt and slowly gripped the first button, working it carefully through the hole. He looked straight into the priest's eyes. He repeated the ritual four more times, and every time the priest's eyes expanded and his breathing becoming shallower. When Stavos got to the last button, Father Michael's panting joined his shaking. Stavos violently pulled the shirttails out of the priest's trousers, exposing the man of God.

Father Michael gasped. A knife quickly made its way under his neck, stopping at the collarbone. The sharp point pressed in, indenting the skin but drawing no blood.

"What are you doing, what are you doing?" Father Michael said, eyes blinking while panting the questions.

"Put a gag in his mouth," Stavos ordered, looking at Kurt.

Kurt looked around and saw thong underwear on the floor next to the bed. He picked it up for the group to see.

"Will this do?" Kurt said, smiling.

They all laughed except for the priest. Kurt quickly stuffed the improvised gag in Father Michael's mouth, its smell and taste familiar.

"Hold him tighter," Stavos said to Markos.

Stavos pressed the knife deeper and the skin broke, trickling blood. The priest's muffled cries followed the knife's path across his chest to his nipple. The priest's head dropped, his knees buckled. Then he looked up, his eyes unfocused and nodded his head up and down toward Stavos.

The muffled sounds from the priest coming through the gag sounded like, "Okay, Okay, I'll tell."

Stavos smiled and brushed his hair with his free hand.

*

Father Michael turned toward the noise in the nearby brush. *What was that?* Something scurried along the ground, shuffling through dead leaves and wet grass toward the dock. More noises approached from the same direction.

Stavos, Markos, Kurt and Michelle came into the shed's light and stopped in front of the priest. Michelle wiped her brow and took off her jacket, revealing her too-snug tank top. The ink work on her shoulder glistened under the shed's light.

"The dock will work fine," Stavos said, "let's go."

The group started walking back toward Michelle's car and Markos's vehicle, parked farther down.

In an unlighted upper-story window in the center wing, Sister Anne stood behind Sofi. The nun's hands lay gently on the little girl's shoulders. They both quietly observed the night visitors and watched them walk away, disappearing down the driveway. Sister Anne pulled Sofi backward and they retreated into the dark.

16

"Mom, wake up, we're going to be late for school. You said we didn't have to take the bus this morning," Sebastian said, standing by his mother's feet stretched out at the end of the couch.

His fingers, wrapped around her toes, shook her whole foot. June, at the other end, peered over the armrest and looked down at her mother's face. Cybil opened her eyes to see her pixie-faced daughter smiling at her.

"Hi, Mommy," June said. "See, I'm all ready."

Her little hands pushed the straps of the overstuffed backpack off her chest.

"Shit!" Cybil said, sitting straight up like a rake being stepped on.

Sebastian and June looked at each other and smiled at their mother's outburst.

My mouth's like mildewed chalk, aarrggh. "That's a bad word, Mommy shouldn't have said that," Cybil said as she jumped off the couch.

She stopped for a second to stretch, before moving to the bottom of the stairs.

Going up two steps at a time, her voice faded as she went, "I'll be down in a minute, get in the car. Grab my phone and put it in my purse, please."

Quickly dressing in her running shorts, Georgia Bulldog jersey and flip-flops, Cybil stepped down the stairs as fast as she could but had to hold on to the handrail for support, last night's effects still lingering. She got in the car and turned, looking in the backseat at both her kids.

"Seat belts on?"

"Yes, Mom," they said in unison, each looking out a window, Sebastian left, June right.

Cybil rested her head on the steering wheel. *Need coffee.*

Fifteen minutes later, her kids dropped off, Cybil bought a drive-thru Starbucks venti iced vanilla latte with a double shot of espresso for the ride back home. Pulling into the garage and turning off the car, she stayed in it as the garage door dropped. She leaned back and took a long pull on the straw. *Ah.*

She blinked a few times and stayed still. After a few more sips, she began to remember last night and the last thing she saw before slipping away.

Cybil stared through her windshield looking at nothing in particular. In front of her, two large black vinyl-covered wire grids with coated hooks stretched horizontally, one above the other. The grids held yard tools, hoses and other various gardening supplies in structured order, by size, left to right. No clutter, everything in its place.

She quickly reached over to her purse, grabbing her phone. She scanned the texts, seeing nothing important, and moved to the e-mails. A quick look and she moved nonurgent to her MAYBE folder, deleted others and answered the rest.

E-mail from Celeste Raven: call your mother, want to talk about June's visit and camping trip!

Pressing Reply she typed in: soon promise, too busy, then pressed Send.

E-mail from PremierModels: You aced the audition! Commercial shoots in Miami next week. Bring several of your outfits from your resort casual line in case they screw up costume.

Cybil smiled. She remembered flubbing several lines but had three good takes after the first one, each better than the last. And on a hunch she left them a fresh gallery of photos including shots of her in resort casual outfits.

Pressing Reply she typed: Yes! Tell em I accept!: then pressed Send.

Cybil grinned, thinking, *William's in Miami next week!* She scrolled to the last e-mail.

E-mail from CoveredDish: Your request for additional product information has been completed and is accessible at the research link. Your response will be secure.

Pressing Reply she typed in: CR2011243636B : then pressed Send.

She smiled. Her ACK code would automatically download her research-bot findings to the unit's secure server. She'd be able to finish her assignment for Sonja on time, before going to Miami next week.

Taking a deep breath she scrolled and found Anne's number. Pressing Contacts, she saved it under Holden. She could hear her blood in her ears. *Control.*

She thumbed a quick text message and hit Send. still pissed, will help, but need time, will call when able ~CR

17

"Ow!" Sister Anne's shin scraped against the edge of the box lid as she entered her room. She frowned at the untaped open cardboard container holding her clothes, next to the door. Stepping around it, she picked her way through several closed and open boxes strewn around her and Sister George's room to get to the dresser. She had to finish her packing.

One small crate lay empty, under the window, unusable. Tim, the innkeeper, had donated all the boxes and crates he could find around the inn including those from the kitchen. The lettuce crate couldn't be used; several slats were broken, exposing ragged splintering edges, plus it smelled. Whatever it had carried, something remained unseen that continued to rot.

Clothed for packing day, she wore jeans with a light long-sleeved dress shirt and sneakers. At the dresser, she opened and emptied the lower drawers, thinking about what she and Sofi had seen the week before. The vans would be here in two days. Shaking her head about the night visitors, she stopped packing and walked to the window and looked down to the empty driveway where Father Michael, the men and woman had stood. *I need answers.*

Tired, Sister Anne went to her bed and sat down. Her completed, taped and clearly marked boxes lay neatly stacked at the foot of the bed. A large rolling suitcase stood next to them. An open overnight bag lay on the floor next to it. She had moved many times with the Army and was an excellent packer.

Retrieving her cell phone tucked into her jeans pocket, she scrolled and found Cybil's text. *At least she'll help.* She lay back to rest, feet still on the floor. A shuffle of feet on the hallway wood floor made her lift her head toward her open door.

"Cecilia's boxes are still empty," Sofi said.

The little girl stood in the door entrance, smiling at Sister Anne and clutching Robby, her one-eared rabbit. Her mouth chomped up and down on gum or some candy. Sister Anne sat up and her eyebrows rose.

"Annnndddd, what about yours, how are they doing?" Sister Anne said.

Sofi looked down and puckered her lips. She tilted her head side to side, a slight grin spreading across her lips.

"Ooohh, I don't know, okay, I think," she said.

"Let's take a look, maybe I can help," Sister Anne said.

"Good, maybe we can play too," Sofi said and held her hand out.

Sister Anne grasped it. It was warm, soft and slightly sticky. Gripping hard, Sofi led Sister Anne to her room, shuffling her sock-covered feet along the floor without lifting them. Sofi flicked off her shoes whenever she could. She liked to glide more than walk along St. Rita's wooden floors. Sister Anne's sneakers squeaked while Sofi shushed like a skier. Sister Anne quit trying to get Sofi to stop this practice. All of her sock bottoms had turned black, accumulating dust and dirt, and washing did little. The damage had been done.

They got to Sofi's room and went inside. Sister Anne looked into the four open boxes: one large, two medium and one small. Sofi had placed a few toys in each box in no particular pattern. The small box was filled with books that had been dumped, not stacked, to overflowing. *This is going to take more time,* Sister Anne thought.

"Sofi, you've hardly put anything in these boxes. Did you forget what we talked about?" Sister Anne said.

"Are you mad?" Sofi said, her eyes searching.

Sister Anne knelt down to her level. "No, I know you are a smart big girl who wants to help. Packing your own boxes will be a big help."

"I forget," Sofi said. She looked away toward the window opposite the door.

"Let's try something," Sister Anne said. "I'll put some stuff that's supposed to go into each box and you follow me and try to put the same kind of stuff for each box. Does that sound like fun?"

"Yes, it does!" Sofi smiled and ran quickly to her closet.

After 30 minutes of intermittent packing by the easily distracted child, who at times dropped to the floor to play with an old toy, Sister Anne managed to get most of the little girl's few belongings into three boxes, leaving one unused.

"Sofi?" Sister Anne said.

Sofi, playing with a wheel less Barbie car too small for Robby to drive but who was stuffed into it anyway, answered without looking, "Yes, Sister Anne."

"We're all done now. I'm going to the garden outside until lunch. You can join me if you like."

"Robby wants to drive some more. Maybe later," Sofi said. She continued to push Robby across the floor, the plastic edges scratching harmlessly, leaving no trail on the wood.

Sister Anne got up, patted Sofi on the head and walked out of the room. Down the stairs with a quick stop in the kitchen to make a cup of tea, she picked her favorite, Red Zinger, which had a touch of honey. She carried her hot drink out into the garden, the small clouds of steam forming above the cup dissipating quickly in the slight breeze. She sat on the bench facing St. Rita, the view familiar. The large oak tree stood tall near the shed, its huge massive limb reaching out. The footpath near the shed led to the dock. *What were they doing here?*

Sister Anne lifted her head, closed her eyes and took a breath. The smell of blooming jasmine filled the air, sweet and delicate. Opening her eyes to the sky, she saw a little patch of blue through gray overcast. Her lips moved and she grasped the cup with both hands, the comforting heat reaching through the porcelain. Every few minutes her eyes closed and opened slowly, as if looking at something that was coming into view. Her cell phone interrupted the quiet.

She placed the cup down next to her and took her phone out. Recognizing the number, Sister Anne's heart picked up its pace and her breathing quickened.

"Cybil."

"Hi, you have a minute?"

“Yes. It’s good to hear from you.”

“Look, I’d like to help. The other stuff, not now, okay? I have a lot going on. Next week I’m in Miami but I cleared my schedule after that.”

Anne could hear a smile through her voice. “Thank you. I’ve been thinking about what you said, and you’re right, not now. Are you really going to help?”

“I’ll try. I’m leaving town tomorrow, but tonight I have a networking meeting with The cSpot crew at The Mirage Grill. Blitz Thompson, he’s a well-informed defense attorney in town, almost a friend. He’s usually there. I’ll see what he knows,” Cybil said. “I’m on my way there now.”

“Okay, what do you want me to do?” Anne said.

“Give me a quick summary, no editing, everything you can think of in ten minutes. Brain dump stuff. If you think of more, you can e-mail or text me later. I’ve texted you my private e-mail address.”

For the next 15 minutes Anne filled in Cybil about St. Rita’s recent past, strong financial position when she got there, and Sofi and Cecilia and the other children. Then she talked about the unforeseen financial issues, strange new board members, Father Michael’s behavior and the recent nighttime visit.

“About the visit, did you recognize anyone with him?” Cybil said.

“Maybe. It was dark but when the group passed under the driveway light, I think I saw a woman who looked like the new board member. Don’t recall her name, but she’s young, not quite our age.”

“Ouch. Okay, any little detail helps. I have to go now. This is good. E-mail me if you think of anything else,” Cybil said.

“Wait, one more thing,” Anne said, “the woman had tattoo work, quite obvious, on her shoulder, and it looked like some type of animal head biting her, that’s all I can remember.”

“That will help.”

“Cybil,” Anne said.

“Yes.”

“Thank you. I appreciate the effort no matter where it leads. And, and … I’m, I’m glad you called,” Anne said, her voice cracking as she finished the sentence.

Following a few seconds of silence, Cybil spoke up. “I’ll try my best. Talk to you soon.”

“I know you will, bye,” Sister Anne said, hanging up.

She placed the cell phone next to the coffee cup. She looked up at the gray clouds now filling the sky … not a patch of blue in sight. Her gaze moved along the path, stopping at the shed. She glanced at the old well and the large oak tree standing huge over the whole area. *Father Michael, what are you doing?*

18

His meeting with Vasily concluded, Mr. Kasen stepped out of the Zatinya restaurant, a block from the Smithsonian American Art Museum, Washington, DC. He adjusted his tie, buttoned the top of his suit jacket, looked left and right before walking to the nearest intersection where he stopped. Looking straight up at the intersection's center traffic light hardware, he found the small, dark glass-covered hemisphere hiding the Homeland Security camera; he smiled. He raised his right hand and a cab quickly stopped.

"Where to, sir?" the cabbie asked. His head turned back toward his passenger, who had leaned forward and rested his hand on the backseat.

The cabbie stared at Kasen's hand for a few seconds before quickly turning back to look straight ahead.

"Reagan National Airport, if you please," Kasen said.

"Okay."

At the airport, Kasen carried his small overnight bag and proceeded to the Delta Airlines counter, but stopped before getting in line. The waiting area had completely filled with single moms pushing strollers, businessmen and families. Kasen walked toward the magazine shop to let the line reduce itself.

Taking his time, he meandered and found himself in front of the magazine stand. Picking up a copy of *The Economist*, he flipped through the articles, stopping to read an editorial about the Arab Spring, how protests about a food vendor's mistreatment by the government in Tunisia led to the fall of Egypt's U.S.-backed dictator and regional unrest. When he returned the magazine to the rack, placing it next to a travel magazine, his eyes grew wide. On the cover of *Condé Nast*, under the headline, "Savannah, Jewel of Georgia," three women were pictured frolicking at the beach. He knew one of them.

Looking around, he spotted a man in a suit at the cash register; no one else was in the store. Stepping closer to the rack, he focused on the beach scene and the young women in casual beach clothes. Two stood posing for the third, who held a camera. The taller of the two posing had deep-blue eyes, eyes he had never forgotten. His own eyes became slits, his teeth pressed to each other. *It is her.*

Grabbing the magazine, he went to the counter, bought it and got into the thinned ticket line. Opening the travel magazine, he looked for the article on Savannah and found the photo and model credits. His crooked smile bared tea-stained teeth.

"Next, please step to the counter," the red-coated agent said, breaking Kasen's downward stare at the three models' names. *One of them is her.*

He booked two flights for himself, paying cash, fully refundable. Atlanta to Los Angeles, roundtrip next week, Atlanta to Monrovia, Liberia one-way three months out. Next he rented a van from Avis, agreeing to pay the out-of-state driving and drop-off charges. The African American counter agent smiled when Kasen told her he was on his way to Miami. She told him she came from Coral Gables and had relatives there and would be visiting with them soon. He wished her well on her journey and she said the same.

Upon entry into the van, Kasen punched in the address of his destination in the GPS for Virginia and then Georgia. The silver-gray minivan pulled out of the rental car lot and the GPS expertly directed the driver to I-95 South and informed him he would be arriving in 1 hour and 56 minutes, approximately 80 miles away.

Kasen settled in for the drive. His open overnight bag sat in the space between the seats. On the passenger seat his leather zipped binder lay open, contents inside stacked and layered, the *Condé Nast* on top of everything. Keeping his eyes on the road, he leaned down and pulled one of three disposable cell phones, this one blue, the other two, red and black. He pushed the Speed Dial button.

"Hello, this is Sam," Safir answered.

"How are you, Sam?"

"I am well. It is good to hear your voice," Safir said.

"Yes, it has been some time. How are preparations for your son's birthday party going?"

"Very good, but I am having some trouble with booking the right venue. I could use some help."

"Is the issue the date of the event or is your preferred location unavailable?" Kasen said.

"My cousin works for the hotel and should be able to get access, but in our last conversation he was not sure."

"Perhaps you and I should talk with him together."

"I think that would be a good idea," Safir said, smiling, his voice lighter.

"Then it's good that we'll be together soon," Kasen said.

"Yes, I look forward to seeing you. Travel safe. Goodbye."

Kasen hung up the blue cell phone and placed it in the bag. He retrieved the red cell phone and dialed Abdul's number.

"Andy," Abdul answered.

"How are you, Andy?" Kasen said.

"Teacher, it is good to hear from you." Abdul spoke quickly and excitedly.

Kasen clenched his teeth and exhaled a burst of air, his eyes narrowed. He had warned both of them several times during training about their speech. National Security Agency electronic ears are always listening with pattern-matching algorithms seeking key words and phrases. Addressing someone as "teacher" is unusual American idiom.

"No need to call me that anymore, we are friends now. Do you understand?" Kasen said, his voice steady and monotone.

"I … I … understand," Abdul said in a downcast voice.

"How is the bakery grand opening plan coming? Is Miami everything you expected?" Kasen said.

"Most of the desired equipment has arrived and it is en route to its final destination. We are waiting for more baking supplies to do our first test batches of bread and pastries. The humidity here does seem to affect the dough consistency," Abdul said.

"In my experience a few adjustments to ingredient proportions should suffice," Kasen said.

Kasen thought, *When I get to Atlanta, I'll have to show him how to adjust the drying agent amounts. His premix batch percentages must be off.* He shook his head thinking he should have spent more time on pentaerythritol tetranitrate (PETN) basics during mission training with these two young soldiers.

"Thank you. I look forward to our working together again on the bread. Opening this store has been a lifelong dream," Abdul said.

"As it is mine. I especially look forward to our guests' surprise as we present these tasty gifts to them and their children," Kasen said, smiling, "I must go now, I will see you at the appointed time."

Kasen hung up. He tossed the red cell phone into the bag and gripped both hands to the wheel. He stared unblinking for a second and took a short breath in. *Abdul is the most excitable of the two and careless. He must be more careful. I'll emphasize this when I see him next week,* he thought.

Kasen continued peering through the windshield down I-95. He could see the green mileage road signs coming up.

AQUA HARBOR, VA 20 MILES
FREDERICKSBURG, VA 40 MILES
RICHMOND, VA 80 MILES

Only 40 more miles to his first soldier.

Kasen grabbed his black cell phone, scrolled down and found Vasily's number and pressed Dial.

"Vasily."

"Are we prepared for activities in the near future?" Kasen said.

"Yes, we are. I did as instructed."

"Circumstances have changed. I now will have direct contact with your friend from this point forward."

"That will not be possible. I told you before, he deals only with representatives, like me."

"This situation requires it. I need his local knowledge. Set it up for next week. I will not take no for an answer … and I will pay double," Kasen said, his voice firm.

Vasily did not say a word for 30 seconds.

Kasen repeated, "I will not take no for an answer."

"He won't like it. But he will call, I will give him your number," Vasily said.

"That is acceptable. What is his name, first one only, please," Kasen said.

"Stavos," Vasily said.

"Thank you," Kasen said, then hung up.

Smiling, he gripped the wheel with both hands, his knuckles slowing turning white, his partial right thumb wrapping around as far as it could. "May Allah be blessed …." He paused and looked down at the *Condé Nast* cover and sneered, "He has made a way. Stavos will find her for me. I will like this place, this jewel of Georgia."

19

Her call with Anne complete, Cybil lowered her phone. Lost in thought she nibbled at a corner. *Need to talk to Blitz.*

Continuing her drive along U.S. 16 into downtown Savannah, she craned her neck looking ahead for her fast-approaching exit. She bit her lip and she shook her head at the buildup of rush-hour traffic. Moving together like a cloud, the sedans, vans, freight trucks, pickup trucks and Mini Coopers enveloped her convertible BMW. With the good sunny weather today, she had put the top down. She had slipped on oversize sunglasses and a head scarf. Moving fast through the traffic she looked like a star in a rush.

A roaring, loud speeding motorcycle came up fast in the middle lane. Cybil could only move left. Between her and her approaching exit, tons of steel moved at highway speeds. *Need to get past this*. Cybil's sports car smoothly accelerated, her right foot pressing the issue, the wind rushing faster past her face, flapping the edges of her black scarf.

With a glance in the rearview mirror and over her right shoulder, she faced forward. Weaving her way through she passed several large trucks in a row, each driver smiled as they looked down at the well-dressed fast-driving model. The wind had rode her skirt up revealing sexy bare legs.

Racing by a pickup truck that displayed a Confederate flag bumper sticker and a shotgun rack, the driver gave her the one-finger salute. She grinned and made the exit.

A few minutes later, driving at city speeds, she found a parking spot near Panera Bread and Bakery on Broughton Street and stuffed two hours' worth of coins in the meter. Checking she had her purse and iPad with her, she slung her designer satchel over her shoulder. At the bakery she treated herself to a vanilla latte and slice of lemon cake. Finding her favorite table open she took her treats and sat down to a perfect view through the huge corner picture window, of the West Broughton and Bull Street intersection, the downtown heart of Savannah's historic district.

The front door of The Mirage was within view. Tonight the restaurant-lounge would host The cSpot. Passing in front of The Mirage, couples, bicyclists, students and visitors with cameras formed a steady stream along the street. Every 15 minutes or so, horse-drawn carriages filled with scanning tourists clomped by, their slow pace charming.

The steam from her drink rose and she inhaled the vanilla scent. Raising the cup to her lips, she coaxed tentative sips of the hot liquid. *Aahh.* Cybil turned on the iPad, placed her iPhone on the table and started working.

Head down, she logged into the unit's secure server and began analysis of the research-bot's findings for her assignment from Sonja. After 30 minutes, she found the smoking financial gun, backdated invoices transferred between subsidiaries that overcharged the military for services never rendered. Typing a quick summary of her findings and attaching the research, she sent a secure e-mail to Sonja. *That'll do for now.*

A soft dinging bell alerted her to a Google Chat window's appearance. SouthSeaSailor, William, just got online.

hey, I got a few before the next sail. how u been? - SouthSeaSailor;

good. waiting for cspot. ran your sailboat aground yet? - CRBlue

next time out maybe - SouthSeaSailor

u still in miami? - CRBlue

yep, docked yesterday, why? - SouthSeaSailor

got a commercial shoot there next week - CRBlue

Text me your flight. I'll send a car, stay with me? - SouthSeaSailor

Cybil paused. A slow smile spread across her face.

Could be good for us - CRBlue

We should talk too ... - SouthSeaSailor

Cybil frowned. *About damn time.*

She wanted to continue chatting but could see The Mirage front door with people crowded around, some going in.

gotta go, c u next week - ;) - CRBlue

can't wait! - SouthSeaSailor

Cybil turned off the iPad. Outside the Mirage door men and women, most in business-casual dress, waited to get in—a sure sign The cSpot meeting had begun. She stuffed everything into her satchel and got up. Walking east along Broughton Street, the heels of her open-toed white pumps clicked sharply on the concrete sidewalk. The shoes contrasted with her teal sleeveless, above the knee, one-piece Calvin Klein dress pinched in by a wide black leather belt and huge buckle. She wore this at the Savannah *Skirt!* magazine shoot for the Most Eligible Bachelorette competition. She also wore it at the awards ceremony, coming in first. It was there she'd met Blitz.

*

Separated from his wife, Blitz's date for the evening was Sally McIntosh, a fellow attorney. But he didn't stay with her. Most of the night he cornered every beautiful, well-dressed woman in the room. Cybil had succeeded in avoiding him, almost. She and John Block were having a drinking contest, with several of their friends cheering them on. Blitz handed his number to Cybil while remarking how much he liked the dress and her legs. She wanted to dislike him intensely but felt sorry instead.

*

When she reached the front door of The Mirage, a tall, well-built man got there first, cutting her off. She noted his olive-skin and clean-shaven look as he opened the door to let her in first. As he grasped the door handle, his muscular forearm reached out of his sleeve revealing a sliver of a red-and-black wrist tattoo. She looked up at him, smiled and nodded her head. He said nothing. She walked in and started looking for Blitz Thompson.

"Cybil! Over here!" shouted Judy, raising and shaking her hand high, her many metallic bracelets clinking.

Judy rose from her chair and pointed to an open seat. She and two others sat at the small table near the front window. The street lamps had come on and their yellow-tinged light cast The Mirage stenciling, in light and shadow, from the front window onto the sitting group. Judy, her glossy black hair streaked pink, with her signature nose ring and one pierced eyebrow, had met and befriended Cybil during art graduate studies at SCAD. Cybil modeled for painting and sculpting classes, many of which Judy attended. Now with her own art and tattoo gallery, Judy regularly attended The cSpot to network. With Judy sat two other art community women, one on each side of her. The chair Judy pointed to, opposite the three women, gave a full view of The Mirage's interior.

"Judy, thanks for helping with the shoot. Jimmy and I appreciate it," Cybil said, sitting down.

"Anytime, hon. Look, I added another inch of ink," Judy said, extending her forearm. "Like it?"

Cybil leaned forward and nodded her head.

Judy's arm swept up and in front of the two women as she said, "This is Danni and Jolene. Danni is a performance artist I'm auditioning for my gallery and Jolene is a tattoo model."

Danni, in a sleeveless dark-blue pantsuit with red pin-stripes, sat with legs crossed, stiff and straight with shoulders back. She nodded at Cybil and took a slow sip from a drink and said nothing. Jolene, with blonde buzz-cut hair, wore white pants and a practically see-through white blouse. Tattoo art covered her upper torso including halfway up her neck. Cybil couldn't tell if the bra she was wearing was real or art. Jolene shook Cybil's hand and held it.

"Soft hands," Jolene said, grinning and slowly pulling her hand away, her fingers lightly caressing the underside of Cybil's palm.

"Thanks," Cybil said, her eyes wider.

She took a quick breath through her nose. A strong jasmine scent emanated sharply from one of them.

"So when are you going to have your next showing?" Cybil said to Judy.

"Next week. In addition to showings by local artists like Danni and Jolene," Judy said, again dramatically painting the air, "I have The Art Event Gallery in Atlanta lending me their Women-Now-Expressions Collection for a month!"

"Sweet!" Cybil said, "I will definitely come by."

Looking past her friend, Cybil scanned the crowded restaurant and the bar that ran along its length; the room was maybe 30 feet wide by 60 feet deep. About 10 four-foot round tables pushed to the extreme left held staggered positions. A narrow, two-person-wide space ran between the tables and the bar. The tables were covered with bright white tablecloths set with lit candles, black napkins and silverware. The thick crowd tonight made lots of noise as groups stood around drinking and talking.

Cybil peered around Judy to see if she could spot Blitz. Instead she saw a fast-walking short blonde in a green-flower-print smocked dress approaching their table.

"Cybil! Good to see you again. I must talk to you," Kara said, "Mind if I take her away from you all for a minute? Promise I'll return her in mint condition."

"Of course. Cybil, please come back. Join us tonight! Danni is going to give me and Jolene a private performance tonight as part of the audition. Her show is unique. Protest art with a sexy soul!" Judy smiled and winked at Cybil.

Cybil stood up, excused herself and followed Kara to the middle of the long wood bar and filled an empty space between two couples. Facing each other they leaned against the bar and rested their elbows on the dark wood. Kara ordered cranberry vodkas for Cybil and herself.

"Thank you for rescuing me," Cybil said.

"No problem. If you stay with that group tonight you might end up in a kid's swimming pool full of fake pig's blood morally protesting the meat industry while half-naked. You would also be fighting off one or two of them. They had an eye on you. I could tell from over here."

Shaking her head, Cybil said, "I'm looking for Blitz. Is he here?"

"Yes, in the private dining room, consulting with John Block and his partner."

"John's here? What are they talking about?" Cybil said.

"The city council is threatening to sue Green Block and Tackle Urbana over the downtown renovation project design as unworkable. I think they're having green regret because of the cost. Environmental responsibility sounds good on paper until you have to pay for it. At least that's what my source inside the council tells me," Kara said.

"Interesting. So how is this year going for your Web magazine? I get updates all the time. You guys break interesting news," Cybil said.

"My reporters are wonderful! After two years and a slow start, we now have the inside on Savannah, old and new. Definitely worth breaking into the trust fund to start it. Having a blast," Kara said.

"How's tonight's cSpot going?" Cybil glanced around and then toward the private dining room door.

"Tonight's good. Last month was slow. Lots of new people. Creative types, mostly. The couple over there is involved in community service projects—very interesting—though they seem a bit sad," Kara said, turning her head toward the couple.

The man and woman, each with a hand on a drink, were talking, their other hands touching.

Cybil glanced at them and nodded.

Kara said, "They just moved into the area. Benny from Yellow Tuna Studios invited them. I mentioned your work at the Rape Crisis Center and the economic development council. You should talk to them."

"Maybe later," Cybil said.

Taking a sip of her drink—ice cold, sharp and sour—Cybil glanced over Kara's shoulder, toward the back. She kept an eye on the door while she and Kara caught up on news, the kind not easily fitting in a Facebook status. Kara talked about another angel investor project, this one focused on microloans for disadvantaged African American sections of Savannah left behind in this new Web age. Cybil talked about her kids, said a few vague words about her consulting practice and William, omitting her upcoming trip to Miami. Kara talked about her ever-changing love life. Cybil smiled as she recalled meeting Kara for the first time.

*

The first month after Cybil moved to Savannah, she got an invitation to The cSpot, where she met Kara. Kara's Web magazine had just launched the Most Eligible Bachelorette competition and she urged Cybil to enter. When she didn't, Kara ignored her protests and enrolled her anyway. She won. The exposure helped her land her first local model shoot where she met Jimmy, her favorite photographer. After that, networking at The cSpot kept her connected to the Creatives such as Judy, John and Benny, whom Cybil occasionally hired for special projects. Thin resumes presented no obstacles for this young group who created their own jobs to fit the times. Building careers around their choices and lifestyle required few tradeoffs in the tolerant, business-friendly city. These green entrepreneurs, urban renovation architects, Web marketing gurus, game designers and graphic artists defined a new Savannah and an extended business family for Cybil, with Kara as friend and mentor.

*

Cybil asked, "How's Lauren?"

Kara paused for a second, then said, "Oh, she's fine. But she moved out last month. We're still friends, but it just didn't work out."

"Sorry, hadn't heard."

"Not a problem. I'm seeing Max now," Kara said, smiling.

"Max, the grad student from SCAD?" *He's a kid,* Cybil thought.

Placing both hands over her heart Kara said, "Yes, yes, and I know what you're thinking, but age makes little difference when you find your soul mate!"

Cybil shook her head and placed a hand on Kara's shoulder. "I'm happy for you. Just remember to burp him after cocktails."

Rolling her eyes and raising her eyebrows, Kara responded, "Very funny, I'll ignore that. How about next week you help me and the team on a brainstorming session? Our next issue topic is 'Savannah Women: New Era, New Rules.' I might need a cover model."

"Nice bribe. Not next week though. The week after works. But tonight I need to talk to Blitz," Cybil said, craning her neck to see around Kara.

"Why don't you just go in! They must be talked out by now," Kara said.

Cybil nodded. *Yeah.* "Thanks, I think I will," she said.

She lifted her glass to Kara in a mock toast, drank the rest, set it down and pushed off the bar.

She took two steps toward the back and a hand touched her arm.

"Hi, I'm David Flint. Kara mentioned you had done volunteer work for the rape crisis center and are pretty well connected. Can I talk to you for a minute?"

He was the man Kara had pointed out earlier.

Cybil smiled and shook her head. "Uh, not right now, I need to talk to a friend."

With eyes bright and friendly, he said, "Okay, I understand. Here's my card, can I call you next week. My wife and I would like to talk with you."

Cybil hesitated, leaned back and looked at the woman at the table. She looked up, smiled and waved hello, nodding. Cybil gave him her card and took one of his, which read: Eden Community Village, David and Amy Flint.

At the private dining room entrance, Cybil knocked on the door. Knocked again and a third time. She reached out to grasp the door handle when it swung open.

Blitz Thompson stood there with a drink in hand, wearing a dark suit, tie loosened, and gray stubble on a thin face. With a crooked grin he looked Cybil up and down.

"Cybil Raven! I guess you finally decided to take me up on my offer, huh."

20

Sister Anne stood on St. Rita's porch looking at the graying sky. Moving vans would soon fill the now empty driveway in front of her. The front double doors were open. West of the city the sky continued to darken with large thunderheads building up, typical coastal Georgia weather in the afternoon. Cool ocean air collided with incoming dry air, stacking high white cumulonimbus clouds until they could no longer hold the moisture. Sometimes the rain fell quietly. Other times, thunder, wind and lightning marked the intensity of the conflict between different air masses, each with their own intent.

She stared at the lone light pole standing guard at the driveway's bend. Under its light the recent night visitors had stopped, accompanied by Father Michael. A startlingly loud crack accompanied by a flash of light and low rumbling warned of the approaching storm. A strong breeze kicked up dust that joined leaves swirling in the driveway circling each other higher and higher forming a small dancing dust devil.

"I'm scared!" Sofi said from the lobby.

Sister Anne turned around to see little socked feet skidding to a stop in front of the door. Moving inside, the nun stepped by taped boxes and zipped suitcases positioned near the entrance. Sofi lunged toward her tall protector, pressing her blonde head into Sister Anne's stomach. Another crack, louder, shook the room. The rumbling thunder deepened. The wind against St. Rita's walls and roof increased, bringing creaking sounds. Cradling Sofi's head with one hand, her one free hand reached out and pushed one door closed. She noticed the sweet smell of rain on the air. Shifting her weight, still with Sofi pressed into her midsection, Sister Anne reached out again, pushed the other door closed.

They went upstairs, to a hallway over the chapel where the window overlooked the shed and the path to the dock. They liked to watch the woods from there, especially at night when deer and other critters visited the trash bins. They could observe the large oak tree with the one massive limb reaching toward the house. The wind, now moving faster, tossed leaves up from the ground while torn leaves cascaded from above.

"Look, Sister Anne, a bird," Sofi said, pointing.

She grabbed the nun's pant leg, scrunching the fabric. Sister Anne blinked a few times as her eyebrows rose. A large blackbird sat in the crook of the trunk and large limb, quiet and undisturbed by the chaos. A few leaves blew by the bird's head. It didn't move. After a few seconds it looked upward and flew straight up. They leaned toward the window to look up and follow the bird but an unnaturally bright flash filled the hallway. A second later, a loud, loud BOOM. Sister Anne had never experienced a noise like this. All of St. Rita shook, the window panes vibrated and the oak tree seemed to shimmer. The wind accelerated, the roof creaked louder, whooshing sounds came from all directions.

Sofi hugged Sister Anne, tighter than before. The nun held her close. *No tornado, please, Lord.* Her eyes scanned the crook of the oak tree. From a pitch-black smoldering patch rose a small column of dark-gray smoke that twisted upward.

The massive limb, its leaves like sails, caught the rising wind, rose a few inches and fell back to its previous level. Snap! Sister Anne looked to see if the branch would fall or if any other did. She looked left, right, up and to the ground. Nothing. The tree seemed whole.

The storm's assault diminished, smaller thunderclaps receding into the distance. Soon Sofi relaxed her grip. Standing there they watched as, over the tree line, gray skies gave way to blue and sunlight began to find its way in.

"Are you okay now?" Sister Anne said to Sofi, who had shimmied to the window.

"Where's the bird?" Sofi said.

"Oh, I think it will be all right. God made birds smart so they could take care of themselves," Sister Anne said, smiling.

"I hope so. I'm hungry," Sofi said.

"I think some cookies are left over from last night," Sister Anne said, taking Sofi's hand and walking her toward the top of the stairs.

At the bottom of the staircase they took a left toward the kitchen. Sofi and Sister Anne sat in the kitchen sharing cookies and milk. Sister Anne leaned back and crossed her arms, her fingers rubbing above her elbow. The sound of a cane ticking on wood announced Sister George's arrival.

"The vans are here," Sister George said.

"Good. Can you stay with Sofi? I'll tell Father Michael."

"Sure. Some storm," Sister George said, and sat down.

With her mouth full of cookies and glass in hand, Sofi looked up at Sister Anne. She gave a small wave and drank her milk.

Walking across the St. Rita lobby, Sister Anne felt lighter. *I will know.* She stepped as if on a march, every footfall striking the wood with a clear tap. She reached Father Michael's closed door, knocked twice but didn't wait for a reply. She swung the door open and walked in.

"Father Michael, I need to talk with you," Sister Anne said.

Father Michael sat at his desk, feet up, a cell phone to his ear.

"I understand. Wait a minute, please." Father Michael said as he saw Sister Anne standing inside. He held up his open hand for her to wait. "Let me call you back. Bye."

Putting the phone down on the desk, he said, "Sister Anne, what can I do for you?"

He motioned for her to sit in one of the two chairs opposite his desk, which she did. He leaned forward, placing his elbows on the desk, his hands tented. Both chairs sat lower than the desk so she had to look up at him. She stood up, walked behind the chair and leaned on its back.

"I'd rather stand," she said.

Father Michael frowned. "As you wish. Have the vans arrived?"

"Yes."

"Very good," Father Michael began to rise.

"I need to talk to you about your night guests last week," she said.

Father Michael sat down, his lips pressed tight against each other. His eyes darted to the side, looking out the large four-pane window with a view of the driveway.

After a deep breath he said, "What do you mean?"

Sister Anne stepped forward, past the chair. "Sofi couldn't sleep that night. I tried to tire her with our naming the stars game from my bedroom window. We saw you, and I think three other men and a woman."

"Friends of mine. I was giving a tour of St. Rita's grounds," Father Michael said.

Sister Anne's voice rose with incredulity: "At two thirty in the morning?"

Father Michael stood up and leaned on his desk. A few feet separated them.

"No concern of yours. Your focus should be the move and preparing the children's new housing," he said.

With her brows pinched and voice steady, Sister Anne said, "Why is this happening, Father Michael? Two years ago when I came here, we used to meet as a staff to review monthly progress reports which included finances. Those meetings stopped. Then we had to start economizing, cutting corners. Then all of a sudden, a few months ago you and the bishop told us we were shutting down."

"Need I remind you, my oversight of this institution has been under the supervision of the bishop and the executive board. Everything is in the open regarding minutes and proceedings," Father Michael said as he sat down. Folding his hands in his lap, he allowed a thin smile to break through.

Sister Anne said, "Father Michael, I am not accusing you of anything, but I have to know more."

"Child, you must trust God and you must trust me. I will pray for your comfort," the Father said. "Please return to your duties. I really do not wish to discuss this any further."

Sister Anne said nothing, turned and walked to the door. She put her hand on the door handle and stopped. Turning her head she looked back at Father Michael and said, "Thank you for your time. I'll be praying also … that the truth will be revealed." Sister Anne took a deep exhaling breath.

She slammed the door shut and the loud noise echoed in St. Rita's lobby.

Father Michael blinked at the sound. He puffed twice through his nose before dialing the person he had been talking to before.

"Who was that?" Michelle said. "I heard a woman's voice."

"That was Sister Anne. A bother and worry wart. I sent her away. Church business," Father Michael said.

"Okay, that's good. I have a message from Stavos."

"What now?"

"Don't get mad at me. And don't ruin my mood for tonight or you'll regret it. As soon as everyone is cleared out, he wants you to call him immediately. He has equipment to move in."

"I thought we were going to wait a few weeks. Let things settle, wait until people forget the place," Father Michael said, his breath quickening along with his pulse.

"Why don't you tell Stavos? I'm sure he will appreciate your candor," Michelle said, her smile clear in her voice.

Father Michael started sweating. He opened this desk drawer and took out a fresh kerchief, mopping his brow. "Fine."

"Good. I'll see you tonight."

Father Michael closed his cell phone and placed it on the desk. He slumped in his chair, sighed and shook his head. *What equipment?*

21

"Hello, Blitz, you have a few minutes?" Cybil said.

She walked past him, not responding to his comment, through the open door he was holding. As she passed by, he leaned in, sniffing her hair, his deep breath loud and conspicuous. Unseen vapors strongly scented of gin and tonic reached her nose as she delved deeper into the room. She saw John and smiled.

Standing up from a small table, John Block, dressed in a plaid three-piece suit, lifted his blue-gray fedora in salute. "Cybil honey, how are you? And the kids!"

"Good," she said.

He quick-stepped over to bear-hug her. Cybil, looking over his shoulder, nodded to his partner, Derrin, who stood a few feet away. He co-owned Green Block and Tackle Urbana, Savannah's eco-minded architectural firm, with John. Standing taller than Block, and older, with a thin mustache, Derrin presented a leaner, more aloof look. He was not a hugger. He tipped his head and smirked.

Cybil said, "Sebastian could use some math tutoring. Fourth-grade math seems a stretch for him."

"Architects know a little about math, static and dynamic forces, you know," John said. "You should bring them over. June can play with Lyle while I combine Xbox gaming with Algebra 101."

John and Derrin occasionally provided child-care for Cybil, their way of repaying the favor she did for them the previous year.

"That'd be fine," Derrin said as he handed John a full tumbler.

Cybil looked at the drink. "Single malt?"

"Only way to drink Scotch, honey," John said.

Both stood in front of Cybil, looking at her, John with a big smile. John leaned into Derrin playfully and Derrin looked sideways.

"Too strong for me. I'm sorry to interrupt, could I steal Blitz away for a few minutes?" Cybil said, glancing over her shoulder.

Blitz was still at the door with his drink.

John said, "Sure. We're done talking about the council. Just drinking and listening to Blitz's past football glories. We decided to threaten a countersuit and then we'll settle. No big deal, typical city politics."

Derrin leaned forward and whispered, "He's pretty drunk right now," his eyes indicating Blitz.

"I think one or two on the council don't like us. Ya know. We're not 'their' kind of people. I'm not sure if we are too new or too out there or both," John said.

He raised his tumbler to his lips and took a drink, his smile gone.

"John, we don't care about their opinion, only that they pay their invoices on time. Let's go see Kara and let Cybil and Blitz alone. You think you can handle him?" Derrin said, looking at Blitz.

Cybil smiled. "Sure. Thanks."

She walked to the table they had been sitting at and took a chair. Placing her purse on the table, she pulled her iPhone out and put it down.

Derrin and John stopped to chat for a few seconds with Blitz on the way out. Blitz turned around and starting walking toward Cybil. Reaching the table, Blitz pulled up a chair and sat in front of her.

"What's up, gorgeous?" he said.

"What do you know about St. Rita?" Cybil said.

"What, no foreplay? St. Rita, huh? What's your interest?"

"Cursory at this point. I'm looking into this for a friend."

"Really? A male friend? Should I be jealous?" Blitz said, leaning in with a smile.

"Blitz, ya know you're the only poor tackling ex-Bulldog middle linebacker, scumbag criminal defense attorney with the worst pickup lines – ever, for me," Cybil said, grinning, her eyes focused on his.

He smiled. "That's what I like about you, no bullshit. But this information's gonna cost you."

"And what's the price?"

"A real date," he said, looking her up and down.

"Real date?" she said, turning her head sideways and placing two fingers on her lips in mock surprise.

He sat straight up and sighed. "Look, next month the Savannah Legal Society is having a fundraising ball and I need a respectable date."

"What about Sally McIntosh?" she said.

"Oh, that was a business date. I owed her a favor for pro bono work she did for a friend," Blitz said.

"How about Craigslist? Should find your type there," Cybil said with a small grin.

"Funny. Look, people know you, and plus, having the best-looking woman in Savannah on my arm can't hurt my rep."

Cybil turned her head so one eye was looking at him, her grin replaced with a soft smile.

She put her open hand over her heart and said, “Blitz, I’m touched. Sure. But only the fundraiser. We arrive – and leave in separate cars.”

“Always one step ahead. Always in control. It’s a deal.”

He leaned backward, tipping his chair on its two back legs. Crossing his arms, he nodded, his smile widening, his eyes taking her in. Cybil’s smooth bare legs crossed elegantly, pushing her teal skirt above the knees. Her peep toe black pumps hugged her toes, perfectly painted a complimentary color to offset the teal. Cybil broke his celebration as she strummed the table with her fingers and posed her first real question.

“Why is St. Rita’s closing?” she said.

His smile disappeared. He bent forward and the chair tipped down and landed with a thud.

“I don’t know about the closing, but about 13 months ago I defended a woman named Michelle for a drug-dealing rap. Got a call from her boyfriend, I think his name was Andrew. Got the post arraignment case file and it was pretty bad for her. I’m thinking, not much I can do but I’ll make a quick fee for showing up at trial,” Blitz said.

“What happened?”

Blitz looked behind him, at the door, which was open a crack. He got up and closed it, returning to the chair.

“So the first day of trial, I’m trying my best to argue dismissal on illegal search, a huge stretch. I’m getting nowhere. Then I see the judge look up and stare right past me with huge eyes. He looks down at his papers and says ‘Just a minute, counselor.’ I swear he was sweating.”

“How is this related to St. Rita?” she said.

"I'll get there. So I look over at Michelle, who is looking to the back of the courtroom and she's smiling. I figure her boyfriend, Andrew, came in to support her. I glance back and see Stavos Gruner and his bodyguards, sitting all calm. Stavos is picking his fingernails with a nail file."

"Who's Stavos Gruner?" Cybil said.

"Not someone you really want to know. So the judge takes a minute and then tells counsel to approach the bench."

"Huh?"

"The judge asks the assistant district attorney about the illegal search, using my weak points I was arguing minutes before. The ADA is answering questions and starts asking the judge where this is going. The judge starts quoting some case law precedent I never heard of and says he will rule immediately. The ADA starts arguing but the judge slaps him down. The ADA is furious, gets snippy and the judge threatens contempt of court. I'm keeping my mouth shut, trying hard not to smile."

Cybil uncrossed her legs and sat forward, putting her hands on her knees. "Interesting, go on."

Blitz smiled and scooted his chair closer to her. He put one hand on Cybil's right hand and said, "I'm going to enjoy our date."

Cybil moved Blitz's hand to the table, saying, "Stay focused."

He sighed deeply and said, "So the judge waves us back from the bench and rules in the defense's favor with prejudice so it can't be brought up again. The ADA is fuming, barely holding it together while jamming his papers into his briefcase. He and his assistant walk out yammering to each other. It was great!"

Nodding, Cybil said, "What do think happened?"

"I wanted to know too, plus Michelle's hot. So I ask if she wants to go celebrate, telling her the drinks are on me, but she says no thanks. I'm disappointed but she hands me an envelope with my retainer check. I open it, of course, right there, and the amount is correct. It's not a personal check from her, though, but from Savannah Land and Trust Ltd. I'm a bit confused. She doesn't seem like the corporate type, so I look toward the back but Stavos and his crew are gone. She leaves and I end up drinking alone that afternoon—but a few grand richer."

"So tell me more about Stavos and how all this is connected to St. Rita."

"Just wait. About six months before I took Michelle's case, a drinking buddy of mine over at the Georgia Bureau of Investigation calls me and says he needs a civilian, a lawyer if possible, for an undercover sting. He thinks I would like the assignment."

"What was it?"

"I was to be wired and go into a massage parlor whose owners were suspected of sex trafficking. The place was somewhere in the Macon-Atlanta-Savannah corridor."

"You must have liked that, any places familiar?" Cybil said, frowning.

"Look, I like my dates to be above age and have free will, whether by choice or by fee. This human sex trafficking business is slavery shit, so I said yes."

"Sorry, go on," Cybil said, her eyes opened wider at Blitz's candor.

"Anyway, after two weeks of planning and prep the sting is called off but during the briefings I see pics of this Stavos guy and his operations."

Cybil's cell phone vibrated on the table. Blitz glanced from the phone to Cybil. "You need to take that?" he said.

She saw it was a text about childcare for next week's trip. "Yes. Can you give me a second? Last-minute travel plans."

"No problem. I need another drink." Blitz left the room.

Cybil read Carol's text: Yes, I can watch them-love them!

Cybil texted back: THANK YOU!!! c u 8 am monday. flight leaves @11

Cybil, waiting for Blitz to return, started to smile, thinking of seeing William, but her thoughts darkened as she reconciled Anne's information with what Blitz had been saying.

Blitz entered the room with two drinks in hand and closed the door with his foot. He sat in front of Cybil.

"Here, I got you another. Vodka cranberry right? I asked Kara. Where were we?"

"Stavos?"

"Right. Well, he was small-time in Atlanta, dealing and running guns up I-95 to the Northeast. He came up on GBI radar. His name surfaced after a few sex trafficking stings. Girls from Russia and Thailand were arrested, then deported, some under 16. Most that were shipped to the Macon parlors apparently came smuggled in through Stavos's connections."

"So you think Michelle was one of his girls?" Cybil said.

"Nah, too American and too many tattoos for the parlors. She got busted in Savannah for drugs. The way the judge reacted, I think Savannah is where Gruner operates."

"Okay, how is this connected to St. Rita's?"

"You're ex-Catholic, right?" Blitz said.

"What the hell does that have to do with anything?" Cybil said. Her eyebrows pinched together and her lips pressed tightly against each other.

"What do they teach in Sunday school, yeah, everything happens for a purpose, right?" Blitz was grinning behind a couple of small chuckles.

Cybil closed her eyes for a second. She hated that phrase.

"Hey, you okay? What did I say?"

Cybil sighed deep and loud. "Nothing. Go on."

"Anyway, a few months after the court thing with Michelle, I get a call from Reverend Scott, a board member of St. Rita's. He wants to know about Michelle's case. I tell him I can't discuss a particular client matter—privilege and all. But that it's public record, the case was dismissed with prejudice. I ask why he's interested."

"What did he say?"

"At first he didn't want to. Then I pressed him. He said that St. Rita's board needed new members, something about an unfortunate accident. Important upcoming orphanage business needed a full board. He said Father Michael had personally recommended Michelle but he was uncomfortable with it," Blitz said, straightening up and taking a long drink.

Cybil's heart skipped a beat. William's mother!

"Blitz, you remember the car wreck that killed Mrs. Gaston and her friend over on the Harry Truman Parkway. The car went over the bridge railing. A hit-and-run." Cybil said, speaking as fast as she could.

"Mrs. Gaston, yeah, old Savannah money. They never found the car that hit her," Blitz said, looking curiously at Cybil.

"Wasn't she involved in a lot of charities? Could she have been connected to St. Rita?"

"I don't know," Blitz said.

Cybil grabbed her iPhone and quickly got on the Internet to Google St. Rita and Mrs. Evonia Gaston. Several links came up: news articles and St. Rita's website. Blitz looked into his drink and sat back.

Reading quickly Cybil found the connection. The St. Rita website did list their staff, Father Michael, Anne and the other nuns but the usual board of directors page was missing. A *Savannah Tribune* newspaper article reported that Mrs. Gaston, along with another patron, had been board members of St. Rita and were killed in the wreck. Cybil looked up at Blitz.

"Yes, she was on the board," Cybil said.

Her heart felt heavy, her weekend coming up. *What do I tell William?* Cybil looked at the time on the iPhone. It was getting late.

"Blitz, anything else you can tell me?"

"Nothing, except opinion. Michelle is not exactly charity board member material. Her look is more Girls Gone Wild than Girl Gone Good. I prefer the former. I can't figure out how Father Michael would come to recommend her, but I can imagine," he said, smiling.

Blitz stayed in his seat as Cybil stood up and said, "Blitz, thanks. E-mail the details of the fundraiser. And go on my website to check my modeling photo gallery. If there's a dress you would like for me to wear, let me know. I'll see if I can get it for the evening."

Blitz was silent for a few seconds, surprise in his eyes. "That's a nice touch. Thanks, I will do just that."

They shook hands and Cybil left the private back room at The Mirage. The cSpot meeting had started breaking up. The news of William's mother's involvement swirled in her mind. She made her way through the dispersing crowd, speaking quick goodbyes as she beelined to the door. Walking along West Broughton Street, she turned right and headed toward her car. Her eyes looked down, focusing in front of every step rather than straight ahead as usual, each footfall slower.

William's mother, I can't believe it. Cybil stopped at the corner and put a hand out to lean against the traffic pole. Next to her, grunge-dressed SCAD students holding half-eaten yogurt cups waited to cross. Across the street a family with two strollers waited. She took a deep breath. The orange hand crosswalk signal turned into a walking man, stepping into the crosswalk, she shook her head. *What will I say?*

22

"Please take the next exit, left, 130B, to Route 3 and continue 13 miles to your destination," said the woman's voice from the GPS.

Kasen's hands gripped the minivan's steering wheel tighter as his eyes searched for the exit sign. Finding it, he signaled a lane change and moved from the center lane to the right. He glanced down to the passenger seat and stared at the cover photo of "Savannah, the Jewel of Georgia," where they would harvest the seeds and he would meet her again.

His mind drifted back to Fallujah, Iraq, to her insolence and interference. She had kept him from escaping the tent. His capture and rendition to undisclosed locations within Saudi Arabia led to three years of interrogation hell. He shifted his weight and leaned left to ease the strain off his right hip as the car banked to take the ramp. Hanging by one leg for days had entertained his Shiite tormentors. They reminded him daily of his family's death, which they said was his fault.

Kasen, eager to reach Safir and finish preparations, followed the directions and got off I-95 onto Kings Highway which would take him straight to Almond Grove Mobile Home Park, less than 30 minutes away from Fort A.P. Hill, Virginia. He slowed, keeping a close watch for the upcoming left turn. Passing the farms, country stores and junkyards, he noticed several full corn fields alternating with fallow ones. In the full corn fields the stalks reached high with sprouting ears of corn, the yellow fruit hidden beneath the thick green husks, not yet ready.

Kasen smiled, laughed and spoke out loud: "Harvest will come soon enough."

A few minutes later he slowed the vehicle, Almond Drive just ahead. He turned left on the dirt road. It forked near the end and he bore right to unit 20, Safir's mobile home rental. Unit 20 was at the end, isolated … the units closest to it empty with no one to listen. In its driveway sat a parked recreational vehicle, the insides turned into an improvised workshop. The RV, recently purchased, was equipped with extra-large propane tanks on one side.

Pulling in front of the RV, Kasen stopped the car and stepped out. The mobile home's screen door opened, Safir rushed out, bounding down the wood steps, a big smile on his face. Safir hugged Kasen and they kissed each other's cheek. Safir led Kasen into the kitchen area and pointed to a small table with three chairs. Kasen sat down. In the middle of the table, a pot of steaming hot tea sat underneath a small plastic hanging lamp. The hot vapors rose and enveloped the lamp. Scattered on the table lay printed maps of the nearby military base's camping amenities. Safir went to the refrigerator and pulled out a tray of qatayef pancakes.

"Qatayef!" Kasen said.

"Yes, my father taught me how to make these for Ramadan. I wanted to celebrate our final meeting and these preparations," Safir said.

He grabbed the teapot's handle and poured Kasen's cup first, then his own. In silence they sipped their tea. Kasen reached out and picked up a sweet cheese-filled qatayef and took several hungry bites.

"Your hospitality is most welcome," Kasen said.

"Thank you, teacher. I am most pleased and honored."

Kasen raised his cup but stopped halfway. He looked into his cup for a few seconds and put it down.

"Tell me about your cousin, the army corporal. Will he help us?"

Safir lowered his gaze and stared at the teapot. "I am not sure. We have not spoken or written since we were children. He was glad to hear from me but was unsure about the camping idea."

Kasen lifted his cup and held it again, midway to his lips. "Do you think I should speak with him?"

"I considered it, teacher, but I think that would make him more nervous. Instead, I believe I have a way to persuade him," Safir said.

"How?" Kasen said.

"I will change the camping trip to include his wife and children, as a surprise. That will please him but also supply the additional elements we need."

"I don't understand," Kasen said.

"My cousin loves camping, cooking outdoors. I will tell him we will cook a big feast to honor his service and his family. I will tell him the propane tanks on the RV are not working and could he help. The purchase of extra tanks—we need four more—will be easy and normal for him as an American," Safir said.

"This will not make him suspicious?" Kasen said.

"I do not believe so, he is very sentimental. Even as a child, he loved celebrations at my mother's house. Always wanting to help with the food and cooking," Safir said.

"Good," Kasen said with a nod.

"To surprise his family, we will have to set up the day before to roast the meat slowly. That means we will be in the camping area as scheduled. When talking about this he complained to me he wanted to spend more time with them. This will be his chance," Safir said, looking straight at Kasen.

"Very well, you know your cousin best. The key is getting the RV on base at the right time at the right spot." Kasen grabbed the teapot and filled his cup. He pointed to Safir's cup. Safir motioned "no thank you" with his hand, his cup still full.

"How is the work going on the device?"

Smiling broadly, Safir said, "I am pleased to tell you that I am ahead of schedule."

Kasen leaned back and lifted his chin. "How is this possible?"

Safir said, "One week after I moved in, the three units next to me became vacant. My closest neighbor is almost a half-mile away. I have been able to make the modifications before and after going to work at the convenience store. Allah has blessed my efforts."

"Any problems with acquiring the necessary materials?" Kasen said.

Safir smiled. "As you taught us, I have been careful when and how much I purchased of the necessary items."

"What's left to do?" Kasen said.

"The current dispersal chamber walls are too thick, exceeding your specifications. I have to thin them significantly so that it blossoms as intended. After that, the mechanism is ready to receive the seed of destiny," Safir said

A dark shadow came over Kasen's face as he spoke. "The seed of destiny must be allowed to blossom and the sweet scent it brings must travel far and wide and find its place of rest. Where they rest, no one else will. This, Allah showed me in a dream when I was with the American pets, the Saudis. After the most severe of beatings I was asleep for a long time. Then I awoke and the vision was clear."

Safir sat still for a few moments, his head bowed, and then asked in a soft voice, "How did you escape?"

"Allah was kind to me. I was taken to a hospital to heal. A kind Iranian doctor helped me. We liked the same strong Turkish coffee and he read me some of the Koran while we drank. I came to trust him and I shared my dream with him."

"What did he think?" Safir said.

"He said nothing, but a week later, after I was strong enough, an ambulance came to take me back to the Saudi prison, or so I thought. Instead the ambulance made its way to the airport and a waiting aircraft. I was taken to Tehran," Kasen said, his eyes cold, his voice steady.

Safir leaned forward. "What happened then?"

Kasen's eyebrows rose, his expression brightened. "I received much help from my brothers, but that is past. We are now close to our goal, of giving this special gift, Hadeaa, as we say."

"When should I expect to receive the seed?"

"After here, I travel to be with Abdul and there I'll help him with his task. Together we drive to the final city where we'll work to complete the elements. I'll send him on to you. I'm sorry I can't be more specific, but the less you know, the better in the event you are captured. You can't tell them what you don't know."

"Teacher, I understand. It is wise," Safir said.

Kasen placed his elbows on the table, and tenting his hands, stared with eyes narrowed at Safir. "My contact there assures me our facilities will be ready when I arrive next week. It should not take much time to prepare the seed and send Abdul to you. After that, the plan proceeds as scheduled."

"Would you like to inspect the RV?" Safir said, his excited voice rising.

"Not yet. I want to review our contingency plans. Tell me again what happens when you receive the change of plans signal," Kasen said.

Safir recited from memory. Kasen pulled his chair close to listen, jostling the table, and the teapot, nearly empty, fell over, spilling about a half-cup of cool tea. Safir stopped talking and grabbed a nearby napkin and sopped up the tea. He then removed the partially soaked maps of the camping area. Underneath the maps, there were several brochures of the upcoming Boy Scout Jamboree to be hosted at the Fort, in the camping area known as the Bowl. The Bowl was a small valley between several surrounding hills, a natural stadium that could hold thousands of campers. Safir looked down and then up at his teacher who was also staring at the maps. Kasen lifted his eyes, meeting Safir's gaze, and they both smiled.

Kasen said, "Continue, my friend."

23

On the flight, in first class, Cybil avoided conversation with her row mate by focusing on the script for her commercial. The filming, scheduled for later that day at the Fontainebleau hotel lobby, should not take long. The scene depicted a couple arriving at the hotel for a romantic vacation supposedly booked in a luxury suite. However they found themselves booked into the smallest room in the hotel. He blamed her for the faulty coupon she gave him and they argued. They were about to split up but the bearded travel gnome came to the rescue.

The plane's speakers crackled instructions for the final approach to Miami and she stuffed the script into her bag. The smooth landing and taxi to the gate passed quickly and soon she arrived at baggage claim looking for William's driver.

Cybil's eyes scanned the row of mostly uniformed limousine drivers holding up small signs as she walked to baggage claim. William had texted about meeting her at the shoot but was delayed due to boat maintenance. He would see her later at the marina.

She looked for her name among the black-suited drivers, all attentive, all male except one. She was tall, young, early twenties, full bosom, attractive, hair tucked under her cap. A passing couple pointed and laughed at the sign she held. Cybil smiled as she read the sign: RAVEN BLUE EYES. *William!*

After exchanging names, the driver, Tina, took Cybil's roller case and led her to the parked limo, Cybil slipping into the backseat.

"How was your flight, miss?" Tina said as she drove away from the terminal.

"Good. Are we far from the Fontainebleau?" Cybil said.

"We'll be there in less than 30 minutes. I'm to wait for you until you're done and then take you to the marina," Tina said.

"Thank you." Cybil settled back and reread her script.

Three hours later Cybil was back in the limo, heading toward the marina.

"How did the shoot go?" the driver said.

"Good. Sorry it took so long. I was the only one who knew my lines. Ha! Anyway, could you give me a few minutes, please?" Cybil said.

The driver nodded and reached for the dashboard to flip a switch. "Sure thing, miss," she said, "just press the green button if you need me."

The privacy shield, a dark glass, rose smoothly till it clicked into place.

To her left on the door panel, Cybil glanced as the intercom call switch went from yellow to green.

She pulled her iPad from her bag, onto her lap. She tweeted, which also streamed to Facebook.

Just finished shoot @Fontainebleau, check site next week for behind the scenes shots

Then @undisclosed location in Miami for r&r ;)

Me Halfway by Black Eyed Peas on The E.N.D.

Cybil reached into her purse and grabbed her cell phone to text Carol about the kids.

How's it going. Ready to give up

Carol was going to take the whole crew to Tybee Island Beach for the afternoon; it might be a while before she saw this message. Cybil then found Anne's number and pressed Call. She put the phone on speaker and placed it inside the cup holder in the door panel. She kicked off her pumps.

"Hi, glad you called," Anne said.

"Can you talk now?"

"Yes. I'm here at Trinity Methodist Chapel on Tybee, our temporary home. I was taking some time in the garden."

"So the move is done?"

"Yeah," Anne said in a low, quiet voice.

"I'm sorry this happened," Cybil said.

"Thanks. The vans took what we couldn't to storage. The rest of us will be here for a while until Children's Services can intake Sofi and Cecilia and the last few. The Trinity folks have extra rooms in their shelter that could accommodate us. Where I'll be going next, I'm not sure. God's really pushing me this time," Anne said.

"Hmmm. Listen, do you remember when St. Rita had to elect new board members because of some traffic accident? It was about a year ago."

"Yes. It was very sad. We had a special prayer service in the chapel, I remember. Mrs. Gaston and Mr. Barnard," Anne said.

"Well, Blitz, the attorney I talked to, tells me that Michelle, the board member who replaced Mrs. Gaston, was recommended by Father Michael. Michelle is young, has a drug-dealing record and not exactly charity board material. How does he know her and why would he do that?"

Anne was silent for a few seconds, then said, "I'm not sure. Like I told you before, when I saw Father Michael and his night visitors, there was a young woman in the group along with two men. Maybe it was Michelle."

"According to Blitz, Michelle is connected to a Stavos Gruner, someone local law enforcement keeps an eye on and apparently the FBI as well."

"I knew something was not right! I've been praying that the truth would come out. St. Rita closing has never made sense," Anne said, her voice rising.

"Right, right. Remember the A27 Jump Jet investigation I was involved with back in the 82nd?" Cybil said.

"Yes. I remember. You got a commendation for that."

"I learned then, if you want to find out the truth, follow the money."

"Sure. Is there anything I can do?"

"Sit tight until I get back next week. We can talk then."

"Are you out of town?"

"Uh-huh. Miami."

"Modeling?"

"Just personal business."

"I'm sorry. Didn't mean to pry. Just curious, I suppose," Anne said.

Cybil bit her lower lip and strummed her fingers on her thigh, glancing out the window. "I have a shoot here and then a friend invited me to do some sailing. Sebastian and June are with their favorite sitter. Actually, they are not that far from you. She's taking them to the beach today."

"They should have fun, it's a nice day. I hope you have a nice time with William," Anne said.

"How do you know that?" Cybil said, her eyebrows scrunching.

"Cybil, you are Savannah's top model and quite a bit of gossip is out there on you. After we met, I thought a few Google searches would catch me up. You and William Gaston are mentioned a lot together," Anne said.

Kara's Internet magazine!

"Ha, so you're stalking me now," Cybil said with a laugh.

"I read about his wealth, sailing life and his Miami home base. I may have been trained in a convent but live in the real world," Anne said, "and I'm only trying to understand you better after all this time."

Cybil paused for a second. Her face flushed pink and a small grin broke into a wide smile. "I'm almost at William's place now," she said.

Anne took a deep breath audible over the phone and said, "One more thing. William's last name is Gaston, which is common in Savannah. But the board member that was killed in the wreck was also a Gaston. Is there a connection?"

"Unfortunately, yes. It was his mother," Cybil said.

Anne was silent.

"You still there?"

"I'm sorry. I'm thinking there's something else at work here," Anne said.

"I don't know," Cybil said.

"I don't believe in coincidences, there are purposes for everything," Anne said.

*

Cybil frowned. *During Airborne training, Anne never talked about belief or religion and now she's a freaking nun.* When Cybil's mom took her to church and Sunday school, which was not often, Cybil heard remarks about "She's divorced now" or "Poor child needs new shoes." Judgmental looks and whispers about her mom wearing short dresses to church had stayed in her memory. Other children's taunts such as "Where's your daddy" on the playground ended with Cybil bloodying some boy's nose. Cybil and her mother never found a welcoming church.

*

"Well, maybe. But we're on our own here, so let's stay focused on finding what we need," Cybil said.

"I'm sorry. I know this can't be easy for you," Anne said.

The limo was slowing down. Cybil glanced out the window. They were coming up to the marina clubhouse. With one hand she quickly slipped her pumps on.

"I'll be okay," Cybil said. "I'm not sure I'll even say anything to William. I need to go now, we'll talk when I get back."

"Okay, I'll keep you in my … thoughts, and thanks for calling. Bye now," Anne said.

The limo came to a stop and the passenger door was flung open.

"Well, there you are, luv," William Gaston said as he grabbed Cybil's left hand and pulled her out of the limo. Her cell phone fell and clinked on the asphalt, sliding under the vehicle.

"Sorry about that," William said as he helped her up and stepped close, leaning in to kiss her lightly on the lips. "I am so glad the shoot brought you here and to me."

Cybil smiled. "So am I."

She reached out for both his hands and held them in hers. "You look good. Lots of sun, I see," she said.

William's father, a businessman from New Zealand, had settled in Savannah where he met Evonia Gaston and then eventually married. She kept her name, which William's father didn't mind since it had weight in the city. William took after his father, who had aboriginal roots and whose skin also darkened much during the summer. Today William comfortably wore tan shorts and a white short-sleeved cotton shirt that sharpened the contrast. On the edge of his short sleeve, red embroidered stitching spelled out WMG for William Mason Gaston.

William looked to the front of the limo and called to the driver, who had stepped out and stood at the ready. "Tina, grab the phone under the car if you don't mind, and put her bags on the mid deck, and thanks for picking my luv up."

Tina nodded.

William stepped aside and held Cybil's hand. He led her through the parking lot and onto the walkway. His slip was at the far end since his sailing yacht, the largest in the marina, could only fit there.

"Who were you talking to?" William asked.

Cybil looked down and took a deep breath. She had never told William about Anne. "Oh, just checking in with the kids."

"You're a good mum," William said and winked.

"You miss her?" Cybil said. *How will I ask about St. Rita?*

"Yeah, I do," William said, "but I'll be all right."

They'd walked a few paces when William said, "I'm so glad you're here," as he squeezed her hand and lifted it, pressing it close to his chest.

Cybil felt his lean pectoral muscle through her hand. His grip was tight, firm. Cybil's heart beat faster, her excitement of being with William again starting to build. Looking at him, she noticed motion past him, on the water. Peering deeper into the harbor, she saw two boats heading toward each other. As the larger ship passed by first, closer to her, she lost view of the other.

Looking back to him she smiled. Slightly taller than her, his dark-brown hair was cropped short, but styled. It fit his square face and strong jaw line. Fit and trim, he moved like an athlete and he could keep up with Cybil when they jogged together. She glanced at his legs, thin but muscular, his calves particularly ripped. *We need this, I need this,* she thought.

At the end of the slip they stepped up the gangway onto the *Kiwi Empress II*, William's 60-foot sailing yacht with a crew of eight. Cybil and William made their way to the back. Near the wheel, a small card table stood covered with a tablecloth. On it a small vase of red roses, a large uncorked bottle of champagne in an ice bucket, two wine goblets and a plate of white chocolate-covered strawberries waited for them.

"Let's have drinks before I give you the tour," William said.

"The strawberries are a nice touch, you remembered!" Cybil grinned. William didn't always pay attention to her preferences.

Standing near the table, William poured the champagne. Cybil lifted her glass, clinked it to William's and they both took a deep sip.

"So where is everyone?" Cybil said, biting down on a strawberry.

"Oh, I gave them the day off. They'll be back tomorrow," William said.

"I see." Cybil smiled licking her lips.

She picked up another strawberry, a smaller one, and looking into his eyes she brought the treat to her lips, pausing. Slowly she wrapped her lips around the fruit before pushing it into her mouth with one finger and bringing her lips together.

William coughed twice and smiled. "I've missed you too," he said.

A couple loud thumps turned both their heads toward the middle of the boat. Tina had arrived and plopped the bags on the deck near the top of the gangway. She pulled off her hat and mopped her brow. Her long blond hair had fallen to her shoulders and it swayed in the slight breeze. She smiled, waved goodbye and made her way off the boat.

"So tell me," Cybil said, nodding and looking at the driver walking away, "has this particular hot blond driver worked for you before?"

William looked over his shoulder at her. "Tina? She's the daughter of my first mate. They live here and she's going to the University of Miami. She works the limo service to help pay her way through school. She's taking up oceanography. Smart kid. A kid," William said, "a kid."

"Just checking," Cybil said, grinning. She drained her glass and held it up to William for a refill.

William nodded and obliged. He refilled his glass.

"Let's take these below," William said in a firm voice, his eyes staring into Cybil's. She nodded her assent.

On their way to the captain's cabin, he talked about the different compartments, galley, storage, crew sleeping quarters, engine room. Cybil uttered "Ok," "Um," "Yeah," half-listening as the champagne sped her relaxation. They finally reached his cabin and walked in.

After placing their glasses on a small side table built in the wall, he waved his hand around the room explaining the layout, pointing here and there, his back to her. He was talking about the workmanship of the wood detail. He turned around to look at her but stopped talking.

Cybil had kicked off her shoes and was leaning against the wall near the door. One arm stretched high on the wall, the other rested on her hip. The two top buttons of her blouse were undone, revealing her black lace bra.

"So how do you lock this?" she said, titling her head toward the door.

William smiled and slowly walked over to the door. He stood next to her, looking at the lock. He could smell the strawberries and champagne on her breath.

Turning his head, he stared into her eyes and slid the bolt into place with some force. The thud vibrated through the cabin, and he said, "Like that."

"I thought you might have forgotten," Cybil said. She reached out and touched his sleeve monogram, then traced her finger down his arm, brushing his warm skin gently.

"Hardly, luv," William said.

With one move he placed his right arm around her waist and the other under her legs and picked her up with little effort. Her arms flung around his neck and she pulled herself up to kiss him. His lips were salty; she tasted champagne on his tongue as it explored hers. Her heart raced, her insides began to burn for him. Still kissing, he carried her to the bed, laid her down gently and stretched out next to her. William pulled away for a second and cupped her chin with his hand. Her eyes brimmed with desire, matching his.

"This weekend will be different, I promise. We'll talk. No more holding back, okay," William said.

Cybil nodded, not sure what William had said. She reached out with both hands, palms to each side of William's face.

"Whatever. Kiss me," Cybil said, and pulling him in, kissed him fiercely.

Soon she was escaping into her pleasure joining his while trying desperately to drive the image of Anne's beautiful face out of her mind.

24

Sister Anne took a deep breath and felt the wind's kiss. The warm salt air and ocean smells of Tybee Beach filled her senses. In the deep of night she stood at the edge of the sea, a short walk from Trinity Chapel, makeshift home for the St. Rita refugees. She couldn't sleep.

With her shoes in hand and standing before incoming waves, cool Atlantic water washed over her bare feet. The earlier phone call with Cybil replayed in her mind. Michelle, Mrs. Gaston, William … Father Michael. *Why would Father Michael recommend a suspected drug dealer to the board? What is he hiding?*

Anne stepped back and stood, looking. Immense, powerful, in constant motion, mysterious, dangerous, the sea could swallow her whole. She wriggled her toes in the rough sand, its texture different from the sand at Dubai beaches. Middle Eastern beach sand was fine and lily-white. On the last day of their leave, she remembered sitting with Cybil under a white shade umbrella on the beach, the diffused sunlight allowing them to take off their sunglasses. Turning, she peered into Cybil's eyes. They stayed for hours swimming, drying off, talking, walking and swimming again. When they left and returned to the hotel they took three times as long to pack; they couldn't stop taking breaks, again and again. Traveling back to base, they talked about how different the water felt, how different everything was becoming.

Now, at this beach in Georgia, looking at the ocean, Sister Anne started shaking. Her fear, after that weekend, grew. *It's happening again,* she thought. St. Rita now closed, Sofi and Cecilia soon to be taken away, Cybil again in her life, the future unknown…. She sensed the same mountain of change in front of her.

25

Stavos Gruner, his hands holding on to the penthouse balcony railing, looked out over the horizon. The rising sun, in a cloudless sky, began to warm the cool morning air. From the condo penthouse, he could see the moored *Destiny* waiting for him, refueled and washed, cleansed from last week's activities. Having the Thunderbolt Marina nearby made excursions easier. He watched the river make its way past the marina, through the marshes, as it spilled into the Atlantic. On the channel, a line of boats headed to sea, at river speed: a couple of commercial fishing boats, a large sailboat, a mid-size yacht and smaller leisure craft. He spotted one boat going the other direction, coming in straight for the marina. A thin finger of black smoke trailed from the rear, a sure sign of burning oil, engine problems and trouble.

Stavos glanced over to the *Savannah Morning News* lying on the small glass tabletop, the headline read: "Savannah couple missing at sea." He gritted his teeth and gripped the rail harder. The Coast Guard search would continue for at least one more day. Tonight's planned run to retrieve Kasen's second-to-last shipment had become too risky. He didn't want to have to explain anything to a nosy Coast Guard crew, let alone be boarded.

He bent his head forward and puffed out a breath. Last week's phone call from Kurt explained why the Coast Guard was complicating his plans. A powerless boat had drifted near the *Destiny* as they picked up last week's cargo. The disabled boat owner was about to contact the Coast Guard but instead asked if the *Destiny* could tow them in. Happy for their luck, they offered to share with Kurt and Markos the margaritas and finger sandwiches prepared by his wife.

Leaving them alive meant witnesses. So shooting both, tossing them into their cabin, burning and sinking the boat became a reasonable option his employees had exercised. But that action resulted in a standard procedure, Coast Guard search which fucked up the schedule. This he had to explain to Kasen, who was on his way to Savannah.

I'll call him later. Stavos turned around and leaned backwards on the rail. Through the thin red-and-white flowered kimono wrapped around his naked frame, the cool metal lay across his muscular glutes. He looked at the bed where the girls slept. Both women lay on their side, spooning, Michelle stretched out behind her friend, her arm around her waist, both heads on the same pillow. The sheet covered them from the waist down. Michelle's eyes opened, she blinked and licked her lips. She lifted her head, saw Stavos and smiled. Pulling her friend closer, she woke her up. Opening her eyes, her friend turned her face toward Michelle and lifted her hand to gently caress her. Michelle kissed the back of her neck. Stavos, walking over to the bed, felt his energy returning along with his appetite.

A few hours later the spent threesome talked each other into lunch at Tortugas Grill. Needing to make a call first, Stavos sent them ahead with his order.

After a quick shower, he stepped over to his walk-in closet, water dripping and leaving a trail of wet footsteps along the heavy pile carpet. He stood at his long rectangular center dresser. On the glass top five neat lines of coke remained from last night's fun. Stavos lifted the hundred-dollar rolled tube lying next to the lines and quickly inhaled two of them. His eyes grew wide and he shook his head as the rush grew. After a few seconds, he recovered and dressed in black shorts, a white Greek cotton shirt and sandals. On the dresser a nondescript black prepaid phone, the one Vasily had given him to talk to Kasen, blinked green; no messages or calls. He grabbed it and went to the balcony to sit. The air had warmed, the sky still clear blue. He pressed the Speed Dial button.

"I'm glad you called," Kasen said, the sounds of a car in motion clear in the background. "Nothing but good news has come from you these last months. And I did want to talk with you about a new matter."

Stavos frowned. *Shit, what does he want now?* "Have you been watching the news?"

"Some. Anything of import?"

"The Coast Guard has been searching for a missing couple at sea. They're part of Savannah's rich so there's been at lot of attention, a sad accident. I'm not sure night fishing is wise with all the sea traffic. I was thinking of postponing."

"Hmmm, I see our dilemma. Of course this was out of your control. Let me talk to my friends and see if we can reschedule our fishing excursion. Do you think one day will be enough?" Kasen said.

Stavos's eyebrows rose and he smiled, saying, "I think so."

"May I ask about my special fishing gear?"

Stavos grimaced. The equipment had arrived by a single large truck, delivered to one of his restaurant fronts. Heavier and bulkier than expected, they needed to rent a larger truck to move them to the orphanage. Setup at St. Rita for the special electrical needs took longer, putting them behind schedule. Having electricians come and do work there, and paying them to be quiet, increased the risk.

"Well, it is presenting some challenges but nothing we can't handle. The expenses continue to pile up though," Stavos said. *I'm going to take as much as I can,* he thought.

Kasen sighed loud enough for Stavos to hear, then said, "Being frugal is a virtue but not at the expense of a wonderful experience. If I did not trust your judgment, I would not have chartered with you."

"We are the best at what we do. We will deliver for you," Stavos said. Taking a deep breath, his chest expanded, and he sat up straight in his chair.

"I do have another favor to ask," Kasen said.

"What is it?"

"I recently discovered an old friend of mine, lives in your fine city. I would like to get reacquainted. Could you arrange a meeting?"

"Will she want to see you?" Stavos said.

"Sadly no but I'm certain you can be most persuasive. And if there are any additional, reasonable expenses, I will cover them."

Stavos grinned. "In that case, I'm sure she will be delighted to see you."

"Very good. I'll text you her name. She is quite well-known in your city," Kasen said, hanging up.

Stavos smiled. He laid the phone on the table and leaned back. He rested his left elbow on the armrest, his other hand on his thigh, fingers strumming. Stavos's mind raced to calculate Kasen's past payments, future payments and the extra charges he could fleece him for. This cash positive operation paid like no other. Nothing must jeopardize these payments that would fuel his expansion plans. "Cash is king," his father would say.

*

Stavos remembered his father taking bets at the docks after morning fishing. The shorefront neighbors, fishermen, storekeepers and local cops liked his hard-drinking father, who always paid off on time and in cash. He never took credit slips. One time, a burly dockworker tried to intimidate his father into taking a bet on his "good word." Shouting gave way to shoving, but a knife stab to the thigh convinced the dockworker Stavos's father only ran a cash business.

*

His stomach rumbled, he jumped up and headed for the door. Taking the elevator down and striding through the lobby he exited to River Drive. Turning left, his walk to Tortuga Grill included a symphony of thoughts about the extra cash, lunch and the girls. With no trip tonight and Kurt and Markos doing the move, he and they would have more time together to continue what was started the night before.

26

Cybil's eyes opened to soft morning light coming through the cabin porthole, half-covered by a white vinyl shade. Facing the boat's east wall, she lay on her side, William snored quietly next to her on the round bed. Cybil's left hand cradled her face, the other rested across her stomach. She sighed. *Nice morning*.

The queen-sized bed, custom-made to William's specs, had plenty of room. But he was a sprawler; when he slept, legs and arms went everywhere. She had scooted toward the wall to get away but his warm, hairy lower leg touched hers along the calf. She moved her legs farther to the side, gaining space but nearing the edge.

She took a deep breath and her nose twitched at William's musky smell, still on her. They had made love most of the night, till exhausted, catching up on several months of missing each other. Passion had never been the problem between them; it was about where they were going or, more where William wanted to go. Cybil, always clear about her direction, could only guess at what William wanted. *I need to know,* she thought.

William stirred and rolled over, hugging her close. He nuzzled her neck, kissing it gently several times.

"Hey, gorgeous luv, good morning," he whispered.

Cybil fought the desire to get up. His body heat, always high in the morning, grew uncomfortable. She stiffened by flexing and he felt it.

"Hey, you okay?" he said.

"Yeah, I'm fine. You're just so damn warm in the morning. I don't like to sweat first thing," she said, slipping off the bed.

William, lifting himself on one elbow, watched her glide, naked, to the bathroom. She was beautifully slim, with a muscular back. His arousal began anew but halted when he saw her dolphin tattoo above her bum. The ink, meant to hide her childhood spinal tap needle marks, was a permanent reminder of pain and courage. Her mother's stories, told to William over shots of tequila, celebrated the brave little pistol of a kid, bald, full of spirit, running around the cancer ward.

"How about breakfast at Chico's on South Beach? We can talk there," William yelled at the same time Cybil flushed the toilet.

A few seconds later Cybil walked out in a pink cotton bathrobe and smiled. "I hope you don't mind, I took it out of the closet. It's a bit long for me, though."

"Uh, I asked the service to stock it for guests. Sorry about the fit," William said, his face slightly red.

He moved backward on the bed and sat upright next to the headboard, the bed sheets covering his lower body. He interlaced his fingers behind his head and leaned against them. His wide shoulders, arms and chest formed a large V above his stomach, his thin skin clinging to defined abdominal muscles.

"Why don't we start the morning off right?" William said, smiling.

He lifted one knee high, the sheet draping and outlining his powerful thigh sculpted from hours of sailing and ship maintenance.

Cybil grabbed a small side chair outside the bathroom and sat down opposite William. She leaned back and crossed her legs. She strummed her fingers on the chair's armrest.

"What, we're going to have a meeting?" William said, his eyes searching Cybil's face.

He dropped his knee and the white sheet rustled down on his thighs as his heavy hands landed with a slight thud.

"William, you told me we would talk," Cybil said.

"Yeah, I did, but how about after breakfast. I'm starving. You helped me work up quite an appetite last night, luv."

"Thanks," Cybil said, smiling, "but, this is important."

William pursed his lips, sighed and looked to the side. His smile gone, he glanced downward and then looked at Cybil.

"I know you and I talked about marriage before but …" William said.

"But what?" Cybil said.

"You told me what you wanted, to make Savannah our home base, maybe have a kid or two together. I know at some point you thought about moving into fashion design work and maybe having a place in New York or Milan, travel more," William said.

Cybil uncrossed her legs, leaned towards him and said, "And you always avoided telling me what you wanted."

"All I want is you," William said, raising his hands up and open toward her.

"William, you've told me that before. It's nicely romantic but doesn't have any meaning. All my first husband wanted was me, so much of me he almost consumed me with his obsession and control."

"Yes, I remember, you were quite open on our first few dates. I kept looking over my shoulder for weeks after that. I had never dated a woman with an ex-husband in Special Forces."

"Well, we get along fine now. He and I reached a better arrangement—though he could do more with his own kids."

"Isn't he getting remarried?" William said.

"Yes, he is. Why?"

William took a deep breath and said, "With me mum's passing I feel I can finally leave Savannah with someone I love and chase the sun that never sets. When I think about us, I think about being together on the seas, about exploring different parts of the world, of enjoying each other anytime, anywhere, of not being tied down to a city or anyone else but us. Just us."

Saying nothing, Cybil stared at William for several seconds, blinking her eyes and trying to understand "just us." She closed her eyes for a moment and the carefree image William painted drew her in. She felt the warm wind on her face as she sat on the foredeck in her favorite bikini, the sun kissing her body. She'd glance back at William, his strong hands gripping the wheel, directing the ship to the next port of call, Nice, France, for the Cannes Film Festival. They could winter in Milan during the fashion show season. Then at that moment she heard Sebastian's voice coming from below deck. He was crying, saying he couldn't find his sister … where was June, where was June? Cybil felt an icy coldness climb along her spine.

She looked around the boat's cabin. Trimmed in red mahogany and brass, the ivory painted wainscot, impeccably finished, clung halfway up the wall. Nautical souvenirs and silver-framed photos of William and his crew hoisting trophies circled the room. Her eyes scanned back to William. Hanging over him, on the wall, a loaded spear gun.

"Sailboats aren't very kid friendly, are they?" Cybil said.

"Don't get me wrong, I like Sebastian and June, but they have a dad and with his getting married, I thought some new arrangement could be made," William said, his lips pressing together and eyes opening wider.

Cybil shook her head and then bent forward, putting her elbows on her knees, her head in her hands. She felt queasy, found it hard to breathe. *Control.*

"I've upset you, let's go get breakfast and talk more."

Cybil took a breath and slowly stood up, her voice slow and controlled. "William, I'm not sure what we would talk about. Thanks for being honest. I have to go."

"Ah, luv, don't leave like this."

"Can you call the limo, please, while I get dressed?" Her voice was cool, businesslike.

William's shoulders slumped and his head dropped, chin resting on a bare chest. "Sure, sure thing."

He knew well enough not to appeal further; her voice and eyes warned him off. His brilliant idea for boarding school, yachts in several places and other accommodations would go unspoken, now and forever.

Cybil stepped into the bathroom, with her bag and closed the door. Looking into the mirror, she shook her head. Dressing quickly, she started to brush her hair. After a few strokes she stopped. Leaning closer to the mirror, she looked at the edges around her eyes and mouth. Frowning she reached into her bag for her makeup kit, but when she saw her prescription bottle she grabbed it. She poured two pills into her palm and tossed them into her mouth. Turning the faucet on she cupped her hand, water spilled between her fingers but enough pooled for a drink to help her swallow.

A half-hour later they sat topside waiting for the limo. Neither had spoken to the other after they finished dressing, the quiet interrupted only when William called the driver. They waited silently at the small table near the wheel, looking past each other. On the table the empty champagne bottle lay on its side with pieces of torn gold foil strewn about. A ragged foil strip rested on the edge of the fruit plate; rotting strawberries drew small buzzing flies.

The limo pulled up to the lot, the driver got out and looked at William who stood up and waved at her. Cybil and William left the boat and walked toward the parking lot. He pulled Cybil's rolling carry-on, walking a few feet behind her while she carried her large Louis Vuitton shoulder bag. When they reached the limo the driver silently took the roller and placed it in the trunk. The back passenger door had already been opened. Cybil placed her shoulder bag in the backseat. The driver went to the front and sat behind the wheel, window down. William stepped up to the door along with Cybil. Her back was turned to him.

William put his hands into his pockets and said, "I hope you have good flight." Cybil turned around and William looked at the ground.

"Thanks. Just as well I get back, I've got a lot to do," she said.

He raised his head, looking at her, his half-smile lasted a second before his lips puffed open letting out a long sigh. He turned his head to scan the parking lot.

"Text me when you get back, let me know you got there okay," William said.

"Sure. What's next on the sailing agenda?" she said.

He smiled. "The boat's checked out fine. The crew will be back here tomorrow for a final run-through before we set sail for St. Thomas. There's a small tournament we think is perfect to break her in. What about you?"

"I'm looking into a few things for a friend. Can I ask you a question about your mom and her work at St. Rita?" Cybil said.

William pulled his hands out of his pockets and crossed his arms, leaned to the side and tilted his head.

"Sure. She was fond of doing charity work for the Savannah art community. But she loved the St. Rita work most. She and Father Michael knew each other for a long time before he asked her to help. What do you want to know?"

"Did she ever talk about the finances or if there were any problems?" Cybil said.

"No, not that I can recall. Why?"

"Well, St. Rita had to close, so I was just wondering," Cybil said.

William shifted his weight to his other leg. "Mum started handling all of the finances when Dad got sick, frankly, better than he ever did. My trust fund did wonders after she began directing the investments. If there were any financial problems at St. Rita, my mum would've been right in the middle of it. Nothing got past her."

Cybil nodded her head.

William said, "I'd think she'd been heartbroken to hear St. Rita closed. She would have tried to keep it afloat financially herself until she could appeal to her peers in the Savannah community. Her will provided a decent gift but apparently not enough. I guess we all lost after the accident." He looked at the sky.

"Thanks, this helps," Cybil said, turning to get into the limo. She tripped as she stepped in, the raised height of the limo floor tricky. Her hands grabbed the doorframe and she steadied herself before stepping inside.

"You okay?" William said.

"Yeah, I'm fine," she said, her eyes trying to focus inside the shaded rear compartment. Her stomach felt queasy.

William put his hand on the roof and leaned into the open door. He looked at her, his eyes wide.

"I think I'm almost regretting what I said this morning."

Cybil smiled. "I'm glad you were honest. It would have fallen apart eventually, no matter how hard we tried. We would've had fun, though." She reached out and touched his face, caressing his chin.

William grinned. "That we would have."

Cybil pulled her hand away, leaned back and looked straight ahead. "Call me whenever you're in town. We can have drinks and catch up."

William nodded, stood up and gently closed the limo door. He tapped the limo roof twice. He stepped back and the car pulled slowly away, through the lot to the service road entrance. The limo stopped, waiting for traffic to clear. He put his hands in his pockets.

Cybil turned around and through the rear window watched William. She waved goodbye. William couldn't see through the tinted glass so he didn't wave back. She turned face forward and sat down. Like the flick of a light switch, William was tuned out of her thoughts. The limo pulled out onto the service road and accelerated toward Miami International Airport.

27

Sister Anne stepped to the side of Reverend Sanders's 2002 Buick lime-green Oldsmobile parked near the rectory at Trinity Chapel. A few minutes before she had taken the car keys from the foyer table, fighting the guilt that filled her. Telling Sanders a story earlier at dinner, about leaving personal papers behind at St. Rita, she had to look past him rather than directly. Her mother's words echoed in her mind: "Look me in the eye, I can tell if you're lying."

Illumination from the porch lights filtered through the dirty rear window. Peering inside the car, she noticed the backseat full of several different-sized cardboard boxes. Each was open, spilling over with worn shoes, pants, shirts and hats. Sanders warned her about the mess from the festival clothes drive when she'd asked for a flashlight and he said it was somewhere in the back.

Opening the rear door, Sister Anne leaned inside. She gagged at the concentrated smell of sweat-stained shirts and moldy sneakers. An array of shoeboxes, lids and hats sat next on the rear window ledge. Their outline broke up the incoming yellowish light from the porch, creating shadows and dark spaces. She felt her way around the cardboard boxes and the clothes that had fallen out. Her hand touched and moved wool socks, cotton blouses, ties and unknowns until, nestled behind the largest box, she felt cold metal.

"There you are," she said, and grabbed the cylindrical, ridged flashlight.

Sister Anne pulled herself out of the rear seat and straightened up. Sliding the open switch forward she followed the bright beam that shot straight up. She looked up at the light which faded into the moonless night full of stars and smiled. For a minute her lips moved as if she were talking and then she turned the flashlight off. Opening the driver's side door, she slid in, started the car and accelerated slowly over the gravel driveway, heading toward Tybee Island's main road which would take her back to St. Rita. Near the end of the driveway, her tires ground and threw pebbles backward as she sped away.

After some 20 minutes, the car slowed as it got within a mile of St. Rita's main driveway, a gated entrance now chain-locked, the only key with Father Michael. Sister Anne pulled the car over to the side of the road. Looking down into the drink cup tray she saw a used, frayed pocket-sized notepad with a pencil stuck in the spiral binding. Before getting out she stuck the pad into her pants pocket and pulled the latch to open the hood, then grabbed the flashlight. Outside the car she raised the hood and manually locked the doors, making the vehicle look like it was in trouble and giving it a reason to be on the roadside; the missing driver obviously was walking somewhere for help.

St. Rita's delivery road cut into the woods a quarter-mile before the main driveway. From the parked car Sister Anne walked to the unmarked entrance. This road led directly to St. Rita's east wing, where Father Michel's office and the kitchen were located. A side hallway connected the two areas. Every room had been packed and moved except for Father Michael's office. He had complained about the commute distance from his downtown apartment to Trinity Chapel. Therefore he planned to work from St. Rita one more week before moving to Trinity's temporary lodgings, now home to the children and the staff.

Sister Anne walked along the dark paved delivery road, her flashlight beaming ahead of her, lighting the path. A light wind off the river swayed the treetops, rustling the leaves. She looked up and saw a half-moon rising above the crown of the woods. The thin light fell on the magnolias, oaks and tall pine trees; they looked like guards lining both sides of the driveway. The sharp smell of pine mixed with the sweet scent of blooming night flowers, jasmine and hyacinth. Sister Anne took a deep breath and smiled, the aroma familiar. She frowned, *Will we be back?*

Clack-clack. The sound of wood hitting wood stopped Sister Anne in her tracks. She clicked off the flashlight immediately and turned her head to listen. The noise reached her again. No steps or voices could be heard. Sister Anne kept walking toward the kitchen, no more than 50 yards straight ahead. The rising moon now cleared the treetops. The wind, light and sporadic, insistently moved leaves and limbs. She approached the kitchen and saw the rear screen door open.

Sister Anne stopped and held her breath. She felt the wind brush her and the short hair on her neck rising. The open screen door closed, hitting its frame twice: clack-clack.

Sister Anne put her hand over her heart and glanced up and whispered, "Whew."

Stepping to the screen door, she pulled it open and peered through the four-pane glass door. Reaching into her pocket, she found the backup master key she had borrowed from Sister George last month, who had never asked for it back. She clicked on the flashlight long enough to help her insert the key. Opening the kitchen door, the interior alarm panel began to beep. Stepping inside, Sister Anne punched in the code and the beeping stopped. *Not changed yet.*

She walked through the kitchen and the side hallway leading to Father Michael's office just off the lobby. The hallway wall separated the lobby from the office and kitchen wing. Standing there she stared at his office door. Made from solid oak and ornately carved, it had a small ventilation window above it. Her eyes had adjusted to the dark and she could see dim light coming over the door through the glass; Father Michael must have left the curtains open on the panoramic office window. Looking down, the master key lay in her open palm. She moved her hand as if measuring the key's weight, then tossed the key up and it landed like a coin in her hand. Inserting the key and turning the brass knob, the door opened and she walked in.

28

Cybil looked up through the limo's sunroof and saw a flock of geese flying low, aligned in a V. They were heading in the same direction. She smiled. *Maybe they're trying to catch the same flight.*

It reminded her of helicopter formations in Iraq as they flew into the center of chaos, known on the news as Fallujah. Her eyes dropped and her smile faded as she remembered the captain's body covered in blood, killed during the mission, the one that captured Al-Mahdi, the Snake. He was the only casualty that day, the price paid to stop that threat for good. The geese's loud honking sounded muted due to the thick sunroof glass. She glanced up again and saw them move together, turning right, then left, smoothly, as a team.

Cybil pressed the Intercom button on the door handle. "How much longer before we get to the airport?"

"Not long, about 20 minutes. I have your boarding passes here. William—uh—Mr. Gaston made sure I had them," the young woman driver said.

"Okay, Tina," Cybil said as her lips pressed together and her eyes blinked a few times.

Cybil leaned back and felt a little woozy. She closed her eyes and let out a deep sigh. *I should feel worse.*

Reaching into her bag she pulled out her iPad and began to tweet but could only make two entries, one being a song she remembered hearing on the way home after meeting Anne at Thunderbolt.

Change of plans - heading back to Sav

Bleeding Love (Jason Nevins Radio Remix) by Leona Lewis

Cybil picked up her phone and scrolled through her various lists, then went back through them one by one, deleting when needed.

E-mail from Jimmy: Southern Living studio shoot moved to next month, my place, 1:00 pm - *Good,* she thought, *need more time at home.*

E-mail: Find your ideal match - delete

E-mail: Your Model Mayhem account usage report is now available - delete

E-mail from Tom: Hey, in town next week on business, have time Wed night. Can I drop by to work with Sebastian on KidMars?

REPLY: Sure. S will like that, he has been drawing a lot, 7:00pm, dinner and homework will be over. Travel safe.

Text: where are you! called the house and a strange woman, Carol, answered, I love to watch MY grandkids you know?

REPLY: Mom, too short notice, you live in LA remember, I'll call u soon.

Text: VERIZON MESSAGE: YOUR CHARGES FOR THIS MONTH - delete

Text: got ur coming home early txt, told kids, they r pumped

Voice mail (Cybil pressed Speaker, then Play): Cybil, this is Blitz. I forgot, am I picking you up for the fundraiser early for drinks or meeting you there? *I told him separate cars. Nice try, he never gives up.*

Hi, David Flint here ... we met at CSPOT. Are you free for coffee this week? I am organizing an After the Outrage Event highlighting sex/human trafficking, you'd be surprised how close to home it is. Anyway, Kara had suggested you could help with your connections. You have my cell, let me know if we can meet. - *Huh, After the Outrage event?*

Cybil paused for a second, holding her iPhone, her two thumbs hovering over the keyboard. She turned her head and looked out the passenger window. Shops, apartments, homes, gas stations, numerous billboards, neon signs and other symbols of civilization zoomed by so fast she could hardly notice. Coming up ahead, a large billboard with a smiling Asian woman grew larger. The woman had black hair, was thin, gorgeous, dressed in a sarong, clean-looking, with one hand in a waving pose. The message clearly written in large letters, 15 feet high, shouted: BUDDHA FLOWER SPA, ASIAN-ONLY STAFF, TAKE SW 8TH STREET EXIT, 2 MILES. YOU ARE ONLY MINUTES FROM BLISS.

*

Cybil's brows furrowed, remembering Lucy's story. Six months ago they met at the Savannah Rape Crisis Center. Cybil volunteered time to work on their IT network. Lucy had run away from one of the Macon, Georgia, spas and hitched her way into Savannah. The cops picked her up and brought her to the center because they knew Sharon Lee, one of the founders, who spoke Chinese. Unfortunately Lucy came from Thailand and didn't speak Mandarin, but took to Sharon, who was older and had a kind manner. Lucy spent time at the center with Sharon, trying to learn Mandarin. Cybil suggested taking Lucy to lunch at the new Thai restaurant, that maybe someone there could translate. As luck would have it, they did.

Still, despite the kindness, Lucy stayed skittish, jumpy when people other than Sharon came nearby, especially when the husbands of the volunteers picked up their wives.

Cybil came to work on the networks one day and asked Sharon about Lucy.

"She's doing okay. Not bad for being sold into sex slavery by your parents at 13 and being in a foreign country, not speaking the language," Sharon said. "We're trying to get her into an English as a Second Language class, taking it a day at a time."

A month passed before Cybil came back to do network security testing. Sharon was out so she asked one of the volunteers about Lucy. The gray-haired worker shook her head, telling how U.S. Immigration visited one day and deported the girl back to Thailand. No one in the States would sponsor her, not even the local Thai community. Cybil guessed no one wanted an ex-child prostitute around. *Shame.*

*

REPLY: David, I'm only free tonight. If you can, please meet me at Gallery Espresso on Bull Street at 6:00 pm. I want to know more.

Cybil scanned the remaining messages, then finished dispatching e-mails and texts and composed a final communication, a text to a private group, AVNER, at 11:03 a.m. It read: Flt lands Sav, 4 pm, c u at the lady at 5.

Cybil held on to her iPhone and leaned back. The gentle rocking of the limo's smooth ride relaxed her, her heartbeat slowed, she closed her eyes. She visualized the Creatives meeting at Forsyth Fountain: her, John, Benny and Judy.

*

In her small retail store a few blocks from Savannah's arts college, SCAD, Judy Blair's free gloved hand wiped away small trickles of blood drawn by the sharp tattoo needle. The blue-green butterfly, just above the left hip of her client, looked almost complete. Her phone, lying on the utility table, vibrated.

"Give me a sec," Judy said, lifting the needle from the skin.

Pulling a new glove from a box on the same table, she used it as a napkin to pick up the phone to see her text.

Looking over to her business partner sitting at the cash register under the flashing red-and-yellow neon sign, Judy's Tattoo & Art Gallery, she said, "I'm going to leave around four thirty today. Got to meet a friend."

She put the phone down and returned to finish the last piece of antenna on the butterfly.

*

At a small second-story office on Broughton Street, Benny, owner of Yellow Tuna Studios, Savannah's award-winning web design firm, sat at his desk. In front of him, his three-screen computer setup, all driven by MACs, held his latest Web project designs. A test simulation ran on the right screen with flashing colors, expanding and collapsing windows, music videos, scrolling text insets. They all moved at what seemed like 1,000 mph. On the left-most screen, his messaging window alerted him to a new text from AVNER, which he glanced at.

Taking his hands off the keyboards, he picked up his cell and texted his partner, Sam: Can't make dinner, need to meet a friend at 5, have the leftover asparagus and brown rice.

*

Just off the Savannah river, in the parking lot of a defunct hardware store a few hundred yards past the end of Bay Street, John Block said, in front of a small group, "As you can see, the view to the river is lovely and unobstructed. It will remain so. The city has zoned this area in front as an easement for utilities, so no other construction is possible."

His assembled group of investors all nodded. Green Block and Tackle's new project, GreenSide, an eco-friendly high-end condo project, had become John's next big thing. Speaking intently, he didn't notice the cell phone on his hip vibrating, but it must have registered. As the group walked back up the small hill to look at the soon to be demolished buildings, John reflexively pulled his phone to check it.

Touching the screen, he saw a new text message. He swiped over to his calendar and rescheduled a conflicting conference call. Holstering the phone, he walked toward the investors to talk about the recycling of demolition waste and its reuse in the new construction.

*

Cybil's limo pulled up to Terminal H, Delta Airlines. As the car stopped, Cybil opened her eyes and took a deep breath. She glanced down to her phone to see if any new messages had come in, especially any from Anne. Nothing.

The driver opened Cybil's door and went to the back, hustling the roller case to the baggage handlers, who tagged them for Savannah. Cybil stepped out and walked up to the baggage counter and presented her Georgia driver's license. The handler smiled and said "Thank you, ma'am," even before he saw the five-dollar tip.

Cybil turned around and said, "Thanks for the lift. I hope this extra drive didn't interfere with your studies and classes."

"Classes? Oh, I tried that last year. Not for me. I like working for the weekends," she said, smiling.

Then she turned around and stepped to the driver's side before raising two fingers to her hat rim to salute Cybil goodbye. Ducking in the open door, she sat behind the wheel. As the door closed and the car pulled away, the driver's cap came off and again the yellow shoulder-length blonde hair spilled out. *William will be fine,* Cybil thought.

Cybil looked right and left, evaluating the light foot traffic passing in front of her. By herself at the closed terminal doors, she smiled and stepped forward and the automatic doors opened wide as she stepped briskly through.

29

Sister Anne stood just inside Father Michael's office and reached to flip the light switch on, but hesitated. *Maybe not.* Taking a deep breath she turned on her flashlight, which was pointed down, and watched a bright circle of white light form. The spot moved across the carpet as she lifted the flashlight, first illuminating part of a wingback chair, then up the large desk and finally landing on the seatback of Father Michael's large black empty leather chair.

Anne exhaled and moved toward the desk. Sitting down, she laid the flashlight next to her, pointing sideways. Its light streamed across the desktop and splashed against the bottom of a brass green-shaded lamp. The light reflected off the metal and created a dim mini-glow which helped Sister Anne see. *Where is his planner?*

Working through the items on top of Father Michael's desk, Sister Anne carefully lifted and replaced papers, books, mementos, folders and photographs. No planner in sight. After giving up on the desktop, she tugged at the top desk drawer, which was locked.

"Damn."

Noticing a shiny letter opener sitting next to the lamp base, she grabbed the silver knife-like implement and stuck the tip into the drawer lock, jiggling it several times, twisting the blade left and right until … click, the latch turned.

She pulled the drawer open and there it was, Father Michael's planner. Lifting it, she noticed packs of chewing gum, assorted pens and highlighters underneath. She placed it on top of the desk. Picking up and pointing the flashlight downward, she flipped the pages, working backward from the current date. Every turn to a new white page reflected light up to Sister Anne's face. She recognized most of the entries were related to St. Rita business, nothing unusual except for a consistent weekly entry. She even found the Gaston funeral entry for 2:00 p.m. And on that same day, Tuesday, there it was, M – 8:00 p.m. Sister Anne flipped the pages backward; M – 8:00 p.m. appeared weekly for several months before the funeral. Sister Anne leaned on her elbow and put her chin in her hand. *What does M mean?*

Facing the door, Sister Anne noticed a bright glint coming off the brass doorknob. The room started to get lighter. She lifted her head and the office grew brighter and brighter until everything was visible, including Sister Anne sitting at the desk. Her heart began racing.

Looking outside through the window, she saw four pairs of car headlights shining directly into the office. Sister Anne stared at the intense display. Immediately she dove to the floor under the desk. Her heart beat faster. She could hear the thumping in her ears, her throat became dry. Within 30 seconds, the room went dark again as the headlights shut off. Sister Anne tried to swallow. She had to put a hand to her mouth to suppress a cough. Car doors slammed. *Who is here?*

Muffled sounds coming from the St. Rita lobby made their way through Father Michael's heavy oak door. The noise stayed on the other side of the lobby for a moment. Then she heard steps. After a minute, she scooted out from under the desk and sat down in the leather chair. She placed sweaty palms on the desk. *Steady.*

Looking at the desktop, she put things back in place to the best of her memory. She carefully closed the top drawer. Getting up and moving toward the office door, she crept forward and stopped before getting by the window. She glanced out and then pulled back. One car and one large truck sat parked outside in the driveway. They were near the front door. She recognized neither vehicle. Stepping fast by the window and getting to the door she put her ear to it, straining to listen.

Silence. Sister Anne's breath became the only thing she could hear, fast and short. She put a hand to her chest and closed her eyes. *Please Lord, get me out of here.* Turning the doorknob slowly she cracked it open a few inches. Glancing through the opening, she peered through and could only see the side hallway walls which blocked her view and anyone's view of her. Hearing no sounds at the moment, she stepped out and closed the door gently before sliding to the wall opposite the door. She leaned with her back on the hallway wall a foot away from the corner. After a couple of breaths she leaned around the corner to get a full look at the lobby.

Empty. To the left, Sister Anne saw both lobby doors wide open, dim blue moonlight beaming through. Drifting dust, carried by a slight breeze, cut across the light and floated in. Her eyes followed the traveling mass as it moved across into darkness and then again into illumination. Bright fluorescent light came from the open door atop the basement stairs. They could be back any second.

Sister Anne waited a few seconds. No sounds. She took a step backward, toward the kitchen, at the end of the side hallway. She felt safer making that her escape route. She turned to leave and then heard voices, clear, echoing across the empty lobby. She froze.

"A few more trips and we're done," a male voice said.

"I'm glad we got the heavy-duty hand trucks, this stuff weighs a ton," a second voice said, also male.

Sister Anne heard their feet step and squeak across the wood floor. She crept back to the hallway corner and peeked around in time to catch a glimpse of two men going out the doors.

They're almost done with what? Sister Anne thought, and then glanced down her exit hallway. She leaned back against the wall and took several breaths. *Should just go.*

The nun leaned forward to leave, but pulled herself back and pressed herself against the wall, inches from the corner. She slowed her breathing and focused on listening. Her sweaty hands, pressed flat against the drywall, stuck like paper napkins on a wet table. She heard a rap and a thud, as if something struck something.

"I told you to keep the door open!" the first voice said.

"The door closed on its own. The wind. Just keep pushing. I'll pull," the second voice said.

Both men grunted and heaved to pull their heavy item up and over the door's threshold. A few seconds later a large thud from something landing rumbled through St. Rita.

Sister Anne leaned closer to the edge and looked around the corner. Both backs were turned to her. They looked up and down at the tall, rectangular wooden crate. Wide slats covered the outside, and inside something shiny reflected the moonlight. Sister Anne kept watching.

"This one has to go where the electrical junction box is, according to the directions from the client," the tall, muscular man said.

His shorter, wider companion said, “I know.” He lifted his hand and wiped the sweat from his brow, flicking it to the floor. “It’s stuffy and warm down there. This setup is taking longer. We should turn up the air downstairs.”

“No need Markos. It’ll get cool soon enough with the rigging to the fireplace we have to do,” the tall man said.

“If you say so,” Markos said.

Both men moved toward the lighted doorway leading to the basement. Sister Anne lost sight of them but could hear their steps fade into silence.

She pushed herself away from the wall, took a deep breath and moved around the corner, tiptoeing to the large crate. Sister Anne stopped and glanced over to the basement doorway. Turning back to the crate, she leaned on it. It barely moved. Inside, dark, indigo-colored smooth metal surfaces spread before her with only a few lines of rivets and screws. It looked like industrial equipment, big rectangular with an electrical panel full of dials. The range on the dials read between 200F–1,000F.

Anne standing in the dark didn’t recognize any of it. She moved around the crate, peering inside the slats for any writing or markings, the moonlight barely illuminating the equipment inside. At the bottom she noticed an ID plate with numbers and lettering. She pulled out the notepad from her pants pocket and knelt, putting her face close to the slats to read the information in the low light.

MPM 450 SEP MENESCO, INC. in black metallic stencil was written on the serial number plate. Barely able to read it, she finished copying it when loud footfalls boomed through the lobby—one of the men was at the top of the stairs. Sister Anne did not move, the crate preventing the large man standing there from seeing her.

“Kurt, wait,” the voice downstairs called up.

Peering through the slats, Sister Anne saw the blonde, short-haired man stop at the top of the stairs.

"What? I'm going to get the crowbar in the car."

"We don't need a crowbar, I found a shovel we can use," Markos said.

"Damn it, you wait till I get all the way up here? Shit," Kurt said as he went back down.

As soon as Kurt disappeared down the stairs, Sister Anne stood up and slipped out the lobby doors. She jogged back toward the delivery road, picking up speed as she got further away. Soon she reached a running pace. Breathing hard but steady, she made it back to the road within a few minutes. The car with the open, raised hood waited. Slowly lowering the hood, she almost had it down when it slipped her fingers and slammed shut, the metallic clang reverberating through the woods and darkness.

"Damn it," Sister Anne said.

She opened her door, started the car, kept her lights off and K-turned on the road. Pulling away from her spot, she looked in the rearview mirror to check. No car lights. As she made her way around a turn, she sighed out loud, "Whew," turned on her lights and pressed the accelerator. The car sped away. *Need to tell Cybil, too late to call.*

As Sister Anne drove off, a parked Dodge Dakota truck with lights off sat facing the retreating vehicle. The driver lifted her head and narrowed her eyes. The truck sat off the entrance of St. Rita on the road side. As the third vehicle in the convoy that had arrived earlier that evening, the driver had been assigned as lookout.

Seconds earlier, looking down while playing Texas Hold 'em on her cell phone to pass the time, Michelle heard the bang of a car hood dropping. Her eyes drove upward, through the windshield, in the direction of the sound.

"What the fuck?" Michelle said as she tossed the phone onto the passenger seat. Watching the car move away, she started the truck and crept it forward, lights out, turning onto the paved road. Her vehicle accelerated smoothly, soon reaching the same turn. She spotted the car moving away; it had its headlights on by now. The red rear lights dipped out of sight after passing a small hill, but reappeared on the rise of another.

Michelle accelerated further, keeping her lights out. She closed in on the car enough to see its make when it passed under a bright street lamp … a green Buick POS. A couple of hundred yards ahead, a car pulled out in front of her from a side road. Michelle turned on her lights and raced toward the Buick, passing the car in front of her. As traffic built up, Michelle's dark maroon truck blended into the stream of other cars; she stayed a few cars behind the Buick. It did not speed or make any other turns and did not seem to be trying to lose anyone who was possibly tailing.

Punching the radio on, Michelle leaned back, rested her left arm on the open window ledge, steered with the other and mouthed the words, "You're mine now."

30

Cybil parked her car at the corner of Bull and Gaston streets, near the south entrance of Forsyth Park. Her iPhone showed 4:45 p.m.; she had a few minutes. Lowering the driver-side window allowed street sounds to come in along with the smell of strong coffee drifting from the nearby Gallery Espresso. Foot traffic streaming from Bull Street to the park looked thin for a weekday, even for a tourist-friendly town.

A diesel truck with a rumbling engine stopped at the crosswalk to let a group of pedestrians pass. At the park's entrance, a street vendor wearing yellow pants, a white shirt, a zebra vest and a huge red floppy hat gripped a thick cord of taut strings connected to 25 or so floating balloons. The full rainbow loomed in different sizes, shapes and colors.

Ten minutes passed and she stepped out of her car. Cybil pressed the Lock button on her fob and the car beeped once. She hit it a second time to be sure. Turning toward the park, she squinted to see down the long walkway to the fountain, too far to discern anything specific. *They should be at the Lady by now.*

Walking briskly toward the fountain, Cybil's flats tapped the concrete in rhythmic cadence, each footfall evenly spaced, disciplined. She passed a park bench and glanced at a man in shorts and a soccer shirt, backpack next to him, sitting and looking toward the fountain. He turned his head and watched her pass by; she felt his stare but looked ahead. As she neared the fountain she saw the group.

Judy, Benny and John stood talking in a small cluster next to the iron fence circling Forsyth Fountain. The Lady stood tall in the pool's center as the gargoyles sprayed their water as if to ward away evil.

Stepping up to the group, Cybil smiled.

"Right on time," John, said looking at his Smartphone before snapping it into his holster.

"Hi, guys, thanks for coming," Cybil said, nodding to each one.

Judy gave Cybil a hug, "How ya doing, dear? You look a little sad."

"Just tired from the flight and eager to see my kids," she said.

Benny moved next to Cybil, smiled and nudged her with his shoulder. "How's that handsome sailor of yours? He was such a hoot when he was here last month. When will he be back? Sam always asks about him—maybe a bit too much!"

"Oh, he's quite busy these days with sailing. Thanks for asking. How long does everyone have?" Cybil said.

"I'm good till five thirty," John said.

"Nothing till six," Judy said.

"Same here," Benny said.

"Let me explain why—" Cybil said and then stopped talking.

A small ghost tour group passed by, the guide dressed in 17th-century garb pointing to the fountain. With a practiced script he explained loudly the origins and history of the fountain and park. Cybil, John, Judy and Benny stood quietly, letting the guide finish and waited for the group to walk away.

Cybil said, "Anyway, I need your help to chase down some information for a friend."

Judy grinned broadly. "Who's in trouble this time?"

"No trouble, just something may not be right, but I'm not sure."

Benny chimed in, "What would you like us to do?"

"Let me give you some background first," Cybil said.

For the next few minutes she explained about Sister Anne, the closing of St. Rita, William's mother and the questions she herself had, especially after her talk with Blitz Thompson and his identification of Stavos Gruner. Benny and Judy listened; John Block seemed bothered when Cybil wrapped up the briefing with Blitz's information.

Cybil looked at Benny and said, "I'd like you to contact UnD0x3d and see if you and he can track down a financial transaction history on St. Rita over the last 18 months. It's a private foundation so there are no public records. Summaries and exceptions only, we don't have time for detail. I need to see if there's anything unusual."

"Easy enough. After I whooped him in Call of Duty, I became a tolerable help to him. He is testy, though," Benny said.

Cybil's eyebrows lifted, she leaned back on the fence and crossed her arms. Turning her head toward Judy, she said, "I'm looking for a person with ink work on her shoulder with some type of animal head biting her or something like that. Can you ask your friends in the business, see if you can find a name?"

"Sure. I don't do that type of work, but I have a couple of artist friends who do. I'll check," Judy said.

John Block's eyes looked away, his face turned toward the woods.

"John?" Cybil said.

He turned toward her, his face drained of color, his lips parted. Breathing loud and straining, he leaned on the iron fence with one hand. Benny stepped to his side and cupped John's elbow to steady him.

Judy said, "John, what's wrong, you feeling okay?"

John blinked and straightened up, took a deep breath and said, "I'm okay now."

Cybil said, "Either you're getting sick or something I said got to you, which is it?"

His voice quivering, John said, "Stavos Gruner is not someone you want to have any dealings with."

Cybil stared at John. "And you have?"

"Unfortunately, once. It was a big mistake. I was shortcutting on getting permitting approval for a project. I thought I could expedite things. I had no idea about his methods," John said letting out a deep sigh.

"Really," Benny said.

"I only met him once at a restaurant, Troy's. I think it was his place, by the way everyone treated him. He was charming, I think from Greece, articulate. It cost me a lot to hire him, more to call him off. Big, big mistake. That's … that's all I can share," John said, shaking his head.

Cybil paused, thinking about letting her friend out of this.

Taking a breath she said, “I really need your help,” while keeping her gaze on him.

Benny continued to be at John’s side, rubbing his back. John turned and smiled at him and mouthed that he was okay.

Looking back toward Cybil, John said, “I understand. What do you need?”

“Property and realty information about St. Rita. If it goes under, who benefits, who owns it now, etcetera. We are operating in the dark, so just need a little light. Can do?” Cybil said.

“Sure, that’s easy enough. Information only. That I can do,” John said, his color returning. He nodded toward Cybil and looked at the others, a thin smile on his face.

“If you have questions,” Cybil said, “text or e-mail. We’ll talk again soon.”

They nodded in unison. Each turned toward the fountain and leaned on the iron fence. Without any of them speaking further, Judy and Benny left first, taking the west sidewalk out of the park. After 30 seconds, John took the east sidewalk.

Cybil stayed, waiting for her 5:45 p.m. with David Flint. She faced the active splash pool in front of her. A gentle wet mist floated toward her and landed on her forehead and cheeks, soothing her warm skin. Turning around, she glanced west and east watching the team disperse. She took a deep breath through her nose. Smelling the flowers’ sweetness brought a smile, her memory of morning runs coming back. With the team now out of sight, Cybil pushed off the fence and looked around. Down the boulevard she saw David and his wife, Amy, holding hands.

As they got close, he stepped up and reached out his hand, “Hi, Cybil, nice to see you.”

Amy made a small wave and smiled.

“Thanks, I appreciate meeting on such short notice. Have you been to Gallery Espresso? It’s a short walk from here,” Cybil said.

“Not yet, let’s go,” David said as he reached for Amy’s hand.

Cybil walked south toward the Gallery, David and Amy a step behind. Little conversation passed until they went inside. Standing in line, Cybil bought a double espresso and found a small table with three overstuffed chairs, a staple of the shop’s comfortable environment. Local art for sale hung on the exposed brick walls and the aroma of baked goods circulated through the store. Tall windows reaching the 20-foot ceiling ushered in natural light. David and Amy sat down across Cybil; he held a cup of black coffee, Amy had steaming tea.

Cybil took a sip and then spoke. “Tell me about this After the Outrage event.”

David smiled. “First, let me say thanks again for meeting with us tonight.” He looked over at Amy. “We’re new here and just getting to know Savannah, the area and people. When Kara told me you had volunteered at the Rape Crisis Center, and with your modeling credentials around here, I thought you might help us draw attention to the event.”

“Why did you move to Savannah?” Cybil said, looking at Amy, then back to him.

He began to answer but Amy shifted in her chair and touched his arm. She said, “We’re from Tennessee, a small town, nothing much. We wanted to try someplace different, larger. Savannah is definitely bigger from where we come from and it’s not as big as Atlanta.”

David raised his cup and took a long sip before speaking. “We’re big believers in community outreach. In a small town, that’s limited to bake sales and bailing out the town drunk once in a while. Bigger cities have bigger challenges. Savannah looked like a great place to live and a good next step.”

Cybil looked at her phone. Twenty minutes had passed since they met at the fountain. Sebastian and June were at home waiting.

“I’m sorry but could we speed this up a bit? I just got back into town, haven’t seen my kids yet. Tell me more.”

“How many kids do you have?” Amy said, her eyes widening.

“Two, a girl, 8, a boy, 11. How about you, any kids?”

Amy shook her head, then looked down and sighed. David turned his head toward his wife and put his hand on her arm.

David spoke up, his smile gone. “Not yet, been trying for a while. We’re hoping a change of scene will help. God hasn’t exactly answered those prayers.”

Amy took a deep breath and turned with David to face Cybil.

“I have little problem getting pregnant …” Amy said, her voice trailing off. “David, tell Cybil about the event idea.”

"After the Outrage is a community outreach event designed to connect like-minded activists to address the human trafficking/sex slave issue," David said, his hands animated as he spoke. "Lots of people get outraged when they hear the facts and news but don't know what to do afterward."

"Have you done something like this before?" Cybil said.

Amy turned to Cybil. "Not to address trafficking. We wanted to do something small first and thought about setting up a confession booth at the Savannah Gay Pride Parade here, but we were too late."

"Confession booth?" Cybil said, her eyes focusing on Amy.

David said, "It's a way to apologize for some of the attitudes and vitriol misguided people of faith express toward the LGBT community. We would be in the booth and when parade goers enter, we confess and apologize to them. We got the idea from a great book, *Blue Like Jazz*. We wanted to reach out to all of Savannah's communities, especially now that we live here."

Cybil sat quietly for a second, thinking about Lucy, the young Asian girl at the center. Then Cybil said, "Let's get back to After the Outrage. What happens afterward, are you looking to raise money, awareness, protest, what?"

Amy said, "Not exactly sure at this point, but awareness, sure, money, maybe. We don't want to do another fundraiser, we want people to commit to some type of action afterward. We're still working through the details."

"Would you get local churches involved?" Cybil said, thinking of Anne.

David and Amy looked at each other.

He turned toward Cybil. "It will be open to everyone, but we want to make it community focused. Sometimes religious institutions and their thinking complicate things."

Cybil smiled and nodded. She stood up and looked at her cell phone again and said, "I really must be going, but count me in to help in whatever way you see fit."

David pushed his chair back and stood up. Amy kept her seat and smiled.

"Cybil, thank you, sorry to have kept you from your family. I'll call you next week?" he said.

"Sure, do that. Amy, it was nice to meet you again," Cybil said, opening her purse. "If you want to know more about Savannah, give me a call." She handed Amy a business card.

"I will. Have a nice evening with your kids," Amy said, standing up. "I think I'll get another cup of tea. This is a nice place."

Cybil headed back to her car. Striding quickly, images of little Lucy at the center, working in a coloring book, flashed in her mind for a moment, mixing with scenes of June sitting at the kitchen table, playing with her dolls. *Yeah, I'll help.*

Reaching her car, she got in and before starting it looked at her phone and scrolled through, finding Anne's number. She typed in a text to her: Back in town, any more news?

31

Sister Anne's flats slid in the gravel as she made her way to Trinity Chapel's back garden. Needing time alone after her night visit to St. Rita, the nun knew this place promised solitude. The broken seashells and rock pebbles lining the path gave way under her shoes, putting her off-balance as crunching sounds followed every step.

Extending her arms like a tightrope walker she finally made it to the grass-matted area and the low-profile marble bench. Sitting, she gazed at the angel statue opposite her seat. The statue, four feet tall, stood on a white columned pedestal. The pedestal had sunk into the sandy soil and was leaning. Vines crept up engulfing the legs of the winged cherub. Mottled algae and other fungus spoiled the angel's formerly white robe. Completing the ruined look, the angel's head and face looked dirty from dust and dried bird droppings. Sister Anne stared at the decrepit stone messenger from God and shook her head.

The garden had a short decorative concrete block wall running the length of the chapel's property, separating it from the residential street. Around the corner toward the chapel front ran a short side street connecting to the main road on Tybee Island. The early morning traffic had not started, so the streets remained quiet. Sister Anne sat, hands folded in her lap, looking at the statue. She closed her eyes and lowered her head.

A block away from the garden, a maroon truck turned onto the residential street and parked at the corner. Through the windshield the driver could see Sister Anne sitting with her head down.

Michelle picked up her phone and dialed Father Michael. She put him on the speaker.

"Hey, it's me," she said.

"Hi, I'm sort of busy. Heading over to my office in a few minutes to finish packing. Just poured my second cup," Father Michael said while sipping his coffee.

He sat at his small kitchen table. On the white wall, recently painted, opposite the table a custom-carved wood crucifix hung, a gift from the St. Rita staff when he had arrived several years ago.

"We had a visitor last night during the move," Michelle said.

"WHAT! Who was it, did they see anything?" Father Michael said.

"Relax, I followed her last night to Tybee. I can see her from where I'm sitting. She's at some church, Trinity something. I drove by it earlier."

"Is there a garden in the back?"

"Yes."

"Trinity Chapel. Is she of slim build, athletic, red hair?" Father Michael said.

"You got it."

"Shit, that must be Sister Anne. What is she doing now?"

"Nothing, just sitting. I need to tell Stavos."

"No, not now. Please. I … I … think I know how to handle this. Give me a couple of days, okay?"

"I don't know. Stavos doesn't like being kept in the dark," Michelle said.

"We'll tell him, just not now. Okay. Why don't you get some breakfast, you must be hungry."

"I am. I'll see you tomorrow. I was up all night and am gonna crash as soon as I eat. See you tomorrow night at eight."

"As usual," Father Michael said.

He closed his cell phone and placed it on the table where he was sitting.

The coffee cup still in his hand, Father Michael looked down into the strong and bitter fluid.

"Fuck!" he said, and threw his cup, smashing it against the wall. The black coffee dripped down the white wall, crawling over the crucified Jesus.

32

"Mom!" June cried out.

She ran full speed to Cybil who was standing at the open door of their home.

Sebastian, a few steps behind, almost caught up with her before both kids piled into their mother, who had knelt on one knee to greet them. Her arms grasped her two children; she brought them close, hugging them hard.

Cybil stood up with one arm holding June, who hung like a monkey off her neck. Sebastian held his mother's free hand with his two. The three of them made their way to the living room. Cybil mouthed the words "Thank you" as Carol, their sitter, passed them in the hallway. The sitter waved goodbye without saying a word but smiled and nodded her head. She walked out, closing the door behind her. Cybil, June and Sebastian fell together onto the family room couch, June giggling, Sebastian laughing and Cybil poking their tickle spots.

"Did you guys eat already or should we go out?" Cybil said as she stroked June's hair. The little girl's head rested in her mother's lap, her eyes looking up.

"Carol made cornbread and ribs," Sebastian said, "and I cleaned up already. You don't have to do anything tonight."

"That's my Boy Scout!" Cybil said, smiling and nudging her son with her elbow.

Sebastian sat next to her, leaning into his mother and looking toward the blank TV with his arm hooked into hers.

June, still looking at her mommy, said, "How was your trip and did you miss us?"

"Did I ever miss you!" Cybil said. "Mommy's business in Miami is over. I won't be going back."

Cybil kept as big a smile as she could but her eyes blinked and she looked away for a second.

June's eyes scanned her mother's and then, lifting her hand, she touched her mother's face, gently stroking her chin. "Don't look sad, Mommy. It's okay, you're home now. You'll feel better."

Cybil stared at her perceptive daughter, comforted but a little anxious at how easily she knew her mother's moods.

"I'm home and working in town, so no travel for me, but are you two excited about your trips?" Cybil said.

June sat up, jumped off the couch and said, "I'll be right back!" She ran out of the room.

Sebastian slipped off the couch and sat at Cybil's feet. He reached into his back pocket and pulled out a Boy Scout cap, snapping it on while giving a salute.

"Troop 4284 is ready! Mr. Grayson said at the last meeting that my KidMars project qualifies for a badge. Will Mr. Tom come soon and help me finish it?" Sebastian said.

"Yes, he'll be here this week," Cybil said.

Standing up, Sebastian sprinted to the bottom of the stairs and took the first two steps in one leap while yelling out loud, "Great! I'll bring my stuff down here to work!"

June came back into the room holding a postcard. She walked over and sat next to her mother.

"It's from Grandma," June said, holding the postcard before placing it in Cybil's lap. "She says we're going to camp out like Sebastian is on his trip."

Cybil looked at the photo postcard showing Yosemite Falls and Green Meadow. The California National Park near Fresno, California, was situated close to her mother's home and had been a childhood favorite.

"That will be fun for you, Grandma and Harold. Make sure you pack some warm clothes because even though it's summer, it can get cold there."

She took a deep breath and closed her eyes for a second. *Control.*

*

Summers at Yosemite filled Cybil's childhood with joy until she turned eight. Rivers, lakes and sunny meadows gave her lots of places to run, hike and explore. A natural tomboy and athletic, she'd leave her playmates in the dust when running and climbing. Sitting on a hillside looking at the valley, the restless little girl found this the only place that quieted her. But after her eighth birthday she refused to go anymore with her parents, making horrible scenes until they gave up. Cybil simply didn't want to go to Yosemite because it meant visiting Wolf Creek Canyon Ranch on the way.

*

Sebastian landed with a thud at the bottom of the stairs, and crayons, markers and loose papers fell out of his arms. "Shit!"

"Son," Cybil said.

"Ooooh!" June said.

"Sorry, Mom," Sebastian said, gathering his art supplies.

He moved to the kitchen table, off the family room. He flipped through pages and began drawing and coloring.

"June, why don't you find a movie you like and Mommy can watch it with you while Sebastian works?" Cybil said, looking at her daughter.

June's eyes beamed and her smile grew wider. "You bet!" she said.

"While you do that, I'm going upstairs to unpack and make a few calls. I'll be down in 20 minutes," Cybil said.

Sebastian, at the table concentrating on his task, said, "Sure thing, Mom."

June leaped across the family room and knelt at the small bookshelf underneath the flat screen LCD TV hanging on the wall. Piles of DVDs already lay scattered on the carpet.

"I'll pick a good one, Mommy," June said.

Cybil got up and went down the hallway, grabbed her two bags and made her way up the stairs. She grinned as she took the last step. *June takes forever to pick a movie.* In her bedroom, she placed her bags inside the door.

She pulled her iPad from her shoulder bag and placed it on the dresser. Calling up her auto stream app, custom-modified for her by UnD0x3d, she typed in duration and frequency settings for the next few days, knowing things would get busy from here on. Auto updates would randomize tweets and music recommendations for her. Looking at herself in the mirror afterward she thought, I do look sad. *Need time.* She pressed Activate. Three posts came out.

Fav biz look shot this year, click here ...

Walk on the Wild Side by Lou Reed

Love Kim Crawford Sauvignon blanc especially with a strawberry in the glass!

"Ha! Great suggestion," she said aloud, remembering an unopened bottle of the same in the kitchen.

Sliding the iPad aside, she got her iPhone out, touch-slid to Anne's number and pressed Call. Cybil waited for her to pick up but the call went straight to voice mail, so she left a message,

"Anne, it's Cybil. Did you get my text? I'm back. Call me as soon as you can."

She sighed and walked over to her bed, sitting on the edge. It felt good to be back on her soft foam pad; the boat cabin's firm mattress on plywood made her sleep uneasy. She looked back at her bags near the door.

Her phone rang and she looked at the caller ID. She picked it up.

"Hi, Blitz, and no, we're meeting there and you are not picking me up," she blurted out.

"Hello to you, too. No need to be short. Okay, I'll meet you there but I did decide which dress I liked—that is, if your offer still stands?"

"Yes. Which one?" Cybil said.

"I think the black halter dress that bunches up under your bust line would be very classy, especially with white pearls and French-style pantyhose," Blitz said.

"I'm impressed. That's a good choice for an evening event and I have just the lightweight shawl to go with it. I'm having it dry cleaned but I broke a heel on the matching pumps. Guess I'll need to buy a new pair," Cybil said with a loud sigh through smiling lips.

"I can hardly wait," Blitz said in a low, husky voice.

"Ha, ha, Blitz, you'll be waiting a long time with that voice," Cybil said.

"Ouch."

Cybil said, "I look forward to keeping my end of the bargain. Your information has helped."

"Yeah, about that, you got a couple of minutes?" Blitz said.

"Not really, I'm expecting a call. But go ahead, I may have to hang up on you," Cybil said.

Blitz said, "It's all right, I'm used to it. Anyway, I was in arraignment the other day and had to spend a few minutes in the hallway outside court. I ended up talking to a couple of drinking buddies from Homicide, catching up. They've been working on identifying a partial corpse that washed up on Tybee Island, not much of it left."

"Really, what do you mean by partial?" Cybil said.

"It was not only badly decomposed but only the upper torso remained. It had lots of evidence of animal bites, large and small, if you know what I mean."

"Ewww," Cybil, said grimacing.

"Yeah, agreed. They also said knife marks were found on the few remaining ribs but they couldn't tell for sure. The kicker was the DNA. The report came back from CODIS and get this, the deceased has been in the system for years, quite a criminal record. He was identified as Roger Van Doren, a known associate of guess who?"

Cybil thought for a second, then blurted out, "Stavos Gruner."

"You got it. When the cops visited Roger's place, a rental, the landlord said he hadn't seen Roger or his daughter, for weeks. Apparently Roger was a single dad. The cops searched the apartment. They said it looked like it had been tossed and there was no sign of the daughter even though her clothes and purse were still there," Blitz said.

"How old was she?"

"A teenager, I think."

"Damn. Sorry to hear that, but this is good information."

"Good information? Cybil, this Stavos guy is stone-cold trouble. Look, I know you've got more balls than most of the cops I know, and I half-believe the spook rumors I keep hearing about you. But this fucker is one mean son of a bitch. Are you sure you should be poking around anywhere near him?" Blitz's concern was clearly audible in his tone.

Cybil put one hand behind her and crossed her legs as she leaned back on the edge of the bed and said, "Blitz, are you worried for me or just trying to score points before the fundraiser?"

"Very funny, Cybil. Jeez, I should know better than to warn you. By the way, are you skydiving again on your birthday this year?"

"Sure. Maybe this year I'll have company. Maybe one of my friends, just one, will be brave enough to take me up on my standing offer and jump with me. Tom, my friend from NASA, who's helping Sebastian on his comic project, said he's in this year."

"He's crazy. Count me out. Skydiving is nuts!"

Cybil's Call Waiting buzzer hit her phone: Anne.

"Blitz, I'm getting that call. See you next week at the fundraiser, thanks, bye now," Cybil said.

"You be—" Blitz was cut off.

Anne's voice came over quiet and steady: "Cybil, I think Father Michael has given St. Rita over to criminals."

33

Stavos Gruner took his razor-sharp knife and sliced into the bloody mass, cutting deep and taking off a piece, which he promptly stuck into his mouth and chewed. He had little left of the 16-oz. rib eye sitting on his plate, his favorite dish at Uncle Bubba's Oyster House. Bubba's, not far from Thunderbolt and the moored *Destiny*, had become a favorite. Stavos liked the food though he cared little for the celebrity of the owner, Paula Deen's brother.

Grabbing another roll, he broke off a piece and sopped up the steak juices before devouring it. He picked up his empty water glass and held it high for the server to see, which she did. Stavos, a regular, always tipped well. She came over with a large bottle of San Pellegrino, Italian mineral water, and filled his tall glass. As the sparkling water poured in, tiny bubbles rose from the drowned, half-chewed lime sitting at the bottom.

Stavos took a long sip before setting the now half-full glass down. He bent forward, put his elbows on the table and interlocked his fingers. He extended his thumbs forming a shelf to rest his chin on. He gazed out the picture windows overlooking the marsh and small tributaries off the Savannah River. His eyes turned down to his phone next to the plate. Earlier, halfway through his steak, he'd read the text message from Kasen about her, the friend he wanted to be reunited with. Name, address and website … he didn't recognize her name.

In his peripheral vision Stavos saw a figure approaching from the left; his table, not visible from the hostess's desk, faced the picture window. He dropped his hands under the table and felt down his calf near his ankle. He turned his head to see a worried Kurt approach.

Taking a chair at the table Kurt said, "We got a problem."

Stavos raised one eyebrow and brought his hands above the table. He stared at Kurt without saying a word, drained his glass empty and said, "What is it?"

Kurt looked left, then right, around the nearly full restaurant. Two tables over, a family of four—a mom, a dad, a toddler and a baby sat—occupied in their own world; next to them, an old couple.

"I got a call from Wilber down at city hall. Someone's been poking around the St. Rita records," he said.

Stavos took a deep breath and sighed loudly. "We have not heard from Wilber for some time. I'm glad the assistant city clerk remembers how to be grateful for small favors."

Kurt let out a laugh. "Yeah, he'd be somebody's nightly bitch at State, the little twerp."

"What did he tell you?" Stavos said.

"Over the last week, he's been handling e-mail requests for all kinds of property information stuff from a developer. He remembered you wanted to be tipped off in case anyone asked about St. Rita."

"Good, send him his usual fee," Stavos said. "So who's been asking?"

"John Block," Kurt said.

"I remember Mr. Block, a nervous type. I wonder what his interest in St. Rita is?"

"Block had second thoughts about using your services, right?" Kurt said.

Stavos frowned and said, "We never came to terms on his special permitting and financing for his project. I'm not sure why he changed his mind but he did pay the withdrawal fee. It still upset me. Cost me a deal with Vasily, who was looking to clean some money for his ex-Russian military friends."

Reaching into his slack's he pulled out a stack of bills, Stavos put a one-hundred-dollar note on the table under his glass. He stood up and put on his sunglasses. Kurt looked at his well-dressed boss, who was sporting a black shirt over light slacks and aviator shades.

"Let's go visit Mr. Block and ask him," Stavos said, looking down at Kurt, still seated. "And let's take my car. We'll come back for yours. You drive."

Thirty minutes later Stavos and Kurt arrived at Troup Square in the downtown historic district. Kurt parked the dark-blue Suburban on the east side near Macon Street, near Block's house. They walked the short distance to a three-story Victorian with metal scaffolding on the right side, paint cans and tarps strewn below on the grass. They both went up the porch steps to the double-glass door. Kurt knocked with a heavy fist.

Leaning to one side Kurt looked through the door's side panel said, "Doesn't look like anyone's home."

"We can wait," Stavos said, and pointed toward Troup Square.

They walked toward the small tree-lined park where, in the middle, a large metal model of the celestial sphere, like the kind found in a planetarium, stood supported by six large turtles.

Stopping next to it, Kurt spoke up. "I've always liked this structure. An armillary sphere. Celestial mechanics in metal. From the Greeks, your ancestors."

"Smart they were. An early model of the universe. In the very first ones, the center used to represent the Earth, and later it was replaced by the sun, when the church finally gave up brow-beating scientists," Stavos said, sighing loudly as he looked west through the trees and noticed the high steeple of St. John the Baptist Cathedral a few blocks over.

Kurt looked at the steeple and back to his employer.

Stavos glanced at the sphere and fixed his stare on the turtles, saying, "In the Hindu creation myth, a giant turtle holds up the world. Here six turtles share in the burden. Interesting artistic expression."

"Agreed. Though not true to its Hellenic origins," Kurt said.

Stavos looked at his associate. "Observant. Do you see the cathedral steeple over there?" Stavos's eyes scanned toward the church's highest point.

"I saw it. Church. Never took to it, never made sense to me."

"That church over there is a nice tourist attraction for Savannah and for some a symbol of faith. To me it's the origin of lies. All of the religions of the world sell one thing, a false promise. And people are not buying it anymore. They smell the hypocrisy. My father, a devout Catholic, was one man on Sunday, another the other days of the week," Stavos said.

Kurt pulled his hands out of his pockets and crossed his arms and said, "My parents were Lutheran, used to make sure we memorized our prayers. I never understood what they meant."

Stavos nodded and said, "Back in Thrace, my dad wanted me to become an altar boy. Said Father Andreas would teach me to love God. All I saw was the priest's love for the bottle and his weekly high-stakes poker games, gambling the church's cash with my father and his friends."

Kurt nodded his head.

"But we're different," Stavos said, reaching out with one hand and grasping his associate on the shoulder.

"How so?"

Smiling, Stavos said, "We don't lie to people about their desires or needs, or judge them. We tell them they can reach beyond their wants. We give them exactly what they crave, right here in Savannah."

"Also the true truth," Kurt said, grinning.

"And what is that?" Stavos said, raising an eyebrow.

"Stavos rules Savannah," Kurt said.

Stavos smiled and put his hand on Kurt's shoulder and squeezed.

Both their heads turned to notice a man walking a small dog, coming toward the square, down Habersham Street. They watched him and his dog head toward the pet fountain on the west side of Troup Square. He stopped, letting his animal drink.

"I think that's Block," Kurt said, and started to move toward him.

Stavos reached out and held his associate's arm. "No, let's wait here and see if he heads home."

The two men continued standing by the square's centerpiece as John Block's leashed dachshund, Lyle, pulled him away from the fountain and toward home, his path taking him around the other side of the sphere. John walked by, glanced toward the pair and nodded his head politely, and they returned the gesture. A few steps past them, Lyle stopped to sniff a bush and leave his scent. Waiting, John turned his head back toward them and stared for a few seconds. The poor dog, in the middle of his business, got interrupted when yanked away by John. He pulled Lyle along, walking fast toward Macon Street.

"Let's go," Stavos said as he and Kurt followed Block. They closed the gap and stopped at the bottom of the porch steps as John reached the door. At the door John fumbled the keys trying to unlock the door. They landed next to the dachshund, who was pawing at the door.

Stavos walked up the steps and picked up the keys. "John Block, nice to see you again. May we have a word?" He handed the keys to him.

"I'm … I'm really busy these days with the renovation and all, plus Lyle and I have yet to have dinner. Maybe, maybe another time," John said as he tried to jam a key in the lock, but again he dropped the tangled mass of keys, car fob and metal pill cylinder.

They struck a decorative metal tread lining the top step, the clanging sound ringing out like a bell.

Stavos picked up the keys again, and the dachshund sniffed at Stavos, who patted the dog's head. The animal went back to pawing at the door. Stavos stood up and held on to the keys for a second and then looked up at John. Kurt had reached the top of the stairs and stood next to Stavos, a thin wicked smile on his face. The three now stood together in close proximity, John trembling, his back to the door. He lifted himself on tiptoes to look over their shoulders to the street, to see if any neighbors were out or cars passing by … no one.

"How … how can I help you?" John said.

"Let me help you," Stavos said, holding the keys up for John and pinching the fob between his fingers.

Then, with his other hand he brushed unseen lint on John's arm just below the shoulder. "Just a few questions, we won't be long. I'm sure your dog is hungry. Lyle, right, that's his name? No worries, let's go inside and talk."

Kurt opened up his sport coat, clearly displaying a .45 automatic shoulder holstered.

"I guess so," John said, grabbing the keys, turning them and finally opening the door.

*

An hour later Lyle, leashed to the pantry door, lay in the kitchen, his head on his paws and his empty food bowl next to him. Every few seconds, a water drop landed in the middle of the kitchen floor. Lyle watched: drip, drip, drip. From the ceiling light fixture, a glass half-sphere, another drop formed on the surface and broke free. On the second floor, above the kitchen, was John Block's master bathroom.

"Stop … please stop …" John begged as he gagged and coughed up water.

Kurt had just pulled him up from the water in his bathtub, for the tenth time. Stavos, a few feet away, leaning against the sink, had one foot on the nearby closed toilet seat. He leaned one elbow on his knee, cupped his chin and stared down at John.

"Again, John, why were you looking at St. Rita records?" Stavos said.

He then nodded to Kurt.

Again Kurt pushed the naked architect's head underwater, this time holding him down longer. John opened his eyes underwater: above, blurry images of two dark figures hovered. His bloodshot eyes burned and he felt dizzy. He wanted to throw up; a half-bottle of gin forced down his throat into an empty stomach made him sick. His hands grasped at Kurt's thick, muscular forearms, slipping and sliding, unable to get a grip. Finally Kurt pulled him out.

"Okay … okay … I'll tell you," John said, waving a hand in surrender.

Kurt let go and stood up. The German ex-cop snapped a towel off a rack and began patting down his trousers.

"I'm doing this for a friend … who knows one of the nuns … and doesn't buy the reasons why it closed," John said, his chest heaving as he tried to catch his breath. He gripped the sides of the tub for balance.

"Who is this person?" Stavos said.

"No one important. I just wanted to get her off my back with some city hall paperwork," John said as dismissively as he could.

He rested his chin on his chest, trying to avoid Stavos' stare.

"What's her name?" Stavos said.

"It's not important. Tomorrow I'll tell her the records got lost. She will tell Sister Whoever and then go away."

"Kurt, toss me his phone," Stavos said.

Complying, his associate tossed John's cell phone over to Stavos, who grabbed it in midair. Within seconds he scrolled through the memory, contacts and the texts. John moved his head down further, trying to hide a small smile. He had deleted the AVNER texts immediately after receipt, as was the team's practice.

"Everything here seems normal," Stavos said, "but I don't believe you."

Stavos nodded toward Kurt, who tossed his now wet towel aside. It landed with a thud. Kurt quickly knelt at the tub's end, John's back to him. Kurt's large hands grabbed Block's small shoulders, pushing the architect under the water. John's hands again tried, with little effect, to undo his tormentor's grip. He struggled under the water, his legs kicking, water splashing on the bunched shower curtains and washing over the side of the tub. When John's flailing began to slow down, Stavos motioned with his hand for Kurt to lift him up. Kurt didn't see Stavos and continued to press down.

"Let him up now!" Stavos said.

Looking up, Kurt smiled and said, "Sorry, I was enjoying this."

Huffing, spitting out water and grabbing the tub's edges, John could barely focus what was in front of him, his heart pounding in his chest, his ears. *They are going to kill me if I don't tell them.*

"Cybil, her name is Cybil Raven," John said, his voice low and sad.

Stavos took his foot off the seat and slammed it on the floor. Still kneeling at the tub, Kurt looked up. Stavos crossed his arms and stood there, his head turning right, then left, his eyes blinking.

"What? Do you know her?" Kurt said.

Stavos looked back at his associate. "I don't know her, but I came across her name recently. Our current operations must be allowed to complete, unfettered. I don't like coincidences."

"I agree, I don't like them either," Kurt said.

"In our business, if you start to see the same car several times over the course of a week or notice the same people in the coffee shop, store or other places staring at you, or other innocent coincidences, something is up," Stavos said. "Maybe law enforcement, a competitor, I don't like these unknowns. The best way to control your destiny is to eliminate unknowns."

John Block listened frozen as Stavos finished talking. Stavos stared past John, nodding his head. Kurt gripped John's shoulders tight and pushed him under the water. Kurt smiled while keeping the struggling, kicking Block in place. Soon John stopped moving.

Kurt let go and his victim lay still under the water, eyes wide open. A few small bubbles trickled out his nostrils. They popped to the surface, ignored. Stavos and Kurt walked into the adjacent bedroom. Gruner pointed to an antique roll-top desk next to the sleigh bed.

"Grab the laptop," he said.

Kurt and Stavos walked down the stairs and past the kitchen. Lyle yelped for attention. The pair glanced at the animal and went out, closing the door. They regarded the street, up and down. An empty Old Town Trolley tour bus traveled across their view, toward the square. Coming in the opposite direction, a young woman jogger wearing a SCAD T-shirt ran past them, headphones on. She looked straight down the street, oblivious to the two men.

Stavos looked at Kurt, put a hand on his shoulder and said, "Bring me Cybil Raven."

34

Driving along Tarthal Way following the hearse, Cybil remarked to her friend Tom, riding in front with her, and to Sister Anne, in the back, how the moss that hung from the live oak trees seemed different than she remembered. She had been part of several photo shoots at the cemetery last year. The large granite gravestones, mausoleum arches and tall angel statues always made for dramatic backdrops in all kinds of light. Today, the sun's radiance was muted by a cloudy sky casting a grayish pall.

Along the roadway, massive arched limbs from the live oak trees reached out and covered the roadway. Thicker and heavier than she recalled, the Spanish moss reached down from the limbs and hung above the traffic. As each car passed, wind streaming from its roof pushed the spider web–like moss up and forward only for it to fall back as if waving goodbye to each traveler.

A few minutes later, Cybil stood, silent, along with other mourners around the open pit soon to be John Block's final resting place on the grounds of Bonaventure Cemetery in Savannah. The Block family plot was located about 50 yards north-northwest from the Tarthal Way roundabout. Bonaventure sat high in the Thunderbolt community, which was east of Savannah, on a bluff overlooking marshes and waterways. The oak tree–lined avenues and colorful gardens within the cemetery created a peaceful setting to receive the dead.

Cybil looked around the gathering: about 15 people had made the trip from the funeral to Bonaventure along with Tom and Sister Anne. Kara, Derrin, his partner who'd made the arrangements, Judy, Benny, office staff from John's business, several regulars from The cSpot and a few people she didn't recognize stood around the hole in the ground. At the end of the empty grave Reverend Sanders waited.

About 150 people had attended the early morning service, presided by Sanders, at Trinity Episcopal Chapel by the Sea. Much of the business community had paid their respects at the service; John's work was much respected. John's mother did not attend, her nasty break with him happening after he moved in with Derrin several years before.

Tom, in town to work on the KidMars project with Sebastian, rode in with Cybil from Trinity. They met Anne at the chapel, a temporary home for St. Rita refugees. She wanted to come along to the graveside service. Afterward they planned to talk about Anne's suspicions and what to do next. Cybil finished scanning the attendees as Reverend Sanders started to speak.

"Friends and family, we are gathered here to lay our friend, John Block, to rest. Beloved by many, his untimely passing saddens us all. One of the realities of life is death. From the Scriptures we are told man that is born of woman and has but a short time to live." Sanders paused and looked around the graveside.

Derrin leaned on Kara, who held him up, her hand under his elbow. He sniffled and wiped his nose with a white handkerchief.

"While life is full of misery, it can also be full of joy. John did enjoy life," Sanders said.

A few around the graveside broke into small smiles and nodded while others remained grim-faced.

Sanders said, "While this flower of God was cut down he will bloom again in the heavenly garden of God to enjoy the eternal sunshine of his love."

Cybil clenched her teeth. She hated religious slogans handed out like soothing lollipops. *How the hell does he know?*

*

In Fallujah, after one especially bloody mission, Cybil went to see Capt. Amanda Hershing, a pilot. Her chopper had taken heavy small-arms fire and went down. Fighting the spongy controls because of punctured hydraulics, she had to fly a controlled crash so the bird would land crew side up—their best chance to survive. It worked, except the chopper blade snapped and sliced through the cockpit, practically cutting her in half above the waist. She was triaged along with other dying soldiers.

In the tent, Amanda, an ex-Catholic, between gasping for breath and spitting up blood, kept asking for the chaplain who was standing nearby, to hold her hand and take her confession. Cybil remembered his answer clearly: “I’m sorry, my dear, I’m a Protestant. I don’t take confession, but I’ll read some Bible passages for you.”

Rules and dogma over compassion and comfort, that’s all religion delivered to Hershing that day, her last. Cybil would have none of it.

*

A loud electric motor hummed as the casket lowered into the grave, the mechanism hidden by drapes and coverings. One by one the procession of mourners threw their symbolic spade of dirt on the shiny, gold-foil trimmed casket. Derrin threw the last spade and a bouquet of lilies and started to sob. Kara hugged him and a few others closed ranks joining the huddle.

The mourners dispersed slowly, forming into small groups to console each other. The groups lingered, exchanging mourners so everyone could share in the memory and the pain. Judy and Benny walked toward where Cybil, Anne and Tom stood. Stepping up, Judy raised her head and looked at Cybil.

“Now’s not the time, but we need to talk, I’ve found something,” Judy said.

Benny nodded his head. “Same here. When can we meet?”

“You don’t think this is related to … you know?” Judy said.

Looking first at Judy, then Benny, Cybil said, “Not sure. Let’s discuss it later. Tonight at MacPherson, late. I’ll text.”

“Good, I could use a drink,” Benny said.

"Me too," Judy said.

Both turned around and walked back to the remaining mourners.

Cybil looked over at Sister Anne and Tom and tilted her head toward the car. The three of them began walking.

Sister Anne spoke first. "I'm sorry for your loss, I know John was a friend of yours."

Cybil nodded but said nothing.

"A tough day for Derrin too, though he looks like he has some support," Tom said.

"Yes, he does," Cybil said.

"Listen, I know you and Anne have a lot to talk about. I'll call a cab and get back to the house and finish up with Sebastian. I'll help him pack for his trip."

"Thanks, Tom, Sebastian will like that. Tell Carol to find you his scout duffel bag. He'll need that instead of a roller," Cybil said.

"Sure will," Tom said and took a side path toward the roundabout, an easy landmark for a cabbie to find.

The two women walked silently for several steps before Cybil spoke.

"It's my fault," she said, talking to the air in front of her.

Anne reached out and put her hand on Cybil's shoulder. "Cybil, he drowned, it was an accident, that's what you told me."

Cybil reflexively twisted her shoulder away, slipping it out from under Anne's touch.

"That's what the officer told Derrin, but I don't believe it," Cybil said.

They kept walking, Anne saying, "Why do you think that?"

"John was looking into the St. Rita property records for me. He texted the day before he was killed that he had made some headway."

Anne stopped. Cybil took a step, stopping also, turned and faced her. Anne's head was down. They stood in a space between guardian oak trees, with bright sunlight streaming in from behind Cybil. Anne's head lifted, her eyes catching the light and becoming shiny emeralds.

Cybil stood silent, transfixed. She tried to take a breath but couldn't, then looked away and exhaled.

"Are you all right?" Anne said.

"Let's keep walking," Cybil said, turning and moving toward the car, now a few yards away.

"What did he find?" Anne said.

"I don't know what he found. We were supposed to meet that evening at Matthews for a late meal, after he walked Lyle. It's close to where he lives—lived," Cybil said, her voice trailing off.

"Why do you think he didn't drown?"

"Derrin found the body, poor man. He was out late with a client. When he got home and found John's body in the tub, he called 911 in a panic after pulling him out and trying CPR. When paramedics and police came, they took over and Derrin watched from the bedroom," Cybil said shaking her head.

"That must have been horrible," Anne said.

Taking a few steps Cybil said, "When things calmed down and they declared time of death, the police looked around, asked if anything was missing, usual questions. The only thing Derrin could see missing in the bedroom was John's laptop."

Anne's eyes widened. "You think someone wanted the laptop?"

Cybil nodded her head. "John could drink. I know. We closed a few places down in Savannah. We'd celebrate whenever he helped me finish an assignment. But the idea that he got so drunk as to accidently drown is ridiculous. The coroner's report declared accidental death. I don't buy it. It's my fault."

She sighed and looked into Anne's face.

"John warned me about Stavos, Blitz warned me. Gruner must have found out," Cybil said.

Anne skipped a step to catch up to Cybil and said, "Do you think the men I saw at St. Rita were Stavos's men?"

"I'm sure of it. What we don't know is what they were doing there. What were they moving? Why is St. Rita important to Savannah's worst criminal?" Cybil said.

"And why, why is Father Michael helping them, the son of a—" Anne had put her hand up to her mouth.

Cybil smiled.

They reached the car and Cybil beeped open the doors. They got in and Cybil drove off, heading to the chapel to drop Anne. A few minutes of silence between them ended when Cybil punched the radio on. The song, "Duet," was playing. She turned down the volume.

"Anne, did you have any luck researching the equipment serial numbers, MPM 450 SEP Menesco?"

Anne chuckled. "Wow, I forget your memory skills. I did find something. Didn't understand, though. The numbers match an industrial designation for a high-temp metal furnace, designed to melt lead. Maybe they're recovering stolen precious metals."

"It's easier and more profitable to smuggle and sell drugs than melt gold or lead. It doesn't make sense, but I got an idea. When we get to Trinity I'll make a call," Cybil said.

They drove without talking for the next 20 minutes, the radio music filling the space. Several times Cybil looked at Anne but said nothing. Anne sat, arms crossed and leaning toward the window, looking out at repetitive, boring highway landscape. They arrived at the Trinity parking lot, in the back, next to the garden.

Cybil stopped the car, turning it off before reaching for her iPhone in the cup holder. Pressing a Speed Dial number she put the phone to her ear. She couldn't use the speaker with Anne there.

Anne looked at the weathered garden angel standing silent and said, "It's a peaceful place but not very well kept."

Cybil glanced at the marred cherub and smiled. "Even an angel can't help from getting dirty in this world."

"So true," Anne said.

Cybil heard the voice mail prompt come on. Per protocol, she left a message: "AVNER requesting research inquiry on item MPM 450 SEP Menesco."

Hanging up and turning in her seat partway toward Anne, Cybil said, "Listen, I need to drop Sebastian at the airport soon. I'm hoping Tom and Carol have the packing done. Don't do anything more for now, I need to think about this."

"I understand. I'll see what else I can find out. Rev. Sanders has been friends with Father Michael for some time, so maybe he can tell me something."

Cybil clenched her teeth and sighed. "Most of my 'other' work is out of town and not so in the open. This is right in my backyard, I work here, I live here with my kids. I'm exposed and frankly so are you. Maybe we need to take another approach."

"I'm not going to stop."

"Me neither, I just want to make sure the next step is the right one. Will you promise me you'll stay put until I figure something out?" Cybil said. She leaned over and reached out her hand, touching Anne above her left elbow.

Anne looked down at Cybil's fingers barely touching her blouse sleeve. "It's still there, you know," Anne said.

Cybil pulled her hand back.

"Is yours?" Anne said in a low, quiet voice.

A loud sonar ringtone, Sonja's, blared from Cybil's iPhone.

"I need to take this in private. I'll see you later, I have to go," Cybil said, starting the car. The phone rang again.

"Okay." Anne nodded, opened her car door and stepped out.

Before pulling away, Cybil looked back at Anne, who waved goodbye. She gave a quick nod, then faced forward, pressing the accelerator hard and jerking the car. The phone rang again, seemingly louder.

Cybil pressed Answer on the steering wheel now that she was alone. "Hi, Sonja, I can talk now."

A small delay … Sonja's calls were always encrypted.

She said, "Imagine my surprise when Ops tells me you're making an unauthorized research request when not on assignment. Since I know that is too simple a mistake for you to make, I authorized it, thinking you must be on to something."

"Heh-heh, I knew it. Thanks for helping. I need a small favor, a minor local thing. It'll be out of your hair in a minute," Cybil said.

Sonja huffed loud and said, "I don't think so."

Cybil raised an eyebrow and said, "What do you mean?"

"You know we get regular DHS technical bulletins. Most are boring."

"Okay," Cybil said.

"So, as soon as I approve your request, your equipment serial number MPM 450 SEP Menesco gets flagged as a special item and comes to my attention."

"Industrial equipment? What for?" Cybil said, both eyebrows raised high.

A few seconds pass before Sonja's voice came through. "That is precisely what we are asking ourselves around here. Seems this equipment is innocent enough, except two years ago the Iranians bought a boatload of them."

Cybil chewed on her lip. "Interesting. The Iranians. Any analysis as to why?"

Sonja took a deep breath and said, "I scanned the initial report done last year. Nothing stands out. The logical explanation is that the expanding Iranian nuclear program simply needs lead. Lead hides the radioactive signature of all types of isotopes and material, so if they're trying to hide from our satellite detectors and other remote sensing, it makes sense they'd buy the equipment. Use it to line rooms at Natanz and other locations."

As Cybil listened, the car crossed the island bridge taking her to Savannah.

"Any other demographics on where else this equipment has been sent?"

"Bright girl," Sonja said, "in the U.S., small manufacturers use this equipment and nothing unusual showed up on the maps. Normal distribution and destinations. Savannah has never had any units until two weeks ago … four were delivered."

"Hmm, who was the buyer?" Cybil said.

"A restaurant in Savannah, hold on," Sonja said.

No hold music came from the unit's telephone system, silence with an occasional static crackling. Cybil, now on I-16 would be home soon. She reached her neighborhood. Slowly winding through the residential streets, she pulled into her driveway, pressed the garage door opener and drove in nudging the tennis ball. The door closed behind her and she shut the engine off.

Sonja said, "Sorry. Yeah, the restaurant."

"I'm listening," Cybil said.

"The question is, why is a Savannah Greek restaurant—I think it's called Troy's Wraps—buying the same equipment as the Iranian nuclear program?" Sonja said.

Cybil gasped, remembering John talking about his meeting with Stavos there.

Sonja said, "Hey, you okay, what was that?"

"Nothing. I just got home. I'm going off speaker," Cybil said, opening her door, grabbing her phone and getting out.

Standing next to car she saw the door into the house open suddenly. Tom and Sebastian stood inside and looked at her. She waved at them and motioned she'd be right in and pointed to the phone. They closed the door.

Sonja said, "Getting the answer to that question is why you are now officially on assignment."

"Okay, I'll get on it and get back to you as usual."

"Good, except I don't want you solo on this."

Cybil paused and said slowly, "Sonja, you know I prefer to work alone. No, no way. Especially in my own town."

"Especially because it is your own town. Sorry, no choice, end of discussion. Check your secure e-mail for additional information. Ed Raintree is already on a plane heading your way. I want you both checking in on schedule." Sonja hung up without a goodbye.

Cybil's hand fell to her side and the phone dropped, slapping the concrete floor, the sound echoing in the neatly organized garage.

She yelled out loud, "No, not Ed Raintree!"

35

"Recalculating," the GPS voice announced to the clean-shaven, dark-skinned driver. His narrow-set eyes peered intently, scanning the highway overpass and looking at a pending left turn.

Kasen carefully drove his rental car through the overpass traffic, down the ramp, back onto the highway, I-75 South. His stop at the gas station, at an exit north of Atlanta, replenished his fuel and dulled his hunger. He picked up a plastic bottle from the cup holder and took another long sip of mineral water to wash down the last few bites of the green, not yet ripe banana. The short walk from the pumps to the store and back helped loosen the stiffness in his right hip. Accelerating smoothly at the bottom of the ramp, he disappeared into traffic.

Less than 20 minutes away, in Morrow, Georgia, a small community near Clayton State University East, Abdul sat on the steps of his rental apartment. Highway I-75 passes right through the college town, on the way to Macon and intersecting I-16 giving travelers a straight path to Savannah. In his lap sat a tourist guidebook of that city, which he flipped through for the fourth time. As he turned the last page, he looked up toward the apartments' gated entrance for any sign of Teacher, but there was none. Abdul frowned and started on page one again.

As a foreign student in the engineering program at Clayton, he had done well, made friends, even visited with the engineering fraternity. This year, he excelled in Chem 1211L, Principles of Chemistry Laboratory. Flipping through the book, he stopped on a page showing the bright white sands of Tybee Island, off Savannah's coast. Taking a pen from his shirt pocket, he scribbled notes and formulas on the picture of the white sand, trying to work out some problems he was having with the test batches. Minutes passed. Abdul moved to another page to write notes. Then a car pulled in to the space in front of him. He recognized the driver, the Teacher.

A brief hello in the parking lot and little said between them, Kasen and Abdul walked up the apartment stairs and made their way into 234B. The strong smell of incense greeted Kasen when he stepped in; spicy and aromatic, it helped cover chemical odors of the improvised laboratory setup in the kitchen. Abdul had been busy cooking the plastic explosive PETN.

The Clayton State U student walked into the kitchen and put the tourist guide down next to the stove. After preparing tea, he brought two cups to the small square table just outside the kitchen. The Teacher, already seated, looked up and smiled. Looking past Abdul, he could see the Bunsen burners, mixers, flasks and other lab equipment that had been hard at work but unsuccessful. Abdul spoke first.

"Teacher, I am an unworthy soldier, and ignorant. I am sorry for my failure."

Kasen lifted the steaming cup to his lips, blew away some of the rising vapors and said, "Abdul, there is no shame in struggle, only in surrender. Tell me, what is the problem."

"My first few batches were close to the specifications you provided in regard to volume and density, but the last ones have been getting worse and worse. I went to the woods to test some of them and their explosive impulse ratios were not adequate at all."

"Have you adjusted for humidity, as we discussed? The air back home is dry compared to the American South, especially in the spring," Kasen said.

"I believe I did, but am unsure. Perhaps you could look over my formulations," Abdul said as he scooted his chair closer.

He laid a loose-leaf three-ring binder, with a Clayton State University logo on the outside, on the table, and flipped it open to the last tabbed section, marked with a single G.

Looking down at the pages and flipping them back and forth, Kasen scanned the chemical equations, ingredient amounts and ratios. Stopping every so often, he asked Abdul a question and then continued looking at the pages.

Abdul's leg vibrated as he waited, his hands on his thighs. He leaned back and sighed. Pressing his lips together, he leaned forward to see specifically what Kasen was examining. Finally, the Teacher spoke.

"You see,"—his long index finger reached to touch a specific equation on the page—"here is where the ratio for this climate has to be adjusted with a finer touch."

Abdul turned his head sideways. "A finer touch?"

"Yes, you must use a rolling average of humidity and dew point data over the last 30 days and project forward 30 days based on history. It gives you the best variance. That way, when the base substance forms, it is matched to the current environment."

"I only used one week of data," Abdul said with a soft sigh.

"Sufficient, yes, normally, in drier, more stable climates. But it is more active here than home, therefore you have to adjust accordingly. We did discuss this," the Teacher said, looking at his student.

"I apologize for my lack of attention."

"No need, this is fairly easy to correct and test. We can make a batch this evening to verify. Once that works, and I am sure it will, we can produce the sufficient quantities in the next few days and ship it to Safir. Then we can leave for Savannah to secure the final element," Kasen said.

Before Abdul could respond, a loud knock on the door was followed by the sound of hands drumming the door in some rough musical rhythm.

A voice through the door said, "Hey, Andy, dude, open up, it's Jason. Let's go get some pizza, man!"

Abdul touched his chest with his hand and thumbed toward the door, signaling he would take care of it. Abdul positioned himself next to the door jamb and cracked open the entrance slightly. A sliver of space allowed bright-yellow light from the hallway to shine in.

A red-headed, freckle-faced young man, about 20, with light stubble, stared in at Abdul. He was wearing a CSU sweatshirt and a multicolored stocking cap.

"Hey, Andy, I'm starving. Let's go get some pizza. Let me in first, I need to pee," Jason said.

Abdul, keeping one foot jammed next to the door, smiled back at his friend and said, "Jason, hi. Not a good time. Sort of busy."

"Too busy for pizza! Oh come on, take a break, you can study later. Plus I texted the Delmonico sisters. Tasty twins, man. They may join us." Jason grinned and tried to peek around the door. "Hey, who you got in there?"

"Jason, not a good time," Abdul said, tilting his head and giving a wink.

"Oh, oh, yeah, yeah. I … I … yeah, I understand, cool. Andy, awww right," Jason said, giving Abdul an air fist bump while backing up toward the stairs. "I'll check with you laterrrr."

Abdul closed the door and returned to the table. He saw Kasen writing on the pages they had discussed.

"Sorry, Teacher, for the interruption," Abdul said.

"Not at all. We discussed assimilating into this culture, and the sacrifices we have to make in our faith, to live like them in order to strike with complete surprise. You have done well, from the sound of your friend's invitation," Kasen said, smiling.

Abdul nodded and said, "Surprise is the key to this operation, is it not?"

"Yes, most supremely it is. Imagine the surprise when this special gift is opened for them, in a place they never would expect. It will be quite the revelation, the design of this gift specifically crafted with their children in mind," Kasen said, his eyes narrowed, his breathing increasing.

Abdul hesitated before speaking. He was wary of broaching the subject of Kasen's family directly. Back in Yemen, the imam had advised Abdul to avoid family references.

Kasen saw this and said, "What is it?"

"The design is most ingenious. How did you first conceive of it?" Abdul said.

Kasen looked at the apartment ceiling, closed his eyes and took a deep breath. His lips moved every slightly, and Abdul thought he saw the words "Allah be praised" mouthed in Arabic. The Teacher's head dropped slightly and he looked directly into Abdul's eyes.

"It took me six months to recover from the CIA's questioning done by the American dogs, the Saudis. During my time at hospital in Tehran my brother sent word about the U.S. drone strike in our village. He had been betrayed and was bringing food to my wife and girls. He left minutes before the missile hit my home. Nothing was left," Kasen recounted, his voice cold, detached.

"Teacher, your loss will not be in vain," Abdul said, slowly closing both hands into fists.

"While I recovered, many times I had dreams and a vision of a beautiful flower opening, and when at full bloom it burst forth sending seeds floating into the wind. When the seeds landed, no matter how green or fertile the ground, it turned to sand and then opened up and swallowed everything," Kasen said, letting out a deep sigh. "My wife loved the zinnia and the flame of the forest. She had a garden. My girls brought me cuttings when they could."

"And after you left hospital?" Abdul said.

Kasen put both elbows on the table. "Our Iranian brothers came to me and discussed a prior project that had been abandoned. They heard of my work in Iraq and sought my advice."

"Allah was at work."

"Yes. When they told me what material they had available, my vision made sense. Within days we had agreed to work together," Kasen said.

Abdul smiled. "Where did you work?"

"I traveled deep within their desert to a large underground complex. After several months, the completed design had to be tested. We did. A nearby valley served us well. The wind conditions, the dispersal, the coverage, all of the parameters worked as expected."

Abdul's eyebrows pinched together as he said, "But you did not use actual material, did you?"

Kasen smiled and said, "No, no. We found that talcum powder mixed with a heavier agent could simulate the effects. A beautiful, glorious white cloud drifted and landed as expected. We used the prototype design you studied back home. That is why your work is important. The explosive impulse must create the dispersal cloud with the right density at the right height."

"Yes, I understand now."

"The actual material is waiting for us in Savannah. This material, like the bite of a snake, will deliver a never-ending poison, if we do our work well," Kasen said, nodding.

"Teacher, I am honored to prepare with you the final element. Together with Safir, our brother, we can all be witnesses to this special gift, Hadeaa," Abdul said as he punched his right fist into his left palm.

"Before we start, I have to make a call. Please wait for me," Kasen said.

He got up and walked over to the sliding glass door next to the apartment's balcony. Sliding the door open, he stepped into the small space occupied by a round grill full of ashes and next to it a rusted racing bike with a flat. He pulled his phone from his pocket, the one for Stavos. He pressed the S Speed Dial.

"I've been expecting your call," Stavos Gruner said.

"Are we on schedule?"

"Yes. Everything is in place as requested and security also. You won't be disturbed. I guarantee it," Gruner said.

"Very well. I and my associate will be arriving as planned. I look forward to sampling your city's hospitality as soon as our work is complete. And the meeting with my friend, has it been arranged?" Kasen said.

"It is being arranged. I think she will be delighted to see you and I actually have a few questions for her myself," Stavos said.

"Really? And why is that?"

"It seems your friend for some reason has been making inconvenient inquiries related to the location. I think a coincidence, but I will personally confirm," Stavos said.

Kasen's thin smile spread across his face. "All the better then, that she and I are reunited so I can express my gratitude properly for her past actions toward me. Perhaps that will help answer your questions as well. Agreed."

"Agreed," Stavos said, hanging up.

Kasen moved back into the apartment and nodded to Abdul, now in the kitchen. From a wall hook he grabbed two heavy-duty lab aprons and held one up for his Teacher.

Kasen smiled, joined Abdul and put the lab coat on. From the coat pocket Kasen pulled protective eye gear and slid it onto his face. Abdul had already put his on. Within a few minutes they stood bent over the workspace, mixing ingredients, heating, cooling and remixing as necessary.

At one point Abdul accidentally knocked over a flask containing a reagent, spilling the contents on the Savannah Tourist Guide next to the stove. The paper started to percolate and decompose. With a gloved hand and little thought, Kasen picked up the guide and threw it in trash. He and Abdul returned to work.

36

"Mom, I'll be okay," Sebastian said, wriggling himself out of his mother's grasp. She knelt next to him and held him close after having kissed him several times. They were saying goodbye near the Savannah Airport security zone.

"You look very handsome in your uniform, I'm proud of you," Cybil said as she brushed dust from his merit badges and straightened a camping achievement pin.

Standing up, she glanced at the nearby Starbucks shop where Jay, Sebastian's troop scoutmaster, had been in line. He now walked toward them.

June, standing next to Cybil, said to her brother, "I think you look like a soldier."

"Thanks. You have a good trip too, sis," Sebastian said.

"Grandma says we will be in the woods, just like you," June said, smiling.

Jay neared the waiting family and said, "Sorry to rush. June, here's your hot chocolate, be careful. Cybil, your double espresso vanilla latte. It's on me. Thanks for bringing Sebastian. Picking him up would have meant leaving two hours earlier with all the other stops I had to make."

Nearby, other families were saying their goodbyes to their sons. The troop started out with 10 boys but two dropped out for medical reasons. The eight who would be making the trip were all good scouts. Sebastian had the most badges—like his mother, a highly motivated achiever.

"You guys have fun. June's flight is some time from now, so we'll sit here for a while," Cybil said.

Jay looked at June and said, "Is this your first big-girl trip?"

The little girl shook her head and held up three fingers. She smiled proudly and looked down at her child-sized pink rollway covered with round-faced, round-eyed Hello Kitty cartoons. Several stickers from different states also decorated it.

"I see," Jay said. "Well, have a safe trip. Sebastian, you ready?"

Sebastian grabbed his scout-logo duffel bag, slung it over his shoulder and firmly declared, "Yes, sir!"

Cybil's heart rose and sank as she watched her uniformed son, duffel bag slapping his back, walking away. The rest of the troop joined him, surrounding him as they followed Jay. Her gaze followed her son through the snaking security line as he approached the TSA screening agent. She tried to take a sip, coughed, found it hard to swallow. He had been to other jamborees, even one overseas. This jamboree was only a few states away, in Virginia, on a military base no less.

She could see through the security glass partitions; he had made it past the scanning machines. Her breathing got shallower, she gritted her teeth. The image was too close to her Iraq memories, of friends leaving, walking away with their duffel, only to come back in a body bag. She tossed the nearly full cup in a nearby bin and let both hands drop as she sighed deeply. She felt a small warm hand grasp her right one.

"Mommy, Sebastian will be all right, I'm sure of it," June said.

Looking down at her daughter, Cybil said, "Thanks, honey. Let's go sit until it's time. We told Grandma we'd call her before you boarded the flight."

Cybil sat with her excited daughter, waiting for the airline agent for a few hours. The final hour passed, involving three trips to the restroom, two trips to buy water and candy plus several phone calls from Grandma before the airline escort arrived.

Saying goodbye and watching her daughter and the female agent make their way through security didn't bother her as much. June's serene presence came into her life the moment Cybil first held her. Today, that sense eased her concern, unlike what she had felt for Sebastian just hours before. After June and the agent passed from sight she turned and walked back to short-term parking.

On the way to the car, she grabbed her phone from her purse and sent an on-the-way text to Sensei Dan. This planned workout would help her state of mind, especially after Sonja's news of the incoming Ed Raintree.

She shook her head at the thought of working with Raintree again. Texting him to meet at the dojo tonight didn't thrill her. Cybil didn't know a more egotistical, overconfident operative. She heard he had gotten married. Maybe that settled him down. Despite their differences in approach they solved a couple of high-profile cases. This caused Sonja to match them when she could. Cybil reached her car and put both hands on the roof. Her breathing quickened and her head dropped. Cybil Raven expressed few regrets in life … one of them was sleeping with Raintree on their last assignment.

Before starting the car, she texted Judy and Benny.

c u at mollys in 2 hours

She drove out of the airport garage, back to Savannah. Within 10 minutes she had reached I-95 and after 30 minutes arrived at the dojo, at the corner of Bull Street and West Broughton, parked nearby and went in.

Heading to the locker room, she passed by Dan who was behind the sales counter adjusting inventory.

"Ready to get your man-card back?" Cybil said.

"Master will teach student tonight," Dan said smiling.

Cybil glared at Dan then winked.

In the locker room she dressed quickly but just before going out to spar with Dan, she sat down with her phone. Looking down to it she shook her head. *I'm too exposed, I'm sorry.* After a few swipes and touches she shut down the all her tweets and posts and went off the grid except for calls and texts. She had decided.

"Oooohhhaaa," Dan exhaled as both hands grasped high on Cybil's uniform lapel.

Dan, dressed in his traditional white karategi, stepped closer to her. Cybil, in her usual all-black uniform and red silk headband, held her ground. They faced each other in the middle of the empty dojo except for Dan's family members visiting from Japan, lining the room, sitting in folding chairs.

Cybil grunted as she threw her hip into Dan for a shoulder throw, but he succeeding in sweep kicking her one standing leg—the other she had lifted for leverage. Soon he had her on the ground, face planted, in an arm lock. She tapped the mat twice. Letting her go, she quickly bounced up, cursed under her breath and bowed briefly toward Dan. Both crouched down and began circling each other. Dan's family, consisting of an old Japanese couple, three young teens and several smaller children, sat and watched, their heads nodding.

"You're a little off tonight," Sensei Dan said with a grin while circling to his left. "You've been on the mat three times already, one more than me."

Cybil moved to her right, matching his radius, took a quick step in, and he retreated. She moved back and continued circling.

"I'll be fine but you won't," Cybil said, her blue eyes narrowing.

She had noticed that her feints had gotten Dan to move closer to the only matted wall of the dojo. She moved in again and feinted with a wide, high snap kick. Dan moved backward and he looked back for a second to see how far he was before placing one hand on the wall.

Moving fast Cybil got inside position and grabbed his lapels. Dan twisted and countered, forcing her sideways and toward the wall, by using his weight. He thought she would focus on the wall, unaware of a coming leg sweep that would take her to the mat and into his choke hold. *I got her now.*

At what could best be described as a controlled somersault, Cybil used Dan's shoving to step up the wall and push off hard. Lifting herself acrobatically above Dan, she twist-dove over his shoulder while still holding on to him. He twirled like a top right down to the mat, landing with a thud.

"Ayyeeee," a collective sound came from the sitting family members, followed by a short round of applause.

Cybil's wrestling instincts came alive. The only girl to wrestle in her high school, she knew now to grapple. In a flash she had him in a full nelson head lock, his arms immobile, his torso scissor-locked between her thighs, his face smashed against the mat. She had a big smile on her face.

"How you doing there, Dan?" Cybil said as sweat dripping through her headband plinked on the gray plastic mat beneath her.

"Fine," Dan squeaked out.

"You gonna slap the mat?" Cybil said.

"Can't move my arms and I'm still trying to figure out what you did," Dan said while he wriggled a little to see if he could slip the hold.

Cybil pulled tighter, squeezed her thighs more.

Dan had enough. "Okay, If I could, I'd slap the mat twice!"

She let him go.

Dan raised himself up into a sitting position and slowly moved his shoulders, neck and arms to loosen the tension. Cybil moved to a sitting position next to the wall. Dan crawled over and sat next to her. Both sat opposite the family gallery, who were talking about the match. Heads nodded to each other and the smiling adults talked to the kids, pointing over to Cybil.

"I think you impressed them with that last move," Dan said, patting Cybil on the knee. "Me too."

"Thanks, and thanks for working me out tonight, I needed it," Cybil said.

"No problem," Dan said as he lifted one arm and flexed his shoulder. "Next time, though, warn me you're coming in pissed before we work out. I'll wear padding."

"Did I hurt you, Dan?" Cybil said, her voice teasing. She put her hand on his shoulder.

"It's not that, you had an edge during the workout. Not the usual fun. I … I … hadn't seen that before."

Cybil's lips pursed and she looked up toward the ceiling and then at her friend. "Sorry, I … uh … I'm helping a friend with something and it's getting out of hand. I'm going to let her down. I have to stop. Can't do what I want to."

"I can see how that would hard for you," Dan said. "Since I've known you, you've always moved toward what you wanted."

"What I have wanted I haven't always gotten," Cybil said, shaking her head. She crossed her arms, her right hand rubbing above her left elbow.

Taking a deep breath, Dan said, "Aikido has taught me fitness and fighting skills. But Islam taught me that submitting to Allah's will brings peace, first with oneself, then with others."

Cybil turned her face toward Dan. "Submission and peace, huh? Submission, I'm not good at that. Peace? Death is the only peace I've seen people get. Only they get it when they least expect it, like when a mortar lands near you and tears you in half, or a 12-year-old Bedouin sniper hits a lucky shot through your vest and severs your aorta. Or when a wouldn't-hurt-a-fly architect is drowned in his own bathtub because he was looking into business he shouldn't have been. False promises are the currency of religion and I stopped buying that load of crap a long time ago," Cybil said.

Dan looked at Cybil and nodded. "I'm sorry about John, I know he was your friend." Dan turned toward his family, who had left the chairs and dispersed. They were walking around the dojo looking at the different awards and trophies lining the wall.

"Cybil, this world has many, many dark places, even here in Savannah. But whether you think Allah, God, Jesus, the universe or fate is running things, well or poorly, you have to admit, many people have it good. I have heard it said that the sun rises on the evil and the good, rain falls on the just and the unjust. You've done well here in Savannah. You have two great kids, a career, you're beautiful as hell and you can kick ass with the best of them. Someone or something is looking out for you."

Cybil said, "If God or something is looking out for me, I wish he'd look elsewhere once in a while. Thanks for the compliment but if he has a master plan, he forgot to ask what I wanted."

Dan's expression indicated he was a little lost. "What do you want?"

Cybil grimaced and stopped herself from talking. She liked Dan, but his religious view of life irritated her. Conversion to Islam seemed to help him, but like her other religious friends his simple answers to hard facts didn't hold with her. Dan hadn't exactly suffered in life. When your Savannah old-money daddy gives you three blocks of prime storefront as a wedding gift, it's easy to run a dojo as a hobby.

"Dan, how about we pick this up next time?" Cybil said with a thin smile.

Her sweat-matted hair had fallen on her forehead and into her eyes. She brushed it away and tucked it under her headband.

"Okay, sure, next time, beers on me though," Dan said, his voice trailing away, "even though I will have tea."

"You bet, but the food is on me," Cybil said as she stood up and glanced out the glass doors of the dojo.

Dan also looked and saw a tall, handsome, well-built man standing outside, who waved. It was Raintree.

"He's here for me. Can you let him in while I shower and change?" Cybil said.

He rose from his seated position and stood next to her.

"Sure, who is he?" Dan said.

"Ted Randall. We have some business to discuss over at Molly MacPherson's. I won't be long," Cybil said, her voice fading as she walked toward the showers.

37

Stavos Gruner looked into his oversize steel thermos cup. Hot vapors rose above the rim, the hot coffee still too scalding to take a sip. He blew on the surface and then looked down the porch steps to the St. Rita driveway. The gravel driveway circled in front of them, around a large magnolia tree whose base looked white due to flowering blooms from the landscaping. The driveway ran past the tree and connected to the main road. Kurt, Michelle and Markos spread out on either side of Stavos as he stood between the two main Greco-Roman columns supporting the gabled roof of the large porch.

"He's late," Kurt said, shaking his head.

"Patience, Herr Kurt," Michelle said, "Mr. K is loaded and we can get real healthy with this and expand the business."

She glanced at Stavos.

Descending calmly and deliberately, Gruner knelt on his left knee. Putting the cup down, he felt around his right ankle. Perched on a mortared crevasse between bricks, the cup started to tilt. It would have tipped over had not Markos, with a thud, planted his big black boot next to the cup.

Picking up the cup, Gruner stood and turned to his friend and said, "Alert as always."

Markos's left hand reached out and grabbed Stavos's forearm. Markos focused front and center as he said, "They are here."

A silver-gray minivan pulled up and stopped, passenger side facing the porch. Out came a baby-faced young man in his mid-twenties, with dark hair and of medium height. The driver exited from his side and walked in front of the vehicle. He was taller, older, his face clean-shaven but pockmarked, black hair slightly gray at the temples. His nose was off-center, deformed in places, signs of previously being broken. His narrow-set eyes shone dark. He walked with a slight hitch and climbed the porch steps. Standing in front of Stavos, the man extended his hand.

"I'm Mr. Kasen. It is a pleasure to meet you," he said.

Gruner looked at Kasen, tilted his head slightly to see more of his client's face and then said, "Welcome to Savannah, we are ready for you."

Kasen smiled and glanced over at Abdul, who had stayed at the bottom of the steps cradling a leather shoulder bag under his right arm. He exchanged glances with Michelle, Markos and Kurt, but said nothing.

Kasen bowed slightly and with his left hand sweeping toward the front doors, said, "Thank you. Please, I am quite eager to see our rooms and then to start work. We have much to do."

"Follow me," Stavos said.

After a 15-minute tour through the lobby, kitchen and upstairs, the group headed to the basement. Stavos led the way and the group settled at the bottom of the stairs, the only presently lit area. Gruner reached over to a nearby light switch and flipped it. Like flashbulbs popping at a movie premiere, row after row of overheard fluorescent lights, recently installed, snapped on, traveling away from the group, across the ceiling.

Now well lit, the large brick-walled basement, before full of clothes, toys and mildewed furniture, shone bright. Large, rectangular and open in design, it spanned beneath the whole of St. Rita from wing to wing, almost 45 yards in length and 20 yards across. It looked like a warehouse except for the ceiling, only about 15 feet high. Harsh fluorescent light bounced off the chrome controls, glass indicator panels and smooth stainless-steel surfaces of four large industrial lead ovens, each with removable melting pots. They sat side by side, four feet of space between them.

On the wall behind them, the basement fireplace had been transformed. The opening was covered with a thick plastic sheet and through it, like a python entering the room, ran a fat cylindrical aluminum air duct. Near the end of the air duct, four smaller ducts extended out; they had been spliced into the larger one. The smaller ones were connected by duct tape to exhaust fans on the rear of each oven. In front of each oven stood industrial carts with thick heavy wheels to ferry the pots across the room.

At the other side, a long wide trough ran the length of the room, higher at one end; it drained into a large square metal collector standing about four feet high. In front of the collector bucket stood a tall, square partition, six feet wide, seven feet tall, made of metal, with a glass viewport. Two holes cut big enough for arms looked like huge black dots. On the other side, thick rubber handling sleeves protruded—the kind that grip hazardous materials.

At the far end of the large basement, several rows of heavy plastic mesh canvas bags stacked five high and 10 across sat like guardians holding back an unseen river. They filled one-third of the room. The bags had no markings or writing. One of the bags had a tear near the bottom, from which a small stream of lead ball bearings had escaped and scattered, like wayward seeds, across the concrete floor.

Kasen and Abdul walked slowly through the refitted basement, with Stavos, Markos, Kurt and Michelle a few steps behind. Like a new home buyer inspecting a future residence, Kasen turned his head, craned his neck, nodded, looked, touched a surface and at times looked back toward Stavos's group to comment.

"Did you have any issues with power supply, given this place is fairly old?" Kasen said as he looked at Stavos, who promptly looked at Kurt.

"Your specifications were clear and we were fortunate," Kurt said. "There's a sheet metal shop down this road, so the power company already had a suitable transformer nearby. I personally supervised the additional power line and controls upgrade."

Kasen nodded and smiled. He continued walking toward the bags and eventually stopped in front of them. He knelt and touched the scattered ball bearings, picking up a few.

Stavos went and stood next to him, saying, "As you can see, all of the bags made it through the sea drops. We almost lost a whole pallet one time when the ballast failed and they started to sink."

"Truly, what did you do?" Abdul said, breaking his silence.

Kasen smiled but said nothing.

Stavos looked over at Kurt again and said, "Kurt improvises as well as he plans. With plastic tarp, rope and an extra tank of air, we floated the whole damn thing right back up to the surface."

"I am grateful," Kasen said as he fingered and palmed the lead ball bearings, lifting his hand up and down as if to gauge the weight, "but we must proceed quickly, Stavos. If you will excuse us, we must get to work."

"Glad to hear it," Stavos said, thinking of when he'd get confirmation of the final electronic funds transfer. "Markos will remain to ensure you are not bothered. I need to complete your other request."

"Ah, yes, my friend, I almost forgot," Kasen grinned, his eyes lighting up.

Stavos turned and motioned with his hand to his team. He turned and walked toward the stairs. Kurt and Michelle followed close behind but Markos lingered for a second.

Markos turned his head toward Kasen and Abdul and said, "I'll be in the lobby but may be outside from time to time checking the perimeter," before joining the departing group.

Alone now, Kasen motioned to Abdul to sit on the canvas bags with him.

"And what do you think of our associates?" the older man said.

"They have done well," Abdul said.

Kasen said, "Has Safir received the shipment?"

Abdul pulled out his phone and scrolled to a text message reply; it was short and from Sam, RECV YES.

"Yes," Abdul said with a satisfied smile.

"Very good. We will do a test run of three bags and observe how long it takes to extract and refine the final element," Kasen said. "We can then calculate a production schedule."

Kasen got up and walked toward the ovens. Abdul nodded, bent down and grabbed a handful of lead ball bearings before heading to the collector metal bucket. Reaching it he walked behind the safety partition and stood over a small work table in front of the partition. He reached his hand over the table and let the ball bearings trickle out of this palm. They fell heavily, clinking on the table with a dull thud.

Abdul smiled as he watched a small mound soon accumulate, although one or two had escaped and fallen, rolling to the concrete floor. Laying his shoulder bag on the table, he unzipped it and pulled out a plastic bag full of AA batteries. Next he extracted two small electronic devices, each the size of a paperback. Both had LED displays reading 0.0, the scale millisieverts per hour. Picking one up, he turned it on, and the digital counter rose till it reached the range for normal background gamma, beta and X-ray radiation. He moved the device closer, sweeping over the lead ball bearing mound. The digital counter rose slightly—one or two points—but nothing more. Abdul smiled and looked over at Kasen who was entering data into the one of the oven control panels.

From across the room Abdul spoke out: "Teacher, the shells have worked as planned. We are ready to harvest the seeds."

Kasen's head stayed down while he focused on the panel, his fingers working the controls. In a loud voice he answered, "May Allah be praised, his flower will bloom soon!"

38

Sister Anne took respite in the Trinity Chapel Garden, on the marble bench, the short stone cherub her only company. It had been several days since she had talked to Cybil. Sister Anne thought of their time in Dubai and how quickly she'd decided to leave right after. She shook her head.

Looking at her watch she saw it was ten o'clock, and today another child would be transferred from their care. Her life in Savannah was being reduced, child by child. After today only Sofi and Cecilia would be left. She would also be leaving, again. Leaning forward, her hands gripped the cool marble seat edge and as her knuckles began to turn white, her green eyes flashed dark. *Father Michael, what have you done?*

"Sister Anne, Sister Anne!" Reverend Sanders shouted out from the sidewalk across the garden. He had stepped outside the chapel door.

She got up, smoothed her dark slacks and walked over to Sanders. Passing by the dirty stone angel, she patted it on the head.

"Yes, Reverend Sanders, what is it?"

"Your cell phone, on your sleeping bag, kept ringing. It happened several times in a row so I figured someone must want to contact you," Reverend Sanders said as he produced the cell phone and handed it to her.

"Thank you very much," she said.

Reverend Sanders went back inside. Sister Anne recognized the number: Father Michael. She hit Call Back.

Sister Anne left the garden and walked on the sidewalk that paralleled the garden, down to the corner. The phone rang once. She looked up across the main road on Tybee Island. She could see all the way to the ocean, across the white sand, to the beach. The phone rang a second time and a voice answered.

"Sister Anne, thanks for calling me back. How are the transfers going?" Father Michael said, his voice stiff.

"Well."

After a slight pause, Father Michael coughed and said, "Good. I'm sure it's hard on everyone. Who's left after today?"

"You know full well who, Sofi and Cecilia," Sister Anne said.

"Yes, that's what I'm calling about. Since you are very close to them and they are hard to separate, I thought perhaps we could discuss doing something different."

Interested, Sister Anne lifted her head. "What do you mean?"

"This is best done in person. Can we meet in 30 minutes at the Breakfast Club, it's down the road from Trinity, walking distance for someone as fit as you. We can have an early lunch," Father Michael said.

"Of course, see you soon," Sister Anne said, hanging up. His comment on her fitness made her uncomfortable.

She pocketed the phone, turned and went inside to tell Sanders of her meeting. Going over to her sleeping bag and luggage in the improvised shelter, she changed shoes from flat pumps to gray sneakers, then slid on a thin cardigan over her white blouse, the morning air too cool for her. Soon she was walking toward the Breakfast Club at a brisk pace.

From her vantage point in the maroon truck parked up the street from Trinity, Michelle saw Sister Anne turn onto the sidewalk and head toward the Breakfast Club. She picked up the phone from her lap and hit Redial.

"Has she left?" Father Michael asked.

"Yeah."

"Good, let's get this over with. Meet me at the Breakfast Club before she gets there."

"Sure thing, honey," Michelle said and hung up.

Michelle then dialed another number.

Stavos Gruner barked, "What now, I'm busy!"

"It's about the matter of Father Michael's inquisitive friend. I told you he's gone crazy," Michelle said.

"The last thing we need is news or attention. A dead nun from St. Rita will only create questions. But we cannot take the chance she will go back to St. Rita when operations are under way or that she'll be talking to people," Stavos said.

"What do you want me to do?"

"Bring them both to me, I'll decide," Stavos said, and hung up.

Michelle pressed on the accelerator and pulled into the street, did a U-turn and sped away. She parked near the Breakfast Club and got out of her truck. Standing by the restaurant entrance, Father Michael saw Michelle and walked over to her.

Looking over her shoulder, Michelle said, “She’s a few minutes away. Where are you parked?”

“On Fourth Street.”

“I think we should both talk to her,” Michelle said.

“WHAT! No.”

“She’s looking for answers, right? Let’s use that to get her in your car,” Michelle said, smiling.

“I don’t know, I’m not sure,” he said.

She put one hand on Father Michael’s arm. “Trust me,” Michelle said with another glance over her shoulder.

Sister Anne, no more than 20 yards away, looked straight at Father Michael.

“Okay,” Father Michael said and moved around Michelle. He stepped toward Sister Anne.

Michelle turned and leaned against the white stucco wall of the small beach restaurant to open her purse. Reaching past her 50v Taser, she pulled a pack of cigarettes and lifted out a single stick. With a butane lighter, she torched the end and took a long puff. She blew the smoke out when Sister Anne and Father Michael stepped up next to her.

“Michelle, I’d like you to meet Sister Anne,” Father Michael said.

Sister Anne remembering the name stared then said, without smiling. “Hello.”

“Yeah.”

Father Michael, his hand on Anne’s back, gently pushed her into a huddle with Michelle. “Sister Anne, we can talk about Sofi and Cecilia later. Michelle has some things to tell us but this is not a convenient place to talk.”

Sister Anne’s eyebrows rose. “Why?”

Michelle spoke up and she glanced down the street. "I have information I think you'd be interested in. But I'd be a more comfortable if we had some privacy, maybe in Father Michael's car?"

Father Michael said, "That sounds good. Sister, this way."

"All right, if that helps you," Anne said looking directly at Michelle.

Father Michael and Michelle, on either side, walked her to the car. Michelle, casually dressed, wore jeans and a lacy short-sleeved blouse under a dark jacket. Sister Anne noticed tattoo work under the blouse but couldn't make out what.

Sister Anne's pulse raced and she tensed her shoulders. The last time she'd had this feeling was back in Iraq whenever the sirens warned of incoming mortar fire. Getting to the car, Michelle opened the rear door to let Sister Anne in and she followed immediately.

Father Michael got into the front, driver's side, and turned around to address Michelle. "Please tell us what you know."

Michelle had taken off her jacket and was fumbling in her purse. Sister Anne glanced at the leopard's mouth devouring Michelle's shoulder.

Sister Anne looked back at Father Michael and said, "Wait, how do you know—" Her question went unanswered as Michelle pressed the taser hard into Sister Anne's shoulder long enough to knock out the inquisitive nun.

39

Cybil and Ed walked without speaking for the first 50 yards after leaving the dojo, heading over to MacPherson's. The breeze had picked up; the inland evening temperature around Savannah dropped fast, drawing in the Atlantic's moist air. They headed west on Broughton toward Barnard Street; Molly's was about three blocks away. Just before they left, she texted Judy: on the way.

Ed broke the silence. "So, I guess your ass is still chapped that Sonja sent me to babysit you on this, huh?" Ed smiled and added a chuckle. With his right hand he brushed his dark-brown, medium-length hair that had been blown in the slight wind.

Cybil gritted her teeth but kept her gaze forward. "Tactful as always, Ed. This is my town and don't screw it up like you did Cyprus."

"That was not my damn fault. I had no idea the driver had been switched. All cab drivers there looked alike to me," Ed said.

"Maybe if you had read the briefing instead of trolling at the hotel bar, you'd have seen the cab company's name on the alert list," Cybil said.

"Ah, you're just sore I got married," Ed said, grinning. "As hot as we were together, I'm taken now." He held up his hand, toggling his wedding band back and forth with his thumb.

Cybil shook her head, unsuccessful in shaking the memory of the quick tryst, the result of too many drinks after an end to a tough case. At the bar they went to he acted like a jerk talking about his family's money and Harvard law. After several rounds, he became the lounge's comedian. She laughed at the lame jokes and his smile became more appealing with every martini he bought her. When he kissed her at the hotel door, she kissed back instead of slapping him. For a month afterward he kept making it more than it was, until she threatened to bring Sonja into it.

"I'm happy for you, now let's get back to business. Did you *read* this briefing?" Cybil said, her voice rising.

"I did. Sorry about your friend, John. Now tell me about the rest of your team here," Ed said.

"Judy and Benny are local tech entrepreneurs who are part of the New Savannah, but have connections through parents and uncles to old money. I've done pro bono modeling and voice acting to help promote their small businesses, and they return the favor when I need information. They don't know anything about the agency work," Cybil said looking around.

Ed nodded.

"Sonja messaged me about using the Ted Randall cover. You know, the ex-cop from Atlanta discharged for excessive use of force, now just a dick," Cybil said, looking sideways at Ed.

"Private Dick. Love you too. What's tonight's meeting for?" Ed said.

"Before the funeral I got texts that they wanted a face-to-face. We couldn't talk there. I'm not sure what info they have."

They stopped at the Jefferson Street intersection. A ghost tour carriage pulled by a weary horse passed before them, headed south, hoof clops landing heavy on the paved road. A smiling tourist couple in the carriage waved at them. After 30 seconds, Cybil and Ed stepped off the curb and stopped in the street. Horse manure in front of them blocked their path.

"Cute little town," Ed said as he stepped over the smelly pile.

She did the same while frowning.

Cybil turned the corner and headed north on Montgomery Street. "It's two blocks down and then a right. Been here three years, love the city, people. But working without a cover leaves me and my kids exposed. Tonight I'm telling Sonja to cut me out of this."

"She's not gonna like it. I'll take lead," he said.

Cybil kept looking straight ahead. "Ed, that's not my call. After you meet the team and we figure out what they have, report in. Sonja will know what to do."

Cybil stopped in front of the large glass-paned door of Molly MacPherson's Scottish Pub and Grill. The inset windows were foggy and condensation clung to the glass. Molly's always had the air down too low. Knowing this she had changed into dark skinny jeans, sling-back heels and a form fitting black long sleeved blouse.

Ed reached for the door and opened it, letting Cybil in first. Looking left, then right, she saw Judy and Benny sitting at a booth, side by side, in the far corner. *Good and private,* she thought.

Ed slid into the empty bench seat, Cybil next to him. She placed her small clutch next to her.

"Guys, this is Ted from Atlanta. Ted, Judy and Benny," Cybil said as the three shook hands.

Ted reached into his front shirt pocket, pulled out two business cards and slid one to each. TED RANDALL, PRIVATE INVESTIGATIONS headlined the card.

Cybil leaned on the table and said, “What have you guys found?”

From her purse, Judy pulled out a photo of a woman’s naked upper torso tattooed with an elaborate snow leopard biting the shoulder. She slid it across the table in front of Ed and Cybil.

“It took me a while,” Judy said, “but I found the shop and artist that did this. He’s a talker, loved to go on about his work and his former party habits. Swears he’s clean these days. Told me all about his client and gave me a copy of his work.”

“Who is she?” Ted said.

“Her name is Michelle. She used to hook him up with what he needed, as he said, in the old days. Two years back he owed her money and did the tat as a favor. Not bad work for a meth head,” Judy said.

“Anything more?” Cybil said, keeping her eyes steady.

Cybil recognized the name from her conversation with Blitz at The cSpot.

Judy looked over at a smiling Benny who was holding up a finger to his lips. The server approached, and they stopped talking as she stepped to the table.

“What can I get you to drink?” the server said. Noticing the photo she added, “Hey, that’s a nice tat. Been thinking of getting another, on my ankle.”

Cybil ordered a cranberry vodka martini, Ed, a lager. Judy and Benny already had their drinks. After the server left, Benny leaned forward.

Shaking his head, he said, “I got a hold of UnD0x3d and had to promise him a rematch before he’d help.”

“Sounds like him,” Cybil said.

“Yesterday I get an encrypted download from him, a huge zip file of documents, spreadsheets, statements. I haven’t gotten through it all, but I did find something weird,” Benny said.

“Define weird,” Ted said.

“I looked at the auditor reports to see if they highlighted anything unusual for a nonprofit. For private foundations, funding usually comes from investment income, from a single large endowment and/or other large single donations. St. Rita depended on one large endowment and it kept getting smaller every few months over the last two years. The auditor report cited poor performance in the investment fund, which was heavily leveraged in mortgages and in Bernie Madoff securities,” Benny said.

“What’s weird about that?” Ted said. “Anybody involved in mortgage investments and Bernie Madoff would have been wiped out in this marketplace.” He looked to the side as the server returned with drinks.

No one spoke while she placed the vodka martini and lager in front of Cybil and Ted. The server left and Cybil picked hers up and drained half of it.

Ted looked at her and grinned. “Hey, wait for me.” He picked up his glass, blew away a little foam and took a sip.

Benny’s face seemed to widen as he tapped once on the table for emphasis and said, “You’d think so, except I had UnD0x3d drill down on the investment fund allocation, whose disclosure is not normally required. But UnD0x3d did his magic and found that they had very little in the Madoff funds, but over 80 percent in Savannah Land and Trust Ltd.”

Cybil, taking another sip, choked. “Wait a second, did you say Savannah Land and Trust?”

“Yeah, why?” Benny said.

“It’s connected to Stavos Gruner according to what Blitz told me. What else about it?” Cybil said.

“Well, the ownership trail leads to offshore Caribbean companies and accounts, which typically means the owners don’t want to be found or identified, but the fund’s poor performance has drained all of St. Rita’s operating capital. No choice but to close. I’m surprised they lasted this long,” Benny said. “Yellow Tuna studios is my third venture and one thing I’ve learned, cash is everything.”

Cybil leaned back and crossed her arms, her right hand rubbing above her left elbow. She said, “Ted, what do you think?”

He looked across the booth to Judy and Benny. “Okay, all we know is an orphanage ran out of money and had to close. Maybe the investment fund went south, but why, we’re not sure. Could be a hundred reasons why they went offshore … save on taxes, a donor wanted to be anonymous. This tattoo girl has a connection to Stavos and St. Rita which is not good. But we need more before we can start poking around harder.”

“I agree. Judy, thanks. Benny, finish scrounging around the financial information and text or e-mail anything else you find. Send it on to Ted,” Cybil said.

Judy shifted in her seat and reached across the table to retrieve the photo. “I’m going to keep this for reference. I like the work. One thing though, Cybil. Did John find anything before … you know.”

"No, he never contacted me. But the police said his laptop was stolen. Benny, John had told me you helped him last year setting up remote backup. Anything there we can use?"

Benny said, "Absolutely."

Ted's face screwed up as he said, "Why so confident?"

"Last year John's house got hit by lightning and fried his laptop. He lost two months' worth of work, all the drafts and schematics for a large project he was working on. Almost cost him the job. John asked me to help him get an online backup service going. It took a whole five minutes over the phone to hook him up. He couldn't come up with a password so I suggested his dog's name, which he loved. I doubt he changed it and even if he did, UnD0x3d can crack it. We can download his entire backup and scan through it for anything including communications to you, Cybil," Benny said as he rubbed his hands together. "Yep, should be easy."

Cybil looked across the booth to Judy and Benny, frowned and said, "I hate to go through a dead friend's records." Taking a loud breath, Cybil said, "But we need to know what he found—if anything—that can help us. I guess we have no choice. Do it and send Ted what you find."

Judy started to slide out of the booth and, looking at Cybil, said, "Are you going to the Legal Society fundraiser at the Hilton tomorrow? You know my dad's on the board and always wants his whole family there, so I'm going."

"Yes, why?"

"I don't want to go alone. Want to ride in together?" Judy said as she finished extracting herself and stood by the booth.

"I'd love to, but I promised Blitz I'd be his date. He wants me to make an entrance alone so he can meet me at the door and slow-walk me around the room doing introductions. That's Blitz, lots of show," Cybil said.

Benny was looking down at his cell phone and texts. He said, "I just hit UnD0x3d that we need to do more. My iPad's in the car. I'm going over to the SCAD library to get online with him. Their Wi-Fi is uberfast."

"Judy, Benny, you have my card, e-mail and private cell. Text or call with updates, I'll do the same. And one more thing," Ted said, finishing his lager and dropping the glass on the table with a thud, "don't take any chances."

Judy nodded and Benny said, "Understood," as they both slid out and stood up.

Benny gave Judy a hug and they both nodded to Cybil and Ed before walking away from the table. Cybil slid out and took the seat across from Ed. He pushed the martini glass over to her, and she picked it up and drained it.

"Nice team," Ed said.

"Yes, thanks for warning them. I should have listened to John. He warned us, but I pushed," Cybil said, holding her glass up for a refill as she leaned out the booth.

The server, at another table, saw the request and gave Cybil a thumbs-up.

"We need to recon St. Rita, find out more," Cybil said, pulling back in. "Anne almost got caught. Can't believe she tried that, but she did get the info on the equipment. I told her to stay put for now."

"She sounds interesting, an ex-Airborne solider, now a nosy nun. You guys have history?" Ed asked, grinning. "Please tell me you have history. You know, shower buddies, private yoga stretching sessions, Army girl stuff, I'm asking but I won't tell."

Cybil narrowed her eyes at him. "You wish. What's the matter, Ed, need a little imagination boost for your alone time tonight?"

Ed laughed. "No need for that. The wife and I have a nice phone routine when I travel."

"Didn't need to know that," Cybil said, her face scrunching up.

Ed looked into his empty glass. "We could use some real data. Do you think Sonja can get a full-spectrum satellite overpass?"

Cybil shook her head. "Yeah, for a Level 1 threat, not this one. No justification to move space assets over a domestic target unless there's a pending threat. All we have are suspicions. That's what I hate about the movies and TV. They make it look so easy to deploy technology to get information and move a story along. It still takes eyes, boots on the ground, experience and brains to make a decision," Cybil said as she tapped her temple a few times.

The server arrived with two vodka martinis. "Would you like an appetizer?"

Ed looked down at the two drinks and then up at the server. "I don't think my friend is interested in food tonight."

Cybil picked up one of the glasses and made sure her middle finger was out as she took a sip, the sour taste tightening her eyes on Ed. The server left.

"I'd love to join you, like the last time," Ed said, smiling, "I'm going back to the Hilton to report in, tell Sonja what's up. I'll scope out a recon plan. Even though you're out I'll keep you posted. So you really out?"

"Tonight," Cybil said.

Ed nodded and scooted out of the booth quickly. Cybil had finished one drink and pushed the empty glass to the table's edge. She didn't look up or say anything to Ed as he walked out of Molly's.

Cybil looked around. The nearby booths were empty. Opening her clutch she saw the two white pills in a micro-baggie, next to her thin leather wallet, a gift from William. She lifted the plastic bag and placed it on the table next to the wide martini glass base. After a few seconds she put the bag back inside and closed the clutch. Lifting the glass to her lips she sipped the bitter-sweet liquid. As soon as it touched her tongue she stopped and put the glass down.

"What the hell," she said, retrieving the plastic bag again.

Lifting the full glass, she contemplated it and said, "Here's to you, John … and William," and tilted her head back, washing down the pills.

40

"Hmmff, hhhuhh." Sister Anne's slow return to consciousness included muffled attempts at talking through the duct tape wrapped around her mouth and neck. The jammed tape in her mouth prompted saliva that squished out and dripped over dried spit already on her chin. She twisted her neck to loosen the stiffness. Opening her eyes she could see nothing through the tightly knotted blindfold.

Taking a deep breath through her nose, the rank odor of exhaust and rubber stung. She puffed a couple times to clear the offensive smell. Her hands, bound in front of her, hurt due to thin plastic bands cutting into her wrists. Her ankles felt the same way. She lay in a fetal position on her right side. Under the blindfold edges some light sneaked in. She lifted her head to try to peek through the blindfold's bottom, to focus on anything. Suddenly the floor pushed her up into the air a few inches and she crashed down, her head hitting something hard and metallic. A sharp, sticking pain, like the edge of a desk, poked at her rib cage. The movement woke her more. She sensed the rolling motion of being in a car. The car made a turn, and she started to roll. More alert now, Sister Anne braced herself against something with her feet. Her head jostled and landed on rubbery hardness that smelled like a tire. She began to realize: *I'm in a trunk of a car!*

Sister Anne's heart beat rapidly. *Damn it*. Father Michael and Michelle! She moved her hands to her side, trying to feel for her cell phone in her left pocket … it was gone. She exhaled through her nose and closed her eyes to pray. She just finished the words "deliver us from evil" when the car stopped.

She heard a latch give way as the trunk opened, and bright ambient light streamed through and around her blindfold.

"Markos," a commanding voice said.

A pair of massive hands grabbed her around her torso. They hoisted her up; an arm went under her head, another under her legs. She then was placed on her feet, gravel under her shoes.

"Stay still," Michelle said loudly, her hands roughly pulling the duct tape off Anne's mouth and neck. Hair stuck to the tape tore away, hurting her.

Her hands remained bound and the blindfold was taken off. After a few blinks her eyes, fully opened, saw in front of her a medium-height man of athletic build. He was well-groomed, with black hair and dark, scary eyes. Looking down, she saw he wore boat shoes. Lifting her head she saw beside him, the men from St. Rita and Father Michael, who was looking down. Michelle stepped back and joined the group.

Sister Anne gasped as she looked past them to see St. Rita. They smiled.

The dark-eyed man said, "Hello, Sister Anne, my name is Stavos Gruner. I have a few questions for you—and by the way, welcome home."

41

"How about I bring some coffee, miss?" the server at Molly's said as she picked up another empty martini glass.

Cybil leaned forward and started to fall before her hands hit the table to support her. "Why? You asked me that last time," Cybil said, her voice unsteady. "Where's the ladies' room again?"

The server pointed to the small hallway behind the corner booth where Cybil was sitting. "Right behind you, miss."

Cybil leaned out of the booth and turned her head slowly to look back. "Gotcha," and then her hand resting on the table slipped.

The server reached out and caught Cybil's arm and held her up so she wouldn't tumble to the floor.

Leaning on the server she pushed up out of the booth and stood. Cybil leaned to one side, placing a hand on the server's shoulder. She motioned without words to the server for her clutch on the seat, which the young lady retrieved.

"I'm fine, just have another waiting for me," Cybil said as she walked carefully to the restroom.

After entering one of the stalls and taking care of business, Cybil moved to the sink to wash her hands. Wicker baskets with plastic plants lined the spaces between sinks. The restroom smelled like cherries; the automatic deodorizer must had been spraying every few minutes. Focusing on the space next to the sink she noticed her clutch purse missing.

"Damn, where is it?" she said out loud.

Turning around, she went back into the stall. *Where the hell is it?* She stepped out and moved to the next one. A woman leaving one of the nearby stalls looked at her and shook her head. Cybil entered the stall and saw it on the tile floor. She leaned down to reach for it but had to brace herself against the smooth wall. Her hand slipped and somehow she turned herself around. Plopped down on the toilet she thought, *Huh, back here again.*

She reached down, grabbed her clutch and placed it under her arm. Then her hand searched her jeans pocket for her iPhone. After scrolling through several numbers she found the one she wanted. Slowly thumbing a message she sent it. Closing her eyes for a moment, then another, then another, her grasp soon relaxed. The clutch fell first, followed by the phone, slipping to the restroom floor and skidding outside her stall door. Her body lax and head against the bathroom wall, she took a deep breath. In seconds, through the door, a soft snoring sound reverberated.

*

"Cybil, Cybil, you okay? Wake up." A familiar voice intruded into her dream of a sailboat.

Bleary-eyed, Cybil squinted and looked up to see the stall door open and Tom standing there.

"What the hell you doing in the ladiessh room?" Cybil said as she threw her arms across her body and drew her knees together.

"Relax, I thought you might need a little help tonight," Tom said, stepping in and putting his hands under her armpits to lift her.

Hustling her out of the stall, he put his arm around her waist and walked her back to the booth. She slipped a couple of times but Tom had a firm grip on her.

From across the room, the server saw the assist and walked up to them, saying, "Coffee for both of you?"

"Yes, lots, and black," Tom said as he reached into his pocket and placed Cybil's phone on the table.

He took the clutch pinched under his arm and put it next to the phone. He slid in next to her to make sure she didn't fall over.

Cybil folded her arms on the table and plopped her head on them. "I'm going to throw up. Why are you here? Aren't you supposed to pick up someone at the airport?"

"Yes, my wife," he said.

Cybil lifted her head enough to turn it the other direction, away from Tom, and she let out a little moan. The server returned with two coffees. Tom badgered Cybil into drinking half of it before she pushed the cup away and placed her head down again on her arms. Tom sipped his coffee, letting Cybil rest for a few seconds. He then put his cup down with a thud.

Cybil's head lifted up. "Huh?"

"Drink some more, girl," Tom said as he slid her cup toward her.

Sixty minutes passed with this same routine until Cybil now sat up straighter, taking sips every minute or so. Tom slid out over the vinyl bench and moved across the booth to face her.

He picked up his coffee, looked over the rim before taking a sip and said, "You better?"

"Better, no. Sobering up, yeah. Why are you here?" she said.

Tom smiled. "I'm at the hotel, zoning out, watching TV, and I get this text from you. It says: Sonka I oyt, rpln katr, which makes no sense to me. One, I don't know a Sonka but I figured if you're too drunk to text, someone should make sure you get home okay," he said. "Your last Foursquare tweet had you at the dojo. I put on my sweats and headed there. Dan told me you had a meeting here."

"Okay," she said, exhaling and taking another sip.

She turned sideways to look out the booth window. Decorative electric torch lamps shone on empty streets, indicating it was late.

"Who's Sonka?" Tom said, tilting the cup to finish off his brew.

"Friend of mine. She is going to take over something I'm working on. Hate to leave her to it, but I have to," Cybil said, looking out the booth window again.

Tom smiled. "Some of your 'other' work you never talk about?"

"My 'other' work is not supposed to happen in Savannah. Someone I used to care about shows up here, where I live, and needs help. I should have walked away," she said, shaking her head. "Maybe John would still be alive."

Tom stayed quiet for a second, then grabbed his empty cup with both hands and looked into it. "Death and suffering sometimes have a way of clarifying things, but not always," he said.

"What?" Cybil said, her eyes straining to open wider but the bright light from the overhead lamp preventing it. She raised her hand to shield her eyes. "It's a little late and I'm not sure I have the stomach for one of your deep-shit talks right now."

Tom looked down with a small smile. "I hear ya. … Have I told you about Serena's work in Africa?" Tom said

Cybil nodded slightly. "Yes, something about teaching women micro-business skills, reading, counseling, empowerment. Working with some groups over there, I think. Can't remember the country right now."

"Liberia. Well, death over there is ever present, unlike here. Pain and suffering, the same. After 14 years of civil war resulting in a ruined infrastructure, broken families, orphans and 95 percent of the women having been raped, you have a deeply wounded society where expectations about life are different from here."

The server stepped into view with a full coffee pot and refilled both their cups.

"Thanks," Tom said.

Cybil said, "Yes, thank you very much."

The waitress smiled and left them alone.

Tom took a deep breath then said, "You know, the kids are given flowers on their birthday to enjoy because the saying is, give them a flower today, they may not be here next year. Life is lived in the moment rather than for some future which may never come," he said. "That makes long-term thinking hard and decision making impulsive."

Cybil frowned. "I almost didn't make it out of childhood. I dealt with death and suffering all the time in Iraq, I lost plenty of friends. Don't tell me I don't understand death and pain," she said, snapping the last word out harder than she wanted.

"Still," Tom said, "what we consider normal or our birthright, which is plenty of food, medicine, 40-hour work weeks, vacations, cars and a long life, all dulls death's sting. That's one of the reasons why religion is waning. The death and hell scare tactic doesn't work anymore. I'm not sure it ever did. People need more than fear to understand the bigger picture."

Cybil thought of her conversation with Dan about submission and peace. This was beginning to sound like a sermon.

"Look," Cybil said, irritated, "the big picture? What kind of picture is it when a drunken son of a bitch crashes into the family van and wipes out everyone except the drunk. Or the creepy stepfather 'visits' his new daughters at night while the wife, in denial, is sleeping. What about the Russian sex trafficker buying the 14-year-old because she has larger breasts than her 16-year-old sister? Did they have any choice what picture they were in?"

"My point exactly," Tom said.

"What do you mean?" Cybil said. Her fingers began strumming on the table.

Seeing it, Tom said, "Bear with me. Choices imply some type of possible order. We expect order and in a sense we expect Heaven on Earth, especially in the West. When we don't get it, God, the universe, your higher power or whatever it is, is dragged into our court of judgment."

Cybil rubbed the corners of her eyes, scraping away the gunked up mascara. She yawned at him while picking up her iPhone.

Tom continued. "We recognize that there should be more to the world than there is. There is more than we know. We sense that the big picture is broken and needs to be fixed. We struggle with that insight. … Who are you calling now?"

Cybil looked down. “No one. I’m checking messages.”

“Okay, mood change,” Tom said, grinning.

“What do you think my mood is now?” She stared at Tom, her eyebrows high.

He said, “Pissed off and wanting to go home.”

“Correct. Thanks for coming out, but I can find my way home,” she said.

Tom smiled and held up a set of keys, jangling them in front of her. “Nice try, but I’m driving you home. No argument. You need your beauty rest. Don’t you have a fundraiser tomorrow?”

“Shit!” Cybil said, slapping her forehead. “I never picked up the dress Blitz asked for, from the dry cleaner.”

“Oh, the silly problems of the young, beautiful and well-dressed. Let’s go,” Tom said, getting up from the booth.

Stepping outside of Molly’s, they turned right. Cybil’s car was around the corner, about 30 yards away. Tom put his elbow out and Cybil hooked her arm in to steady herself. The cool air felt nice, the small breeze lifting her shirt off her back for a second. She noticed a tall man walking in front of them, well built, with a short haircut. Every few steps he looked back. She and Tom took a few more steps and then footfalls echoed behind them. She glanced behind her and saw a stocky man walking with a much younger woman who was wearing a dark jacket, fishnet hose and a purse slung over her shoulder.

They turned the corner. Cybil’s BMW came into view on the side street. A large SUV was in front of it, which had not been there before.

Tom escorted her to the passenger side and pressed the fob, beeping to unlock the doors. The man who had walked in front of them stopped at the SUV and opened the back door. He then took a step toward them.

Cybil's heart rate increased. Her breathing quickened, like back in Iraq when the incoming mortar whistle screamed for everyone's attention. She tensed her shoulders and legs but weaved a little, not having fully recovered. Behind her she heard the scuffle of feet and the click of heels moving quickly toward them. She turned to see a smiling Tom looking at her. Behind him, moving fast, the stocky man had raised a thin black metal baton high in the air, the kind the cops extend from nowhere to subdue subjects.

The baton came crashing down on the side of Tom's head, just above the ear. Cybil felt a warm spray on her face. His eyes glazed over, red liquid flowing and covering his face. The image of the captain on the mission to capture the Snake flashed in her mind. Tom crumbled to the sidewalk.

To her left, Cybil's eye caught the woman approaching fast. Turning, she saw an outstretched hand coming toward her neck with a small black device making loud snapping and crackling sounds. *Taser!* Cybil took a quick side step. The Taser flew by her ear, the sound even louder. A metallic smell reached her nose. She threw a forearm block and simultaneously grappled the arm holding the Taser. This allowed her to slide her hand down to start a bending wrist hold. Cybil used her body, pushing hard and slammed the woman into the side of the car.

A look of surprise didn't last long on the woman's face as she turned red and gritted her teeth. Taller, full-breasted and with a strong upper body, she pushed back with some force, using the car as leverage and tried to slip the wrist hold. Cybil drove her knee into the woman's stomach. She bent over but still had the Taser button pressed down, the blue arc snapping.

A large shadow moved into Cybil's peripheral vision. The short, wide assailant stepped over Tom's body and closed in on the two women locked in a struggle. He got within arm's length and reached for Cybil. The woman gripping the arcing Taser tried to angle it into Cybil who, sensing the opportunity, twirled herself and lifted the woman's hand, redirecting the blue spitting points right into the approaching man's chest just above his heart.

She held it there, and the man's head, inches from Cybil's face, snapped up, his eyes opened wide. She could see his irises shrink. Then he started to shake and rock before stiffening. He stood suspended for a second, perfectly vertical, before falling backward like a tree severed at the base.

Cybil had had enough. She bent forward, jamming her rump into the woman and with both legs drove her back into the car. She bent the wrist further, waiting for the bone to snap. A sickening crack followed.

"Aaaaahhhh, you bitch!" the woman screamed as the Taser fell, hitting the curb and sliding under the car.

Cybil spun around and threw an elbow uppercut that found the woman's chin. Her head flew back. Her eyes closed as she went limp. She slid down the BMW's side and landed with a thump. Cybil took a step back and reflexively looked toward Tom lying on the sidewalk, not moving.

That was the last thing she saw before her vision went black. The man from the SUV struck the back of Cybil's head with the butt of his .45 and watched her fall, landing across Michelle.

42

"She's late!" Blitz Thompson groaned to himself as he stood in the lobby of the Hilton Hotel on Liberty Street. Noisy with guests and brightly lit, the Hilton and the fundraiser had become the center of Savannah's legal society for the night.

Again he watched another extended black limo pull up and disgorge well-dressed, coiffed and jeweled patrons. The annual fundraiser benefiting the United Way had taken in over $100,000 in donations last year from criminal, civil, patent, corporate and other attorneys. Half of the participants sitting, drinking and listening to speeches had helped the other half in settling divorces, keeping drunken sons and daughters out of jail, setting up trusts and reaching some accommodation with the law. Money could always bend the law to favor the rich and Thompson bent it well.

"Blitz, Blitz!" Judy shouted across the lobby, hand in the air. She had just left the restroom and moved toward him.

Blitz turned and recognized her from The cSpot meetings; they had talked several times, a little too hard-rock for his taste, plus the tattoos. But he waved at her to come on over; maybe she knew where Cybil was.

"Hi, Judy, you look nice," Blitz said.

"Thanks, it's a new outfit," Judy said, twirling around.

Blitz smelled strong musky perfume in the air coming from her. He smiled and looked out again through the lobby doors.

"Has Cybil arrived yet? I heard she's your date tonight," Judy said.

"Supposed to be. You don't know where she is?" Blitz said.

"She should be here. We met at Molly's for drinks yesterday. She was hitting it hard, though. Maybe to get ready for you." Judy reached out and gently slapped Blitz's upper arm. "Oh, still working out, Mr. Football?"

"Trying to keep the middle-age spread in check," Blitz said, patting his stomach.

Jazz music drifted from the back of the hotel, live from the fundraiser to entertain early guests. Judy looked out the door and then down to her large watch connected to rows of teal and azure beads strung together to make a watchband.

"It's still five minutes before the dinner, so technically she's not late, though she is usually early," Judy said, pressing her lips together.

She dropped her arm and the beads clinked. Her eyes scanned the lobby in case Cybil had snuck in through the side. Judy stopped and stared at a guest, dressed in casual clothes, in the sitting area looking at a laptop, his ear buds in and head nodding as if listening to music. He looked up and saw Judy. He lifted his hand and waved.

"Huh, he must be staying here," Judy said, waving back.

"Who?" Blitz said.

"That guy over there, that's Ted. He's a friend of Cybil's, an ex-cop from Atlanta. I met him last night," Judy said.

"Really," Blitz said, coughing, "Are … are they an item?"

"Not that I could tell, but you never know," Judy said, looking back toward him.

"She was supposed to be here early so we could mingle. There were a couple guys I wanted her to meet," Blitz said.

"Let me guess. Potential clients who would stammer at meeting Savannah's top model on your arm?" Judy said.

Blitz looked over at Judy and smiled. "Whatever it takes."

Judy faced the automatic lobby doors that swooshed open, then closed. "I'm sure she'll be here soon, she's always on time." She glanced to the side and said, "I wonder if Ted knows anything."

Ed Raintree had been keeping Judy and Blitz in his field of view, sneaking peeks as he worked his iPad. Ed sat with his back to the wall, no one near, his check-in with Sonja in progress. When communicating in the open, for appearances you listened but typed to talk.

Nothing new to report. Cybil didn't talk to you last night, did she? I'm hanging in the lobby until the fundraiser. I wanted her input on the recon for St. Rita, Ed typed in, then hit Send.

In the secure video chat window Sonja shook her head and said through Ed's earphones, "No she didn't. Make sure your recon is solid. No risks. Remember Cyprus and the hell I caught from State to get you and her out of there. I don't want to have to deal with Bubba Gump with a badge."

Ed typed: The deal on Cyprus wasn't that bad. Got a nice nap till the lawyers bailed us out.

"Shit, Ed, don't make me regret sending you. Find me something, anything, so I can send a team there or a least order a full electromagnetic spectrum remote scan," Sonja said.

Okay, okay, see you at the next checkpoint. we done? Ed typed.

On the screen, Sonja nodded her head and then immediately the video window closed. Ed looked up and saw Blitz and Judy still standing in the lobby, being passed by women in flowing gowns and men in tuxedos. Blitz looked at his wrist and then up at the doors.

Ed frowned and thought, *Cybil's never late.*

43

Cybil felt stuck, like sitting on a deep soft couch, unable to get up. Yet she was being pushed side to side; her stomach felt the motion. She took a sharp breath, and a sweet vanilla scent punched through. "Huh?"

Her eyelids opened a crack and she thought she heard Anne's voice, which was impossible. Slowly her hearing sharpened, the voice urgent, maybe angry: "Cybil, wake up." But she closed her eyes again and was out.

Anne's appeal failed again. Sitting in a metal folding chair, Anne's zip-tied hands chafed against the too-tight binding. The unconscious Cybil had been placed next to her, bound the same way, by Markos. After he plopped her down, she ended up leaning on Anne, out cold. He grinned, looked at the both of them, turned and walked out of Father Michael's office.

Cybil's head, hot and sweaty, rested on Anne's shoulder, quiet, at peace. Anne moved her body to nudge her, but stopped. The warmth pressing through Anne's sleeve made her pause. She closed her eyes. Dubai came rushing back and their long, deep talks about the future in between intense intimacy. She had never seen Cybil so happy, while her battle with doubt continued to wage. *Not now.*

Anne nudged Cybil several times with her shoulder, a couple of times knocking a leg into hers. Several times she said "Wake up," but in a soft voice. Finally she raised her voice and pushed as hard as she could, tipping both chairs off the ground an inch.

"Cybil, wake up!" Anne shouted and looked up immediately to Father Michael's office door.

"Huh, what?" Cybil said.

Her lips smacked and her jaws flexed before she drew a deep breath and then sat straight up. Her eyes struggled to open. Morning sun streaming in from a large panel window behind them brightly lit the room. She shook her head. The sweat from her forehead flew off and landed on the wood floor, several droplets forming a single line. Cybil took another deep breath in, her chest expanded and she tried to lift her hands up to touch her face. She couldn't.

"What the hell!" Cybil said, shifting her body against the restraints. The bound chairs resisted her energy and barely moved. She looked sideways and her eyes snapped wide open.

"Anne! What are you doing here?" Cybil said.

Anne smiled. "Nice to see you awake. I'm a guest, as you are."

"Shit, where are we?" she said.

"At St. Rita, in Father Michael's office," Anne said.

Cybil blinked, then closed her eyes for a second. "Who else is here?" she said.

"I've been here a couple of days. Father Michael and Michelle delivered me to Stavos. He has two big guys working for him, scary. The short, wide one is Markos. The other, Kurt," Anne said. "Hey, you've got some blood on your face. You okay?"

Cybil remembered the scuffle at the car, breaking Michelle's wrist and pushing the Taser into the short wide man who cold-cocked Tom. "Damn, I hope Tom is okay."

"What happened?"

"Tom was going to drive me home. I … I … needed a little help."

"I see," Anne said. "I remember."

Cybil's eyebrows rose. "Yeah, yeah. I think Markos and your Michelle attacked us at my car. They hit Tom on the head and he collapsed. I disarmed her, then I blacked out," Cybil said, and now she felt a throbbing on the back of her head. "Oh, my head." She craned her neck up.

"Turn around, let me look," Anne said. "Yes, you've got a nasty cut, dried blood and a bump."

"He must have hit me, the man next to the SUV," Cybil said

"Sorry … I think there are other people that I haven't seen. There is so much noise and commotion coming from downstairs. That basement was for storage and now it sounds like a factory. Plus this room gets hot off and on during the day and night. Sometimes I feel like I'm in an oven," Anne said.

"Interesting," Cybil said.

Anne looked at her and said, "What do we do now?"

Cybil paused for a moment. Her memory flashed to Dubai as she looked at Anne, whose very same words, "What do we do now," were spoken after an unforgettable weekend back there. Cybil had tried to bury that phrase in the months and years after Anne's sudden unexplained departure.

"What, what's the matter? You okay?" Anne said, searching Cybil's face.

Cybil exhaled. "I'm okay. I was supposed to go to a fundraiser and meet up with Ted Randall, someone who is helping us now. He'll know something's wrong, plus you'll be missed too."

Anne looked down and shook her head gently. "No, no, I won't be missed. Father Michael took care of that. He told me he had called Reverend Sanders and let him know I was doing a task for him out of town and would be gone for a few days. I guess they are almost done here, and then I don't know what happens to us." Anne's shoulders slumped as she finished her sentence.

Cybil's heart ached at Anne's words, "I won't be missed." She had been. Cybil and Anne didn't talk for a minute. Then Cybil leaned over and nudged Anne.

"Hey, remember the insurgent mortar attack the week before Dubai. We took cover behind the captain's Humvee," Cybil said.

"Yeah."

"One round came so close, the headlight shattered from the concussive force and your helmet flew off. You looked at me and started laughing. Freaked me out for a second, thought you lost it," Cybil said.

Anne let out a small laugh. "Yes, I remember."

"Do you remember what you said after that?" Cybil said.

Anne's eyes looked to the side and up, searching the ceiling for an answer. "No, do you?"

"Yes, you said I was thinking of changing my hair before our trip, but I won't have to with my head blown off," Cybil said, starting to laugh.

Anne laughed too. "Okay, I remember. I also peed in my pants but didn't tell you that!"

"Good thing, I wouldn't have let you live that down," Cybil said.

Anne smiled and nodded her head.

Smiling, Cybil said, "We still need to—"

She and Anne looked up toward the door, hearing footfalls and voices coming closer. The wooden lobby floors of St. Rita had given them audible advanced notice.

The brass knob turned. The large, ornately carved door cracked open slowly at first, then swung quickly the rest of the way. It pushed air into the room and a warm draft swept over Anne and Cybil.

Fully alert, Cybil recognized all three of her assailants from Molly's. They preceded a handsome man, well-dressed in boat shoes, tan slacks and a white short-sleeved fringed shirt. He had a tanned, athletic build and an olive complexion.

Anne whispered under her breath, "That's Stavos."

Cybil instinctively lurched forward a second toward him, the man she was sure had killed John Block. Her chair inched forward, the force strong enough to pull Anne along.

Stavos stopped and turned and appeared to talk to someone behind him, the open door blocking Cybil's and Anne's view of the trailing person. Stavos looked back to the pair and focused on Cybil, whose eyes narrowed, locking with his.

Stavos nodded his head and said out loud, "I see what you mean by the eyes, Mr. Kasen. I'd love to see them in a more friendly setting, but we shouldn't delay your reunion."

The procession in front of Stavos moved toward the desk and stood there, all with arms folded. Stavos took a step to the side and with his right arm made a sweeping motion to usher in his guest.

Mr. Kasen stepped casually into the room, moving past the door and coming into full view. He limped a few steps before stopping. Dark-complexioned, with closely spaced eyes set in a triangular face, his head seemed to float over a tall, thin neck. He wore a lab coat over dress slacks and a long-sleeved shirt. On his chin, a thick, twisty scar curled downward. He looked at Cybil for a few seconds, before smiling.

Cybil's mind raced, her heart beating faster to catch up. She saw his smile, gasped and screamed inside her head: *The SNAKE! Al-Mahdi Al-Rashid!*

44

Ed Raintree snapped open the window curtains. He squinted from the dull morning light, cloudy and gray despite the sun fully risen over the Atlantic. From the top floor of the Savannah Hilton on Liberty Street, he viewed the city. From here he could see over the historic downtown district to the Savannah River Channel. The channel ran close to the city's edge, to Veterans Park and the touristy Bay Street. A large tanker moved slowly out through the channel.

At street level, you can't see the water, so the ship would look like it was motoring down the street, a crazy thing. This tanker moved out toward the sea, stacked five containers high, maybe filled with cargo, maybe empty. *I wonder where this one is going*.

The distinct "ding, dingle, ding" alarm tones he had set for his check-in call with Sonja sounded from his iPad. He rubbed his eyes and took a deep breath. The coffee and Red Bulls he inhaled all night to keep him going lost their effect around 4:00 a.m. and he still had not found Cybil.

Ed sat down at the small desk next to the window and stared at his screen. He reached out and finger tapped the unit's icon, the Japanese kanji symbol for stealth.

忍
術

Sonja's idea to use the symbol as an informal unit moniker displeased her superiors, as juvenile. The team liked it since it paid homage to half of her heritage and personalized the sometimes faceless work. Within a few seconds the secure connection formed and Sonja's face appeared in the chat window. He leaned forward.

"Report," Sonja said, normal opening banter gone.

No earphones were needed; he was alone in the hotel room.

Ed spoke in a low voice: "Cybil's missing. None of her Creative team has heard from her. Judy and I saw her last at Molly MacPherson's. She was drinking when I left. Her cell phone GPS track signal is off the grid, she's not at home, her car was not in the garage. Her tweets and Facebook streams are off. I hit most of Savannah's clubs last night looking for her. Maybe she was blowing off steam. I found her car parked down from Molly's. I saw some blood splatter on the car door."

Sonja nodded her head. "Damn. What about the St. Rita recon?"

"I never got to that as planned. When she didn't show I gave her an hour before starting the search. Do you think you can send a team now?" Ed said.

Sonja shook her head. "No exigent circumstance exists yet—almost, but not quite."

"What do you mean almost, what about the blood splatter?" Ed said, leaning closer to his iPad and staring into the video window.

"Inconclusive. Could have been from someone else or road kill the night before. We'll get back to that. Something else has come up," she said.

"What?"

"A facial recognition flag connected to Cybil's file popped up yesterday. I had to get additional permission from the director for resources to do a correlation analysis. He now has an eye on this assignment," Sonja said.

"Is the analysis complete?"

"Just finished reading it this morning," she said.

"Keep talking," he said.

"Cybil's Airborne unit in Iraq smashed a sophisticated IED operation outside of Fallujah. They captured the leader, called the Snake, Al-Mahdi Al-Rashid, a Yemen-born Sunni Muslim. Al-Mahdi was an American-educated chemical and electrical engineer who left to return home before the fighting began and found his way into Iraq to fight for the cause. We renditioned him to the Saudis. He died in a Riyadh hospital after a particularly 'thorough' interrogation," Sonja said.

"Yeah, thorough the Saudis are," Ed said.

He leaned back and grabbed his shoulder and rubbed it. During an exchange training visit, he spent one hour in simulated interrogation at a Riyadh airbase. They apologized profusely for dislocating his shoulder.

Sonja said, "His face gets a hit at Reagan Airport, Washington, DC, of all places. It took longer because the software focuses on living terrorists first, then scans dead ones—"

"Because sometimes they are not dead, like our 'deceased' deep-cover operatives," he said.

"Right. Worse, the doctor, who signed his death certificate, moved to Iran to practice medicine. Tehran, I believe," Sonja said.

"Iran again. Now is this enough for a team?"

"Nope, all we have is a missing agent known to go on benders and perhaps a long-dead terrorist now alive in the U.S., maybe. Yes, Al-Mahdi is an expert in explosives, but the facial recognition match barely passed the 85 percent threshold with a clean face. When they scanned bin Laden after Team Six got through with him, his match went over 95 percent even with a hole under his left eye," she said.

"Ninety-five percent? Must have been a small hole," Ed said.

"In the front, not much left in the back. Anyway, I can't authorize more resources on what I have now. I need more. You need to find Cybil and recon St. Rita. Have you talked to Sister Anne?"

"No, didn't get a chance. I'll find her this morning and see if she's heard anything," Ed said.

"Good. Forget the check-in schedules, keep me updated as you go along," Sonja said and hung up, the video window closing.

Ed stood up and, looking through the window again, over the city, said, "Cybil, why didn't you tell Sonya and where the hell are you?"

45

Cybil's deep-blue eyes flashed, boring in on the Snake's face. Her breathing picked up, she shuffled her feet to get up but could only lean forward, straining against her bindings. The metal chair creaked. The last time she'd seen Al-Mahdi was in Fallujah. She had barreled into him, helmet first, at high speed and stopped his escape from the captain's tent—but too late to save her commander.

A thin smile crawled across his face. He had followed Stavos into the wood-paneled room. Another man, in a lab coat like the one Al-Mahdi wore, stood behind him, younger, also Middle Eastern–looking. Al-Mahdi passed a clipboard he held in his right hand to his associate. His left hand, holding a pen, rose. He clicked the pen, retracting the point and slid it into his coat pocket like a knife into a sheath. Hanging off the pocket was a small badge-like device, thick, which enclosed a milky, translucent plastic.

Al-Mahdi came closer to Cybil, every step sounding out on the wood floor. He stood before her, and she looked up. Their eyes met, his dark, narrow slits closing.

"Late again," Al-Mahdi said, raising his hand and striking her hard across the mouth.

The slap echoed.

The strike turned Cybil's head sideways and her lip spilt. Licking it, she tasted blood. Turning her face back toward Al-Mahdi, she glared but said nothing, glancing at the device on his pocket.

Anne had muffled a gasp at the slap. She closed her eyes and bent her head forward. Her lips moved but she did not speak. Her tied hands moved up, wanting to touch Cybil, but couldn't. Opening her eyes she looked to see Cybil staring at Al-Mahdi.

"I see you noticed this," Al-Mahdi said, tapping the badge device twice with a long, thin finger.

He smirked, turned around and walked over to Stavos and his group. His associate trailed behind.

Stavos, relaxed, sitting on the edge of Father Michael's desk, leaned over, looking past the approaching Al-Mahdi, at Cybil and Anne. He shook his head and smiled.

Kurt laughed, Markos nodded his head.

Michelle sat on the desk, her fishnet-stocking legs dangling and swinging. Her bandaged wrist lay in her lap. A black-and-blue bruise shone prominently on her chin.

Stavos looked at Michelle and said, "Go get Father Michael. He's working on the preparations I told you about. Make sure he finishes, and check his work. I want the rest of this place cleaned up and ready for the next client."

Michelle popped off the desk, her heels striking the floor loud. She left the room.

Al-Mahdi moved closer to Stavos and the group assembled at the desk. They huddled close; Cybil and Anne could barely hear them talking. Then they walked out of the room together, closing the door.

Cybil lifted her head and swallowed a couple times. Her throat parched, she grimaced through the effort. She licked her lips again. The congealed blood had bandaged the split.

"Who is the man who hit you?" Anne whispered, looking at the door.

"The Snake, Al-Mahdi. My unit captured him in Fallujah and smashed his IED factory network. Turned things around in the region. Gave us time to work with the village elders," Cybil said.

Anne's eyebrows scrunched together. "I don't remember that mission."

Cybil turned to her. "That's because you left a week before I was picked for that operation," Cybil said, her eyes staring into Anne's.

Anne sighed and looked down. "I'm sorry, after Dubai, I couldn't … I …"

"Now's not a good time to talk about it. I need to figure a way out of this."

"Got an idea? Let me help, I can do more than pray," Anne said.

Cybil laughed. "Maybe we need more prayer." She tilted her head toward the door. "Al-Mahdi's god seems to have things his way. Maybe yours and his can come to an agreement."

"Don't laugh," Anne said, her face close to a scowl.

"Sorry, but I've gotten along fine without him and when he seems to be in the mix, I get less than what I want. Been that way from the start," Cybil said.

"What do you mean?" Anne said.

"Oh, never mind," Cybil said, shaking her head.

"No, I want to know," Anne said.

Cybil frowned. “I don’t have use for a God who cannot even hear a child’s prayer.”

“Cybil, God hears all prayers,” Anne said, her voice softening.

Cybil paused, her face lost a little color, and she spoke slowly. “Not mine, not while hiding in my closet while my parents fought. Or while chemo was being poured into my veins. Doctor’s cured me, not faith or prayers.”

Anne blinked as she looked at Cybil. “You have been blessed with more than just survival. You have friends, a career, beautiful children, you love them and they love you. It’s a miracle to be alive and to be loved.”

Cybil’s shoulders slumped. Quiet for a few seconds, she looked at Anne and her chest ached. Then she thought of Sebastian and June, alone, being raised by someone else. *Damn it to hell!*

“Are you okay?” Anne said.

“Alive! For how much longer? Thankful? I’d be a lot more thankful if others were doing their job, because I am not hearing any helicopter gunships and a SWAT team about to fast-rope down here.”

“Cybil, I don’t want to argue, especially now,” Anne said, her eyes moist. A thin smile grew into a confident one. “But I believe we will be fine. I trust in him. He has shown me. Just don’t try to control everything. Can you be patient?”

“What did you just say?” Cybil’s eyes opened wider. Both her pupils moved up and she remembered.

*

Cybil's radiologist nurse, kind faced, soft and plump, always talked to her gently during the many radiation sessions. Cybil recalled lying down on the table, getting ready again, to travel down the tube. Something dangled from the nurse's lab coat, and the little girl reached out to touch it. It was plastic, cold. The nurse said, "We have to be patient in this room. The invisible rays need time to work so they can help you. But they can hurt me if I'm not careful, so this helps me be careful. Can you be patient?"

*

Cybil's mind raced—IED factory in Fallujah—lead-melting ovens from Iran. Lead shielding—YES.

Cybil turned to Anne and said, "I'm going to see if I can get us out in the open, might have a chance then. Maybe Ted, a friend helping me, might be looking for me. Hang in there, it might get rough."

A grouping of footfall noises began coming through the closed door. Approaching closer and closer the noise built until the door opened. The group had returned, except for Michelle. They moved back to the desk, where Kurt unrolled a set of sea maps, and the group bent over to examine them.

Cybil's head turned toward them. "Al-Mahdi, I see you managed to escape our hospitality. Tell me, how are your Iranian brothers doing?"

Al-Mahdi stopped talking in mid-sentence and looked over his shoulder at Cybil, then turned back to the maps.

Cybil spoke louder, her voice dismissive: "I doubt the dirty bomb you're building will work. When we smashed your factories in Fallujah, our analysis showed your detonation device design was pretty flimsy. All this effort, too bad."

Al-Mahdi spun around. His eyes locked onto Cybil.

Cybil leaned over and whispered to Anne, "Hold on."

Al-Mahdi walked over to them, Stavos and his group followed. Abdul stayed at the desk. When Al-Mahdi stopped, Stavos moved to his left, Markos and Kurt to his right, forming a semicircle that surrounded the women.

"You know nothing," Al-Mahdi said.

"We know enough," Cybil said, scanning the room. "The lead-melting ovens downstairs are distilling cesium or U-235 your Iranian brothers gave you for your dirty bomb. Our satellite radiation sensors are more sensitive than you planned. The trace smoke coming from this place probably lit up their monitors at Space Command in Colorado. I'm sure you had to vent the hot air from downstairs. "

Kurt, looking surprised, turned and looked at Al-Mahdi, who held his gaze on Cybil.

Al-Mahdi laughed and clapped his hands in front of him. "I have spent some time in your cities studying. Even your Sin City in the desert. You make sport of everything to numb the empty materialism of your lives. I believe good poker card playing involves bluffing. You bluff because you think luck or fortune will soon be on your side—typical of American arrogance. You are sadly mistaken this time."

Cybil thought, *I need to get out in the open.* "You can't take the chance," she said to him. "They will be here soon. Stay. Suits me fine. I'd move out if I were you."

Al-Mahdi crossed his arms and leaned to one side, looking relaxed. "Mr. Stavos tells me your investigation that brought you here had nothing to do with my operation. I could tell from the look in your eyes when you first saw me. You were not expecting me. I doubt your government knows anything that is actionable," Al-Mahdi said, chuckling and clapping his hands again. He shifted his feet and stretched his arms and yawned.

Stavos stepped forward. "John Block eventually told us about you. Give him credit. He protected you as long as he could. But Kurt is very persuasive."

Kurt smiled at Cybil.

Her teeth grinding, she tried to stand up but couldn't. She struggled against the bindings, jostling her and Anne.

Al-Mahdi turned around and slowly walked in a circle around Stavos, Kurt and Markos. His lab coat rustled as he moved. He rubbed his chin, tracing the scar beneath it, and then stopped, looking down, then up.

"No, your government will be completely surprised when my gift blossoms for them. They would already be here if any radiation leak had been detected," Al-Mahdi said, chuckling.

Anne said loudly, "You dishonor Allah and Islam by this violence. As you did in Iraq. I was there with Cybil. We saw."

"The nun speaks! What do you know of Allah and Islam? Your being there was an affront and interference. You started jihad! We will end it. Islam is strong. Your God is weak, as is his supposed son, dead on a cross, a fake prophet offering false promises, unlike Mohammed, who speaks truth," Al-Mahdi said.

Admiring the outburst, Cybil looked at Anne. Cybil now turned to face the group. "Look, I've been missing and they *are* searching for me. Eventually the satellites will detect my radioisotope ID—we get the injection for just these occasions. They will find me and your gift, whether I am breathing or not."

Al-Mahdi turned and faced Stavos and said, "She's lying, I am sure, but it is probably a safety precaution to take her to sea. Let them search the oceans for her. I would come with you but I need to secure the final element and leave with Abdul."

Stavos smiled and glanced over to the women. "No bother, consider it a complimentary final service. As I told you, we received notice from Barbados of your final payment. It will be my pleasure to ferry our guest. We moved the *Destiny* this morning to the dock outside."

"What about the nun?" Kurt said.

Al-Mahdi stepped toward Anne and bent down to look into her face.

"Bring her downstairs. I want her to watch as we prepare this gift. She will learn," Al-Mahdi said.

Anne stared back in silence.

Stavos turned his head toward Kurt. "Do it."

Kurt approached the women and a knife appeared. He cut Anne's bindings and stood her up. With his knife at her back, he walked to the door. Before she went out of the room she looked back at Cybil. Kurt shoved her past the doorway.

Cybil's heart sank as Anne disappeared.

Al-Mahdi nodded and faced Cybil again. He crossed his arms, one hand underneath the badge. His eyes grew wider and a crooked smile spread across his face.

"I am looking forward to watching your news broadcasts and propaganda outlets try to explain how such a gift could be opened right in the middle of one of your military bases, in the middle of a group of boys playing soldier. The ground they died on will be poisoned for 1,000 years. No one can approach the soil to build memorials or mourn their loss. Our jihad will be reborn, bin Laden's death no consequence, all because of Allah's will and Al-Mahdi's hands," Al-Mahdi said as he closed his eyes and look upward.

Cybil froze. The room started to spin. She couldn't hear anything. Her lungs forced a breath. The memory of Sebastian's duffel bag slapping his back rushed into her mind. He was walking away but didn't turn to see his mother, his mind set toward Virginia, to join others at this year's Boy Scout Jamboree, held again at Fort A.P. Hill. This Army base with scenic campgrounds, nestled behind tall fences and tight security, designed to hold thousands at a time, was chosen for the promise of safety.

Cybil looked up, wanting to speak, but couldn't. A thick fear filled her mind for her son and she fought hard just to breathe. Stavos put his hand on Marko's shoulder and nodded toward Cybil. Markos moved away from the group and approached her slowly, his face expressionless. In his hand he held an arcing Taser, its blue light jumping between the points, the smell of ozone preceding him.

Stavos's voice broke through her daze: "Put her on the boat and stay with her. We'll be there in a few minutes. Should be easier for you to handle, unlike last time, huh?"

He and Kurt laughed.

Markos looked back and frowned, with lips grimly pressed together. He nodded and turned to Cybil, jamming the Taser into her neck.

46

Darkness surrounded Cybil. She felt weightless, rocking back and forth like a baby in a mother's arms. Her face felt wet, then she felt a few drops fall on her skin. *Tears? Who is crying*? Becoming more conscious she felt the whole of her slow down. She took a breath, and the smell of diesel fuel raked her nose. Her eyelids cracked opened and she heard a man's voice: Stavos? Slowly her hearing came back, the voice mocking.

"Looks like our sleeping girl is awake, stand her up!"

Cybil blinked several times and took some quick breaths through her mouth. *Where am I?* A pair of large mitts grabbed her arms and jerked her upward, landing her shoeless feet on wet vinyl. The slanted floor she stood on made it difficult to balance. Her legs wobbled. As her vision cleared, she saw bright sun, blue sky and greenish water past Stavos in front of her. The acrid smell of rotting seaweed hit her nostrils. Her face felt sticky. She licked her lips … they were salty. She blinked again with the realization.

"Welcome to the *Destiny*. We are so glad you are our guest, though only for a little while," Stavos Gruner said as he opened his arms in a welcoming gesture.

She glanced around and saw Kurt at the helm of the boat. The boat had slowed and was now drifting. He punched a button and the clanking anchor chain threading down to the water shook the boat. Kurt, dressed in a wetsuit, looked ready to scuba dive and was using binoculars to scan the horizon. Next to him, leaning on a side wall near the wheel, an M16 assault rifle.

Cybil tried to take a step back but her feet were bound, along with her hands, and she fell backward. She felt the same large hands grab her again. Turning her head to look back she saw Markos. He squeezed tighter. A small wave hit the back of the boat, where they were, and splashed up, the fine spray settling on her and Markos. The water stung her neck, burning in two spots … *the damn Taser!*

Marko's eyes met hers. His bald head, wet from the spray, shone in the bright sunlight. His thin, almost white eyebrows seemed to disappear. He nodded twice to her as his eyes pointed to Stavos. He leaned in, tightening his grip further on her shoulders. He turned her to face Stavos, who had circled left.

Markos put his mouth close to her cheek; she could feel his warm breath on her ear.

He whispered, "Don't fight. It will hurt less and be quicker. Then you will swim and sleep."

Cybil started breathing faster. Her eyes focused on Stavos, who stepped closer. Her heart pounded. She could barely swallow. Sweat poured down her neck, sticking her wet shirt to her back. Her chest tightened and she began shivering. She felt cold. Icy hands reached around her waist, pushing her toward Stavos. *Sebastian, June… Anne.*

Then over Stavos's shoulder, her eye caught an object in the air, distant, hard to see the shape, it looked all black. It grew larger and larger as it approached and its speed increased. About 25 yards away, it stopped in midair. Cybil could now see wings of a large bird flapping as it hovered. Not a white-and-gray seagull, which would be expected. Without a sound, the blackbird stayed in place, its wings beating methodically, not slow or fast, as it stared in their direction. Cybil blinked a couple of times, her face relaxed.

"What?" Stavos said, noticing the change in Cybil.

Following her gaze past him, he started to turn. The blackbird's wings moved quicker and quicker as it gained altitude. Higher and higher, faster than Cybil had ever seen a bird fly. By the time Stavos had turned completely around, it had gone from view, high in the bright sky above the sea. He turned his head side to side, searching. Nothing.

Cybil felt Markos's grip loosen, his hands shaking. Stavos turned to look at her and noticed Markos's expression.

"What the fuck's wrong with you?" Stavos said to his associate.

Markos shook his head, indicating nothing, but he had seen the blackbird along with Cybil.

Cybil took a deep breath. *Control*. Her heart began to slow. She tensed her knees, flexed the bottom of her bare feet, her toes trying to grip on the wet, slippery deck. Turning her head toward the helm she saw Kurt had stopped scanning and looked in only one direction. He lowered his binoculars and faced the group.

"Stavos, they're here," Kurt said out loud.

Stavos smiled and with the same volume, said, "Good, we'll be done here in a few minutes. Can't keep our new client waiting."

"I'll raise the anchor as soon as you're done," Kurt said.

While they were talking Cybil's eyes scanned the elevated bridge area where Kurt stood. At the foot of the door, beneath the helm, rested a single scuba tank, regulator attached and waiting. A loaded spear gun leaned next to the tank.

Stavos said to Cybil, "I'm feeling good today. Today, I get a new client. Mr. Kasen, who has paid us so well, will be leaving the day after tomorrow. Business is good."

Cybil turned her face to Stavos. He approached and stepped close. Cybil smelled alcohol on his breath. Markos's grip remained loose, his hands still shaking.

"Markos, let's give her a fighting chance when she goes swimming. Roger, after all, was an employee and knew the rules. Here we can be gracious with our guest," Stavos said as he smiled and stepped away. "Cut her pretty feet loose."

Markos knelt behind Cybil. She had to lean on his shoulder trying to keep her balance, and the sight of her almost sitting on his shoulder drew a smile from Kurt, now watching the scene.

A serrated knife appeared in Markos's hand and he cut through the ties with little effort. Cybil spread her feet apart, shifting her weight from right to left, feeling her body again. The deck had dried somewhat, and the glassy sea was quiet. Her toes gripped the ridged vinyl; she had traction. Markos stood up and held her again, but not as tight as before.

Stavos again approached Cybil, stepping close and then with his right hand, brushed over his black hair. He looked straight at her. She stared back. His head moved slightly back, then he leaned forward.

"Stavos," Kurt said.

Stavos looked over to him. "What?"

"I'm going forward to check the anchor guides. The chain got stuck last time. I don't want to be late screwing with it," Kurt said as he slid down the bridge ladder to the deck.

He grabbed the M16 and made his way to the bow of the boat.

Stavos nodded to Kurt and then faced Cybil. His eyebrows rose. "Would you like to say something? Perhaps a last request, though an unreasonable one is unlikely to be granted."

Cybil needed more time to think. "Yes, I do have a request."

"Go ahead," Stavos said, stepping back and opening his arms wide.

"Can you do me a favor, though I am not sure you can deliver on it," Cybil said.

"A favor? What can I grant?" Stavos said, his chest puffing out.

"Do you think you could get a message to my children? Just a written note. I figure even a monster like you might want to let a kid know what their mother's last words were," Cybil said.

"Of course, please say it to me and I will remember and write it down," Stavos said with no intention of doing so.

Cybil paused for a second in thought, then looked up and started to speak, but stopped. "No, wait, not that. I'm thinking."

She glanced back again to the scuba tank and spear gun. Kurt had gone to the front of the boat. She looked at Stavos directly.

"Tell them … tell them … that when they grow up, they can honor their mother by finding your sorry ass and shooting you in the balls before they put one between your eyes. Got that?"

Stavos's eyes grew darker, his face red. His shoulders pinched up and he quickly stepped up and jammed himself close to Cybil, pressing his chest into hers. Grabbing her head with both hands, all of his fingers closed around her face. Her facial muscles contracted against the pressure of his tightening grasp. One of his hands slid down to her throat, closing around it so that she could hardly take a breath. His eyes, no more than a few inches away, filled her view, yet she stared back, deep-blue eyes flashing defiance. Suddenly he relaxed his grip and took a small step back.

Exhaling, Stavos said, "No. I'll take my time."

He slowly knelt on one knee in front of Cybil, as if tying his shoe. Stavos seemed to be adjusting his pant leg. He started to rise and Cybil saw her chance.

She threw her head back as hard as she could. She heard Markos's nose breaking, followed by a loud grunt. She leaned back into the stunned, bulky Markos to add leverage for her next move. Her front leg lifted and she piston-kicked Stavos, catching him in the middle of his chest. She couldn't enjoy the look of surprise on his face long because he stumbled backward and over the side, the force too much for him to handle. A fountain splash of water rose above where he landed and loud yelling quickly followed.

Cybil stepped forward, putting space between her and Markos. She back-kicked Markos in the groin, her bare heel smashing deep. Another loud grunt and Markos fell to the deck in a fetal position, one hand on his nose, another on his crotch.

A gunshot rang out and whistled by her head. Kurt, at the front of the boat, had taken a shot but didn't have a clear line of sight, the bridge being in the way. He began moving along the side; soon he would have a straight shot.

Cybil sprinted toward the scuba tank. Another shot rang out, cracking the bridge glass panes next to her but they didn't shatter. The bullet lodged in the bulletproof glass. She reached the tank and spear gun.

Kurt, seconds from a clear shot, stopped and looked over the side at Stavos, splashing in the water and yelling to be pulled out.

"Stavos, I'll be right there, I'm going to kill her first," Kurt said.

That was enough time for Cybil to decide. Her tied hands could not grip, therefore the spear gun was useless. She knocked it aside. Bending over, she gripped the tank nozzle and dragged the heavy tank to the side. With an extra-deep breath and yank, she pulled the tank up enough to clear the side and tossed it into the blue-green water.

Kurt had cleared the bridge and stood no more than 15 feet away from Cybil. Nothing was between them. She saw him lift the rifle to fire. Cybil smiled, bent her knees into a runner's squat and jumped backward over the side just as she heard the loud crack of the M16 firing at point-blank range. The bullet whistled by her chest as she lay prone in the air before splashing into the sea.

"Shit!" Kurt yelled as he raced to the side and began firing into the splash wake from Cybil's dive.

Cybil's eyes stung as she opened them underwater. She dolphin-kicked to dive deeper, to get away from the bullets hitting the water. Air trails ended a few feet under the surface but she was now deep enough to be safe. She looked up to see a wavy outline at the edge of the boat, but then it disappeared.

After firing several rounds into the water and seeing no blood or body, Kurt threw the M16 onto the deck and raced to the stepladder at the back of the boat, where Stavos was heading. Waiting to give Stavos a hand, he looked over his shoulder to where Cybil jumped over the side. He shook his head.

Cybil swam and kicked hard, forcing her body to cooperate. Making distance between her and the bullets, she somersaulted around underwater and headed back to the sky, chasing the daylight. Slowly breaking the surface of the water on the opposite side of *Destiny*, Cybil inhaled through her nose without making a sound. *Control.* Taking some breaths, she crept down the side, toward the back. She listened to voices coming from the top of the boat, then dove again under the boat toward the propellers.

She looked down and could see the faint outline of the scuba tank slowly sinking, a few feet below. She had to get her hands free. Holding her breath, and with a few kicks toward the propellers, she reached the blades. She could see Stavos's lower body and legs kicking, swimming a few feet from her while trying to get out of the water. Putting her hands to the blades she worked the zip ties against the worn metal. After only a few strokes the ties gave way. She frog-kicked back toward the front and surfaced, trying to quiet her gasping.

"She went over that side!" Cybil heard.

She took a huge gulp of air, sunk down under the water, twisted and placed her feet on the boat's underside and pushed herself under as hard as she could. She had to reach the tank before it got too deep.

The blue-green water turned darker and darker the deeper Cybil kicked. Slowly blowing air out her nostrils, her lungs ached. Her sight hampered by the murky water, she swam at a downward angle in the direction she thought the tank went. The water cooled as she kicked again, diving deeper. She'd have to surface soon. Then she felt a stream of bubbles gently caressing her cheek. The tank floated directly underneath her but was out of reach and still sinking. Doing a tuck-dive that thrust her downward farther, she committed to the depth. She got closer to the tank, which was sinking only inches away. Reaching for it she missed. The tank slipped farther away. Her reflex to breathe, to take in water, grew stronger. She was seconds from her brain forcing her to take a breath, to bring water into her lungs and start the process of drowning.

She thought about turning and reaching for the surface, but there was no time. She dove again, legs kicking and arms reaching for the tank. Closing in fast, the shiny chrome of the nozzle appeared in front of her. Her fingers closed around it and stopped its descent. Lifting her body out of the dive her legs kicked to stay at the same depth. Grasping the air tube she pulled the regulator and mouthpiece toward her and jammed it into her mouth. She took a breath. Nothing. *The valve!*

Holding the tank between her legs, she found the valve and turned it. A burst of air filled her mouth and she took a breath. A few coughs followed, expelling water that had gotten into her mouth and lungs. Her breathing became regular. In, out. In, out.

Cybil looked up to the surface to get her bearings. Her heart, ready to burst seconds before, began to slow. Her frantic kicks to tread the depth became smooth and regular. The bottom of the boat looked small. *I must be deep.* In, out. In, out. She surveyed the dark water while breathing. Suddenly thin trails of air broke the surface and then slowed to stop a few feet underwater. *Bullets!* All she could hear was a low thumping sound every time a trail entered the water. Eventually the shooting stopped.

Standing at the back of the boat, Stavos said, "Stop shooting, Kurt. Just wait. She's been under five minutes already."

Using a large towel, he patted himself dry. Markos sat a few feet away, holding a bloody towel on his face, pinching his nose through it. He was shaking his head.

Stavos looked at Markos. "Serves you right."

Kurt, one foot up on the side of the boat, had the M16 pointed at the water. He scanned right, then left and back again. He moved to the other side of the boat and did the same. Repeated the pattern twice until about 10 minutes had passed.

Glancing at his gold Rolex, Stavos shook his wrist to fling water drops off the dial. "We need to leave. She's drowned already. And even if she got the tank and is waiting us out, we are 15 miles out in strong currents. She's a goner." Stavos moved toward the helm.

Passing by Markos he stopped in front of him.

Stavos pointed at his face and then to the water. "Throw your towel in the water. It will draw the sharks. Get a fresh one. Go below and lie down. I want you ready when we meet the new client."

Kurt punched the Start button and the dual Mercury inboard engines rumbled to life. With anchor raised and the propellers churning water, the boat pushed to its appointment.

Stavos stood next to Kurt at the helm and looked past the stern, to the water they were fast leaving behind. He bit down hard and ground his teeth, glad to be rid of her.

*

The distinctive sound of propellers starting up had reached below. Cybil had been checking the regulator gauge, which showed near empty. She looked up toward the sound and saw the boat moving away. The farther it got from her, the faster she kicked toward the surface.

Breaking through the surface Cybil spit the mouthpiece out and took a deep breath—*Aahhhh!* Treading water, she turned toward the boat, now a small blob on the horizon moving away to the east. The aluminum tank, near empty, floated on the surface. Cybil thought, *Lucky break, most steel tanks sink like rocks whether empty or full.* The aluminum ones didn't. She hugged the tank, using it for floatation. She wanted to take her water-logged jeans off but they would keep her warm. Hypothermia would not pose a threat in southern Atlantic waters but with little body fat, the always cold model had a cool, wet night pending.

Looking up she found the setting sun obscured behind a thin veil of clouds, off the horizon. No land in sight. She had been unconscious during the transit and had no idea if she was north, south or parallel to Savannah. With maybe two hours of daylight left, she started paddle-kicking toward the western sun, hugging the tank. She took a left angle, assuming she was north of Savannah to compensate for the Gulf Stream's northern flow. The adrenaline in her system began to dissipate. Her stomach rumbled. Her split lip from Al-Mahdi's strike throbbed, the intrusive salt water burning the soft exposed tissue. She had not eaten since yesterday. She could feel fatigue creeping into her shoulders and legs. Every kick took more and more effort.

Cybil lifted her head to see any landmarks but there was only water. She kicked again and again, trying to keep a steady pace, unsure how long her strength would last. She kept going as the sun set and darkness fell, no moon in the sky. For another two hours she paddled. The sea stayed calm helping her make steady progress yet she could feel her pace slowing. She was so tired, thirsty. Her lips were cracked. She thought, *I must look like hell.*

Hours passed, she lost track of time. A half-moon had risen above the sea, its soft light blanketing the water around her. Finally, she stopped kicking and rested her head for a minute on the tank. The cool metal soothed her sweating cheek. She fell asleep, floating peacefully in the gently rolling sea.

About 500 yards away a dark shape moved underwater, toward her. When it got within 200 yards, it circled her position in a wide loop. With every completed pass it drew closer.

47

Awake a few minutes, Sister Anne shook her head sharply to the right. Her fine red hair, wet and matted, rose off her brow. Drops of sweat flew from her twilled ends and plopped a few feet away on the St. Rita basement floor. Her shirt under the vest was completely soaked.

After moving her downstairs late in the evening, they had tied her wrists around an old metal support pole near the stairs, thankfully in front of her and not behind. She slid down to a kneeling position sometime in the night, exhausted. Her wrists and forearms ached; they were reddened, splotchy with dried blood from scraping against the rusting metal.

Al-Mahdi and Abdul worked with relentless focus, except for when they put out their mats and prayed. She watched until her eyelids grew heavy. They closed once, twice. She fought to stay awake. From her position, she could watch them except for the area directly in front of her. Several times in the night, they stood there, backs to her. Side by side, they stood in front of what looked like a three-panel room divider. It was made of metal, with a small, thick glass window and two holes where they put their arms in to work.

She couldn't remember when she fell asleep. The last thing she recalled, besides the heat and the constant low rumbling that shook deep in her chest, was the red glow coming from the ovens' open melting pots. The glow rose to meet the bright fluorescent light in midair.

Morning light now streamed through the narrow, rectangular basement windows, each no bigger than a car's square headlight. Sister Anne watched the swirling dust hang in the air, barely moving through the incoming sunshine. The sharp smell of burning metal overpowered the room. Still kneeling, she struggled to rise, careful not to hurt herself again because of the bindings. Across the room, Al-Mahdi and Abdul, both in lab coats, stood at the middle oven. Abdul looked at Al-Mahdi, who nodded once. The younger man moved a sliding knob control from high to low. The rumbling noise from that oven ceased and the melting pot retracted to a recess matching its shape. They moved to the other two ovens and repeated the procedure. When the last oven shut down, the room became quiet.

"Allah, be praised!" Abdul said, reaching out to hug Al-Mahdi who returned the affectionate gesture. Patting each other on the back, dust flew off with each strike. Both coughed.

"Yes, you have done well, my friend. Come, let's secure the final element and rest. Tonight we return to Virginia and begin preparations to deliver our gift," Al-Mahdi said.

Abdul patted his chest twice, over his heart, and looked up. He then turned and walked behind the thick metal room divider area. His face appeared in the small window. Turning his head he looked at Sister Anne. His crooked smile disappeared as he bent down. After a few seconds, he walked out with a shiny metal briefcase, thick and wide, with a padded handle. Appearing heavy it swung slowly at the end of Abdul's spindly arm. In his other hand he gripped a small electronic device with an LED display which flickered red with numbers.

Walking over to Al-Mahdi, Abdul handed him the device. He struggled to lift the case to chest level while standing in front of Al-Mahdi. He began sweeping the device all over the metal briefcase, along the edges, on top and below it. He smiled as he looked at the display.

"A perfect container for our harvest," Al-Mahdi said.

Abdul lowered the case slowly and gripped the handle, muscling it down and onto the floor.

Facing each other the two shed their lab coats, letting them fall to the ground at their feet. Stepping away, they turned toward the stairs to leave. Sister Anne looked at Al-Mahdi with a soft face as he walked by her, Abdul preceding him. Abdul took one step before Al-Mahdi's hand reached out to his associate's shoulder.

"Wait," he said.

He turned where he stood and faced Sister Anne, a few feet away.

"You said I dishonored Allah and Islam, did you not?" Al-Mahdi said.

"Yes, I did," Sister Anne said.

"Do you think that is evil?" Al-Mahdi said.

"Evil can come from our choices. Sometimes there are other forces at work," Sister Anne said.

Al-Mahdi, turning his head left and right, his eyes looking around as if to find something, said, "Allah is the source of all good and evil. We are honest about that. Your religion lies to you that your God is all loving and good, yet evil somehow escapes his notice."

"Nothing escapes God's notice," Sister Anne said, "including what you're doing."

"What I am doing I do for my family, Allah and to awaken jihad within this land. This is but a spark to the flame. We have many here ready to spread these seeds," Al-Mahdi said, speaking quickly, his eyes narrowing to slits, his tongue licking his lips.

Sister Anne stared into his eyes and said, "Would your family be proud of you?"

"If they were alive, yes!" Al-Mahdi said.

Sister Anne paused for a moment and her eyes softened. "I'm sorry about your family," she said.

Al-Mahdi bent forward to answer, but stopped. His eyes shifted and his face grew red. "They are in paradise. This work remains for me," he said.

Sister Anne's gaze stayed on Al-Mahdi. She smiled and said, "I understand."

"You understand nothing, spare me your mercy. It is a thin disguise of your pity. Mercy, grace, forgiveness, weak offerings from a weak God who couldn't even avoid death," Al-Mahdi said.

"Love is never weak, it's much stronger than the cowardice of hate," Sister Anne said, taking deep breaths. Her body rose, her legs bracing her up.

"Americans do not love. They war—for oil. They seduce—for commerce. They proclaim their exceptionalism while spreading a voyeuristic, materialistic culture like a virus infecting everyone with lust and greed," Al-Mahdi said. He raised a fist and shook it slowly.

"I agree with you," Sister Anne said.

Al-Mahdi's head jerked back. He blinked and glanced at Abdul sitting on the last step, the case resting on the floor. Abdul had a blank expression.

Turning back toward Sister Anne, Al-Mahdi said, "You lie."

"No, there is much wrong with this world. All of it, including America. God is working hard to make it right. He is doing the best he can, working with what he has, flawed, imperfect people. He calls on all of us to join him, to help him, to do good, to restore what was lost, to make this world better. What you are planning to do, whatever it is, cannot be good, and adds to the cycle of hate," Sister Anne said, her appeal soft, her voice gentle.

Al-Mahdi turned his face away. He reached out and leaned on the wall next to the sitting Abdul. He took a step sideways to find his balance but his foot hit the case, which barely moved. Al-Mahdi looked down at the case, his head bent forward: 10 seconds, 20 seconds, 30 seconds passed.

Finally, Al-Mahdi, his back turned to Sister Anne, lifted his head and looked straight up. He opened his arms wide, lifted them high as if to pray and then lowered them. He turned around.

His eyes, narrow and dark, stared at Sister Anne. "The best place to start fixing this world is to break the will of the great Satan. Attack what he cherishes, what he spoils and dotes on. Then he will retreat. We will start with the little ones first. Your future, nun, is this basement, now your coffin. Your God has forsaken you."

Al-Mahdi smiled and turned. Favoring his stronger leg he stepped carefully past Abdul up the stairs. Abdul stood up fast but struggled carrying the case up the stairs. Their steps faded and the basement became quiet.

Sister Anne leaned against the metal pole. Closing her eyes, her lips moved in prayer for Cybil, wherever she was; for Al-Mahdi, their enemy, that he would be stopped without more bloodshed; for Father Michael, that his conscience would take hold. Lastly she prayed for strength.

She took a deep breath through her nose. The musty basement smell mixed with the acrid odor of rust. Her cheek brushed against the rough, flaking crust encasing the pole. She leaned back and looked at the stairs. No sound, no one around. Staring at her hands bound around the pole, she slowly moved her wrists up and down, side to side, her plastic zip ties heating up, bits and pieces of black plastic snapping off. *This might work.*

*

Father Michael stepped hard on the brakes of the St. Rita van as it stopped in the front driveway. The gravel under the tires crackled under the weight of the slowing vehicle. His cell phone rang. Michelle sat next to him and coughed. She tapped her fingers on the windowsill and her leg twitched piston-like. She hadn't smoked in two hours.

Pressing Answer, the priest said, "This is Father Michael, how can I help you?"

"Yes, this is Ted Randall, an old friend of Sister Anne. We served in Iraq together. I found her on Facebook but there was just a work number. I am in town this week. Thought you might help me get a message to her to call me, maybe give her my number. We had lost touch." Ed Raintree's voice came through warm and sincere.

"Oh, yes. Sorry, but uh, Sister Anne is helping me relocate some of the orphans to a shelter, a safe house. It's a domestic violence case. She left her phone with me, it's out of charge. She'll be back next week. I'll tell her you called, I have your number here," Father Michael said.

"Oh, oh, okay. Well, thanks then, goodbye," Ed said, hanging up.

Ed turned to face Reverend Sanders, who stood a few feet away brushing moss from an angel statue. They were in the Trinity Chapel garden.

Ed walked over to him and said, "Thanks for suggesting I call Father Michael. He was quite helpful."

"I'm glad. Sister Anne should be back from the Catholic Children's Conference soon. She's so nice to do his speech for him since he has to finish closing out St. Rita business. He was very grateful for her help. Wouldn't stop praising her," Reverend Sanders said.

Ed smiled. "Yeah, you were right, that's what he told me. I'm sorry to bother you. Say, is the Breakfast Club nearby? I think I'll have a bite before going back to town. No reason not to enjoy your beach area before leaving."

"It's not that far from here, walking distance, if you like. Go down four blocks and then take a left. You'll enjoy it, Ted," Reverend Sanders said.

"I think I'll drive. Thanks again."

While heading to his car he thought, *Anne's missing too? Shit!*

48

In. Out. In. Out. Cybil's back rose and fell with every breath she took, her chest pushing down against the tank. Instinctively hugging the half-submerged aluminum cylinder, they both floated with the current, drifting farther out to sea, the progress made earlier, when awake, erased. Through the night she had slept. Now the increasing daylight touched her eyes. Soon it would brighten enough to wake her. In. Out. In. Out. Her legs, like fishing lines, hung underneath, bare toes twitching. Her eyeballs moved under closed, fatigued eyelids, tracking something. Cybil dreamed.

*

She walked on hot desert sand, her eyes wide open. Recognizing the beaches of Dubai, or so they seemed, she smiled. The soft landing of waves drew her attention. She turned her head to look at them. Small, gentle ones, typical of Gulf beaches, licked the wet sand. Turning again to look down the beach, far away, someone, a woman, wearing a big straw hat, reclined under a large black umbrella.

Without reason Cybil ran toward the woman, shouting "Anne, Anne," but she wasn't sure it was her. The woman kept looking out to sea. The umbrella closed and then opened again. The smooth cloth turned into feathered wings and a head appeared, then clawed legs. The whole thing became a bird of impossible size. It flapped its wings and hovered. Sand swirled around the woman like when a helicopter lands, yet calmly she stared at the sea. Then she looked up.

Lifting her arms she reached for the bird causing her hat to fall off. It blew into the waves. The creature bent down, opening its mouth wide, wider than made sense. It swallowed the woman whole. She never made a sound. Then with a few flaps of its wings the bird flew straight and fast up into the sky and disappeared.

By then Cybil had arrived at the spot, the sand in the air had fallen. All was still. She looked down to the blanket where the woman had been; it lay crumpled and twisted. Bending down Cybil picked up the blanket, flapped it once to get rid of the sand. Underneath, buried in the white grains, except for a corner, a black cell phone lay there. She knelt on the sand and started folding the blanket, ignoring the phone. Surrendering, the blanket folded under her movements, corners meeting corners, sharp creases smoothed down until she was done, inspection ready. She put the blanket on the sand. Then the cell phone rang. Cybil picked it up and pressed it to her ear. Sebastian's voice screamed through: "Mom, help!"

*

Cybil kicked violently, pushing herself and the tank halfway out of the water. "Sebastian!" she yelled out before splashing back into the water.

Losing her grip on the tank it floated away. Groggy from the dream, she treaded water without thought of swimming after the tank. Wave after wave passed by her, every rise and fall moving her and the tank farther and farther away from each other. She shook her head and realized the tank had gone.

"Damn it! Just great," she said.

After a few minutes she alternated from a hanging float to moving forward. Lifting her head out of the water to exhale, she took a deep breath, inflating her lungs. She turned on her back and floated on the surface, looking straight up. Army water survival training had kicked in.

Cybil floated, looking up. A few thin, white clouds moved slowly across her field of view.

In a soft voice, she said, "Not sure if you're paying attention. After all, it's not like you've done me any favors lately."

Backstroking a few times, she turned, put her face in the water and swam for a few minutes, the water feeling cool. Her shirt floated up, rising above her waist and revealing half her dolphin tattoo, her jeans covering the rest of it. Again she turned on her back, floated, thought of Sebastian with the scouts, Anne back at St. Rita and Al-Mahdi.

She gritted her teeth. "Even YOU have to care about those kids. You can let me drown but do something, damn it!"

To the left, very high, appeared an aircraft contrail. *Doubt anyone can see me.*

A few more minutes passed while Cybil floated on her back, breathing regularly. A splashing sound came from her right. She raised her head above the water and saw a dark shape, just under the surface, moving toward her.

Her heart beating faster, Cybil looked back up toward the sky. "Really?"

Moving off her back, she scissored her legs back and forth. Clouds on the horizon had dulled the rising sun but the morning light shone enough to let Cybil see the approaching figure.

A few feet in front the shape veered off and disappeared into the depths. She waited a few seconds then nothing. Then a minute passed.

Cybil exhaled, smiling, and said out loud, "Hell of a lot better than a pack of sharks."

Looking up, she slowly treaded water making a 360 degree turn to check. In the distance she saw a small white cloud hugging the surface about a half-mile away. She squinted, looking deeper into the cloud which seemed to be expanding and contracting. It didn't make sense. She thought, *Wait, it's a flock of seagulls feeding, maybe feeding on chum from a fishing boat!*

Cybil started swimming toward the seagulls, her arms beating the surface, her legs kicking strong and smooth, but uncertain how long this burst of energy would last. She settled into a regular rhythm, head moving to the side to take a breath, head down, arms reaching, grasping the water, her legs propelling her forward. She had to get there fast.

Bbbrrrrrrrr! The low, loud rumble of a foghorn greeted Cybil as she got within 100 yards of the twirling, flying mass of white and gray. A small fishing boat, packed with nets and tall poles, floated on the other side of the mass of diving, cackling birds. They flew away at the sound of the horn but soon swirled back to feed.

Just then a large swell pushed her and the boat apart. Then another took her further away. She gritted her teeth and swam hard against the waves. After a minute of determined stroking, she neared the side. She swam around to the back, under the aerial dinner party, and reached the stern, where she came to a long pole with fishnet stuck on the end.

"Get a hold, miss! He's a lot stronger than he looks," an old voice called out.

Holding the pole's other end stood a young boy in tattered shorts and a yellow T-shirt. Next to him stood a thin old man in painter's overalls with no shirt, his gray hairs sticking out from behind his suspenders. His thumbs looped under the straps. She grabbed at the coarse net and held on. She gagged at the smell of mildew and fish guts.

The boy pulled her closer and the old man reached down, his scaly, rough hands grasping Cybil's prune-like fingers, then her wrists. He pulled her up and into the boat.

"Don't just stand there, get a blanket and some water," the man barked at the boy.

The man, one hand on her shoulder, pointed with his other to a padded vinyl bench built into the side. Weathered, with ripped edges and holes of varied sizes, it had one smooth spot big enough for her small rear end to sit.

"What in heaven's name are you doing out here?" the man said.

The boy appeared with a worn blanket and a bottle of water. The old man threw the blanket around the shivering Cybil. She twisted the cap off and drank.

"Thank you, thank you for picking me up," she said.

"Glad to. I'm sure happy we came your way. Wasn't supposed to be here today at all, except for the cancelled charter. Was about to head back to shore, nothin' happening. Chumming didn't do a thing, no big catches around. We threw a couple of lines maybe to catch dinner. We saw the flock of seagulls feeding and the big blackbird," the old man said, smiling and scratching his head.

Cybil's eyes opened wider. "What did you say, a blackbird?"

"Yep, we were watching the flock feeding and in the middle a big blackbird, way out here. Didn't belong. Me and the boy stared at it. It flew straight away, up into the sky. Strangest thing. When we looked down, we saw you, barely. Had to get the binocs. You were far away but swimming toward us," the old man said. Nearby, the boy nodded.

Cybil shook her head. She took a sip, finishing the water. Smiling, she handed the empty bottle to the boy and looked at the old man, saying, "Do you have a cell phone or ship to shore?"

49

Cybil sat at the back of the fishing vessel, surrounded by the high-pitched sound of twin Mercury engines. The outboard power plants churned water, pushing the boat fast toward shore. Throttled at top speed, the engines whined, exerting themselves as the boat rose and fell, cutting across the waves. The wind had picked up. Salt spray from the bow cutting through the building swells pelted her face and stung her lips.

Cybil's hand grasped the edge of the bench she sat on since the last boat fall had almost knocked her to the deck. The mounting winds stirred the shallow waters off Savannah's coast. Low dark-gray clouds appeared to her right and moved toward them.

"Looks like a rare summer Nor'easter," the old man shouted over the noise as he steered the craft.

The boy stood next to the aging mariner, whose scraggly gray hair whipped backward in the wind. His floppy yellow hat held on for dear life, pulling at his neck, its frayed drawstring down to thin strands. It looked like a parachute about to fail its passenger. Cybil smiled, recalling her first jump.

*

Scared shitless, she took in the wind from the aircraft's open door. The C130 rambled through air level ready to drop this group of first time jumpers. Time slowed as she looked out. First in line by jumpmaster design, she would lead her brothers into the blue. Smiling she simply took the biggest step of her life.

*

Cybil looked down to the fisherman's cell phone in her hand, an old model, simple, no text capability and, worse, no signal.

"How close are we to Thunderbolt?" she shouted to him.

He didn't hear. She stood and carefully made her way forward. The boy saw her approaching and tugged at the old man's sleeve. He turned his face but kept steering.

"Yes, miss?"

"How far away from Thunderbolt? I need to call ahead," she said.

"Not far, maybe 10 miles from the point, 30 minutes max," the old man said, looking down to the phone and then to the left, toward a lonely lighthouse appearing to float in the ocean. "Should work in a few minutes, always does when we pass the point."

Cybil returned to her seat, waited a minute and checked for a signal. Nothing. Another minute. She checked again, nothing. Frustrated, she clenched her free hand into a fist and slammed it onto the vinyl seat. The force of her strike on the cushion squished the wet foam and water spurted in a small geyser.

"Great!" she said, and looked up to see the boy laughing.

She laughed also. *Sebastian would have found that funny too,* she thought. Her chest ached, she missed him and June. But she was still alive and coming back. *I hope Anne is okay.*

The boat slowed, the waves became calmer; they had moved into the Savannah channel. It would lead them straight to Thunderbolt Marina. She looked down at the cell phone: three bars. She dialed Ed Raintree's number.

"Cybil," Ed said at the sound of her voice, "where the hell have you been!? Are you all right?"

"Yes, I'm okay. Listen, we don't have much time," Cybil said.

"Time! I've wasted a lot of time looking for you. Sonja won't send a team until she knows more. She thinks you're on a bender—hope not. And I tried to find Sister Anne, she missing."

A boat passing them, heading out to sea, blared its horn. Cybil waited and then said, "I know where she was last. I don't have time to explain. We can brief Sonja on the way to St. Rita, after you pick me up. But first you need to go to my house. Now shut up and listen!"

Cybil instructed Ed to retrieve her go kit, a black leather bag filled with essentials. A change of clothes, backup cell phone, energy bars, combat footwear, three microphone/earpiece communication units that used a secure channel, her two knives, a Glock, backup .38, four explosive, magnetic disks with timers, a small backpack, GPS tracker and a few other classified items. She gave him the guest combination for the security system and rear door electronic lock.

Since he was eating at the Breakfast Club on Tybee, Ed would have to hurry to cross back over the bridge, get to her house and travel back to Thunderbolt to meet her when the boat arrived at the marina. He left his half-eaten breakfast and a $20 bill as he bolted out the door.

Approaching the marina, the old man expertly guided his vessel through the channel and slowed it as they got closer to the docks. Finding an open slip, he backed the boat in with a gentle bump. He kept the idle going, pressing the craft's rear and side against the floating tires until the boy jumped onto the dock and tied the guide ropes to the dock's metal cleats. Turning the engine off, the old man motioned for Cybil to join him on the dock. Standing, she shed her blanket and stepped away from her seat, following the mariner off his boat. The boy came and stood next to the old man. Both looked at Cybil and smiled.

"I can't thank you enough for your help," she said, holding out her hand.

He shook it gently. Cybil turned to the boy, bent over and leaned closer to shake his hand.

"Kind of you," she said.

The boy nodded and looked up at the old man. He tilted his head toward the end of the dock where a hose attached to a water faucet hung, its nozzle resting on the wood deck. The boy left, walking toward the hose.

"I think your ride is here," the old man said, looking past Cybil to a tall, muscular man standing next to a black SUV.

Ed waved wildly to get her attention. Cybil waved back and motioned with one finger for him to wait. He stopped waving and leaned back on the SUV and crossed his arms.

"I'd like to thank you, and the boy. Are you moored here?" Cybil said.

"Nope, we're from St. Mary, just north of Jacksonville. Up here for the week. Like I said, someone chartered our boat, paid us ahead of time but never showed up. We leave tomorrow, a day early, figure the no-show lost his chance. Fishing's no good here. Wasted trip—expect for helping you out, of course," the old man said, smiling.

Cybil drew closer to the old man. He pulled back but then accepted her hug.

"Thank you, miss, was nothing," the old man said, his face pink.

Cybil turned and walked toward Ed. She reached the security gate and opened it. The dock, lower than the parking lot, had steep stairs connecting the two. Taking a few steps up she stopped. *Never got their names!*

Turning where she stood she yelled, "What's your name! I'm Cybil Raven, I need to know your name!"

Cybil continued walking backward up the steps. She had to get going.

The old man had moved toward the boy, who has hosing down the side of the boat. Giving directions, he walked along its length, showing the boy where to spray.

She reached the lot, about 25 yards away from Ed. His arms stuck out, palms up and he yelled, "Hurry up, Cybil!"

The old man had reached the back of the boat. Cybil yelled out the request again. This time he raised his head, put his hand to his mouth and shouted back. His other hand pointed to the back of the boat, to a name in red paint.

"I'm Jonah Castor, captain of *The Kikayon*!"

*

Raintree pressed the accelerator of the black Suburban. It jerked forward, nearly hitting the yellow striped posts guarding the marina entrance. Cybil sat in the front passenger seat, her black bag open at her feet. She pulled off her damp shirt. Underneath, her damp black lace bra stuck to her. Reaching into the bag, she grabbed a black knit GORE-TEX® pullover and slipped it on. Her hands went under the pullover and unclipped the front clasps and pulled her bra out before slipping her arms through the shirt's holes.

"Ahh, that feels better," she said.

Out of the bag came a pair of black pants and a small, metallic-looking square in a plastic zip bag. She opened it and unfolded the paper-thin emergency thermal blanket, laying it over her legs and waist.

She turned her head toward Ed, her left eyebrow raised.

Raintree kept his eyes forward. "Keep going, don't let me stop you," he said with a grin.

Cybil repeated the procedure, pulling her damp jeans and panties down and slipped on dry GORE-TEX black pants with a black leather belt. Ed let out a deep sigh and smiled.

Looking straight ahead she said, "Enjoyed the show? Good, now dial Sonja and let's brief her. We need NEST support from Homeland Security. Fast."

"I did enjoy it, and you smell better. No insult intended," Ed said.

"None taken, dickhead," Cybil said, smiling at him.

Ed puffed out a small laugh. He pressed his steering wheel cell phone control and the voice commanded, "Dial unit … Speaker."

Continuing to change and before the fourth ring sounded, Cybil completed her transformation: black Velcro-binding sneakers flew onto her bare feet; her Glock slid fast into a back-side belt holster which also held her military-issue knife; above her ankle, she strapped on her calf knife under the knit cloth.

The calf knife, along with the flask, had been gifts from the captain, back in Iraq. Slim, its black onyx handle tapered where it met black steel. Hand-forged in Fallujah, the edge worked so it cut without effort and the sheath was specially designed to sharpen the blade with every pull and put. The captain had bought it at a local market; it was of Shiite origins, the only one in the booth. The seller weaved a tale, said this was a one-of-a-kind knife; so sharp that should you cross paths with the devil, you could cut his soul out, provided he had one.

"Ed, any news on Cybil?" Sonja's voice sounded tired. The cell phone speaker vibrated with her low voice.

"You sound like you miss me," Cybil said, a slight smile lining her comment.

A few seconds of silence. "Just didn't want to lose our investment, that's all," Sonja said, lying.

"Well, now that we're all caught up, can we get to it?" Ed said, his fingers strumming the steering wheel.

For the next 10 minutes, Cybil relayed everything she knew: Sister Anne's capture, St. Rita's conversion into some type of processing lab built around lead ovens; about the badge and how similar it was to the ones X-ray techs wear during radiation treatments.

She talked about Stavos's crew, Al-Mahdi's boast of pending triumph, Sebastian's connection and her whereabouts the last 14 hours before her recovery at sea. Cybil finished by asking Sonja to call local Savannah PD and see if they had heard anything about Tom, who was with her when she was captured.

Sonja updated Cybil on Al-Mahdi's Iranian connections and then provided new information about a recently intercepted shipment from North Korea to Iran of chopped-up, spent rods encased in lead weightlifting equipment.

Sonja concluded, saying, "It makes sense that he is building a dirty bomb or bombs. But what we don't know is how many, how far along he is and the target or targets." She paused a moment. "Do you think Sebastian is a target?"

Taking a deep breath, Cybil said, "No, no, this is not personal. Sebastian being there is only a coincidence, but it helps us identify a possible strike target."

Ed reached the intersection to turn south to St. Rita. The car leaned, going around the turn, and Cybil's hand gripped the door's roof handle.

Ed spoke up: "Do you think this is enough to get the Nuclear Emergency Support Team going, plus a strike team to help us at St. Rita?"

"Give me a minute," Sonja said. A long pause followed. "There, it's done."

"What?" Ed said.

"I've notified the director I'm going to declare a Radiological Event Threat in the Eastern Corridor. The last RET was a false alarm and caused a shit-storm of finger-pointing. He'll be in my office in about 10 minutes to confirm and escalate, or put me on suspension for not knowing my job. We don't have much time. Cybil, why do you think the scouts are the target?"

"Al-Mahdi talked about boys playing solider and how this gift opened in the middle of a base would poison the ground for 1,000 years or something, I can't recall word for word," Cybil said, pausing to take a breath.

She then said, "Fort A.P. Hill in Virginia, where Sebastian and the other scouts are, is the only military base hosting a scout event this year. I remember his scoutmaster telling us at a parents' meeting."

Raintree said, "That's pretty fucking ballsy, trying to penetrate military base security, a base within 100 miles of DC. He must have inside help."

"I agree, he must have. That can work for us," Sonja said with rising excitement in her voice. "We can access military records quickly and work inside out to find any connections to recent immigrants, students, diplomats."

Ed said, "How long before NEST and strike teams get here?"

The car hit a deep pothole, the interior sound rose as the contents inside the car jostled around. Ed gripped the wheel harder to maintain control. Cybil braced herself against the dashboard.

"What was that?" Sonja said.

"Nothing," Cybil said. "Keep going, how long on the teams?"

"Procedure says four hours to wheels up, then transit time to location. Virginia is driving distance for Team One. Best case, five hours to on-site at Fort A.P. Hill. Alerting base security could be tricky. Al-Mahdi's people could be watching and then things could go bad real fast. We made a lot of progress on inter-agency cooperation but we still got 10 freaking government departments coordinating on a RET. For Team Two, Savannah, seven hours. Could be less, but that's what the book says. This ain't Hollywood, real life takes time."

Cybil said, "Sonja, Ed, think of the psych impact of a dirty bomb going off on a secure base, close to Washington DC, and turning the center of a military installation into a radioactive dead zone for years, a constant reminder of their victory. Shit, they could say it was bin Laden's revenge from the grave. It would embolden enemies worldwide to step up these types of attacks. We need to do whatever it takes to end this."

"Cybil," Sonja said.

"Yes."

"You know we can't evacuate the scouts until we know more. The bomb could be there now and if we try to do something, it could be detonated by remote. We don't know how many eyes Al-Mahdi has watching. We could try to pull Sebastian out—"

"Only if you think you can pull it off safely. I … I … know you'll try." Taking a deep, loud breath, Cybil said, "Ed and I need to get to St. Rita, set up an observation post and wait for the strike team and their equipment, before we go inside to secure whatever hazardous or radiological material is there. There may be another device at St. Rita. He could have the place booby-trapped. We have to get Al-Mahdi, alive. Give me 15 minutes with him and he'll tell us everything. And I won't need buckets of water."

Ed looked over at Cybil and nodded his head. She returned the nod, acknowledging his support for what they had to do, what they must do when they got the Snake.

"Sounds like a plan. Wait …. The director's knocking on the door. Here goes. Report when you're set up at St. Rita," Sonja said as the call ended.

Cybil looked at Ed. "Where's your recon package?"

Ed tilted his head to the backseat. "Leather briefcase, combination 014 on the left, 021 on the right."

Cybil leaned in between the seats to reach back and grab the briefcase. Doing so, her body pressed against Ed, his elbow into her abdomen, his upper arm between her breasts. She paused for a second, her face close to his; she bit her lip, fighting the memory of their short but intense time together. He smiled. She found the briefcase and pulled it over the seatback.

"So, 014 on the left and 021 on the right? Really, Ed, twice and three times 007?" she said.

Ed said nothing as he nodded his head slowly and grinned.

Opening the briefcase, she searched through his papers, multiple passports and *Maxim* magazines. A small 4 x 6 photo in a cheap plastic frame had a picture of a smiling Ed with a big busty blonde, looking drunk, sitting in his lap. They each had umbrella drinks in their hands.

"The wife?" Cybil said.

"Yep, honeymoon picture at Cabo, my favorite," Ed said.

Cybil laid it aside and found a white 8" x 11" envelope marked "St. Rita." It contained a summary page; Internet printouts of St. Rita's website; Web photos of the staff, including Anne's, which was circled; aerial photos and topo maps and photographs of the St. Rita grounds, plus blueprints of the interior. Cybil noticed the service road entrance, so marked on the map and its distance from the intersection.

The car slowed ahead of the turn onto Wylly Island Road. The sun had almost set, dusk giving way to dark. Ed kept the car lights off.

Tracing her finger along the map, she said, "Drive about one mile, then park on the side. This area looks promising as an entry point."

50

Dry leaves crunched under Cybil's weight as she crawled forward, low to the ground. She came across a fallen log about 18 inches wide, with broken branches sticking out of it. The log lay just inside the forest which spread from the road to the river. She jutted herself on it between a long and a short branch. Leaning on the scratchy bark she felt it through the breathable GORE-TEX. Propping herself with one elbow on the log, she lifted her single lens monocular to her eye, pointing it at St. Rita's front porch.

Markos filled the lens. He had been walking the grounds, looking around. This was the fourth time he'd made the circle around the orphanage, like clockwork. Reaching the front, he stopped, then looked around one more time. The porch lights lit the entire front including about 20 feet outward, before fading into the dark night. He turned and lumbered up the steps and into the building, closing the door behind him.

Cybil said, "How many minutes this time?"

Ed, lying next to her, looked at his watch. "He's consistent. Every 30 minutes he appears and takes 10 to make the circle around the grounds. Left to right."

"Good," Cybil said.

Zooming out, the whole of St. Rita came into view. Corner spotlights between the first and second floor circled the three-story building, creating illumination circles on the grounds. Like a skirt of light surrounding her waist, St. Rita shone in the night.

By panning left and pressing Zoom, the image of the chapel magnified and filled her view. Beside the chapel towered a huge tree. Underneath it a shed with a small light and a few feet farther, a vine-covered brick well. Both sat next to a loose gravel path leading to the dock. Their observation spot angled 45 degrees left from the place of worship. From that spot, the dock, pathway, chapel and left front of St. Rita came into clear view. A small door halfway down the side was opposite the well.

Slight movement at that door drew her attention; she zoomed in further. A furry raccoon darted from the woods, passed under the light and reached the front steps of the chapel. It crawled across the steps. The masked visitor stopped, stood on its hind legs and sniffed the air. Then it jumped off the steps into the green, fully leafed bushes to the side. The three-foot-high bushes shook and leaves flew off. The raccoon emerged, scampering across the steps and back into the woods. Clutched in its mouth was a writhing rat with a long tail, which fought to get loose.

Cybil smiled and lowered the lens from her face.

Ed looked over. “What did you see?”

“Nothing. You see Stavos’s boat at the dock?” Cybil said.

“No, give me the glass,” Ed said.

Cybil handed him the monocular and watched him work the controls. He nodded. “Yeah, I see it,” he said.

"Watch the front door and porch. There're plenty of woods to hide my way to the dock. Talk to me over the comm if anyone comes close so I can take cover. Won't take more than 15 minutes, plenty to spare before Markos does his prison guard routine. No water escape route for these bastards," Cybil said.

"I like the way you think, work fast," he said.

Nodding, she checked inside the small backpack. She said, "Should only need two."

Cybil reached behind her and pulled her Glock, placing it on the log.

"What are you doing?" Ed said, looking down at the gun.

"I'm going in the water. I need this dry for later," she said.

Ed nodded and returned to glassing St. Rita's front door.

Cybil looked at Raintree, intently watching. He had aged a few years, a wrinkle or two around the eyes. He had changed clothes when they parked. Pulling on black combat fatigues with pockets everywhere, he looked dressed for stealth. His long lean body lay prone, like a missile aimed forward, still fit as when she first worked with him. Despite their repartee, his concern when driving back from Thunderbolt felt genuine. She smiled at him.

"It's clear. You can go, you have 25 minutes now," Ed said without taking his eyes off St. Rita's front area.

Cybil rose to her feet and jumped over Ed and into the woods, toward the river. Her eyes adjusted to the light, the half-moon overhead helped keep the woods from being completely dark. The dense woodland next to St. Rita had enough gaps and clear spaces that could expose her position. Tracing a line 20 yards parallel to the gravel path, she went deeper into the forest. Cybil bent low, darting from tree to tree.

Ed talked over the comm every 30 seconds: "Still clear."

The wind continued its shift inward, toward Savannah. The steady breeze through the trees partially covered the sound of her walking over dry forest floor. With every breath the smell of the woods filled her nostrils. Every 10 yards or so she leaped onto one of the many cut stumps, leftovers from the lumber harvest used to thin the forest. She crouched like a cat surveying from a safe height. Stepping off, she carefully watched her footfalls to avoid stepping on the many dead, dry branches littering her path. The resulting noise would reach anyone outside of the buildings.

At her halfway mark, a gap in the woods opened and she could see the well under the huge tree. A single wide limb reached across the space between the woods, over the bricked source of water and almost to the St. Rita Chapel. The limb's center area was dense with leafy branches. The limb grew wider and thicker as it reached the end. It looked like a forearm with a hand reaching out, Cybil thought.

Snap! The loud sound traveled through the woods and bounced off the brick wall of the chapel. She had stepped on a dry, dead branch.

"Damn it!" She said under her breath.

Kneeling down into a runner's squat, she froze.

Through her earpiece, Ed whispered, “Shit, Cybil, I heard that way back here … don’t move … I’m looking ….”

After five minutes of quiet breathing over the comm channel, Ed said, “It’s clear, no one’s come out, keep going.”

More focused, she picked her way carefully, making sure to step on thick pads of leaves. Increasing her pace she closed the gap to the edge of the river. She knelt, facing the rear of the *Destiny*. Her shoe slid on the muddy embankment and dipped into the cold water. Cybil’s free hand reached out to the ground to hold her up and her fingers sank in the gooey mud.

“Any movement?” she said into her mike.

He said, “None. Hurry, you got maybe 15 minutes.”

Cybil crept along the embankment. Reaching the dock, a single L-shaped structure just big enough for the *Destiny*, she grappled one of the thick, slimy algae-covered posts. She slowly slid into the water. A tall, thin metal pole fastened to the outer post had a single bulb lighting the area. Sinking her body down, only her blue eyes and top of her head broke the surface of the water as she moved toward the boat.

Frog-swimming with a soft stroke to avoid splashing water, she made her way along the dock, to the stern. The draft to the bottom easily spanned 15 feet. Treading water there, she pulled her waterproof backpack to the front and took out the first charge. Round, with a circular magnetic ring around a sticky pad, it was designed to attach to anything above water, underwater, under a bridge, anywhere an operative wanted it. In the middle of the charge a small, black arming toggle switch was located; it had a white LED dot on one end. After placing it below the waterline, near the rear fuel tanks, she pressed the white dot down. It started flashing red, armed for detonation one hour from now.

Swimming again, this time to the bow, she noticed ripples farther out in the water. A small head poked out, followed by a larger hump behind. A turtle had joined her in the water. Soon its head disappeared under it.

Reaching the front, Cybil placed a second charge near the bow, again under the waterline. Pausing for a second as her hand rested on the side, she recalled her struggle, less than 24 hours ago, on the deck above and under this boat.

Setting the timer slide to synch with the other charge so they would explode within seconds of each other, she pressed the white dot down; it began flashing red.

She mouthed the words, "One bitch down, one to go. Michelle, you're next."

Five more minutes passed as she had made her way back to the river's edge and climbed up on the embankment. Water dripped from her back, legs and chest. Shaking her head as if looking left and right on a runway, water flung from her chestnut hair, landing behind in the river, ripples moving outward from the bank. Lifting both hands, she ran her fingers through her hair. Her GORE-TEX knit immediately began to evaporate the moisture; she would be dry by the time she reached Ed. Glancing down the bank to the boat tied to the dock, she stared at the Greek lettering. *I'd love to see Stavos's face when it blows.*

Ed's voice told her it was clear, but to hurry. She turned her face toward the woods. Mentally retracing her steps, she leaped up the bank and headed back to their observation spot.

A few steps later the communication channel crackled: "Freeze. Someone's coming out of the chapel side door! … Wait. … It's a woman. I think it's Anne!"

Cybil, deep into the woods and halfway to the chapel from the riverbank, couldn't see anything. She picked up her pace and taking some chances, ran, making noise to move up and get a look. Using her hands to knock aside branches and leaves, she made her way toward the wood's edge.

After passing a large cluster of pines and oaks, the view opened up and she could see the chapel side door open. Anne stood just outside, crouched halfway down and looking left and right. One hand was behind her on the doorknob, the other on her knee. Her red hair looked matted. On each wrist plastic zip ties hung loosely. Cybil wanted to shout for her, but couldn't. It would compromise her and Ed's position. She had to get closer.

Moving fast toward the chapel and cutting sideways, Cybil ignored the noise under her feet. Sliding on a mat of loose leaves, she regained her balance and kept going. If they got Anne out, it would eliminate a hostage scenario, she thought. She told Ed her intention while he kept sounding out his observations.

"She's starting to move away from the chapel, to the woods," Ed said.

Cybil said, "Yes, I can see now, it looks like I can intercept her once she's under cover. This is good. Keep your eyes on her."

Taking a few more steps, Cybil saw Anne's slow progress toward the woods. Another 20 feet and she'd be within whispering distance.

"Shit! Someone just ran out of the chapel after Anne, she won't make it," Ed said over the communication channel.

Cybil took a few steps forward to clear a tree in front of her and stood up from her stooped position. She saw in horror, Michelle making a flying tackle at Anne. Landing on the ground, the pair struggled. Without hesitation, Cybil ran toward them. Tearing through the woods, her arms brushed away anything in her path. As she broke into the clearing, she saw Michelle on top of Anne, choking her and slamming her head into the ground, yelling at the escapee.

"You fucking little bitch!" Michelle said as she slapped Anne across the face.

Anne's hands fought to block the assault and then she stopped her flailing. Her eyes looked up, above her head, to a pair of legs.

Michelle looked up and said, "What the—" but never finished.

Cybil's front ball kick caught Michelle flush in the forehead, snapping her head back. She tumbled backward and landed flat on her back. Stunned, she rolled to her side and placed her hand on the ground to get up. She slipped as her bandaged wrist gave way. Cybil leaped high over the prone Anne and landed her full weight on Michelle, who let out a huge huff. The force of the impact knocked Cybil's earpiece out. Moving around on the ground like a wrestler, Cybil got in position behind Michelle. Cybil's legs wrapped around Michelle's torso like a python squeezing while her arms circled the neck for a classic choke hold.

Michelle's garbled throat sounds trickled out as she struggled to free herself. She clawed at the arms around her neck, her red nails from her good hand scratching deep into Cybil's forearms, drawing blood. Focused, Cybil squeezed further to cut off the blood flow. She had not noticed her earpiece was gone.

Ed, watching the fight through the glass, smiled at Cybil's quick action. *Michelle will be unconscious in 30 seconds*. Ed glanced down at this watch: 30 minutes had passed. He swung the monocular to St. Rita's front door.

It opened and Markos appeared. Short, stocky, with powerful legs, he immediately started his routine, moving left toward the chapel.

Ed swung the lens back to the side of the chapel and said, "Markos is out. He's approaching your position. Get yourself and Anne into the woods for cover, quick!"

Cybil, still holding Michelle, who struggled less and less, didn't react to his warning. Anne, standing up, brushed herself off and stood with her hands on her knees. Then she stood straight up.

Ed, seeing Markos halfway to the chapel, shouted into his mouthpiece, "Get cover now!"

With no reaction from Cybil, Ed leaped up and raced through the woods. He angled his approach to emerge from the forest's edge by the time Markos turned the corner. While Markos's attention would be on the group in front of him, Ed planned to nail him from the back. Ed pulled his steel baton from his belt. He snapped it to the side and it extended 18 inches. Ed twirled it around a few times, getting the heft. He had to make sure to hit him hard the first time. It may take a few thumps to drop this gorilla, he thought.

As Ed approached the edge, he picked up speed; Markos had reached the corner. Markos, having turned the corner, kept walking. Ed broke through the wood's edge. He had 10 yards to close and sprinted on his toes, trained to approach quickly and quietly. He raised his baton waist-high.

Markos's head jerked up when he saw Cybil rise and stand over Michelle motionless body.

Anne, seeing past Cybil's shoulders, shouted, "Behind you!"

Cybil turned and put herself instinctively between Markos and Anne. She crouched into a ready position, scanning Markos's gait and planning her next move.

"Stay put. When I hit him, run into the woods. Wait there. I'll be right behind," Cybil said to Anne as she focused on Markos's approach.

Anne put her hand on Cybil's back. "No way. We take him together." She moved right a few feet to bracket him.

"Damn it, Anne, don't argue with me, I can handle him," she said.

"Not without me you won't, plus it will keep his attention, understand," Anne said. She dropped into a combat stance and watched Ed approaching behind Markos.

Markos, seeing Cybil, and glancing over to Anne, stopped and said, "You have no chance."

He took several long strides toward them as his face grew red. Grimacing he bared his teeth as his hands dropped to his sides. Moving forward, his head turned from Cybil to Anne and back again. Both his large, powerful hands were flexed, fingers wide apart, and ready to wring their necks.

Cybil feinted right, then left. Anne did the same. When Markos looked at Anne when she moved, Cybil reached behind her and pulled her military knife. Markos looked back at Cybil, saw the knife and stopped for a moment. Ed stepped closer, raising his baton high.

Pffst! Pffst! Two shots came from the left. Soft, silencer soft.

Ed caught two rounds in the side of his chest. The force of the .45-caliber bullets twisted him and knocked him away from Markos. He hit the ground and grabbed his side and front, his hands searching for wounds. He moaned, stunned and bleeding.

Markos spun around and saw Ed lying on the ground writhing in pain, blood pouring out, spurting through fingers pressed against the wounds.

Kurt stepped out of the chapel side door waving his gun and said, “You two don’t move.” He looked straight at Cybil and Anne.

Cybil looked at her friend Ed, lying on the ground. *Not like this, he just got married.* Anne moved to her side. She put her arm around her shoulder.

Kurt walked up to Ed, who was crawling on his stomach, toward the woods. The baton lay by his feet. Kurt kicked it away.

“Enough,” Kurt said.

He lifted the gun up and pointed it to the back of Ed’s head.

“No!” Cybil shouted.

Pffst! Pffst! Ed’s head slammed into the ground as the two .45 shells finished the kill. Cybil turned her head away. *Ed, Ed.* Anne’s hand squeezed her friend’s shoulder.

Kurt addressed Markos: “Get Michelle inside and cleaned up.”

Michelle, lying on the ground face up, had started to move, her knees flexing, one hand on her head.

Glaring at Cybil and then Anne, Kurt waved the gun toward the chapel door. “Inside, the lobby, you know the way. But first, drop that knife.”

Cybil let the knife hanging limp from her hand slip to the ground.

The two women walked toward the chapel door. No light came from inside; only a dark rectangle lay before them. Glancing at the dock and the boat, Cybil could see the storm clouds coming in, as Captain Jonah had predicted. The wind picked up rolling leaves in front of them, like a flock of flightless birds trying to escape.

Cybil mentally calculated the time left before the charges exploded. *Be ready.*

51

Cybil followed Anne inside, through the chapel and into the adjoining hallway leading into the lobby, which was lined with black-and-white prints. She glanced at the various photos: larger pictures of kids, nuns and priests were followed by smaller ones with fewer children and staff. The last part of the hallway had no portraits, just a blank white wall.

"Keep moving!" Kurt said as he shoved the .45's silencer muzzle into the small of her back.

She turned her head to glare at him. Unmoved, he simply jammed the gun into her back again. Turning forward, she saw Anne had also turned to look. Cybil nodded, her chin lifting forward telling her to keep moving, her eyebrows lifting. She mouthed the words "It will be all right." Anne's little smile and quick nod signaled she understood. She turned forward and quickened the pace.

Anne entered the lobby, and her nose twitched at the unfamiliar smell. The musty, old wood scent remained, but gone was the lemon accent from the floor waxing. Instead, the tang of burned metal hit her nostrils. The group stopped in the middle of the lobby. Cybil looked down. They stood on the hand-carved, worn seal of St. Rita's Children's Home, open since 1875 to house Savannah's abandoned children.

The clock in her head kept ticking: *30 minutes*. She stood next to Anne, their shoulders touching, hands to their sides. Heavy footfalls from the stairwell drew their attention. Stavos, Al-Mahdi and Abdul stepped down toward them. Al-Mahdi and Abdul, casually dressed in suit jackets, reached the lobby floor a step ahead of Stavos. Both had small overnight bags over their shoulders but Abdul also carried a metal briefcase.

"She appears quite alive. I am most disappointed," Al-Mahdi said as he made the last step.

He wore brown boots with thick soles that landed heavy on the wood floor. He put his hand on the carved pinecone knob at the end of the handrail. Gripping it, his knuckles turned white.

From the chapel hallway where the group emerged, Markos, holding Michelle up with an arm around her waist, bulled his way in. Sporting a dark bruise on her forehead, Michelle stumbled forward despite Markos's support, her heels scratching on the wood floor. He moved her to the bench next to the lobby doors and helped her sit. Stepping away, he joined Kurt, standing behind the women. Pulling a .38 pistol from a shoulder holster under his jacket, he pointed it at the women and glanced back at Michelle. She reached for her neck and rubbed it. Her eyes, blood-red from the capillary bleeding that choke holds produce, stared at Cybil. Cybil glanced over at Michelle and grinned. Michelle licked her lips, sneered and glared back.

Stavos joined Al-Mahdi on the lobby floor. Abdul moved to the side, just in front of the last step. The briefcase he held looked heavy because his fingers dug deep into the padded handle. The ridged, silver-metallic briefcase measured thick, about 8 inches wide. He rested it on the bottom step, not letting go but needing help to mitigate the weight.

Stavos and Al-Mahdi moved together toward Cybil and Anne. The women each took a small step backward into Kurt and Markos, whose combined bulk formed a wall behind them. Anne's hand reached for Cybil's, they locked fingers and clasped tight. Anne looked across the lobby to the stained-glass window, to the white dove that had looked black before. She remembered her conversation with Sofi, about God taking care. She gripped Cybil's hand harder. Anne looked at her, her eyes intense as the last time they were this close, in Dubai.

Cybil leaned into Anne's ear and whispered softly, "Stay close, you'll know when to move."

Her lips touched Anne's ear when she whispered, her breath blowing Anne's fine red hair. The scent of vanilla filled Cybil's nose. She remembered Dubai, the intensity of all she'd felt. Then the image of her dream, when at sea, flashed in her mind, of the beach, the umbrella, the bird. She gripped Anne's hand again, and she squeezed back.

Stopping a few feet away, Al-Mahdi and Stavos looked at the women. Stavos looked over at Michelle on the bench where she rested. She shook her head several times and took deep breaths. Stavos turned to Al-Mahdi, who had crossed his arms and shook his head slowly side to side.

"I tire of this. Abdul and I must leave immediately. Yet I am uncertain if you can handle these loose ends. I cannot have loose ends as I finish my business up north," Al-Mahdi said, uncrossing his arms.

A voice came from the side: "The basement, lobby and upstairs bedrooms are ready. Do you need anything else?" Father Michael walked over to the group from the other side of the lobby.

"Not now. Did you tell the bishop about your sabbatical?" Stavos said.

"Yes, I e-mailed him that I'm leaving tomorrow and would see him in a month." Father Michael smiled, looked over at Michelle and thought, *But I didn't tell him she'd be with me.*

"Before you go, Mr. Kasen left an overnight bag in his room. Can you please get it as a favor for our guest?" Stavos said.

The priest frowned but said, "Sure."

Father Michael turned his back to the group and took two slow steps upward. His hand gripped the rail for support. He glanced over his shoulder toward Stavos and then looked up the steps.

Stavos looked over at Kurt and causally pointed a finger at Father Michael going up the steps. Kurt took two steps to the side and pointed his .45 at Father Michael's back.

The bullets hit the priest's upper torso and his body slammed against the wall next to the stairs. His hand on the railing slid down, pinning his arm between it and the wall. He stumbled down the stairs, sliding his arm down the wall but it jammed against one of the supports. He spun around. Grabbing the rail farther down for support with his other hand it too slipped behind the rail. Kurt took a step closer and, lifting the gun, pointed it at the priest's face.

Looking over at Al-Mahdi, Stavos said, “No loose ends here.”

Kurt pulled the trigger. With another “Pffst!” a single bullet entered Father Michael’s forehead and exited the back, exploding the priest’s gray matter into a tight red-and-white pattern on the wall that trickled down. The priest’s head fell forward, his chin resting on his chest, his arms spread wide open. He hung on the railing like a doll left behind by a child no longer wanting to play.

Anne gasped as her eyes widened. She tried swallowing but her throat was dry. She didn’t want this for Father Michael. Cybil shook her head and squeezed Anne’s hand.

Kurt stepped back behind the women. He looked at Michelle who was sitting up, both hands on her knees. She shrugged her shoulders, tilted her head and smiled sideways as if a funny joke had just been told.

Al-Mahdi raised his eyebrows and, leaning toward Cybil and Anne, said, “Shoot them now.”

“No! Too quick. There is a deep well outside, on the way to the dock,” Michelle yelled from the bench, “they’ll spend hours looking for them and not us. Maybe never find them.”

Stavos looked over at Michelle, then at a smiling Al-Mahdi.

Al-Mahdi said, “Poetic. An unmarked grave no one will ever mourn over. To the depths of the earth we will send them both. Let us proceed quickly.”

He turned toward Abdul and waved his hand for them to leave. His associate picked up the case, bending his knees for leverage. Abdul stepped up next to Al-Mahdi.

“Markos, get the priest’s body and bring it. Michelle, take his place,” Stavos said.

"Gladly," Michelle said. She stood, rubbing her neck, then walked over behind the women. She stretched out her hand to Markos.

Handing her his gun, he went toward the stairs. She pushed the women toward the lobby door. Her hardest shoves went to Cybil, who bit down hard. *Not yet, but soon.*

Michelle and Kurt pushed the women through St. Rita's double doors, onto the porch and past the ribbed white columns and onto the steps. Behind them, Stavos, Al-Mahdi and Abdul followed, with Markos carrying Father Michael's corpse. The group moved off the porch, onto the gravel driveway. The crushed rocks—small, irregular and colorless in the night—gave way under their feet. They turned toward the chapel like a funeral procession, silent. Only the random crunch of steps filled the air.

Turning the corner past the chapel, the group walked toward the well. Beyond it was the floating *Destiny*. The incoming Nor'easter winds had churned up the inland waterway, small waves melting into larger ones, the chop bobbing the yacht like a toy. The boat began to knock hard into the dock's rubber tires, the thunking noticeable as they kept getting closer. High up, the half-crescent shone behind low, fast-moving clouds. Luna hung over the boat and the agitated Savannah River channel, lighting the planned escape route to the sea.

As the group approached the well, the breeze increased again, the nearby forest noise building. The wind rushed through treetops scraping leaves against each other. Tall, thin pines leaned into the crown of neighbor oaks before creaking back into a straight posture. Scurrying small animals tunneling through underbrush caught Kurt's ear and his head turned to the dark woods. He craned his neck and squinted to see, but then turned back to shove his gun hard into Anne's back while Michelle slapped the back of Cybil's head.

"Keep going, bitch!" Michelle said.

The breeze picked up and became steady. More often now, dry lightning flashed as if a camera somewhere took a snapshot. No thunder was heard only the wind's steady rustling. Tree limbs jostled by the breeze creaked, a few dead ones longing to fall, broke off and tumbled through the canopy, their progress to the ground audible as they found their final resting place.

The group reached the well and stopped. A flash of light, dry lightning, no sound, illumined the entire party. Stavos, Al-Mahdi and Abdul stood just past the well, closer to the boat. In front of the well, Cybil and Anne stood with Kurt and Michelle behind. Cybil looked at Ed's body lying a few feet away, before turning her eyes back on the well. It was round, about six feet across, the surface a dark black disk.

Missing was the overhead bucket and pail mechanism, long ago replaced by a steel hand pump on the side. Running city water had reduced the well to an unused decoration. Cobwebs laced the handle to the spigot. Cybil shifted her feet and lifted up on her toes to see inside. Nothing but blackness waited for them.

The insistent wind had cleared a space in the sky to let moonlight reveal the stage. The huge single limb from the massive oak tree, above the well, scattered the night beams. Through its many snaking branches lush with leaves, shadows fell on everyone. Light and dark patches, like camouflage, settled on each figure. Then a single loud caw sounded from the woods.

With Father Michael's corpse still over his shoulder, Markos pointed at the large oak tree, his hand shaking. On the tree limb, near where it joined the trunk, sat a large blackbird.

All heads turned to see. Anne took a small breath. Cybil's eyebrows scrunched together and she leaned her head to one side. Michelle and Kurt glanced up, then returned to eyeballing the women.

"Markos, Markos!" Stavos said, raising his voice above the wind that was now whooshing through the area, "It's nothing. Throw the priest in."

Markos hesitated, but then shook his head and stepped forward to the well and tossed the body in. A long interval, then a splash. It was deep.

Glancing from Stavos to the bird, Markos drooped his head and shoulders as he walked toward his boss.

"Better. Now dump him too," Stavos said, pointing at Ed.

Markos moved to the dead agent's corpse and with little effort and no expression, picked up the body. At the well, he leaned over the edge and tossed in the remains. Another splash.

Stavos looked at Michelle, who stood behind the women, and smiled. "You pick the next one."

Michelle's head turned left to Cybil, then right to Anne, then back to Cybil. Both women faced forward but listened intently.

Michelle said, "The bitch goes in first. Kurt, hold the other till I'm done. It'll be fun dragging her fighting ass and throwing her in. Markos, help me."

"No! Me first," Anne said loudly, turning around to face Michelle.

Cybil looked over at Anne angrily and said, "What are you doing?"

"You're stronger, I can't … can't watch you get hurt," Anne said.

Anne said to Michelle, "I'll jump in. I won't fight back. Please give me a minute to pray first."

Michelle looked at Stavos, who nodded.

Kurt jammed the gun in the back of Cybil's head. "Don't move!" he said.

Wrapping his large arm around her neck, he pressed her into him and jammed the gun muzzle into her temple.

"It will be over for you soon," he said.

Cybil struggled but couldn't budge. She began to breathe harder and sweat. She saw Anne walk in front of Michelle as both headed to the well. Cybil's mind raced. *This is going too fast, the charges will be too late.* They had run out of time.

Anne turned and looked at Cybil. Then she took a last step near the well and fell to her knees. Michelle, with her gun hand hanging by her side, stepped beside Anne.

Anne folded her hands, bent her head down and started to pray silently. After 30 seconds, she fell face first to the ground.

Cybil shook hard against Kurt's grip, wanting to reach her, be with her at this last moment. His grip tightened, she coughed, her mouth dry. Her eyes glanced upward at the sky and down to Anne. In the moonlight, on the ground, she looked like a corpse. Cybil did not want this as her last memory of Anne. She wanted the Anne of Dubai, fun, sexy, vulnerable, free, unfettered. Her fingers grabbed at Kurt's large forearm, and he flexed tighter. Her eyes moved up, looking at the moon. She thought, *Damn you.* Then a small dark figure passed in front of the moon, almost eclipsing it. The blackbird had flown across Luna's face.

Anne rose to her feet and looked at Michelle and then at Stavos. She peered into the black darkness of the well. She had a peaceful look on her face.

Al-Mahdi said, "Finish it, now. We must leave. The ship will be meeting us at—"

He never finished his sentence as a brilliant white lightning discharge struck the massive oak tree limb at the trunk joint. The deafening thunderclap was louder than anything anyone in this group had ever heard. Then a crackling, crunching sound, slow at first, rushed to a loud, sharp snap as the joint gave way. Tree sap smoking from the 3,000-degree strike fell to the ground near the base, along with flaming wood shards and charred shavings trailing smoke. The limb, hanging over the group, lurched downward. The whole massive arm, complete with leafy side branches, fell and landed on the group, all four thousand pounds.

Before losing consciousness Cybil watched Michelle being propelled forward. A thick, round jutting branch had struck her in the back as she stood near Anne. It toppled her into the well, screaming.

Dark blackness, then a deep sigh. In. Out. In. Out. Cybil noticed her breathing, steady, regular. For a moment she thought, *I'm at sea.* Flexing her fingers, she felt dirt and grass under them. Blinking, her eyes opened. On her back, she looked up. Soft moonlight fell through leaves and thin branches sitting a few feet above her head. The wind rustled the leaves above her. Stars flickered in the space above. The stillness bothered her.

She moved her legs and feet, wriggled her shoulders and arms. Under the limb's fallen canopy, Cybil lay in a small crawl space with enough room to sit up, which she did. Taking a deep breath she twisted to look behind her.

Kurt came into view a few feet away. She tensed up. He did not move. Staring closer, she saw why. A baseball-width branch lying across his neck had him pinned but that didn't kill him. The thin, knife-like branch sticking out of his chest had done the job. The branch end curled up like a bent accusing finger. Blood dripping from its tip landed every few seconds, splattering onto his chest.

Whoa. Cybil turned and reached up for an overhanging branch to pull herself up. Pushing through the leaves, her 5'6" frame barely cleared the fallen tangle. Looking around she saw Markos a few feet away. A two-foot-wide branch, bent like a flexing bicep with a huge knot for an elbow, sat on the back of his skull. His head, twisted and misshapen, had been crammed into the ground.

Still recovering, Cybil thought, *Who else …*"Anne! Anne!" she said.

"Over here, I'm okay," Anne said.

Cybil's soul expanded. She looked over a side branch separating her from Anne, who had been knocked several feet to the side. Her waist and legs remained hidden underneath thick, leafy cover, the rest of her visible. She sat up.

"Anything broken? Can you move your legs?" Cybil said, standing on her toes, her hands gripping the rough bark for leverage.

"Yes, I can move fine, I just need to wiggle out of here. I feel good," she said.

"Ahh, ahh," groaned a male voice from the other side of the well. The leaves shook and moved. No one stood up.

"I fucking can't move! My legs are broke. Kurt! Markos! Michelle! Where the hell are you?" Stavos's voice came through the brush.

An approaching, then receding whoosh of something large and fast in the sky gave Stavos an unwelcome answer. The fast-beating rhythm of helicopter blades raced around the corner of the chapel. Lining its brick edge from the ground to the third floor, a bright white glow was followed by swirling dust. The chopper's landing lights and downward wind created a tumult that would not soon settle.

Cybil looked at the light, smiled and then turned to the unseen Stavos and said, "My team's here. Time's up, you …"

She stopped in mid-sentence as a figure rose from a crouch, on the farthest edge of the fallen limb, past where Stavos lay. A briefcase in hand, he took a step, limped, took another and stumbled toward the dock on unsteady legs.

Cybil turned to a wriggling Anne, making progress, only her ankles lay underneath the brush. "Someone is getting away, are you—"

"I'll be fine, go," Anne said, smiling at Cybil.

Cybil leaned over, reaching her hand to Anne, but a thin, leafy branch separated them, jamming itself into her stomach. Anne reached back the same, their fingers inches from each other.

"Go," Anne said again.

Cybil's eyes flashed deep-blue and she took a deep breath. *Yes.*

Turning, she grabbed the branch in front of her, her arms flexed in sync with her legs. With a single powerful thrust, she lifted herself and swung her legs over the branch, clearing the area that had boxed her in. Landing on pressed leaves and snapped branches, she had a clear path to the figure fast moving away from her. His legs churned toward the dock. She took several fast steps toward him, then BOOM! A huge sound stopped his advance. Cybil halted.

A second later another boom, followed by intense light rising fast into the sky, a tumbling, swirling ball of burning gas and smoke, red and black, hung over the *Destiny*—blown in half and sinking in front of them.

The flash outlined a body a few feet to the left of Cybil. Abdul. He lay underneath a gnarly 10-foot-long branch that rested on him. The tree section had chopped into him, along his torso, his body unnaturally pressed into the ground. He was not moving.

Looking back toward the dock, in the explosion's light, Cybil saw Al-Mahdi stare at the fireball expanding and folding into itself. His face turned to hers, his eyes burned red as the fireball. Hugging the case, he turned left and raced into the woods.

52

The explosion's noise receded, and Cybil's legs sped her to the spot where Al-Mahdi had entered the woods.

Crashing through brush, jumping over fallen branches, she stepped her way through the woods fast. Dried brown leaves clung to her hair; she brushed the clinging vegetation away. About 30 feet into the woods she stopped. The dark canopy filtered most of the moonlight, casting a pale blue tint over the small trees and palmettos. She squinted, looked ahead, to the right and left for Al-Mahdi, but couldn't find him. Cybil knelt and rested both hands on the forest floor, touching the dry leaves and damp soil. Staring into the woods she turned her head to listen.

Falling leaves like huge snowflakes slowly descended. A bird's call echoed, followed by tree frogs serenading the forest before it became silent again. Tiny scratching sounds to the left grabbed her attention, but it was probably only a small animal. Then the sound of leaves being crunched reached her ears. A couple of seconds passed, then the same sound again. … A few more seconds, the same sound. The intervals were spaced too much like a man stepping slowly over the forest floor. She looked toward the sound.

Her eyes had adjusted fully yet she couldn't see an outline or anything. Another crunching step and her eyes fixed on the position. *Where is he?*

Another crunch but this time Al-Mahdi stepped into a thin shaft of moonlight, his upper torso partially revealed; he was no more than 20 yards away. He stopped and lay the briefcase down next to his feet. The leaves again crackled.

Cybil's eyes focused. *Gotcha!*

Drawing a straight line to the target, she saw he was in a small clearing with a clump of bushes to the left, a fallen pine tree straight ahead and a grouping of short oaks to the right. The fallen pine had nestled on another fallen log, creating a barrier. It would be a five-foot hurdle to jump over that log. Cybil looked ahead and saw her solution in front of her, near the fallen pine.

She waited for a breeze to provide sound cover. Her breathing accelerated. *He'll start moving again and I'll lose this chance,* she thought. Then a strong, blasting wind came through, rushing between them. She lifted her fingers off the forest floor, leaned forward and broke into a sprint.

Her legs blurred as she ran straight toward him. A few feet from the fallen log she leaped onto a tree stump about two feet high. Her right foot balanced on the stump while her left hand landed on the rough bark. Pushing off hard, she went airborne, twisting toward Al-Mahdi. Her right foot swung around and headed toward him.

Al-Mahdi had heard something but had to pick up the case. He looked down to it, then looked up in time to see Cybil's foot slice through the moonlight, hitting him flush in the chest.

"Umpf, ahh," Al-Mahdi groaned as he toppled backward and to the ground.

He slid a few feet on his rear end, the pine needles providing a sliding platform.

Cybil's other foot landed square on the case. It broke open and a small ball, softball size, of metallic blue rolled out. She had planned a cat landing but the metal briefcase tripped her. The case slid toward Al-Mahdi while it pushed her backward into the fallen pine, where she hit her head.

She rolled over on her hands and knees trying to focus, but brown, black and dark blotches tinted with blue swirled before her. Still groggy she saw that the metal softball lay just underneath her chest. She reached out to touch it. It felt warm despite its cool metallic color. She crawled a few inches and drew a deep breath. The smell of rotting leaves mixed with pine made her blink. Her hands flexed to grip the moist ground, leaves squished between her fingers. *Woods! Al-Mahdi!*

Cybil looked up and rose onto her knees. She reflexively raised an upper arm block to protect her face from Al-Mahdi's boot coming at her.

Her block, effective enough to prevent real damage, couldn't stop the force from knocking her over. The kick was powerful enough to lift her off her knees and lay her out. She thumped onto her back, to the forest floor like a log. Putting her arms behind her to get up, her hands slipped on the wet leaves and again her back hit the ground. Before she could get up Al-Mahdi jumped on her chest, his knees pinning her arms, his hands reaching around her throat. Cybil could hardly breathe from the weight, and then his hands tightened their grip. She tried coughing but couldn't.

Al-Mahdi smiled, his triangular face hovering over her as he said, "This will end soon for you. You are not as important as my schedule. My gift must be delivered."

He tightened his grip. She couldn't take a breath.

Cybil bucked herself up trying to shove him off, but he was too heavy. She lifted her knees toward Al-Mahdi's back, thrusting upward. Her lower legs were almost to her hands.

"Oh, the American whore thinks I will fall for her charms. Are you offering yourself to me?" he said.

She shook her head and tried to speak, moving her mouth, but no sounds came out; her vocals cords were slowly being crushed. He squeezed tighter, then relaxed his grip a bit.

"Tell me then, before I send you to your God, if you have one. What final words do you have for yourself?"

Cybil coughed and started to speak, but then coughed again. Al-Mahdi relaxed his grip more. She nodded her head.

"I have … have no words for myself. But I do for you," she said.

Leaning in, he looked into her eyes. "And what are they?"

Staring at him, she nodded as her fingers traced the top edge of the blade handle of her black steel calf knife. *Just an inch more.*

"They are about your target. We know about the device. It will not reach Fort A.P. Hill in Virginia," she said, gritting her teeth.

Al-Mahdi's eyes narrowed to slits. He moved his face, nose to nose, to hers and his breath hit her. It flashed her back to the tent where the captain had died.

"It matters little what you know. I will not be stopped because it is Allah's will. That is the truth," he said, looking upward.

"The last truth you will know is that I killed you," Cybil said as her fingers fully gripped the calf knife's black onyx handle.

Sliding it out, she twisted the blade and jammed the tip hard toward his butt cheek, cutting through his pants and breaking deep into the skin. She ripped it out quickly. He twitched and rose to get away from the blade. It was enough to free her arms. Her left hand reached up and grabbed his jacket, holding him. With a sweeping motion, like a boxer's wide right hook, she punched-slid the blade across this neck, slicing his left carotid artery and gashing open his throat, bisecting his trachea. He rocked back and his hands reached for his throat. Al-Mahdi started to make gurgling sounds as the blood flowed into his windpipe.

She lowered the knife to the front of his chest. Her other hand, palm open, rested on top of the handle.

Plunging the knife in, the upward angle slid the blade under the sternum. The hilt of the knife thudded onto his chest. She twisted the blade. Blood flowed over it onto her hands.

Al-Mahdi's eyes snapped wide open, his gurgling sounds ceased. His hands dropped to his side. His chin dropped onto his chest. He fell over, one leg still on Cybil. She pushed it off and rolled over to her knees.

Bobbing, weaving light beams typical of gun-sight flashlights shone from positions all around her.

"Stay down, hands over your head. Identify yourself!" came a voice from the forest shadows.

"Really, you couldn't have shot him while he was choking me?" Cybil said, wiping her hands on the ground.

A SWAT team of black-uniformed men closed on Cybil, all the beams on her. She squinted into the light.

"It's her, stand down," an older voice said.

The beams immediately shot to the ground. All the men were dressed in commando uniforms, no markings, with masks and eyes shields. Some of them stepped back into a rest position, the others turned toward the woods, still at the ready.

"Sorry, Miss Raven. With the night scopes we can only tell so much," the older voice said.

He stepped toward her and removed his mask. With a gray buzz cut and a five-o'clock shadow, this soldier looked experienced, Cybil thought as she stood up.

"What's the situation?" Cybil said, glancing toward the orphanage.

"The location is secure," the older commando said, pointing over the treetops. "We've set up a command post and processing area."

The glow of artificial lights illuminated the sky over St. Rita.

A SWAT team member approached from the dark. The leader shone his beam into his face. He lifted his mask only enough to clear his mouth to speak.

"NEST has secured this area. They found the material. Small, softball size. They think it was cesium. Classic dirty bomb scenario," he said.

"Damn, that stuff is extremely hazardous. How was it being transported?" the leader said.

"Lead shield case but it cracked open. You're right, the amount was highly enriched, the millisieverts are off the scale. It was in the open but now secure. Central has been updated," he said.

"Good, be careful with that. If anyone got exposed, they need to be checked out," the man in charge said.

He turned to Cybil. “Miss,” he said, his voice soft, while shining the beam in her face, “You’ve been in a hazmat zone. We should take you to the hospital to be checked out. We’ve set up a secure section within the ER, our own doctors.”

Cybil put her hand on the man’s arm. “There’s a survivor, she’s—”

“No worries, miss. Sister Anne identified herself and told us where you had gone. She’s fine, but they’re taking her to Memorial Medical to be checked out,” he said.

Cybil smiled and said, “Thank you.”

“One more thing,” he said.

“What?”

“I’ll brief you on the way to Memorial. It’s about Fort A.P. Hill and your son.”

53

Three black SUVs drove in close formation east on US-80, Victory Drive, toward Savannah. Minutes after leaving the island, the middle vehicle reached the bridge over the main tributary, the channel off the river that flowed past Thunderbolt and into the Atlantic.

As the thick, heavy tires bounced over the threshold from highway to bridge, Cybil's finger pressed the window control down. Fresh air streamed in. A deep breath took in the familiar scents of her city. The river's smells mixed with fried food aromas—probably from Bubba's or Tortugas Grille—made her smile. Peering farther along she saw the lights of Thunderbolt Marina, where she and Anne had met after so many years. Now waiting for news on Sebastian, Cybil began to cry.

The loud vibration of a nearby cell phone forced her to take a quick breath and wipe her tears. When he got in the car earlier, the team leader told her that Sonja would call. He himself knew little. Sitting next to her he pulled a phone from a front thigh pocket and put it to his ear.

"Huh. … Huh. … Yes. The area is secure. Gruner is in custody, the Feds have him at Memorial. The material and other remains are being transported as instructed. … Yeah, she's right next to me. … Okay," he said.

Handing the phone to Cybil, he said, "It's Sonja."

"What about Sebastian?" Cybil said as she started puffing, her palms sweating.

She leaned forward on the edge of the passenger seat, her back tense. Her grip on the phone tightened.

Sonja said, "He's fine. Relax. He's coming home as scheduled. All the scouts are safe. He and all the troops are coming home not knowing a thing."

Cybil exhaled and slumped back into her seat.

Closing her eyes, she took another audible breath and said, "Thank you, thank you, thank you!"

The leader sitting next to her smiled and leaned back. He pulled a small pack of gum from a chest pocket. Looking out the car window, he put a piece in his mouth and started chewing slowly.

Cybil listened to Sonja's briefing. It lasted until they pulled up to the hospital emergency entrance. Al-Mahdi's operative near Fort A.P. Hill, Safir, had a cousin, a lieutenant on the base. The lieutenant had purchased an unusual amount of propane that got flagged for a closer look. After a records sweep, they found this lieutenant had a great military record but his family connections in Yemen had triggered a higher alert. The FBI interrogated him on base, but he knew nothing. When he mentioned that their only plans were for a picnic on the same day as the scouts' closing ceremonies, the FBI asked for details and Safir's location.

With the trailer park under surveillance, the joint strike team moved in after the target left the RV. Delay road blocks from local law enforcement were set up to prevent an untimely return. It didn't take the team long to discover the mobile RV had been rigged as a moving dirty bomb of unique design. They got inside easily—finding no perimeter booby traps to deal with—and tore it apart. A first-pass analysis of the device and its design concluded the conventional explosive yield was massive, but the ingenious construction to maximize dispersal of radioactive material made this special. The first explosion would have killed many instantly and the radiation fallout many more for years to come.

The softball-sized cesium shell, when vaporized, would have reduced the stadium valley into a radioactive dead zone for centuries. With the geography and wind patterns, adjacent exposure beyond the valley would have reached another 10 to 25 miles. Initial calculations had the damage much worse than what happened to the four reactors at Sendai in Japan after the quake and tsunami. Those were contained somewhat; this would have been a worst-case scenario and graver than 9/11, since 5,000 scouts had been in the valley.

Safir was taken into custody at one of the roadblocks. He folded like a map during interrogation and confirmed they built only one device and were waiting for Al-Mahdi to deliver the "seed of Allah"—his words. The rest of his story checked out.

The car slowed to a stop. Cybil, phone still next to her ear, got out and walked toward the hospital's glass doors which slid open before her. She sat in the empty waiting room that smelled of bleach and cherry, while the team leader approached the desk.

Still on the phone, Cybil said, "Did you ever find out about Tom?"

"He checked out this morning from St. Joseph's Hospital. The cops took him there after finding him passed out in his sweats and smelling of bourbon, in an alley near Molly's. They thought he was a homeless drunk," Sonja said.

"They must have dumped him there after taking me," Cybil said.

Sonja chuckled and said, "Lucky they didn't shoot him in the back of the head. We intercepted the police report. He did not have any ID, but they ran his prints. Since he worked at NASA in the early '80s his prints were on file. I called him, posing as Savannah PD for follow-up information, and said you were fine and would be in contact. He's leaving today to pick up his wife in Atlanta, but wanted me to give you a message."

"What?" she said.

"You sure know how to show a guy a good time!" Sonja said, laughing.

Cybil laughed, the concern about her friend dissipating with every chuckle and smile.

A nurse called her out of the waiting room and escorted her to the secure section past two armed guards dressed in black unmarked combat fatigues. The doctor in the emergency room never smiled as he gave Cybil a complete exam, treating her cuts and scrapes. He then sat down opposite her in a chair as she sat on the table, hospital gown over her pants.

"They gave me no details on your potential radiation exposure and you don't measure anything other than normal background," he said. "I don't believe the rash is related. It looks like a sunburn only."

"That's good. After all the radiation I took as a child, I should be glowing," she said, smiling.

Her legs swung on the edge of the table.

The doctor remained glum. "Keep to your regular check-ups. You may want to consider spacing out your mammograms as well, in case this incident has increased your risks. Plus, treat that sunburn on your chest. Does it hurt?" the doctor said, getting up from the chair and stepping closer to her.

Cybil looked down and, pinching her gown between her fingers, lifted the covering. About a hand-width wide pink rash covered the space between her breasts, climbing a third of the way to her nipples. It felt cool, she thought.

"Not at all, can I go?" she said.

"Of course," he said.

He walked out of the room and closed the door. She jumped off the table and got dressed.

Finally ready to leave, Cybil left the ER hallway, heading to the lobby. She glanced sideways down one of the perpendicular corridors. Outside a room, two large uniformed Savannah PD officers, with feet apart, stood in guard stance. A man in a dark suit and dark glasses walked out of the room and toward her. She waited for him to reach her. As he approached she saw he had an earpiece in and a lapel mike.

"What's going to happen to Stavos?" she asked, standing erect, arms crossed, leaning on one leg.

"Miss Raven. Mr. Gruner will be transported into Federal custody as soon as his thigh casts are set. Bastard broke both legs. Not sure how that happened," he said.

Cybil smiled. "Me either. What are the charges?"

"Well, aside from standard criminal conspiracy, illegal material transports, import violations, murder, etcetera, the federal terrorism connection tops the lists. It would have put a needle in his arm if it weren't for the deal."

"What fucking deal!" Cybil said, dropping her hands into fists at her side.

"Relax, Miss Raven. This son of a bitch will never see the light of day outside of club fed, but he avoids the death penalty by cooperating with our ongoing terrorism investigation into Al-Mahdi's network," he said.

"He's dead, by the way," Cybil said, grinning.

"Yes, I know, my congratulations," the man said, "but some networks are designed that even if you cut off the head of the snake, another grows to replace it. We'll find out soon what kind of network he built."

The man bowed slightly and walked away. Within a few feet from her, he touched his finger to his ear and talked into his suit.

When Cybil stepped into the waiting room, the team leader greeted her.

"Miss, we're ready to take you home. I believe you have an early pickup at the airport tomorrow morning," the team leader said, smiling.

Cybil smiled back.

54

"Mom! I haven't been gone that long," Sebastian said, gently trying to loosen his mother's grasp.

Kneeling on one knee, Cybil held him tight. June stood behind her, all three in the airport central area, past security. The red-faced scout, in full uniform, looked over his mother's shoulder, into his sister's face and raised his hands palm upward with a quizzical look. June smiled and shrugged her shoulders.

Giving up, he melted into her arms, embracing her and leaning close to her ear. He said softly, "I missed you too, Mom."

Cybil closed her eyes. Her fingers gripped her little man's back around his waist, her head in his chest. She smelled spilled Coca-cola and airline peanuts.

He tapped her on the shoulder and said, "Can we go now, Mom?"

Sniffling once, Cybil rose and said, "Sure, honey, we're going straight to Forsyth Park. Mom's got a meeting there, plus it's a beautiful day."

June, stepping to her mom's side, tugged on her arm and said, "I told you he'd be all right."

Cybil looked down at June, nodded her head once and said, "Yes, honey, thanks. You were right."

"Mom," Sebastian said, "can we get real hot dogs this time and not the tofu kind?"

"Sure, and ice cream too. It's a great day for the family!" Cybil beamed, grabbing both her kids' hands and led them out of the airport on a half-run.

No more than 30 minutes later, Cybil found a spot on Gaston Street, slipped four quarters in the meter and walked, hand in hand, with her children down the park's center lane. They strode toward Forsyth's landmark fountain. She looked right and left, taking the familiar scene in, squeezing June and Sebastian's hands tighter as they walked closer to the waiting Lady. A steady, low rumble of grass mowers in the flat fields was a familiar background noise. Laughter, squealing and screaming, from the playground near the clamshell stage, promised morning playmates for her children.

Her nose detected a bouquet of sweet hyacinth mixed with fresh-cut grass. She slowly exhaled and inhaled again to savor the scents. They reached the active fountain. Each water feature, hard at work, meant a cool mist floated as a fine spray around the fountain. Mother, son and daughter craned their necks and placed their faces flush into the invisible cloud. Cybil's forehead and cheeks gathered a wet film, which soon evaporated due to her warmth from the fast walk. Her face felt cool, rested.

Stopping, her kids slipped their hands out of hers and started circling the large central fountain, their hands slapping the iron fence surrounding the pool. A quick low ringing followed each blow and then dissipated. Sebastian and June smiled, looking back at their mother. They would make it back to her in a few minutes if they kept their course and pace.

On one bench to the right, an older couple sat, holding hands, the woman holding a leash. At the end of the leash a small dachshund lay drinking from a small plastic bowl.

Cybil looked down briefly, closed her eyes and mouthed, “Goodbye, John, we’ll miss you.”

A voice cried out, “Cybil, Cybil, hey!” It was Judy with David Flint and his wife Amy.

“Hey, how you feeling?” Judy asked, reaching Cybil and hugging her.

“I’m good. Here with the kids,” Cybil said, tilting her head to the circling duo.

Judy waved and yelled, “Hey, June, Sebastian!”

“Hi, Aunt Judy!” Sebastian and June yelled back together.

“I hate when they call me Aunt Judy. Sounds so damn old. Just Judy is fine. I need to talk them again,” the tattoo artist said with a fake frown.

David reached out and shook Cybil’s hand. Amy stepped in and gave Cybil a hug.

“Thank you so much for telling us about Sofi and Cecilia!” Amy said.

Cybil smiled and said, “So what’s happening?”

David said, “Well, if we pass the interviews we can start by fostering them first. We want to take them both. Amy’s sister was special needs, so that is not a problem. We are hopeful.”

Cybil said, “Wonderful! What about the After the Outrage thing. Is it still going on?”

“Yes, we’re setting up for the event for later today—and thanks for agreeing to help,” David said.

“What time does it start?” Cybil said.

Amy reached out her hand, placing it on Cybil's arm. "We have a lot of people asking about this project. Your presence will help raise awareness about this and the Eden Community Village idea. I'll introduce you on stage around 6:00 p.m."

Cybil took Amy's hand, smiling, and cupped it between her own. "I look forward to it. Okay if I bring my kids?"

Amy smiled back. Sebastian and June had completed their circle and stood next to their mother.

"Hi, I'm Amy. Your mom is going to help us tonight at the event. Lots of kids will be there and we'd like you to come."

June looked up at Cybil, as did Sebastian. Cybil smiled and nodded.

"Sure!" Sebastian said.

"Hey punks, I bet I can make it to the jungle gym before you," Judy said, turning and jogging slowly toward the playground.

June and Sebastian broke into a sprint, laughing and chasing after Aunt Judy.

Amy and David watched the two children as they raced away. Amy nudged closer to David and her hand slipped into his. Cybil saw Amy's smile.

David beamed at his wife, then turned to Cybil and said, "Your kids seem great. Thanks so much for agreeing to help. See you at six?"

"You bet," Cybil said with a wink.

She watched David and Amy walk toward the clamshell stage, hand in hand.

Cybil turned toward the iron railing and looked across the fountain's pool. Arcing streams of water from the four trumpeting gargoyles dove through the water's surface, roiling their landing zone and sending ripples in every direction. Cybil watched a large ripple followed by several small ones travel toward her. Reaching the cement edge, they splashed against it and disappeared beneath the surface.

"Beautiful Lady at the top of the fountain looks like she's ready for a fight." Anne said from Cybil's side.

Cybil didn't move as she stared into the water. The waving, floating image of the statue danced again on the surface as another set of waves traveled through.

"Yes, she is," Cybil said.

Cybil turned around and leaned on the iron railing, her back to the pool. She had a tank top on, her thin but muscled arms bare, which displayed her twin dolphins tattoo above the elbow. Anne stood next to her, her hands gripping the rail, looking up at the statue. Anne, in jeans, wore a camisole under a sheer, white long-sleeved blouse. Her twin dolphin tattoo was visible beneath the white fabric. Anne glanced at Cybil's arm.

Anne said, "It hurt like hell. I had never had one before, or since. If you hadn't poured those shots down my throat, I'm not sure I would have." She smiled, shaking her head.

"It was your idea! Then you chicken out," Cybil said, laughing. "You just needed a little courage … in liquid form."

Anne's smile left. "Leaving the way I did … not very courageous."

Cybil pointed to an empty bench a few feet away. "Let's sit down or else we'll need towels soon."

Sitting next to each other, they both leaned back.

"I saw your kids as I walked up. They are beautiful, like their mother," Anne said.

"Thanks, their dad's handsome. But it wasn't enough," Cybil said.

She turned sideways and placed her arm along the bench's top plank, her hand stretching toward Anne.

Anne turned and did the same, placing her hand on Cybil's and said, "I'm sorry, people do disappoint, don't they."

Cybil nodded.

Anne closed her eyes and took a slow breath. "I want to ask you a question."

"Okay."

"Any more thoughts on what happened, how what a miracle it is that we are alive, what we went through," Anne said, her eyes brightened.

Cybil shook her head. "I don't know. We were lucky, I guess."

"Lucky? That's one way to look at it. Studying different ways people approach the spiritual, I've learned we need to give each other time, space and respect to find out what we believe."

"You never talked about God or the church or anything spiritual when we met," Cybil said.

"I should have, but I was confused. Before we met I had decided to go into the order after my tour. Meeting you changed my mind, at least for a while, but my doubts came back, especially after Dubai," Anne said.

Cybil turned back to the fountain and moved to the edge of the bench and said, "I'll never forget what we shared there."

Anne turned also and scooted up, sitting next to her and placing her hand over Cybil's.

"Neither will I," she said.

They sat for a minute, silent, Anne's warm hand over Cybil's.

"You sure what happened at St. Rita wasn't a random coincidence?" Cybil said.

"I'm sure," Anne said.

Cybil shook her head. "If it wasn't random, then it wasn't really fair."

"What do you mean? I don't understand," Anne said, her eyebrows scrunching.

"From my viewpoint, most of the planet is ignored by fate or the universe. Bad happening all over the place. A flash flood sweeps away a family campout, leaving one child alive. An earthquake of the millennium kills thousands of the world's best-prepared people. Warlords massacre hundreds, starve thousands and then transition to become political leaders. A child who should die from leukemia survives, another chokes on a pb&j sandwich. This is a pretty fucked-up place. Why would we, in our little corner, rate any attention?"

Anne, quiet for a moment, leaned back on the bench and turned sideways, placing her arm on the seatback again, her hand stretched out.

"Deep questions. I've been asking them myself," Anne said.

"Any answers?" Cybil scooted back and turned, mirroring Anne's position.

"Not really. But what we experienced at the well, it seems more than luck, don't you think?" Anne said.

"I don't know about that, I feel pretty damn lucky!"

They smiled, taking each other's features and details in, their hands clasped lightly until Anne gripped Cybil's hard before releasing it. Anne turned, sitting forward on the bench putting both hands in her lap.

Cybil didn't understand, yet mirrored Anne's body shift. A minute of silence became unbearable to her, so she spoke.

"What's wrong?"

Anne's hands gripped the edge of the bench, the rough wood ridged and uneven under her palms.

Cybil stared at Anne; the rest of the park receded into the background.

"After Dubai, I knew there was nothing wrong with me. I finally understood who I was. But I … I couldn't stay with you," Anne said.

Cybil groaned. Her face began to get warm, her color turning red. She cleared her throat, then saw out of the corner of her eye, a bird zip by. Small, gray, probably a sparrow. She froze.

She remembered her dream, at sea, about the beach, with Anne sitting under the black umbrella. Cybil closed her eyes and took a deep breath. And another. In. Out. In. Out.

When she opened her eyes, Anne was looking at her.

"You okay?" Anne said.

"I am. Are you?" Cybil said, biting down, her jaw flexing. Control. She wanted to cry.

"Where to now for Sister Anne?" Cybil said, looking forward, to the fountain.

"The bishop says that St. Rita would have shut down eventually. The mainstreaming trend away from group homes to foster homes is changing the way orphans are housed and placed. It's better for them. David and Amy, taking Sofi and Cecilia, is an example."

"I glad I was able to connect you," Cybil said. "The Flints look like they really care."

"The Philadelphia diocese has five group homes that need to transition. The bishop thinks I could be of use. After the sex scandals, they wanted a nun in charge," Anne said, standing up.

Turning to Cybil, who was still seated, Anne said, "Thank you for your help. You will be in my thoughts, always."

"Thought only, no prayers? He and I are not exactly on speaking terms so I could use a good word now and then," Cybil said.

Anne smiled. "Sure, especially in the line of work you have."

"MOM! MOM!" June said, running up to her mother and sliding onto her lap. June looked up at Anne.

"Hi," June said.

"Hello. You are very pretty, like your mother," Sister Anne said.

June blushed, leaning into her mother and said in a quiet voice, "Thanks."

Anne, her eyes becoming moist, looked at Cybil. Exhaling a deep sigh Anne said, "Goodbye, Cybil."

Cybil, her arm around June tightening, tilted her face upward, her lips parted slightly. She licked them, then biting her lip, she pushed the words out: "Goodbye, Joy Anne Holden, my friend."

Anne turned and walked away, down the central lane of Forsyth Park, past the wood benches, through the tall pines and leafy oaks. Her pace quickened when she got farther away. As she disappeared Cybil slowly closed her eyes.

"She seemed nice. Will we see her again?" June asked, rocking in her mother's lap.

"I don't think so. Some friends you never see again," Cybil said, moving sideways as June slipped off her and onto the bench. "Where's your brother?"

"Aunt Judy bought him an ice cream and they're sitting and talking. It was boring," June said.

"Let's go join them," Cybil said, smiling.

Walking toward the concession area, Cybil held June's hand tight. As they approached the seated Aunt Judy and Sebastian, Cybil glanced over her shoulder, back down toward Gaston Street. With nothing to see, she took a deep breath, smiled and sat down. Pulling out a 10-dollar bill, she sent Sebastian and June to buy drinks and an ice cream sandwich for their mother and whatever they wanted for themselves, splitting the change, which they could keep between them. She looked at Judy and smiled.

Two tables over, with his eyes on the Raven family, an olive-skinned man wearing a soccer jersey over jeans extended his arm to write into a black 5" x 8" notebook. As he extended his arm, a sliver of a red-and-black wrist tattoo peeked out from under his sleeve. At his feet lay a hiker's backpack. After finishing his record keeping, he stood up, finished his drink, slung his pack on his shoulder and walked toward the north end of Forsyth Park.

55

"The seed's universe folds into itself, dividing it must die so reuniting it may live, to change and become what it was meant to be."
—Adamic Scrolls, First Verse, Seventh Scroll

After a minute of staring into the tiny video camera, the hiker hears multiple door locks click open. He pushes his way through.

Open before him is a large rectangular courtyard. The air feels cooler than outside. The hiker looks up and sees it is five stories high, each level with a wide, deep balcony circling the courtyard. Birds are flying all around near the top of the courtyard, chirping and calling out to each other. The sound of their beating wings is amplified in the enclosed space.

At each level closed doors sit behind the stone balcony railings; they are spaced evenly, about 10 feet apart. Looking back down to the courtyard, he sees the six gardens, each full of plants, flowers and small trees, each of different size. All six gardens surround an empty square plot of land twice the size of the largest garden, filled only with dirt. Benches surround the empty plot. On one sits a monk, bent over, hooded. He is tossing something to a blackbird at his feet.

The hiker walks toward the monk and sits next to him. The bird peeks at the man but does not move. He picks at and swallows the food the monk is tossing, seeds perhaps. The hiker takes the backpack off and lays it to the side. He leans forward, elbows on knees. He turns his head and notices the wispy gray hair trailing out from the side of the hood, longer than last time. The monk's hands, wrinkled, fingers bent from arthritis, struggle to retrieve the seeds from a crumbled paper bag.

"Did she survive?" the old monk says.

"Yes," the hiker says.

"Did you interfere?"

"No."

"Are you sure?"

A slight pause from the hiker while he thinks about the boat charter he never showed up to enjoy, then says, "I did not interfere."

"And the children."

"Safe."

"Good."

"Why can we only watch but not act?" the hiker says.

"We pray, God acts. That is our duty. We can do nothing else until it is time. It has been so, as the Watchers have done, since the first Adamic scrolls were found," the old monk says.

"When will it be our time?"

"Patience and faith, my friend. The children are the key to our acting."

"A lot can happen. It will be many years before—"

"Speculating wastes energy. We must be focused. They must be with her until it's their time. They are not ready yet. She will make them ready."

"Does the scroll say what is next?"

"Hard to say. It took years for our banks of super computers to decipher." After a pause the old monk says, "The first prophecy."

Both sit up, open their arms, palms up, close their eyes and recite together in one voice:

"The seed of the tree will usher the forever of the city,

the seed of the tree will usher the endless flow of the river,

the seed of Raven will usher the age of the tree,

the seed of the tree will reveal the seed of the woman."

After they finish, the men return to their positions. The old monk tosses a few more goodies to the blackbird before speaking.

"Our Chinese brethren's schematics stolen from the TIHANE-20 project have been invaluable to speed our progress, but these upgrades to the super computers are making them run hotter. The latest depths of the new mine shafts to house them have tapped into massive ice veins, remnants from the last ice age. It has allowed us to cool them more effectively, producing less of a thermal footprint. We don't have to run the super-cooled nitrogen pumps, which produce observable heat, as much. We must not be detected by Those Who Scatter," the old man says.

"Is there anything new from the deciphering programs?" the hiker says. He watches the bird twisting its head back and forth for food.

"We have deciphered the core of the next sequence," the old monk says.

The hiker shifts, his voice rising. "What does it say, please tell me!"

"Hard to understand," the old monk says. "What we recite in open took 50 years to decode, starting with the first mainframes recovered from Van Braun's laboratories at Peenemunde. They were never destroyed, as the Allies thought. The Nazis had advanced computing much more than anyone knew. He sabotaged their operation and slowed them down even though he was one of them. His younger brother, one of our own, convinced him to let us take the machines."

"Again, another divine assist to our quest," the hiker says.

"Yes, we are now 16 years into the next sequence. Just the core has been deciphered. Our scribes sometimes produce interpretations that can have multiple meanings. What the council has determined is that it speaks of the children of Raven. That they must be allowed to be with their mother and not be taken prematurely, as we have the others," the monk says.

"And what of Raven?" the hiker says.

"And what of Raven?" The old monk shifts his feet, cranes his neck, stretching it, and sits up straighter.

He says, "The divine spark within the human heart is golden and warm, forever flaming the resilient passion of enduring hope. Scratch the surface of life and you find deep realities underneath, of pain and joy mixed in an uncertain elixir from which we have no choice but to drink. The world is more than we know. Her world is more than she knows."

The hiker turns his head toward the monk, who stops speaking, his face now turned to the ceiling of the courtyard. Spanning the whole courtyard length, it displays similar carvings, as on the arch, but in larger relief. Small and large birds dart and fly around near the ceiling, chasing each other. Some bird droppings land at their feet.

The hiker smiles, suppressing a chuckle.

The monk lowers his head and says, “It’s all right, son, some think life is a divine joke foisted on us by a mean-spirited God playing with the lives of men and women. Some on the council think I am full of what landed near us.”

“I don’t think that,” the hiker says.

“I know. To answer your question, and what of Raven,” the old monk sighs and says, “she is the key to breaking the hold of Those Who Scatter in our time. And it must be broken now, so they do not succeed then.”

He stands and says, “I must rest now.”

The hiker remains seated as he watches the old monk shuffle slowly away. His sandals scrape along; he can barely lift his feet. He heads toward a gleaming stainless steel door of an elevator on the first level, near the front doors. Reaching it, the monk feels for the Down button and pushes it. The doors open.

Stepping slowly inside, the monk turns around and uses his fingers to read the Braille on the control panel. He finds and presses the last button, marked L150. The doors close. The elevator speeds downward.

The hiker turns his head and leans forward. The bird tilts its head looking for food and when none is produced, it flies out through the opening above the front. The hiker stares at the empty dirt plot before him.

Author's Notes

Cybil Raven: Miracle at St. Rita is an original, copyrighted work. The third full-length novel in the series, *Cybil Raven: Valley of Souls* is due for release in the fall of 2012. Visit www.cybilraven.com to learn about this compelling, close to real-life character and her upcoming adventures.

"What of Cybil Raven?"

Fictional stories take us to a safe place in our minds where we can play with words, ideas, concepts and events that can actually help us understand the world we live in and maybe other worlds that could be out there.

Crystal and I have tried to make this story an entertaining starting point for the Cybil Raven Chronicles. Cybil Raven is a deeply interesting character with unique life experiences who is searching for the same thing all of us are … some meaning to it all.

While all fictionalized stories are based on some facts, the Cybil Raven Chronicles are more so because my coauthor, Crystal Craven, is the model for Cybil. Yes, Crystal is an actual Iraq War veteran who served time in Fallujah with the 82nd Airborne. Yes, she did jump out of perfectly good airplanes. Yes, she also did covert work and, yes, she is a beautiful fashion model (that's her on the cover) and, yes, she is a technology specialist and a single mother of two.

We hope you follow along with us as we journey into future stories, because there will be many; we have just scratched the surface.

The e-book experience and Savannah Notes

The embedded links in the e-book edition are intended to enhance the reading experience. In the print edition they have been made the same color text, with an underline, so as not to distract too much from the reading experience in the main text.

For print readers who wish to experience the e-book links, you can go directly the Cybil Raven Website, www.cybilraven.com and access this section on the website, called by the same name, and all of the links will be live and interactive. Just remember to please add your name to the mailing list so I can keep you posted on the next Cybil Raven book coming out.

So you can continue reading here and go to the website later or stop and go there now. It is your choice!

So to continue this section, most of the links point to actual Savannah locations that are integral to the story and the character of Cybil Raven. I have summarized them here with some back-story I thought you might find interesting.

But first a little about Savannah.

The beautiful city of Savannah, Georgia, has changed from the eccentric hamlet made famous by the best-selling novel, *Midnight in the Garden of Good and Evil*, by John Berendt. While still very much a charming southern city with deep historical character, today's Savannah bustles with commerce, academic excellence and entrepreneurial energy, making it a go-to destination for many.

In numerous research trips to the city, I discovered a much younger and vibrant Savannah than I had expected. Savannah provides a vast menu of choices regarding living, lifestyle, work, education and entertainment. Daytime activities are inviting to families and tourist friendly. You can spend all day visiting the many unique parks dotting the city. The nightlife on Congress Street bustles into the early morning hours with both upscale urban professionals and SCAD undergraduates and graduates mixing it up on the dance floor and in the lounges and eateries. I love the city and therefore weaved it into the fabric of the novel.

Following are excerpts, with the embedded links, from the novel, with a little back-story.

Enjoy!

Chapter 1:

"The wedding gown she wore, a form-fitting pearl white Vera Wang, a rental for the shoot, restrained her." – Vera Wang gowns need little introduction to those who follow fashion. As a father of two 20-something daughters, I've learned more than I thought I wanted to about weddings from them, as they watched shows such as *Bridezilla* and *Say Yes to the Dress!* The reason the wedding dress element is in the story was that my coauthor, Crystal, had invited me to a shoot at the Forsyth Park when we first started working together, but it got cancelled. She went on to do another shoot in Daytona Beach where she modeled her mother's wedding dress. I wanted that visual in the first chapter to start things off.

"Her eyes settled on the top of Forsyth Fountain, to the classical Greek figure of a woman in military stance holding some sort of rod or flag. Cybil cocked her head slightly. *Good to see you again, lady.*" – Forsyth Fountain is beautiful! It is the centerpiece of Forsyth Park, which is the centerpiece park of Savannah. On another research trip we met at the fountain with her photographer, to shoot the cover art for the first two books and she suggested the white Greco-Roman clothing style.

"With a large following eager for Cybil Raven Tweets, Facebook Posts and Music recommendations, she did not want to disappoint." – Cybil Raven is a Greek goddess fashion model, a child of these times, completely connected through social media and the Internet to her fans. She especially loves music and posts her favorites, often reflecting her many moods, such as with this song,

Ladies (Put a Ring on it) by Beyoncé

Chapter 3:

"He disdained the crowded Fridays and Saturdays filled with SCAD (Savannah College of Art and Design) college kids and overdressed over-30 cougars in heat prowling for young men." – Savannah's changing demographics are due in large part to the impact of the expanding arts university located in Savannah, GA. Many graduates, from all over the country stay and either find work or start businesses so as to remain in the city they have come to love.

"He took the tumbler from her and drained the anise-flavored ouzo, on ice, allowing it to flow over his tongue. It was his third of the night." – Stavos Gruner, the Greek, learned to savor this drink while learning to fish with his father. Stavos drank directly from the bottle he'd pry from his passed-out father's hand, but was careful to leave some in it, less he earn another beating.

"He squeezed his arms inward so he could feel the presence of his Heckler and Koch HK45 Compact." – Kurt favors the HK45 Compact now available through the U.S. branch of the German gun manufacturer. Kurt likes the reduced kickback from the lighter than standard HK45 handgun. It allows him to stay on target as he squeezes round after round.

" 'STAV! STAVOS!' A voice boomed. Its owner He had just made his way through the sparse dance floor at the Saya Lounge." – The Saya Lounge is a great destination for late-nighters. The good and fun crowds start to come in around 11:00 or so, and the drinks are very well made ☺!

Chapter 7:

"Sister Anne thought she saw the top of St. John the Baptist Cathedral." – One of the landmarks of Savannah, this Catholic church founded by French colonists in the 1700s, has seen the city grow and mature. Renovated in 2000, it stands tall in the middle of the historic district, sitting next to Lafayette Square.

"Crossing Abercorn Street she reached Lafayette Square." – One of my favorite spots during my research trips, the small fountain makes a particularly good spot for a meditative break.

"She parked behind the Hamilton Turner Inn, a three-story bed-and-breakfast next to Lafayette." – The inn, right in the middle of the historic district and walking distance to many locations, is ornately adorned and impressive.

Chapter 9:

"It was too far to see the Aikido Savannah Dojo on Broughton Street." – Cybil Raven received combat fight training in basic training during her service with the 82nd Airborne Division. She received additional advanced martial arts training when hired by the UNIT and excelled in many separate disciplines, but was unusually adept at Aikido. She has kept up her skills by training often with Sensei Dan in Savannah, GA, at the dojo.

Chapter 11:

" 'The St. Rita Children's Home board meeting will come to order,' Father Michael said as the clock in the conference room at the Oglethorpe Club reached 2:00 p.m." – Housed in a historic building, the Oglethorpe Club is Savannah's exclusive members-only club.

"Still wearing his golfing shoes from his morning round at Henderson Golf Club he saw the group looking at them." – Henderson Golf Club remains Savannah's best public golf course.

Chapter 13:

"The wail of the tower horn signaling prayers echoed across the city, deep in Yemen, on the Arabian Sea." – Yemen, a troubled Middle East country, is a place of political turmoil and home of an evolving terrorist network with links to Al-Qaeda.

Chapter 17:

" 'I'm leaving town tomorrow, but tonight I have a networking meeting at The cSpot at The Mirage Grill.' " – The young entrepreneurial energy of Savannah is on display at The cSpot networking meeting every month. Old and new Savannah money mix and mingle along with stiff drinks and tasty appetizers. If you want to know what's happening with the under-35 set, this is the place to be.

Chapter 18:

"Mr. Kasen stepped out of the Zatinya restaurant, on Ninth Street NW, near G Street, a block from the Smithsonian American Art Museum, Washington, DC, his meeting with Vasily complete." – The nation's capital has numerous outstanding restaurants to suit all types of ethnic tastes.

"He shook his head thinking he should have spent more time on pentaerythritol tetranitrate (PETN) basics during mission training with these two young soldiers." – PETN is a favorite homemade explosive used by make-it-yourself bomb makers worldwide.

Chapter 19:

"A few minutes later, driving at city speeds, she found a parking spot near Panera Bread and Bakery on Broughton Street and stuffed two hours' worth of coins in the meter." – I spent many an afternoon in this bakery, observing the foot traffic going up and down West Broughton, taking notes and writing. You really do get a feel for the city and the many people passing through.

"The front door of The Mirage, within five minutes' walking distance on West Broughton, was within view; tonight the restaurant-lounge would host The cSpot." – The Mirage is a great ethnic restaurant and occasionally hosts The cSpot networking meetings. The cSpot is a real organization that provides an excellent networking forum for young and not-so-young professionals.

"I mentioned your work at the Rape Crisis Center and the economic development council." – Cybil Raven has a heart that she matches with deeds. Because of her past experiences, especially what happened at Wolf Creek Canyon, Cybil is sensitive to victims of abuse.

"Cybil hesitated, leaned back and looked at the woman at the table. She looked up, smiled and waved hello, nodding. Cybil gave him her card and took one of his, which read: Eden Community Village, David and Amy Flint." – An urban, city-centric church started in 2011 in Savannah, GA. Progressive, socially liberal but biblically conservative, this young group of spiritual travelers moved to Savannah in 2010 to become part of the community to try to make a spiritual but not religious difference.

Chapter 22:

"Kasen, eager to reach Safir and finish preparations, followed the directions and got off I-95 onto Kings Highway which would take him straight to Almond Grove Mobile Home Park, less than 30 minutes away from Fort A.P. Hill, Virginia." – Fort A.P. Hill is a large military base not far from the nation's capital and hosts annual scouting events.

Chapter 23:

"Cybil pulled her iPad from her bag, onto her lap. She tweeted, which also streamed to Facebook. Meet Me Halfway by Black Eyed Peas on The E.N.D." – Cybil's social media connection to her fans includes music recommendations which often reflect her moods.

Chapter 28:

"Reaching into her bag she pulled out her iPad and began to tweet but could only make two entries, one being a song she remembered hearing on the way home after meeting Anne at Thunderbolt.

Change of plans, heading back to Sav, Bleeding Love (Jason Nevins Radio Remix) by Leona Lewis" – Cybil's social media connection to her fans is ongoing, with many music recommendations.

Chapter 30:

"Lowering the driver-side window allowed street sounds to come in along with the smell of strong coffee drifting from the nearby Gallery Espresso." – One of Savannah's premier local coffee shops, this eclectic bistro also provides local artists the opportunity to showcase their work. But there is more than coffee; the kitchen is grade A, offering pastries, sandwiches and other treats for the constant stream of visitors and regulars. It's one of Cybil's favorites.

"We got the idea from a great book, *Blue Like Jazz*." – One of David and Amy Flint's favorite books is *Blue Like Jazz*, by Donald Miller. Its take on nonreligious spirituality is personal and insightful and has helped young persons of faith understand the difference between spirituality and religion, the latter often having little to do with God and his love for the world.

Chapter 32:

"The California National Park near Fresno, California, situated close to her mother's home, had been a childhood favorite." – Cybil, a California girl and beauty pageant winner, learned to love Yosemite National Park near her childhood home.

"The report came back from CODIS …" – CODIS is the national offender database used by law enforcement to keep track of the criminal element.

Chapter 33:

"He had little left of the 16-oz. rib eye sitting on his plate, his favorite dish at Uncle Bubba's Oyster House." – Paula Deen, Savannah's famous southern cook, has a brother named Bubba who is not a slouch in the kitchen. His restaurant, on the way to Tybee Island, from the mainland, is a favorite location for foodies going to or returning from the beach. It is also Stavos Gruner's favorite place for steaks and shady business deals.

"Thirty minutes later Stavos and Kurt arrived at Troup Square in the downtown historic district." – One of the smaller but more interesting parks, it features a unique central astronomical device used in early celestial studies. Also, it is a pet-friendly park with pet-accessible drinking spots. It is near John Block's home.

Chapter 34:

"A few minutes later, Cybil Raven stood, silent, along with the other mourners around the open pit soon to be John Block's final resting place on the grounds of Bonaventure Cemetery in Savannah." – Bonaventure Cemetery is both a haunting and beautiful place to visit. Overlooking the city, the landscaping and gravestone architecture awes and inspires as one walks the grounds.

"Looking first at Judy, then Benny, Cybil said, 'Not sure. Let's discuss later. Tonight at MacPherson's, late.' " – MacPherson's is one of many of Savannah's Irish-themed restaurants. Savannah, known for the largest St. Patrick's Day parade second only Boston, has a deep Irish heritage.

" 'I don't know what he found. We were supposed to meet that evening at Matthews for a late meal, after he walked Lyle. It's close to where he lives—lived,' Cybil said, her voice trailing off." – Matthews Bistro, just off Bay Street, near Troup Square, is a gourmet eating destination for locals and out-of-towners looking for excellent food and good times. Small, cozy and wood-themed, Matthews's reputation continues to grow as does its variety-filled menu. The Sunday brunch is not to be missed if you're in town. It is also the place where the author and coauthor first met to discuss working together on the series, Cybil Raven Chronicles.

"A few minutes of silence between them ended when Cybil punched the radio on. The song, 'Duet,' was playing. She turned down the volume." – Music keeps Cybil company and echoes her moods, which can vary greatly.

Chapter 35:

"Less than 20 minutes away, in Morrow, Georgia, a small community near Clayton State University East, Abdul sat on the steps of his rental apartment." – Hiding in plain sight is an advanced technique usually taught by sophisticated Western security agencies. Unfortunately it has been adopted by terrorist organizations worldwide.

Chapter 36:

"She drove out of the airport garage, back to Savannah. Within 10 minutes she had reached I-95 and after 30 minutes arrived at the dojo, at the corner of Bull Street and West Broughton, parked nearby and went in." – Cybil Raven excels at hand-to-hand combat, taking to the training like a natural. Making men twice her size fly through the air or slap the mat for mercy, she keeps her skills honed. She especially favors Aikido, which uses your opponent's momentum against him. The Aikido Dojo in Savannah is run by Sensei Dan, her friend.

Chapter 37:

"Next he extracted two electronic devices, each the size of a paperback. Both had LED displays reading 0.0, the scale millisieverts per hour." – This unit of measure is the international standard recognized to evaluate the biological damage of radiation.

Chapter 38:

" 'This is best done in person. Can we meet in 30 minutes at the Breakfast Club, it's down the road from Trinity, walking distance for someone as fit as you.' " – A local favorite on Tybee Island, the Breakfast Club is a classic American diner within walking distance from the beach. Small, with few tables and a Formica counter from the 1950s, you will not only enjoy great food and but also a great atmosphere.

Chapter 42:

" 'She's late!' Blitz Thompson said to himself out loud as he stood in the lobby of the Hilton Hotel on Liberty Street." – The Hilton Hotel on Liberty Street is a centrally located premium hotel providing easy access to the historic downtown district while providing class A accommodations. One of the taller structures in the city, it provides breathtaking views from the top floors.

Chapter 47:

" 'He is doing the best he can, working with what he has, flawed, imperfect people.' "– One of author Tony Timbol's favorite books is Susan Isaacs's *Angry Conversations with God*, a spiritual memoir from a talented actress, comedienne and personality whose brutally honest insights about life and her relationship with God, explored in unique therapy sessions, has spoken to thousands.

Chapter 49:

" 'We need NEST support from Homeland Security.' " – Acronym for Nuclear Emergency Support Team. NEST is a team of scientists, technicians and engineers operating under the United States Department of Energy's National Nuclear Security Administration (NNSA). Their task is to be "prepared to respond immediately to any type of radiological accident or incident anywhere in the world."

" 'No worries, miss. Sister Anne identified herself and told us where you had gone. She's fine, but they are taking her to Memorial Medical to be checked out,' he said." – One of Savannah's two main hospitals, it is an award-winning academic medical center.

Chapter 54:

" 'We have a lot of people asking about this project. Your presence will help raise awareness about this and the Eden Community Village idea.' " – An urban, city-centric church started in 2011 in Savannah, GA. Progressive, socially liberal but biblically conservative, this young group of spiritual travelers moved to Savannah in 2010 to become part of the community to try to make a spiritual but not religious difference.

ISBN: 978-0-9831333-1-5 (eBook)
ISBN: 978-0-9831333-3-9 (Paperback)
LCCN: 2011927033 (eBook)
LCCN: 2011934654 (Paperback)

Published by Verilogos Publishing, www.verilogos.com
St. Johns, FL 32259

Second Publishing Date March 2012

Author: Tony Timbol, www.tonytimbol.com
https://www.facebook.com/TonyTimbolAuthor

Author: Crystal M. Craven, www.crystalmcraven.com

Cover Photo Credits: Photographer: Ron Brewer of Ron Brewer Images www.RonBrewerImages.com
Cover Art: Crystal Bos, Unbound Photography, www.unboundphotos.com

Acknowledgments

The author first and foremost AGAIN thanks his loving and beautiful wife, Shelly Timbol, for her support and grace during this process, along with his two daughters, Emily and Stephanie, equally supportive. Thanks also to test readers in my circle of family and friends, who encouraged me with positive feedback.

Also much gratitude to gracious friends and professional colleagues who provided insight and perspective, such as accomplished industry guru Jerry Simmons, writing coach Diane O'Connell, publicist Gary Roen, the best copy editor ever, Beth Mansbridge, who did the first copyediting pass and my daughter Emily, who did the second editing pass.

Finally, to my coauthor and creative partner Crystal M. Craven, who, in the middle of a busy personal life, did much reading and revision, making the story more realistic and believable. Her significant artistic and other substantive contributions are more than appreciated; they are invaluable to the creative process. I look forward to working with her on future entries in the series.

Tony Timbol and Crystal Craven

Cybil Raven Chronicles:

Cybil Raven Beginnings: Volume 1

Cybil Raven: Miracle at St. Rita, Volume 2

*

A NEW FULL-LENGTH NOVEL
COMING 2012/2013

Rough, Ready and Ex-Airborne:
this is one fashion model you want on your side!

Cybil Raven: Valley of Souls

Volume 3

http://www.facebook.com/CybilRavenChronicles

www.cybilraven.com

To contact Tony Timbol or to be placed on a mailing list to receive updates on new releases, go to the www.cybilraven.com website and enter your e-mail address on the home page or click the website Contact tab

11796001R00247

Made in the USA
Charleston, SC
21 March 2012